Burnt Silver

H. A. Titus

To my family and my "framily"
Because all of you are awesome

TABLE OF CONTENTS

Prologue

JOSH

Due to various deaths, dismissals, and betrayals, it seems I've become the de facto recorder for the Museum. How this has happened is a tale "long in the telling," if I want to get Tolkien-esque about it. I'll try to make some sense of it.

As I've already written of my first experiences in the Underworld and the beginning of the fight against Fear Doiricht, there's no need to go back and rewrite that—everyone seems satisfied with the accounts, even though at the time I'd only written them to record memories for myself, and not for use in any official record.

But since these accounts forward are official, I can't focus only on my experiences. Others will have to have their say—whether it makes the narrative clearer or muddier is not my place to say.

Chapter 1

JOSH

Four months to the day since my life had been turned upside down.

I rocked back on my heels, staring at the rectangle of dirt with new, delicate green blades of grass. It seemed like the grass should have grown faster. Marc had been buried nearly four months ago. I thought I'd never be back, but I hadn't been able to resist the pull to the gravesite today.

They'd put the headstone up. It was simple—a rough-cut block of gray granite with the words *Marc Gillam. Beloved son and brother. Loyal to the last.*

Loyal to the last. He certainly had been that.

Marc had given his life for his people. He'd given his life after I'd messed up the plan he and Eliaster had come up with.

We can't let that eat at us, I'd told Eliaster at Marc's funeral. But I still hadn't let go. And most days, I figured I never would.

Four months since my best friend had died, defending the world from a threat most would never know existed. I swallowed and curled my arms in against my stomach, as if to protect myself against the tightness in my chest.

A flicker of movement in the corner of my vision. I

blinked, and in that brief darkness, saw again the white stone of the relic bashing into David's head. The burst of red. I flinched and drew a deep breath into my prickling throat. Would I never be able to stop dreaming about that moment?

And then there were the other nightmares that haunted me when I tried to sleep.

Nightmares of Marc, a rusted iron knife slicing into his flesh, the pain in his eyes as Eliaster worked to squeeze the poison from his veins and give him another hour of life. Nightmares of David's blank eyes, the blood pooling under his skull, caved in where I'd bashed it with the pathstone, the crumbled white rock mixing with the blood.

The ones with Larae were the worst, though. Larae, slicing open my wrist, draining my blood for her dark magic. Larae, her body pressed against mine, her soft lips trailing against my jaw and neck. I'd never even touched her—she'd been my best friend's girlfriend. Off limits, even if she *had* been flirting with me. But she'd betrayed me, Eliaster, Marc—even David, who had joined her in her treachery, who had died because of her.

I hadn't gone to anyone about the dreams. Who could I tell? Eliaster would just scoff at me. My parents would think I'd lost it or started on drugs those two weeks I'd been missing. I wasn't about to draw my brothers or sister into this strange new world I was living in.

I could have told Roe, Marc's grandmother. But I hadn't seen her since the funeral. And I didn't really know how to approach her now. She seemed to think I was some kind of paragon who would save the fae. Like I needed that kind of pressure.

I stood up, rubbing the back of my neck. Sweat smeared under my palm. I breathed deep and focused on the weather. Anything that took my mind away from Marc, or David, or any of my other nightmares. The day was warm, and the clouds overhead offered no relief, serving only to make the air more sticky than usual. Summer in Missouri. We'd probably get rain before the afternoon ended.

My phone vibrated, and a moment later, the tinny sound of Survivor's "Eye of the Tiger" blasted through the quiet cemetery. Eliaster. The jerk had changed my ringtone again. I pulled the phone from my back pocket and hit the screen.

"Yeah?" I said, starting for the paved road that wound through the gravestones a few yards away.

Instead of Eliaster, a softer, more sibilant voice echoed through the phone's speakers. "Josh?"

"Angel." I took a deep breath, glad he wasn't here to see me flinch. The ex-Unseelie fae made me nervous. "What do you want?"

I could imagine the sarcastic grin on the dark fae's face. Angel may have been Eliaster's informant, but he was no fan of mine, and to be honest I didn't care for him all that much either.

"Someone requested a meeting," Angel said. "Eliaster said he's busy, so he wanted you follow up on it."

My heart rose to my throat. Eliaster wanted me to meet an informant?

Before my mind could stop spinning, Angel said, "Relax, tightwad. Eliaster wouldn't just throw you in the deep end like that. I'll be there with you, holding your hand the whole way."

Okay, that sounded more likely. I rolled my eyes. "Great. Where do I meet you?"

"The front entrance to the Market. See you in a few minutes."

Well, it was going to be more than a few, but Angel hung up before I could let him know.

I sighed, replaced the phone in my pocket, glanced back at Marc's grave. The back of my throat felt tight and dry. I'd been in the Underworld since Marc had died, sure, but only back and forth to the Tyrone rath. This would be the first time I'd willingly stepped foot among a large number of fae in months.

How would I react? Ever since that night in April when Marc and I had been attacked by a troll, I'd been seeing through fae glamour. Now I could tell who was human and who was pretending without even trying.

So far it hadn't gotten me more than a few dirty looks, and once even a come-on from a gorgeous fae girl with green hair and the perfect hourglass figure, the type of girl most nerds like me never see outside of a video game. I'd turned her down.

Overhead, thunder rumbled.

I glanced at Marc's grave once more. When Marc had died, I'd promised him I would keep fighting. In his memory. Roe had told me she believed I was destined to be a part of the Underworld.

I didn't know if that was true, or if this was utter stupidity on my part. but I couldn't just walk away, not without trying my best to help.

I grabbed my helmet, pulled it on and started the bike.

The curvy road leading back into Springfield had no shoulder, not even a gravel strip. Typical of country highways in this area. I hunched close to the body of my bike and took the curves way too fast, forcing myself to concentrate on staying upright.

Before long, I crossed into the city limits, and traffic forced me to slow down. I pulled up to a red light and planted my feet on the pavement. It was stupid, riding a bike with no protective gear other than a helmet and boots, but I didn't care.

I turned into a parking garage and guided my bike down to the lowest level. Few cars were parked down here, though I spotted Eliaster's sleek supercar near the back.

I pulled up to the back wall and opened the black electrical box that sat on the far side. I put my left hand inside, and felt a cold chill as something—I assumed it was fae magic—washed over it. With the whine of grinding mechanisms, the wall receded, revealing a tunnel strung with wires, pipes, and dim orange light globes.

I drove my bike through, the wall rumbling closed behind me.

My engine's roar echoed in the tunnel, thrumming loudly even through my helmet. This time of day—mid-morning—the Underworld tunnels were quiet, at least close to the surface. Most sidhé, I'd discovered, preferred to conduct their business during the night, especially the fae. Sometimes I wondered if fae were the basis for vampire legends humans had eagerly been devouring—no pun intended—for centuries. Eliaster insisted they weren't, but if I knew him, the grumpy, blond fae didn't want to be thought of as a blood-sucking, sparkly fairy. Bad enough that some human cultures saw him as a three-inch pixie with wings.

I spotted a couple of goblins scurrying along the side of the road. Their pale, saggy skin, edged in ragged patches of fur, stood out against the dark walls of the tunnel. All goblins had sharp, claw-like fingernails and slit-pupiled eyes, but these guys had distinctive pointed ears rimmed in fur at the sides of their heads. Cat-sidhé.

I slowed as I went past them, watching them carefully. One of the cat-sidhé actually dropped on all fours and hissed at me through jagged teeth.

I didn't have my sword, but I dropped one hand down to my side, feeling the outline of my nine-mil pistol through my jacket. The goblins backed away, their eyes glowing green in the dim overhead light.

I shook away a chill as their eyes vanished into the distance.

I parked outside the distinctive metal gates of the Market and walked in, tucking my helmet under my arm. It was as loud and vibrant as ever, the large square of open space inside the gates milling with sidhé and humans. I paused, letting the noise wash over me. Glamour ghosts flickered over faces, the lights from the Market booths making them glow like streetlights in the rain. My stomach flip-flopped, and I pushed down the sudden urge to turn my back and run. Angel was waiting for me. His dark clothes, inky black skin, and sardonic smile were hard to miss in the crowd's riot of color.

"Josh!" He threw his arm over my shoulders.

I froze. This was weird. He was acting way too friendly. My feet dragged in the powdery dirt as he pushed me forward.

"Relax." He spoke through a gritted smile. "We're being watched."

I stumbled a little as my feet caught up and forced a smile of my own. "Great to see you again, Angel." My neck itched. I really wanted to figure out who was watching us, but I knew I couldn't.

Angel steered me through the crowd. I ducked under a troll's heavily muscled arm as it swung a box over our heads, then pushed Angel to the side to get out of the way of three leather-clad punks giving everyone else nasty looks as they plowed through the throng. Angel talked loudly about this fortune teller he'd met who specialized in human fortunes and how I just had to try her services. That was our cover, right? Maybe this informant didn't want it well known that she spoke to close associates of the Tyrones? I bobbed my head, watching as the twinkling lights and brightly festooned booths swept past us.

Before too long, I was standing in front of a brightly-colored tent. It was draped in purples, oranges, greens. Gauze-covered Christmas lights wrapped around the front poles and entryway, and a beaded curtain served as a door. Just like I'd expect a fortune-teller's tent to look like. Maybe if she catered to humans, that was to be expected. It seemed like most humans who knew the Underworld existed were the superstitious types—all except me.

Angel planted his hand in my back and pushed me forward. "Go on!" He said, the grin still frozen on his face.

"You, uh, wanna come in with me?" I asked. My stomach curled in knots. Why had Eliaster sent me? What was his game here?

"She said she would only speak to Josh MacAllister." Angel shrugged. "So I guess that means I'm out. I'll be here if you need backup though."

Yeah, gee, thanks a lot.

I sighed and pushed aside the beaded curtains.

They rattled back into place behind me.

Once again, the interior of the tent was pretty much just like I'd expect from movies and books. Racks of fancy metal shelves lined the walls, stuffed to bursting with books, loose papers, carved wooden boxes, bottles with mysterious smoky substances swirling inside of them. A red parrot screeched from a cage in the corner, beside a back entrance covered in sparkly black cloth. Incense curled from a little brazier at the back of the tent, making the thick air smell of sweet patchouli and cinnamon. In the middle of the room sat a little round table with a crystal ball mounted on it.

I rolled my eyes and crossed my arms over my chest. "Hello?"

A fae woman brushed the black curtain aside. She looked young, like all fae, but the slight lines around the corners of her mouth and eyes told that she was old—Roe's age, maybe older. Dark makeup outlined her dark eyes, and she'd left her hair in loose waves over her shoulders. She stopped, her eyes narrowing. Although she definitely looked the part of a sultry fortune teller, her ready stance and narrowed gaze told me that she knew I could see through her glamour, and she wasn't going to put on an act for me.

"Josh MacAllister," she said matter-of-factly.

"Yeah. And you are?"

"Maira." She gestured to the round table. "Have a seat."

I crossed the room cautiously, placing my backpack at the floor by my feet and sitting in one of the upholstered chairs. It was deeper than I thought, and I sank back into it for a split second before jerking forward. My heart pounded, more from being startled than scared.

She pulled the other chair around the table and sat in front of me, then held out her hands. "Let me see your palm."

"What?" I said.

She grabbed my wrist. "For show. In case anyone walks in ..." Her voice trailed off.

I looked down. She'd grabbed my right hand, and, peeking from the edge of my jacket sleeve, the thick black scar left by Larae's dark magic was clearly visible. I tried to wrench my arm free, but she had a tighter grip on it than I thought. Thanks to Larae's magic, I had no feeling in that hand anyway, but I could imagine my fingers tingling from her hold on my wrist.

"So it is true," she said quietly. "That you had a brush with a sorceress—that she took your blood—and yet, you survived."

I pressed my lips together and waited.

"Does it still hurt?"

I couldn't help the shiver that crawled down my back. Before I could stop myself, I blurted, "Have you seen this before?"

"No. I feel something ... off. Something wrong."

She might as well have dropped acid into my stomach. I shivered. "Is—is that really bad?" No one I knew so far had any idea of what to make of the scar. Not Cormac, not Eliaster, not even Roe. Maybe this fortune-teller knew something.

"I could not tell you." Maira sighed and bent forward, running her thumb along the lines in my palm. "If it is true that you survived battling a sorceress, then I also assume what else I've been told is true. That you work for someone who would be interested in relics of a certain kind."

My pulse quickened. Okay, time to switch gears. I took a few seconds to steady my breathing, shove away her words about the scar. I'd deal with it later. I leaned forward, lowered my voice. "Potentially. Depends on who's asking and what the price is."

"The one who is asking is the one to whom you owe a life debt. As for the price ..." She shrugged.

Life debt? It took me a few seconds, and then it felt like an iron band tightened around my chest. Cori. Coriander Airgead.

A few months ago, he'd saved my life in Chicago. Out of

curiosity, he'd said. Out of an interest in getting a favor from someone close to the Tyrone family, I figured. I'd never told Eliaster. Was Cori cashing in the favor now? Why would he be the one giving me information?

My brain stutter-stepped. "What … does he want me to do?" I stammered.

Maira shrugged. "I was only told to pass this information on to you." She sat back, released my wrist. A quick motion, and a folded slip of paper appeared in her hand from out of nowhere.

I rubbed my wrist. My scar ached. "What's this?"

"A request."

"For?"

She shrugged. "I was merely asked to be the messenger."

I got up, waited. But Maira merely turned away from me, pulling her sleeve over her hand and using it to rub a spot away on her crystal ball. I nodded in thanks, snagged my backpack, and walked from the tent.

"Well?" Angel asked.

I shook my head. "I'm not sure." I wasn't about to tell him what she'd said. My mind spun. How was I going to explain this to Eliaster?

Someone bumped into my arm, causing me to stumble against Angel. He elbowed me upright. I glanced back in time to see a human, his shoulders broad and his hair a dark blond, duck into Maira's tent. Another sucker for her to tell her fortunes to.

I shivered and flexed my right hand, wincing as a twinge—the first feeling I'd had in my fingers for months—shot through my hand. I slid my thumb between the folds of the paper and flipped it open.

Meet me at the coffee shop tomorrow, 10 AM. No tricks, no traps.

"You okay?" Angel asked.

I shoved the paper in my pocket and glanced up at him. He was watching me out of narrowed eyes, interest showing in the flickers of gold at the edges of his dark irises. Of course he hadn't asked out concern. He was trying to figure out an angle, as always.

"I'm fine, thanks."

His eyes narrowed even more. "If you're hiding something from Eliaster—"

"Hope you've changed the passcode to your garage, Angel," I said, grinning. "Although I figured it out last time, so I'm not sure how much good it'll do anyway."

The muscles in his jaw bunched, and he spun on his heel and walked away. I watched him disappear into the crowd of the Market, my stomach churning a little from all the fae and the glamour swirling around me.

Some days, I thought I'd taken to the Underworld just a little too well.

Chapter 2

ELIASTER

I parked my motorcycle in an abandoned lot and walked the last two blocks to the ramshackle buildings in the outskirts of the Underworld. It had been a while since I'd visited Blaise, an older goblin who mostly kept to himself, but still somehow knew all the shady happenings in the area.

I skirted around a barrel with an open flame, then eyed the wooden buildings that leaned forward over the street. The entire slum area of the Underworld was a medieval wreck. One spark and the entire collection of greasy wooden buildings would go up in ashes. I lifted my head, sniffed, and cringed as I caught a whiff of the nearby sewer system.

Thankfully, not that many people lived in this area any more.

I walked up rickety steps to the second floor of a building that tipped precariously to one side, and gently rapped on the door. "Blaise?"

Nothing.

I leaned to the side and tried to see in the one tiny window, but the usual tattered blanket was tacked in front of it. As I moved, I caught a whiff of a heavy, almost-sweet smell. My throat clenched. Something was rotting. Had he abandoned the place and left it full of garbage?

I rattled the door, and the entire structure shook in response. I eased away and gnawed on the inside of my cheek. Kicking the door down might very well bring the entire building down on top of me. Man, I should've brought Josh with me. Even when he'd been essentially useless, he'd been able to pick locks.

I grabbed the doorknob again and gently jiggled it up and down, hoping the wood was loose enough that I could slip the bolt free. "C'mon, Blaise, open up! It's Eliaster."

With a *ka-thunk*, the lock slipped, and I pushed open the door. It thumped into something and would only open halfway. My skin prickled. I gripped the sword at my side and eased partially into the room. Something reeked.

The inside of the single-room apartment was sparse, just a bed and a ratty camp chair with a single-burner camp stove on a metal box in front of it. A large storage shelf stood to one side of the bed, stuffed full of books, and a crate at the foot of the bed had spilled, scattering a tangle of grayish clothing and blankets across the floor. There was a stack of tinned foods in the corner behind the camp chair, and another pile of empty cans in the other corner.

I stepped fully inside the room and let the door swing shut behind me. Something bumped into my shoulder and I spun, heart hammering. Blaise's bloated face met mine, skin a dark purple, tongue hanging from his mouth, eyes black sockets. I gasped and backed up. The stench hit me full force and made me gag.

Blaise's body swung from the rafters of the room, a rope around his neck. I hunched my shoulders and pressed my fist to my mouth, forcing bile back down my throat. I pulled my flashlight from my pocket and clicked it on. The beam shook as I played it over the goblin's body. Lividity had settled the blood at the goblin's feet. He'd been hanging there for a while. A *long* while. My shoulders sagged, and I stepped back, feeling a burn in the corners of my eyes.

I turned the flashlight beam to the goblin's face. Metal coins flashed in the light. That explained why I'd thought his eyes had been gouged out at first. I stepped closer. Dark metal disks, stamped with a half indistinguishable ogham, had been wedged into the goblin's eye sockets. I gritted my teeth and reached out, trying to pry one free. The metal seared my fingers and I jerked back, hissing in pain.

Iron.

Whoever had done this was one sick bastard.

Using the edges of my fingernails, I picked the coins free, wrapped them in a scrap I tore from the blanket on the bed, and stuffed the bundle into my pocket. Josh or Roe could look at them later.

My phone buzzed, and I retrieved it from my pocket. One missed call from Josh.

Met with the informant. Are you coming back to the rath soon?

I sent him a quick confirmation and looked around the room, feeling sick to my stomach, and not just from the smell. Blaise had never been a dear friend, but the old goblin had been helpful, always giving me enough hints that Angel and I could keep tabs on the Lucht Leanuna's movements.

Who could've killed him? Llew? It didn't feel like the Unseelie's style. Phantom pain flashed through my shoulders, and my right fingers spasmed into a fist. There were no signs of torture, no broken fingers or cuts riddling the goblin's body. Llew liked breaking fingers, and he had a sickening attachment to knives. Besides, Llew would've made it obvious. And I couldn't feel any of the stomach-churning unease I got at the slightest hint of Larae's dark glamour.

Neither of them would've dared to debase a fellow sidhé's body by shoving iron coins into the eyes. Blaise had been hung, plain and simple. Judging by the state the apartment was in, maybe there had been a bit of a struggle first, but it was hard to tell.

I lifted my head, held quiet and still for a moment.

Great. The last thing I need is an unknown enemy out there, gunning for my informants.

Why had Blaise been killed? I walked to the shelf of

books and ran my fingers down the stack of paperback spines, more for something to do. Anything to do. The paperbacks were squeezed in tight, no indication that anything had been hidden in them recently. Besides, everything Blaise had ever given me had been verbal. The goblin had been paranoid … for good reason, it seemed.

I stepped out of the house and crouched on the rickety little balcony, leaning my back against the unsteady wall, hands covering my mouth. I didn't even know who Blaise's next of kin had been. I squeezed my eyes shut, then just as quickly opened them again. Blaise's body had been cold, but there was no telling if someone was watching the place. I didn't need to make myself an easy target.

I stood and walked down the steps, reaching into my pocket for my cell phone. I'd have to let Da know. He could send someone to deal with the body. I glanced up again at the door, then lowered my head and trudged back through the slums to where I'd left my bike, my chest tight. Blaise hadn't deserved that. No matter how evil, no sidhé deserved iron in the eyes.

Chapter 3

JOSH

I skirted the outside edge of the Underworld city, passing through a neighborhood that consisted of falling-apart shops and the remnants of a once-grand Victorian home, before hitting the rich section of the town. Mansions dotted the expanse of green grass-like moss, all looking pale and washed out under the orange light. For the life of me, I could never figure out why the rich fae wanted to live down here. I guess they liked the mystique and elusive aesthetic. It *was* atmospheric, I'd give them that, but I'd trade it for a house in the sun any day.

I pulled up at the wrought-iron gate of Cormac Tyrone's rath. From the outside, it looked like your typical Tudor mansion, but when I glanced up at the roof, I spotted the sniper, hunkered down beside the false chimney, rifle trained on me.

I grinned and lifted my fingers from the bike in a half-wave.

The gate buzzed and swung open enough to allow me to pull through. I motored up the gravel drive and stopped at the foot of the front steps.

The front door opened and Lukas, Cormac's head of security, stepped out. No matter how many times I met the fae, my stomach still clenched a little. I gritted my teeth.

"Joshua," Lukas said evenly, staring at me.

I returned the stare, all the while willing my breakfast to remain in my stomach. Some fae affected me more than others—Eliaster compared it to a fight-or-flight instinct that kept most humans away from the sidhé and out of danger. With some fae, like Eliaster, the sensation had faded the more time I spent around them, until I could barely feel it. Maybe I just hadn't been around Lukas enough.

Or maybe he really did pose a threat to me.

"I didn't know you planned to come today."

I pulled my helmet over my head, hearing a crackle as static pulled my already-crazy hair skyward. "Hadn't planned on it, but you know how plans tend to change." I offered a smile.

Lukas did not smile back as I jogged up the steps, leaving my helmet on my bike seat. For a moment, I didn't think he was going to let me in. Then he stepped aside, holding the door open. As I brushed past him, his hand darted to my side, snatching the pistol away.

"Hey!" I spun to face him again, but didn't grab for the gun.

Lukas examined it, thumbing the safety on and off and releasing the clip. He snorted at the caliber. "This wouldn't stop a troll or a rager."

"Well, hopefully I won't run into too many of those." I held my hand out.

He ignored it.

"Give it back to him, Lukas," came Cormac's voice from the side of the foyer.

I raised my head. Eliaster's dad stood at the library door, hands clasped behind his back, his green eyes narrowed at Lukas. Lukas shrugged and extended his hand toward me, the gun clutched loosely in his fist. I grabbed it.

Lukas gave me one last dirty look and walked further into the house.

"Please come in, Josh." Cormac stood to the side of the

door, gesturing inside the library.

I walked past him, placing the gun on a side table near the library door, and entered the library. The last time I'd been here, the place had looked neat and precise, like I'd always imagined the Diogenes Club would be. Rather than the neat configuration of chairs and tables this time however, some of the furniture had been shoved to the side, making room for a new desk and several cardboard boxes, each stamped with the logo of a popular computer company.

Cormac said something to Lukas in a low tone that I didn't quite catch. I rubbed the back of my neck. I'd expected to find Eliaster here. Having Cormac greet me instead was ... uncomfortable.

As Cormac closed the library door, I raised my eyebrows and nodded to the stacks of computer equipment, hoping a joke would crack the ice. "Hope you don't let Eliaster near this."

Cormac chuckled, lines crinkling the corners of his eyes and betraying his age. "If Eliaster torches any of those computers, accidentally or not, I might just kick him out on his ear."

Well, at least he and Eliaster shared a sense of humor.

Cormac walked over to a cabinet housing a coffee machine and several types of liquor. "Drink?" he asked.

"Just coffee, thanks."

He nodded and pulled a single-serve pod from one of the drawers. The coffee machine burbled to life, filling the once again uncomfortable silence. Cormac was a bigwig in the fae Underworld, at least in Springfield. He hadn't spoken to me since we'd gotten back from retrieving the pathstone in Chicago. He hadn't even spoken to me at Marc's funeral. I'd gotten the impression that he thought his son had made a mistake in dragging me, a human—an Overworlder—into the sidhé world.

So what did Lord Cormac Tyrone want from me now?

He handed me a mug, then pulled another chair across the fireplace and sat down. The scene reminded of the first night I'd ever met any fae—only instead of the silver-haired, immaculate Blodheyr, it was Cormac I was speaking to. He blended perfectly with his surroundings in the library, his button-down shirt, tie, and slacks immaculate. The only incongruous thing was the stack of computer boxes in the background—and, of course, me.

I sipped my coffee.

"I was impressed by the work you did with those hard drives. It can't be easy to pull hidden information from them in the way you did," Cormac said.

I shrugged. "It's not hard."

"I also hear you can do some hacking."

I felt my neck and face go warm. How had he found that out? I cleared my throat. "I'm not that good. Got caught each time. I'm better at the whole math angle."

"Nevertheless, you have a much different skill-set than most people I know."

The understatement of the year. While most fae glamour wasn't as extreme as Eliaster's—which caused him to fry most electronics he came in prolonged contact with—it still interfered enough to make tech difficult for fae to grasp.

"I want you to work for me."

It was a good thing I hadn't taken another drink, otherwise Cormac might have had it all over his face. I stared at him. "What? Why?"

"Because the fight is far from over." Cormac rubbed his hands together. "Roe needs a research assistant, now that she's actively searching out the pathstones. And, like I said, you have a unique technological skill set no one else I employ does. The last time we ran into the Lucht, they were using a message board on the Internet—something no one had thought of until you came along. I know you promised Marc you'd help, but I also know that you can't do so pro bono. Therefore, my offer."

Apparently, the two Tyrones had been talking to each other. Well, that was better than their relationship had been a few months ago, so, baby steps I guess. I blew out a deep, gentle breath. "So what you're saying is I'd basically be a glorified IT guy."

Cormac's lips pursed. "I'm not familiar with the term."

I took a sip of my coffee. Then I set it on the side table. "So what do you want hacked?"

Cormac raised an eyebrow. "Perhaps you'll want to negotiate terms and conditions, and then actually accept the job, before you ask that question."

Oh. Right. I rubbed the back of my neck. Stupid fae and their stupid word games.

Cormac set his cup to the side. "It's not even a guarantee you'll need to hack anything. But I want someone who has the ability to keep track of online activities that might be related to the Lucht Leanuna. Before you discovered their forum, I didn't have any idea something like that could have existed." He smiled wryly. "Maybe I should have listened a little to my son." He glanced up at me, eyebrows raised. "Is that something you'll be able to do?"

I paused, working it out in my head, then nodded. "I should be able to find or write some webcrawler programs that could—"

He held a hand up. "No need to explain it to me. I couldn't understand anyway." He glanced at the door. "I believe Roe had planned to stop by here this afternoon, so you could talk to her, see what kind of help she needs."

"Actually, sir ..." I tugged the piece of paper the fortune-teller had given me out of my pocket and handed it to him. "That came through an informant today."

His eyes flicked over the paper and he nodded. "Did the informant mention what this was in relation to?"

"She hinted that her employer knew where a pathstone could be found."

"Excellent." He handed the paper back to me. "Well done. I'll be in my office if you need anything."

I nodded, even though his praise felt unearned. I hadn't done anything but talk to Maira. And he probably wouldn't be too thrilled when he learned where the information had come from.

I pulled out my phone and sent Eliaster a text. *Need to talk. Are you home?*

A few minutes later, his reply came in. *Be there in five.*

Well, I could get started on the computer in the meantime. I pulled the top box off the stack and slit the tape open with my keys. Mostly, I just wanted to see what Cormac had given me to work with.

After a few minutes, I heard the sound of a motor outside. I closed the lid of the box and headed outside, grabbing my gun on the way. I nearly took Lukas's head off as I swung open the front door. He spun around, scowling at me.

"Why are you still out here?" I asked.

His scowl deepened. "None of your beeswax."

Dude, what is your problem? I bit back the words. Right now, I really didn't feel like getting into a confrontation with him. "Where's Eliaster?"

"Why do you ask?"

"What are you, the bouncer? Where is he?"

Lukas sighed. "He just pulled around to the workshop. Should I show you there?"

"Nah, you've got more important things to do than play butler, I'm sure."

The fae glared at me, but I just gave him my most innocent smile as I walked out the front door. The workshop was attached to the garage, but mostly hidden around the corner of the house. As I got closer, I heard the faint sounds of some classic rock song playing in the building.

I pushed open the side door.

Eliaster already sat at the worktable that ran along the back wall, tightening a bolt on some piece of engine sitting in a puddle of grease on the wooden surface. A pitted, rust-splotched motorcycle frame sat in the middle of the cracked, stained concrete floor, parts scattered around it. The bike's original color might have been red, but I couldn't tell for sure.

As I got closer, I could hear Eliaster singing along under

his breath. Something about not feeling something, or not fighting a feeling, whatever. Classic rock wasn't really my thing.

I cleared my throat.

He spun around, wrench half-raised. "Josh. *Amadán*, one of these days I'm gonna split your head open before I realize it's you." He hit pause on the mp3 player sitting on the table, and then grabbed a rag and started scrubbing his hands. "So what'd Maira have to say?"

"She was just passing along a message. Said that if we were interested, we'd find evidence of relics in Illinois. And she gave me this." I held out the scrap of notepaper she'd handed me.

Eliaster took it and glanced at the message. His scowl deepened. Eliaster straightened and stepped into the garage. His supercar's engine was still ticking, loud in the quiet, metal-sided building. He opened the passenger door and pulled out his backpack. "Did she say who this information was from?"

I rubbed the back of my neck and looked away. "Coriander Airgead."

Silence met my admission. I looked up, and Eliaster was staring at me, one eyebrow raised.

"Coriander Airgead. Son of Drake Airgead?" he asked.

I was pretty sure it was rhetorical, so I kept my mouth shut.

Eliaster's eyes slowly darkened to a forest green. "Why would the son of an Unseelie lord who lives in New York of all places contact you—and specifically ask for you *by name*—to tell *you* that he has a lead for us about relics?"

"Maybe because I owe him and he wants to cash in on the favor," I muttered.

"You owe him a favor? Since when?"

"Since he saved my life in Chicago."

Eliaster's gaze flicked back and forth, and I could tell he was putting the pieces together. "He was the one who saved you when Llew grabbed you away from us?"

I nodded.

"Okay. I get not telling me at the moment, especially since we were suspicious of Larae and David. But this is the first I'm hearing about it, and it's been *several* months at this point."

I shrugged. "I just … didn't want to think about it after …" After Marc's death.

Understanding crossed Eliaster's face. "Look." He plunked down on the bike seat. "I know you're regretting that you got mixed up in all this. But the simple fact is, the Underworld has you now. You won't—"

"Won't escape. Yeah, yeah, I've been given the grand tour."

He smirked. "Dude, you've been given the CliffsNotes version."

I groaned. Of course he picked up right away why I'd been reluctant to talk about it. I was dragging my feet, hoping that I'd drop off the radar. Sure, a couple of months ago I'd been all gung-ho, but I was still scared.

Not that I'd admit that to him.

"So, what do you think?" I asked.

Eliaster smoothed the paper between his fingers, gnawing on the inside of his lip. "Right now, Blodheyr and Larae have a jump on us. They knew where to find one pathstone—they very likely know about others. We can't afford to not chase this lead." He handed the note back to me. "I'll back you up, don't worry."

I nodded, feeling my stomach tighten. This would be good, right? If we found relics, and Cori was telling the truth, maybe we'd get hold of a pathstone before the Lucht. Everyone was convinced that the Lucht Leanuna getting their hands on the pathstones was a bad idea all around, seeing as how they wanted to use them to open a portal to the fae Otherworld and free a monster. After seeing the havoc Larae had wrought just to find one, I tended to agree. I'd promised Marc I'd help. So that was what I'd do.

But I still couldn't shake the feeling in my chest—that

something was going to go horribly, horribly wrong.

Chapter 4

JOSH

I stood on the street corner, staring at the café across the road. It looked fairly harmless from here, just a cinderblock building painted brown, built back from the street a little to allow room for a tiny patio crowded with metal chairs and tables. The patio was deserted this morning, everyone preferring to get their daily caffeine fix indoors rather than letting the gray skies drizzle on them.

The place still got my hackles up, even now, four months after Marc's death. And now, my first time back, I was walking into a meeting that could very well be a trap.

I leaned against the stoplight, waiting for the signal to change to "walk." Water dripped into my jacket collar, and I shook my shoulders as the cold droplets slid down my neck. I tried to psych myself up. Eliaster was just across the street. I forced myself not to look over my shoulder at where he sat in my old beater of a car instead of his fancy supercar. I'd be fine. What could a fae do to me in public, with so many witnesses?

Even as I thought it, the edges of my vision started going black. The back of my neck itched, and what felt like warm, moist breath huffed over me. I spun. No one stood behind me. But I could almost feel scaly fingers clutching the back of my shirt. I reached back and pulled at the collar of my jacket.

Stupid question. Stupid, stupid question.

The light finally changed, and the cars slowed to a stop. I dashed across the street, puddles soaking my sneakers and the hem of my jeans, and headed around the building to the front entrance—ironically at the back of the building, away from the street. The parking lot was full, and I felt a brief flash of jealousy for all the people who could still come here without shaky hands and shortened breath.

Relax. It's Cori. If he wanted you dead, he wouldn't have gone to all that trouble setting up this meeting. I shoved open the glass door. The bell jingled overhead, making me jump. The patrons at the tables closest to the door gave me curious glances, but their interest was quickly pulled away by their friends, their computers and smartphones. I stood just inside the doorway, my clothes dripping on the welcome mat, scanning the inside of the café.

No faces had a glamour ghost blurring their features. Everyone was—weirdly enough—human.

"Hey, buddy." One of the baristas leaned over the counter, her pierced eyebrows raised. "In or out."

I let the door swing shut behind me and stepped up to the counter. I ordered quickly, just a regular cup of black coffee that I could've gotten a lot cheaper elsewhere. This wasn't really about the coffee, I reminded myself as the barista took my cash and handed over a scalding hot paper cup. This was about proving to myself that I could come back. That I'd made some kind of progress. Judging by the acid turning in my stomach, I had to guess that I still had a long way to go.

But today, I wasn't going to run from memories.

I chose an empty booth by the front windows and slid into it. It wasn't the same booth Marc and I had sat in, that night back in May, but it was close enough to make my nerves strung out like the wires on a violin. I glanced over at the table next to me and found the receipt someone had left, a brown ring of coffee marking the white paper. Five-seventy-two. The table beyond that, I could see a paper slip attached to someone's coffee cup. Two-fifty. I rolled my shoulders and sipped at my coffee absently, then gasped from the pain the burning liquid shot over my tongue.

"Stupid, stupid," I muttered, pressing the back of my hand to my mouth. *Pay attention, idiot.*

"That looked like it hurt," someone said.

I glanced up as a slim girl with copper-colored hair slid into the booth across the table from me. I blinked, waiting for a glamour ghost to slide away from her face. Nothing changed. I blinked again. A lock of hair over her ear changed from red to white, the coarse, straight hair in bright contrast to the curls surrounding it.

"Careful with that," the fae said, pointing to my coffee.

I glanced down at the cup in my hand. I'd crunched in the sides, and coffee burbled between the rim and the lid. For a second, I didn't register the pain of the hot liquid.

Then I gasped again and jerked my hand away, shaking it. I grabbed napkins from the edge of the table and dropped them on the spreading puddle of coffee, then looked back up at the fae. "Of all things, why the glamoured hair?"

She smirked. "Yeah, you're as good as they say you are."

My first thought was, *she's kinda cute.* My second thought was to trap that first thought, shove it into a mental box, and put a padlock on it. She didn't exude that sexy, over-friendly vibe Larae had—in fact, she gave off a distinctly *un*friendly vibe—but I'd learned my lesson. I dropped my hands, moving my bag from my right side to my left, as if getting ready to bolt for the door. "Who are you?"

"A friend."

"Yeah. Sure. I bet." With my bag concealing the rest of my movement, I pulled my gun from the hidden holster at my waist and rested it on my leg. Over the ambient noise of the coffee shop, I was pretty sure no one else would hear as I thumbed back the hammer.

The girl rolled her eyes. "Really? We're going that route?"

Okay, so she'd heard. Dang fae and their keen hearing. I shrugged. "Can't be too careful, not with the crowd I usually hang around."

"You're picking up Eliaster's paranoia. I don't blame you. Based on what I've heard"—she whistled—"your entry into the Underworld wasn't exactly a cakewalk."

"Just tell me what you want and then get out of here."

She rolled her eyes.

Before she could answer, a more familiar voice said, "Good grief, Aileen, just answer him."

I glanced up. Standing beside our booth was a tall, slim fae. I almost didn't recognize Coriander at first—the last time I'd seen him, he'd been wearing dark clothes under an outrageous red leather tuxedo jacket, and his blond and red-striped hair had been spiked into a Mohawk. Now he wore his hair slicked back under a baseball cap, and the jacket had been replaced with a nondescript gray hoodie.

He nudged the girl. Aileen rolled her eyes and scooted over, letting him slide in the booth.

Cori tucked his hands into the pocket of his hoodie and grinned at me. "Forgive my sister. She's the dramatic one of the family."

Aileen smirked.

I could definitely see the family resemblance—the same nose, similarly shaped eyes, and jawline. "I think you both probably inherited the fae drama gene, at least." I squinted between the two of them and frowned. Cori was unquestionably full fae, with sharp features and pointed ears. But Aileen's ears were rounded, like a human's.

She noticed me looking and touched the top of her ear. The multiple rings on her fingers clicked on her cartilage piercings. "I know. We're only half-siblings. I'm three-quarters fae—he's full. Good eye."

"And your brother?" I remembered the shorter, broader fae I'd seen Coriander with in the Chicago marketplace. What had Eliaster said it name was. "Gray? Gren?"

"Gren," Cori confirmed. "Again, full fae, but still only

half sibling."

I tucked the information away. Maybe Eliaster or Angel or Roe would find it useful. "Okay. So, you two care to enlighten me as to what's going on?" I gently released the hammer on my gun and slipped it back into my holster.

Cori whistled softly and elbowed Aileen. "He had a gun on you? You're losing your touch."

She rolled her eyes again. "You're the charmer of the family." She leaned forward, clasped her hands together on the table. "Josh. Have you ever heard the name Galen Shaughnessy?"

It didn't ring a bell. I shook my head.

"He's a relic runner who lives in Kansas City. Track him down, find his hideout, and the trail will lead you to a certain relic you and Eliaster might be interested in."

I wanted for the rest, but she didn't say anything more. "That's it?"

"That's all I can tell you."

"Okay." I leaned back, crossed my arms over my chest. "Why? Just tell me where the relic is, and we'll go retrieve it."

"I can't."

"Why not?"

She tipped her hand from side to side. "It's complicated."

"Uncomplicate it."

The corner of her lips twitched, as if she was trying not to smile. Aileen glanced at Cori.

Cori met my eyes. "I wish we could, but this meeting alone is a huge risk for us. I'm not even supposed to be here. The original plan was to lure you in using my name."

Lure me in? I shifted. It was hard to ignore the prickling on my neck as he talked. I hunched my shoulders, forcing myself not to look out the window and search for Eliaster. He was okay. He'd take care of himself.

"I was supposed to warn you off searching for more relics," Aileen said softly. "Threaten you, if necessary. That's all I can tell you right now. We're running out of time." She leaned forward even more. "We need help, Josh. But we know that without a gesture of goodwill on our part, Eliaster won't listen to us. That's fair, I get it. So this is our offering to you."

They both stared at me, eyes flickering just a little, both looking tense and ready to bolt. I tapped the edge of the table trying to find anything about their body language that said they were lying. *One-two-three…four…five-six. One-two-three…four…five-six.*

Aileen suddenly opened her right hand, laying it flat on the table, palm up. "Do you know the rule of three?"

I racked my brain for a second before I dredged up the information. It had been in a book Roe had given me. "It's sacred, isn't it? If sidhé say something three times, it must be true?"

"It's sacred and binding by glamour," she said. "Take my hand."

Cautiously, I reached across the table and laid my hand in hers. As her fingers closed around mine, her thumb brushed the edge of my bracelet. The contact sent a sudden, brief jolt or shock or *something* down my arm, so quick I didn't even have time to react. What *was* that?

Aileen didn't seem to notice. Instead, in a low voice, she said, "I swear to you by my soul and by the Allfather above in heaven, and all his *aingeals* there and here on earth, I am speaking the truth to your ears." She repeated the phrase a second, and then a third time.

A frisson of glamour swirled around our hands, purple and so faint I could barely see it. I glanced up and saw the glamour reflect in her eyes, intense and gray, flickering bits of blue and purple sparking in her irises.

I had no doubt that she was telling the truth.

With the ritual completed, she leaned back, withdrawing her hand and staring out the window. Her eyes continued to flicker.

Cori glanced between us. "Do we understand each other?"

I flexed my hand, staring at my fingers as the final bits of purple glamour sank into my skin. It was weird to see someone with such control over their glamour. The only two fae I'd so far seen with a similar amount of control had been Eliaster and Larae, and neither of them had that tight, finely-tuned look or feel to their glamour. I wasn't even sure if Eliaster could manifest his any time he wanted—so far it had mostly seemed to arc out of nowhere when he was upset, destroying any electronics he was touching.

I took a deep breath. "Yeah. I can't promise anything, but I think the promise Aileen just made will hold a lot of weight with the Tyrones."

Cori nodded and stood up, tugging on Aileen's arm. "Follow the information we gave you. If it proves correct, let Aileen know, and she can meet you to provide a more thorough explanation."

Aileen flicked her fingers in a subtle motion.

I followed the small burst of glamour until it puffed against the dry corner of a napkin that I'd put over my coffee spill. A single line of digits scrolled out on the paper, as if an invisible hand had written it there as I watched.

She said, "This is my burner phone. You're the only one who has the number, unless you give it to someone else. Use this from now on."

I waited as the brother and sister made their way out the front door, then stood to leave. When I stepped out into the parking lot, it was empty. They'd disappeared, far quicker than they should've been able to.

I blew out a deep breath and ran my hand through my hair, then looked down at the scrap of napkin in my hand, the purple, shimmery ink spelling out my only lead to a pathstone.

I just hoped what I'd told them would be true. I just hoped that I could convince Eliaster to chase this lead with me, and that I hadn't just lied to a couple of really desperate fae.

Chapter 5

ELIASTER

I leaned back in the passenger seat of Josh's old beater car, idly scrolling up and down through the tracks on my mp3 player.

I glanced up, watching as Josh crossed the street at a jog. He looked miserable, and not just from the rain dripping down his hair and glasses. His hands were shoved deep in his pockets and he just looked *done*. He hesitated in the doorway of the café, then stepped inside.

I kinda felt bad for him. This was the last place he'd seen his best friend, Marc, before his world went crazy. Well, the last place he'd seen him normal, anyway. Marc had been a half-fae, and he'd died because an insane fae had decided to shove a rusty iron knife into his gut. I knew Josh blamed himself, and while there wasn't anything I could do about his guilt, I personally couldn't wait until I got hold of Llew again. Preferably with an iron knife in my arsenal. The burns on my hands would be worth it.

As soon as the thought entered my mind, I closed my eyes and took a deep, slow breath. In. Out. *That's not who I am anymore.*

I got out of the car and hopped over the ledge of the parking garage. Not far from where I stood, a couple of benches sat under the overhang of the garage, a metal trashcan with an ashtray on the top separating them. I rummaged in my jacket and pulled out the package of cigarettes I usually carried. I didn't smoke, but sometimes, pretending to gave me an excuse to hang out in one spot for a bit. Just something Angel had taught me.

I tapped out a cigarette, lit it, and watched across the street. Josh had settled in a booth near a window, just as we'd agreed on. After a moment, I noticed a fae girl walk beside the booth. Josh jumped, and the girl laughed and said something to him. I tensed. He was supposed to be meeting Cori, not a random fae girl.

My neck prickled, and at the same time I heard footsteps echoing in the parking garage behind me.

"You know you're not fooling anyone, right?"

I turned my head just enough to see out of the corner of my eye. An unusually broad-shouldered fae leaned on the barrier of the parking garage. I eased my hand down to the knife at my side.

As he hopped over the barrier, the chains strung along his jeans pockets clinked.

I dropped the cigarette and turned, angling my body into a defensive stance.

The fae held his hands up. "I'm unarmed. I just want to talk."

I scoffed. "Yeah. Gren Airgead just wants to talk? I'll believe that when I see it."

He raised an eyebrow. "I know who you are, but how do you know me? We've never met before, right?"

"Right. But those are a pretty distinctive look." I gestured to the chains. Now that he was closer, I could see that his belt had multiple tiny loops in it, with one end of the chains fastened there, and the other end disappearing into the large front pockets. I had never met anyone who knew precisely what he kept in the pocket watches on the ends of the chains. Some people said bombs, some said poisons, some said they were family heirlooms and he just wore them all for the aesthetic. All of them or none of the above were also legitimate answers.

Whatever it was, I didn't care to find out the truth today.

Gren leaned against the barrier beside me and crossed his arms over his chest. "Let's cut the small talk."

"Suits me."

"I'm here to discuss your hunt for relics."

"I thought that might be it." Relics, or specifically pathstones? I guess I'd have to listen to find out. I relaxed my stance but didn't drop my hand from my knife. "So that's why you've been following me." I glanced over at the café and noticed that Cori was now sitting in the booth beside the girl, and Josh seemed really intent on what they were both saying.

"So you noticed," Gren said.

"Of course I noticed."

He accepted the snark with a nod. "But you didn't tell your human buddy."

I frowned. Of course I hadn't told Josh. He was already amped up enough—telling him that we were being followed would've made him more nervous. But Gren couldn't know that for sure. "So who's the girl?"

"Our sister."

I raised an eyebrow. "Whoever's yanking your chain sent three of you against one human and one fac? Paranoid much?"

Gren shrugged. "He wanted to get the message across clearly."

"Okay, and what's that?"

"We know about your work with the curators. Hunting down and destroying relics." Gren looked me in the eye. "We know about Emily and Iain."

Those two names set instant knots in my gut. I had to fight to keep my hands unclenched. "Everyone knows about that," I snapped. "That's supposed to be a threat? To scare me off?" Ice trickled down my spine. Did he know my true purpose for hunting down relics?

Gren glanced over to the café. "Wouldn't want a repeat

of that mess."

A chill rolled over my face and neck, followed immediately by a hot flush of rage. They were threatening Josh.

My phone dinged in my pocket, the special three-chirp tone I'd set for Josh. I glanced at the screen. *Need to talk.*

"Ah, looks like my siblings are done talking sense into your partner," Gren said amiably.

I shoved the phone back into my pocket.

"So what'll it be, Eliaster Tyrone?" Gren asked. "As you prepared to listen to reason?"

I snorted. "Have you heard anything about me?"

Faster than I could duck, Gren grabbed the front of my shirt and slammed me into one of the parking garage's support columns. "Ready to listen now?" he growled.

I grabbed at his wrists, tried to pry his hands free. When that didn't work, I tried to drop my hands and go for the knives under my jacket.

But my hands stayed fixed in place.

I ducked my chin so I could see what was going on. Flames of yellow-green glamour wound around my wrists and hands, pinning my fingers in place against Gren's arms. A slight electric buzz ran along the backs of my hands, making the hair on my arms stand on end. My vision narrowed, and I fought the sudden panic that surged through me like a live wire. The last time I'd seen this much glamour, it had been from a crazy Unseelie witch trying to kill me.

I gasped. Spread my fingers and tried to pull glamour into my own hands. Tried to sear away the fire wrapping my arms. A burning warmth spread over the backs of my hands and arms. Faint blue flame flickered from between my fingers and then died.

Gren laughed, a sharp staccato sound. "That's pathetic."

I looked up, gritting my teeth, and started. Gren had changed. His skin had been clear, but now I could see the glowing tattoos on his cheeks and brow, down each side of his neck, poking from the hems of his shirt sleeves. I could've sworn that he hadn't had tattoos before … had he been hiding them with glamour?

I drove my knee into his gut.

Gren's smile turned into a pained expression, and he gasped out a short breath. The cords on my wrists vanished. I twisted free of his hands and swung, hard, at his face.

He dodged and my knuckles slammed into the concrete wall. I swore and turned, swinging again with my other hand.

He grabbed the collar of my jacket and threw me backward into the parking garage. I curled up, wrapping my arms around my head. I hit the concrete floor hard on one shoulder and rolled several times before I could stop myself. I looked up. He'd thrown me close to ten feet away from the entrance. I swallowed, clenched my hands. He was a *lot* stronger than I'd thought.

Gren stepped into the garage. Here, in the darker space, I could see the flames of yellow glamour misting from his fingers.

I staggered to my feet and drew my knife. Crap. Stupid idea to stay and fight—with that much glamour, he could easily give me a beating. But if I ran, he'd hit me in the back with glamour, then step in to finish the job with his fists. Either way, I was probably getting some bruises and maybe a broken bone or two. My shoulder twinged.

Gren leaned across the doorway, blocking the nearest exit, and crossed his arms. "I'm serious. Stay out of this. You can chase the Lucht Leanuna to your heart's content, but stay away from the relics. You hear?"

"Do you really think that's going to stop me?"

"No. But you're setting Josh up, if you're not careful." He smirked. "And I don't think you want any more blood on your hands."

The words sucker punched me hard. I clenched my free hand. "He can take care of himself." But he couldn't. I knew that, and I saw in Gren's expression that he knew it as well.

"Fine, whatever you have to tell yourself to sleep at night." Gren started to turn away, then said over his shoulder,

"And for Danaan's sake, get yourself a focus tattoo. The next time I see you, I actually want this to be a fair fight."

I waited until he was out of sight before I collapsed onto my knees, hands shaking as I sheathed my knife. My mind spun. What danger to address first? The threat against Josh, the control over glamour that I'd never seen before in my life … *What's a focus tattoo?* I stood, brushing my hands against my jeans. My left hand throbbed with the movement. I winced, glanced down. Blood dripped from my knuckles. I flattened my right hand against the wall in an effort to steady myself.

Out of all the sidhé I'd ever met, I was pretty sure that Gren scared me the most.

Josh came around the corner of the parking garage, head up, eyes scanning the interior of the place as they adjusted to the dimness. He smiled when he first saw me, but the smile quickly faded as his eyes widened. "What happened to your hand?"

I glanced down at my hand. "I left some skin on the wall."

"Who were you fighting? Did Llew show up again?"

"Might be worse than Llew," I said quietly.

Josh's face went white, and I realized my mistake.

"Not Larae," I clarified. I walked toward the car, massaging my hand. "Let's talk when we get home."

Josh was weirdly quiet on the way back to the rath. I glanced over at him once or twice. He kept his head ducked down, his eyes on his phone, and his thumbs tapping away like mad on the tiny touch screen. Something had clicked in his techno-brain; I could tell by his intense focus on whatever it was he was doing.

What had happened in the café? Who was the fae girl I'd seen sitting beside Coriander?

Gren had said *our sister*. So the Airgead brothers had a

sister.

Strange how, after pushing people away for so long, I'd gotten attached to this weird human in such a short time. I'd always wanted to protect humans from other fae—that was part of what had driven me to working with the curators and seeking out relics in the first place.

Josh made me think of some of the curators I'd worked with. Sharp as a new dagger, adaptable, but still somehow clueless at times.

As we parked, got out of the car, and headed up the steps of my father's rath, Josh suddenly looked up from his phone. "What can you tell me about the rule of three?" he asked.

I blinked. Hadn't been expecting that question. "The, uh … huh. Haven't heard that for a long time."

"So what is it?" Josh learned forward. His eyebrows rose just a touch, and he grinned.

"It's an old sidhé thing. You know how our eye colors fluctuate with our emotions? The d'anam fuienneog?" I barely wait for his nod before continuing. "That makes it easy to guess emotions. Makes it difficult to lie, but we still can. So our ancestors found a way to bind all the fae with the rule of three—when a fae repeats something three times, it must be true. Otherwise …" I trailed off. Truth was, I didn't really know what would happen if a fae tried to lie *and* invoke the rule of three. "It's a holy number. Fae are pretty suspicious regarding anything holy."

Josh nodded. "I'll see if Roe has any ideas."

"Good plan. She'll know more than me." I paused on the steps of the rath. Where had he heard that? "Why'd you ask?"

"Aileen—she's an Airgead, Coriander's older sister—invoked it when I met with them."

I raised an eyebrow. "What'd she say when she invoked it?"

"She just used it to swear that everything she'd told me was true." Josh pushed his glasses further up the bridge of his nose. "She swore by the Allfather and the angels."

I made a skeptical noise.

"I think it was the real deal, Eliaster. I felt this … shock or something when she took my hand, and I saw the glamour when she said it."

Since when had he been able to see glamour? I rubbed the back of my neck. "Well, while you were chumming around with the nice siblings, I got to visit with Gren Airgead."

"The one with the pocket watches?" Josh's face scrunched and he shrank back. "You got into a fight with him?"

"Sort of. But what's more important is that he warned me off. Said Cori and Aileen were doing the same to you."

"Funny way of warning me off." Josh chuckled.

I smirked, but didn't laugh. "So what happened, if they weren't telling you to stop hunting down relics?"

He pocketed his phone, still smiling a bit. "You ever heard the name Galen Shaughnessy?"

I shook my head. "Should I have?"

"Cori and Aileen said he's a relic runner who lives in Kansas City. They wouldn't give me much—they acted really scared about something—but they said that if we found Shaughnessy, we'd find a trail to a pathstone."

Vague promises, using the one thing we really wanted as bait … yeah, this didn't have *any* red flags at *all*. "Sounds like a trap."

"That's what I said, and I pressed them for more info. They seemed really scared about something. Aileen said that she'd been sent to Springfield to keep an eye on us, and that Cori wasn't supposed to be there at all, but that they were taking a chance and sharing this info in good faith."

"Did they want something in return?"

"I guess? I don't know, they didn't outright say anything."

I grunted. "So they were just sharing this out of the goodness of their hearts?"

"C'mon, Eliaster, what's it gonna take for you to trust them?"

"Oh, I don't know, maybe their brother not threatening the life of my friend?" I snapped. "My *human* friend who can't defend himself as well? Who still lives aboveground? Who now trusts the siblings of the guy who threatened him?"

Josh stared at me, wide eyed. "What?"

"Gren threatened your life, Josh. You really think I'm going to believe what Aileen and Cori say now? Like I said, this is some kind of trap. I bet they're working for Blodheyr. Gren sure seemed okay with the idea of killing you to get me to shut up."

Josh's shoulders hunched. "Then why go to all this trouble? Why not just gank me right then? Why try to draw us into some big conspiracy about black market relics?"

His questions were making too much sense. Way too much sense—and I didn't want to hear it. Not right now. My hands trembled. I shoved them into my pockets.

Josh sighed in frustration. "Well fine then. I guess we'll ignore this lead, that's the only info we've found in months mind you, to *play it safe*."

I rolled my eyes, then turned and jogged down the steps before I smacked the snot out of him. "I'll be in the garage." That was probably a lie. I needed to talk to Angel, see if he'd heard any rumors about Blaise's death. If Josh didn't come chasing after me in a few minutes I'd go track Angel down.

"Great. Awesome," Josh said sarcastically. "I guess I'll see you later. Maybe."

The *maybe* stung, but I gritted my teeth and kept walking. He might not like it, but this was to protect him.

Chapter 6

JOSH

I didn't stay at the rath long that night. I tried working on the computer stuff Cormac had shown me, but Eliaster's flippant dismissal of the information we'd gotten from the Airgeads grated on my nerves. I quit after about an hour of work and headed to my family's house aboveground.

By the time I got home, everyone else was asleep, so I went straight up to my room and collapsed on my bed. I turned on a TV show on my laptop, but soon my mind drifted from the problems of five robot pilots to my own issues.

Even though I was tired, my nerves felt like they were on fire. I felt ready to jump out of my skin, and my hands kept twitching of their own accord. It had been like this at night ever since I'd recovered from the trip to the Chicago Underworld.

I finally fell asleep, an almost physical weight dragging my limbs to stillness.

And I awoke to silence. The house was dark, silent. Moonlight filtered through my window. My computer had gone into sleep mode, so I must've been out for a while. I got up and tapped the mousepad to check the time. 2:30 AM. I walked over to the window and glanced out. Hadn't the curtains been closed when I'd fallen asleep?

My stomach sank. We'd been about to go into a new moon, but the one I saw from my window was full. And it had been shining on me as I'd slept. In ancient Gaelic mythology, that was a sign that I wouldn't live out the year. I swallowed hard and backed away, yanking my curtain shut. As I did so, the moonlight caught my right wrist, and I gasped in shock. The black scar that had been left as a mark of Larae's dark glamour had expanded. Like a thick, dark cuff, it wrapped fully around my wrist and extended a couple of inches up my arm. I could move my fingers, but I no longer felt my hand.

A jab of pain shot into my left wrist. I looked over and gasped again as the metal bracelet on my left wrist dug into the flesh, cutting deep lines of red that trickled down my hand and dripped onto the floor. The smell of iron—fresh blood—rose to my nostrils, and I gagged. The bracelet compressed again, and I dropped to my knees, screaming.

Glowing vines shot from the ground and lashed around me, pinning my arms to my sides. More crawled up my face, filled my nose and my mouth. I thrashed and screamed, but no sound came out. I could feel the vines snaking down my throat, and I started heaving, choking.

Wake up! I screamed at myself. *This is a dream! Wake up!*

More vines dug into my chest, and the cold, misty tendrils curled around my heart. They squeezed. I doubled over, screaming soundlessly, tears dripping down my face. I took another deep breath, felt the vines expand with my chest, and wrenched my arms together in front of my body. As soon as I screamed again, the vines tightened, but my fingertips were touching. I caught the web of my left hand between my fingernails and pinched. Compared to the rest of the pain wracking my body, it was nothing.

Inconsequential.

But it was just enough.

I felt like I'd been physically slammed back onto my bed. I bolted upright, patting my chest, my mouth. No vines.

Daylight streamed in around the edges of my closed curtains. I checked my wrists. The scar was still there, a thin line of darkness on the underside of my wrist, and the metal bracelet was still on my left, fitting just as snugly as it had been before.

I tried to push it off.

It wouldn't fit over the base of my thumb.

My heart leapt into my mouth, and I pushed on it again. The edge dug into my wrist, and a thin line of red trickled down my hand. Just like the dream.

I stopped, dread making my stomach turn. What if blood triggered it? Would it crush my wrist like it had in the dream?

My blood dripped down onto the jeans I still wore from yesterday, but the bracelet did nothing. I was finally able to slide it over the widest part of my hand, and I threw it on the ground next to the bed. It landed with a dull thump. I slumped back on the pillows and rubbed my face, sobbing. It had just been a dream. A dream. That was all. Just a dream.

I laid still for a few minutes, breathing hard, my hands over my eyes. I hadn't had a nightmare that bad since the first time I'd dreamt about killing David.

Someone knocked on my door. "Josh?"

Mom. I got up and opened the door, dragging my fingers through my hair.

She smiled. "Sleepy today? You're usually up and out the door so fast we can't even eat breakfast together."

"Yeah. Yeah, I...I crashed pretty hard last night." My stomach growled, and I remembered I'd been so nervous about meeting Cori and Aileen that I'd skipped dinner last night.

Mom laughed and motioned downstairs. "I'm going to go drag the twins out of bed."

Okay, so they were all still here, so it had to be fairly early. Their school started at 8, and the bus came by at 7:30. I shut the door and gathered everything I'd need for the day. I snatched up the bracelet and turned it over in my hands.

When Roe had given it to me, after Marc died, she'd only said it was an old family heirloom, that Marc would've wanted me to have it, that his sisters and mom had given their blessing for it to be passed on to me. Roe wouldn't have given the bracelet to me if she knew it would terrorize me.

At least, I hoped not.

I shook my head. That was a stupid thought.

Why now? Why hadn't I gotten bad dreams from the first night I started wearing it? I'd have to talk to Roe, see what she thought of this new turn of events.

After making sure my wrist had stopped bleeding, I changed into a new T-shirt and jeans, crumpling the bloodstained clothes into the bottom of the laundry basket. I grabbed my backpack and shoved the bracelet into my pocket. As I stepped down the stairs and into the kitchen, my phone rang. I glanced down at the screen. Eliaster.

My dad looked up from his newspaper. I smiled and waved to him, then stepped across the hall to the living room and answered the phone.

"Roe was attacked last night," Eliaster said sharply.

My face and hands went cold. "Is she hurt?" I asked in a low voice.

"No, just shaken up."

"Okay, well, I'll come anyway."

"Sounds good."

Mom called from the kitchen, "Are you eating with us?"

"Sorry, gotta go," I said, grabbing my shoes from the rack beside the front door.

"You work with computers, not people!" One of the twins—Matt, I thought, but it was getting hard to tell them apart just by voice—yelled back. "Is it really that much of an emergency?"

I rolled my eyes and ignored him. As I headed out the front door, my mom's voice called me back. I looked up, and just like I was five again and starting my first day of kindergarten, she was standing at the door holding out my jacket, a wrinkle of worry between her eyes.

I sighed and went back for it.

As I took it, she stepped forward and hugged me. "You know we're proud of you, Josh? Even though we've had some rough years, we're very proud."

Those words cut deep. I leaned back from the hug and studied her face more carefully. There was a shadow behind her eyes. Was she really that worried about me? It felt weird. I'd seen a lot of emotions I'd caused on my parents' faces—frustration and surrender being the primary two—but never worry. I pulled my jacket on and kissed the top of her head. "Thanks, Mom."

She nodded.

My mind spun as I pulled out of the driveway.

Eliaster met me at the edge of the Market, and together we made our way around the open area to the neighborhood where Roe lived. The first sight of Roe's house sent a cold shock through me. Every window in the place had been busted out. The street in front of it twinkled with glass shards. The door hung open, the upper hinge ripped off the wall. Claw marks scored the doorframe, and something had busted through the porch railing, reducing it to splinters.

"Holy crap," I muttered, stopping at the edge of the mossy yard. From here, I could see the front hallway of the house. Claw marks scored the plaster along the stairs. A shiver crawled down my spine.

Eliaster swore quietly and stepped up to the porch, staring at the interior of the house. He walked inside and pivoted to look at the doorframe, running his fingers along the wood. "The silver's still there." His jaw clenched.

"I don't understand," I said.

"Roe keeps the door and window frames lined with silver. It's not as powerful as iron, but it keeps most nasties out."

"It didn't deter the sluagh in May."

"No, but it weakened it. If it hadn't been weakened, I wouldn't have been able to smack it with that poker and get it to stop chasing us."

I frowned, fighting back a shiver at the remembrance of the sluagh and its gaping, beak-like mouth. "So, what do you think did this?"

Eliaster ran his fingers along some of the slash marks on the wall. His touch dislodged some of the plaster bits, and they pattered to the floor. "Based on how the silver didn't seem to slow it down, and these marks ... *fear dearg*. Redcaps."

I searched my mental files. What I remembered wasn't pretty. Redcaps stood about shoulder-height to me. Scrawny and hairy, with faces that were a nightmare's blend of human and rodent, they sported long jagged talons on their hands. They killed for sport and often wore hats dyed with the blood of their victims as trophies. Some of the legends said that the hats had to be kept soaked with blood, but I wasn't sure if that was true or just the usual Gaelic hyperbole.

"Iron claws," I muttered.

"Yeah," Eliaster said, straightening.

Of course we were dealing with some of the only sidhé not affected by iron. I sighed and looked around. "Lukas?"

The door at the end of the hallway creaked open, and Lukas looked out from the kitchen, a broom in one hand, dustpan in the other. "You two finally decided to show up, huh?"

I rolled my eyes. "Good morning to you too."

"So you're thinkin' redcaps too," Lukas said, leaning on the broom handle.

"Makes sense. They got past a monster deterrent, and when they didn't find a victim, they destroyed the place. I guess the question would be why."

"Or one of your Unseelie buddies decided to get back at Roe for helping you out," Lukas said. "Broke in. Tore it up."

Eliaster tapped the gouges in the wall. "This is a claw

pattern. You'd have to be awfully precise with a really sharp blade to mimic this."

"Or another clawed beastie."

"The faoladh? Come on, Lukas, you should know better than that. Besides, silver is worse than iron to them."

I left them to their bickering and walked over to the library door, easing it open. It was even more trashed than the hallway. The couches and chairs had been ripped to shreds. Papers and stuffing scattered across the carpet. Half-burned books choked the fireplace, and other books had been tossed around the room, their covers torn, pages hanging from the binding. Roe's desk had been smashed and torn nearly to splinters. One of the bookshelves lay facedown on the floor, the back smashed in.

I swallowed and stepped into the room. Glass crunched under my feet. Carefully, I began gathering books and papers into stacks, finding places on the remaining bookshelves. Roe would have to go through it all and sort it again, but I could at least salvage some of it.

I heard Lukas's and Eliaster's voices moving as they walked through the rest of the house, surveying the damage.

What if Roe had been here when the intruders had come? Would we have found her body, slashed open on the floor? The very thought made me feel sick to my stomach.

After a while, the door creaked open. Eliaster stepped into the library and whistled softly. He edged around debris to the couch and cleared a spot for himself to sit.

"Find anything?" I asked, not looking up at him.

"Nothing. I called Marc's mom and sisters. They're all still okay."

"That's good to hear." I picked up another armful of papers, carefully aligning it with a stack on a shelf. A small porcelain owl figurine had somehow escaped the carnage, and I picked it up next, cradling the cool statuette in my hands.

Eliaster heaved a sigh. "Dad and Roe both think we should chase the lead the Airgeads gave us."

I nodded.

"But I don't want to leave Springfield right now."

"Why not?"

Eliaster's mouth twisted. "That's right, I hadn't told you yet." He pulled a bundled cloth from his pocket and set it on the ruined coffee table. "One of my informants, Blaise … I found him dead yesterday. Hanging from the rafters of his apartment. And I found these wedged into his eyes."

I flipped open the bundle. Two small, dark-colored coins clinked together. They were covered in small hash marks. "Iron?"

He nodded. "No fae would desecrate a sidhé body like that. Leaving it to hang, and shoving iron coins in its eyes."

"So you think Blaise was killed by a …" I hesitated. "A human?"

"It doesn't make any sense, but it's either that, or Llew has gotten really, really sadistic." Eliaster snorted and muttered, "Wouldn't be too much of a stretch."

"And you think the two attacks are related?"

Eliaster shrugged.

I stared at the coins. I knew that, no matter who had killed Blaise and attacked Roe, it probably felt personal to Eliaster. Blaise was his informant. Roe was practically family.

But we finally had a lead to the pathstones, to the Lucht Leanuna. I reached out and closed my hand around the coins. My stomach turned, but I knew what I needed to do. I'd promised Marc.

"I'm going," I told him.

Eliaster looked up, eyes wide in surprise. "What?"

"I'm going to follow the Airgeads' lead," I said. "If you feel that you need to stay here, that's fine, but I don't want this chance to slip out of our hands." Eliaster stayed quiet, so I pressed my advantage. "What if this is a distraction by Llew, meant to keep you here while the Lucht find other pathstones?"

"What if it's not?" Eliaster countered, jaw clenching.

"If it's not …" I shrugged. "Your dad believes you this time, right?"

He nodded.

"So let him handle it for a few days. Or stay here."

The look on his face suggested I'd cut him with a knife. Eliaster shoved his hand through his hair, then stood up. I felt bad for pushing it, but we needed this lead.

Eliaster walked back and forth for a minute, rubbing his neck with both hands. Then he finally said, "You're right."

Some of the tension eased from my shoulders. "I'm not trying to force your hand—"

"I know, but I'm not going to let you go by yourself. You wouldn't know where to start. You don't enough about how the Underworld works yet."

"Probably not, but I feel vaguely offended. Thanks a lot," I quipped, trying to lighten the mood.

His smile was there and gone in a flash. "Well. Let's go find a relic runner then, shall we?"

Chapter 7

JOSH

By the time we pulled into a motel parking lot nearly three hours later, the bats kicking around in my stomach still hadn't subsided. I bounced between thinking that this was the stupidest thing I'd ever done in my life, to thinking that I would be helping, making a difference. I knew the way I felt was an overreaction. I kept telling myself it was an overreaction.

Still didn't change anything.

The motel wasn't a rent-by-the-hour crapfest, but it wasn't much higher on the food chain either. I glanced around the parking lot, at the streetlights sputtering along the cracked sidewalk in front and the grimy white paint on the sideboards of the motel.

Eliaster came out of the office and tossed me a key. "Room twelve." He nodded to the line of rooms across the parking lot.

Our room was at the back corner of the lot, furthest away from the road. An untrimmed green hedge scraped against the sideboards, and through the branches, I saw that the next lot over was deserted. I fitted my key into the lock and opened the door. The old, stale smell of cigarette smoke and beer floated out of the room as I pushed the door inward.

"Lovely." I reached to the side and flicked on the lights. The décor screamed generic motel—a few faded prints of prairies on the wall, some weirdly textured wallpaper, and threadbare carpet. "Did you have to pick the cruddiest place you could find in all of Kansas City?"

Eliaster pushed past me, carrying his backpack and a duffel bag. "Better than some I've stayed at."

"What, Dad doesn't spring for five-star resorts?" I threw my bag on the bed closest to the door and sprawled out beside it. My stomach chose that moment to growl.

"My da hasn't exactly approved of these outings in the past, so I try not to make him mad by wasting money on the nicest place available."

I squinted and turned my head to the side. "If I squint right, the stain on the ceiling looks like Chris Pratt's face."

"Should I turn on 'Hooked On A Feeling'?"

I sat up. "Seriously, you know *The Guardians of the Galaxy*, but not *The Lord of the Rings*? It's a classic, dude."

"Yeah, but my *life* is a fantasy novel. Why would I want to read it or watch the movie or whatever, when all I have to do is look out my window?" Eliaster unzipped his bag and pulled out a sheathed knife. He drew the blade and flicked the edge with his thumb.

From the ghosting around the knife, I knew it was another one of Opti's weapons. The glamour imbued in the knife would make human eyes slide right past it, unless they were specifically looking for a weapon.

"Where are your swords?" I asked.

"I could ask you the same question," he said.

I glared at him. Answering that would only open a lot more than I was willing to discuss with him at the moment.

After a few moments, Eliaster dropped the knife back into the backpack. "In my other bag in the back of the car. You can borrow one of them tonight if you want."

"What's on the agenda for tonight?" I asked, ignoring the offer of the weapon.

"Bar-hopping." Eliaster pulled his phone out of his

pocket, tapped the screen, and showed it to me. He'd dropped three pins in a map app, showing the addresses of bars we could easily walk to. "I had Angel get in touch with some people he knows up here. These three bars are known fae hang-outs, mostly the unsavory types."

"So we can find the criminal side of his life, not just the rich, respectable side that the Airgeads told us about," I said.

"Bingo."

Four hours later, it was one in the morning and I was dragging along, hoping the next bar served decent coffee along with beer and liquor. Eliaster kicked a rock off the sidewalk in front of me, muttering under his breath in Gaelic, whether in frustration or just thinking out loud, I couldn't tell.

The first two bars had been a bust, as far as I could tell. We'd gone in, talking loudly, like we were already halfway to trashed, about Shaughnessy owing money to our bosses and any other crap we could think of. No one had even flinched, as far as I could tell.

I rubbed the bracelet in my jacket pocket. The nausea from my fight-or-flight reaction to the fae was worse tonight, and I wondered if it was because I was in a new place, dealing with new fae, or if the bracelet had something to do with it. Once we were back home, I was going to have to test out some theories. Walk around the Market for a bit without the bracelet and see if I reacted the way I was reacting here.

We turned a corner, and I spotted the green neon sign a few storefronts away. Our third and final stop.

Eliaster let me catch up to him, then threw his arm around my shoulders. "Ready for this?"

I nodded. "Yeah, just—"

"We're being followed." The words were so quiet, I almost missed them.

Oh, wonderful. I resisted the urge to look over my shoulder. "How long? By who?"

"Goblins. Three of them, one of them cat-sidhé. They've been trailing after us since the first bar."

"Why didn't you tell me?" I hissed.

"I'm telling you now."

I buried my frustration and took a deep breath. "Okay, so—distraction? I got it. I'll swing around in the next alley."

"I don't—"

Dang it, couldn't he just let me do this already? "They won't follow you. I'm the lesser threat—they'll follow me." I didn't give him time to reply. I shrugged his arm off my shoulder and stepped away, giving him a shove for good measure. I raised my voice. "I'm tired and I'm sick of not getting anywhere. I'm heading back to the hotel."

Eliaster's lips twitched in amusement before he snapped back, "We have a job to do."

"Screw the job. Screw you. I'll talk to you tomorrow morning." I turned and stomped away, striding past the bar. My heart hammered, and my hands shook, so I stuffed them deep into my pockets. Despite myself, I snickered. Maybe I didn't intend to abandon this job, but it had kinda been nice to get out a bit of my frustration by yelling at Eliaster.

Behind me, the door chimed as Eliaster went into the bar. I swung into the alley and slowed my steps, listening. If I focused, I could hear tiny scratching noises, like claws, on the pavement behind me.

I spun around. The three goblins were creeping behind me, spreading in a half circle, knife blades glinting in the street lights. They blocked the mouth of the alley.

"Uh … hi, guys." I stepped further away from them, not bothering to hide the nervousness in my voice. I eased one hand to my side, reaching for my gun holster.

Too slow. The three darted forward. I spun, putting my back to the wall, but that was all I had time for, they moved that quickly. They closed into a semi-circle around me. My mouth went dry. Even though they were only chest-high, they were strong and quick. I did *not* want to deal with these guys on my own.

The cat-sidhé, distinguishable by its patchy fur, stepped in front of the others, angling its blade at my chest. "What's your business with Shaughnessy?" it snarled.

"Oh, so someone did finally notice we were asking about him. Finally. I was beginning to wonder if everyone in this city was just that unobservant." *Any time, Eliaster.* I moved my hand from my gun to my knife.

"Enough," the cat-sidhé snarled. "Answer the question, or—"

"Hey, hey, you can't have all the fun." Eliaster stepped into the alley, twirling his knife in his hand.

The cat-sidhé snarled and hissed something in Gaelic at the other two. They backed off, stalking toward Eliaster.

Well, this was gonna be fun.

I glanced back at the cat-sidhé. It stood with the knife still angled at me, but its head was slightly turned so it could see Eliaster and the two goblins out of the corner of its eye.

I took the chance and darted forward, grabbing the goblin's knife hand. It hissed and twisted, whipping me around and into the wall of the alley. My head smacked into the brick, pain bursting across the back of my skull. I grabbed its arm with both hands as it pressed the knife toward me. Over our struggle, I could hear shuffling and grunts as Eliaster and the two goblins got into their own scuffle.

"What do you want with Shaughnessy?"

I shoved its arm to the side, then drove my elbow straight into its temple. The cat-sidhé staggered, then straightened, baring its teeth at me. Something zipped into its chest, and the cat-sidhé crumpled like a wet piece of cardboard. I staggered a bit, still feeling dazed, and touched the back of my head. No bleeding, but I could already feel a welt rising under my hair. I looked down at the cat-sidhé, at the knife sticking out of its chest. Eliaster's knife.

He was unarmed.

Eliaster yelped, and I looked up in time to see him stagger back, wiping blood from his mouth. The goblin who had hit him shook out its fist, and the two moved in, hemming him in against the alley wall like they'd done to me.

"Josh! A little help here!"

As I started forward, a flashback punched me in the throat. I toppled, grabbed at the wall in a desperate attempt to maintain balance. *I could hear the sharp thwack of fist meeting flesh. Scyrril's deep, gravely voice. Marc's higher-pitched, almost-panicky replies. I could smell rotting banana peel. The hair on my neck prickled. My hand throbbed, aching so much that I curled my fingers into a fist.*

Just make it stop.

I jerked my head up as a goblin landed a punch in Eliaster's stomach, dropping Eliaster to the ground. Eliaster sucked in air and rolled away, narrowly avoiding a kick in the face. He got to his feet and backed away, hunched over. Blood trickled down his chin.

I staggered upright, my hands shaking. Pulled my gun from my jacket. Brought it up and sighted along the barrel to the goblin's chest. I took in a deep breath, held it, squeezed the trigger.

The shot cracked through the alley. The goblin's left leg buckled. Eliaster arched his back and kicked the goblin's other leg, dropping him all the way to the ground. Its shriek echoed off the alley walls.

The last goblin scuttled backwards, gawking at the gun in my hands, and took off running down the alley.

I stood, feeling sick to my stomach. Not from shooting the goblin. From everything else—the adrenaline, the flashback. My hands kept shaking and I nearly dropped the gun. What had I been thinking? I could've missed. Worse, I could've hit Eliaster.

Eliaster grabbed my arm. "Took you long enough. You okay?"

I nodded, not trusting myself to speak just yet.

He marched back to the goblin on the ground. He crouched, grabbed the goblin's shirt and yanked it into a sitting position. "Where's Shaughnessy?" he growled.

The goblin wailed and tried to pull free, his hands scrabbling in the loose gravel at the mouth of the alley.

My stomach churned. "Eliaster—"

"Shut up." He looked up at me, and I took a step back. The *d'anam fuinneog* in his eyes was going wild, shades of green spiking through his irises. He turned back to the goblin. "Where'd your friend run off to?" He punched the goblin in its wounded leg.

The goblin screamed and tried to struggle free. After a minute it stopped, cringing away from Eliaster. "That gunshot wouldn't have gone unnoticed," it rasped. "The police will be here soon."

Eliaster grabbed his knife from the cat sidhé's chest and pressed it against the goblin's throat. "Not in time to save your other kneecap if you don't answer me."

The goblin stared at him, then glanced up at me. I stepped back, holding my hands up.

"Last chance." Eliaster pressed harder, a line of blood appearing under the goblin's chin. "You're going to regret it if you don't answer me. I'll cut you open like I'm gutting a fish."

"Okay, okay, okay! Shaughnessy's probably at the Blue Fire. It's a nightclub—he's part owner."

"And your friend?" Eliaster snarled.

"I can't—I can't—you don't understand, if I tell you and they find out—"

Eliaster slammed his fist into the goblin's temple. The goblin slumped to the ground, eyes rolling back in its head.

I backed out of the way as Eliaster stood and stomped down the alley, motioning for me to follow him. I stepped to the side of the unconscious goblin. It was still out for the count. Rustling quickly through its pockets, I found only a little package wrapped in brown paper. I stuffed it in my own pocket and jogged after Eliaster, skirting around the cat-sidhé's body.

We walked in silence around the corner, then Eliaster held up his hand.

"What was that?" I hissed at him as he crept back to the corner and crouched down.

"Don't. I didn't kill it," Eliaster shot back.

I winced.

He wrinkled his forehead. "Sorry, that's not … You shot him to help me. Don't regret that." He sat, his back to the wall, and ran his hand down his face. He looked … almost scared. But before I could ask if *he* was okay, he started talking again. "I didn't hit him that hard—he should wake up again soon. He'll be hurting, he won't be paying attention. We'll follow him, see where he leads." He nodded to me. "What'd you find?"

I pulled the brown package from my pocket and peeled away the paper, revealing a small jewelry box. Something rattled inside as I turned it, examining it from all sides. I fumbled in my backpack for a small penlight, then held the light between my teeth as I eased open the box.

Nestled inside on a foam cut-out was a glossy, round bead about the size of my thumb, covered in the same type of hash marks as the iron coins Eliaster had showed me earlier today. I tipped the box, showing it to him. "What are those?"

"Ogham. An old Gaelic writing system." He squinted. "De … *dea-tho* … something. I never learned all of the symbols. Roe would know them. It's definitely some kind of relic, though. Lots of them have ogham on them—that's the medium typically used for imbuing them with glamour." He went back to watching around the corner.

"I thought you worked with curators. If this is something typical to relics—"

He snorted. "I had more to do with the protection side of things than actually dealing with the relics. Besides, I can see the glamour woven around that thing. Can't you?"

I squinted at the stone, then shook my head.

Eliaster frowned. "That's weird. I thought you could see glamour now."

"Maybe it was just a fluke." Or maybe not wearing the bracelet had something to do with it.

Eliaster suddenly went tense and motioned for me to be quiet. Then he rose and motioned for me to follow him.

Chapter 8

ELIASTER

I stalked the goblin for about fifteen minutes as it took alleys and side roads towards the business district, where I could see some kind of factory billowing white steam into the night sky. The goblin wasn't fast—it limped and wobbled, muttering under its breath. Every time it whimpered, I winced.

I'd lost control. I hadn't expected them to put up a fight like that, to get me to the ground. I'd been cocky, and then I'd panicked.

I shook the old fear away and focused on following the goblin.

To my surprise, instead of going for one of the abandoned warehouses we passed, the goblin ducked down a street into an old residential area. This must have been where factory workers lived back in the day—the houses were small cracker boxes, mildewed and crumbling. More than half of them looked abandoned.

I hung back at a street corner, watching as the goblin scuttled up the steps of a house with boarded-up windows. It rapped on the door, and a few moments later, the door cracked open enough for it to slip inside.

I glanced over my shoulder. Josh hung back, jiggling his

unlit flashlight in his hand with major jitters.

"He's in there," I whispered. I dug into my jacket pocket for my own flashlight, then tossed him an extra pair of leather gloves.

He caught them. "So we're going in?"

I glanced over at the house. It sat quiet and dark. "Maybe. Depends on what we see. C'mon."

We crossed the street in a quiet jog and ducked to the side of the house. As I stepped onto the neglected, muddy lawn, I spotted a small window set into the house's foundation. I motioned toward it, and Josh flicked on the flashlight.

Broken pieces of glass glimmered in the grass and dirt around the busted-out window. Josh crouched down to get a better look. I glanced around. The window above us was boarded over. No getting in that way—if I even wanted to get in.

Josh inhaled sharply.

My pulse spiked. "What?" I hissed.

He motioned toward the basement. I knelt beside him and tipped my head to see. The light played over a cement-block room that looked to be the length and breadth of the entire house. On the far side of the room, I could barely see spikes that had been pounded into the wall, chains coiled on the floor next to filthy, tattered blankets.

I could feel anger rising up my chest and neck in a slow wave of heat. I dug my fingers into the ground.

"Think they have any prisoners?" Josh asked.

"Guess we'll find out."

"Are you sure—"

"Yes, I'm sure!" I snapped back. I didn't look at Josh as I lowered myself to my belly and slid backward, edging my legs over the basement window's metal sill. A small point of glass that I'd missed caught and dug into my thigh. I winced and stopped, working my jeans free, then breaking the shard off and tossing it out into the yard.

I landed on the dirty basement floor in a crouch and

paused, waiting to see if there was any reaction to the noise. Above me, voices and muffled footsteps sounded. No one would've heard me over the din the goblin and his buddies were making themselves.

I flicked the flashlight around the interior of the room. It was too small for the house, so it must be a walled-off section of the basement. Tattered remains of a curtain and a cheap metal curtain rod lay on the floor not far from my feet. I motioned for Josh to follow me and crept forward to the blankets. As soon as I touched them, dust rose into the beam of my flashlight. Old, then. And the chains had left rust stains on the fabric. These hadn't been used in quite a while.

Still, the idea of goblins holding someone prisoner down here, likely some poor human who had fallen into their hands, made me grind my teeth.

I heard a light thump as Josh's feet hit the ground. I motioned for him to wait where he was, then crept forward to the door. It was already hanging open just a crack, and I eased it back so I could shine my flashlight into the next room. The beam played over a slightly more well-trafficked room, scattered with random broken furniture, an old, rusty washer, and various other bits of junk that I quickly scanned.

Josh nudged my shoulder and pointed to the side of the basement, tucked between our door and a set of rickety wooden stairs. My heart nearly stopped.

A small wooden workbench stood below the stairs, clear except for a small cardboard box. One of the flaps hung open, and something inside glittered. Before I could say anything, Josh had squeezed past me and opened the box the rest of the way.

I tapped his shoulder. "Don't let them touch your bare skin."

He nodded and pulled on the gloves. After a second, he picked up the entire box. "This thing is full of books, and there's jewelry in here too," he whispered. "I think we have our proof."

"You're sure? They have ogham?"

He pulled out a bracelet and a necklace, holding them out to me. I pulled my sleeve over my hand and accepted the bracelet. In the light of the flashlight I could just barely see ogham carved in the underside of the bracelet.

I frowned, wishing I'd paid better attention when Roe had tried to teach ogham to me a couple of years ago.

"So Cori and Aileen were right," Josh said quietly.

I nodded, feeling slow-witted, my brain scrambling to catch up. Cori and Aileen had been right. "Let's—"

The door hinges creaked. My stomach dropped. *Crap*! I grabbed Josh's shirt and yanked him into the side room, pressing us both into the shadows beside the door. Thumping came down the stairs. After a few seconds, whoever it was began whistling off-key. I glanced out the door. A goblin stood at the washer, dumping dirty clothes into the top. I eased the door shut a bit more, then motioned for Josh to head out the window with the box. As he crossed the room, I eased around the corner again, watching the goblin.

Broken glass crunched under Josh's feet. I winced and grabbed for my knife. The goblin paused. My heart seized in my chest and I squeezed my knife hilt.

The goblin sneezed, sniffed, and resumed loading the clothes into the washer.

Once Josh had safely climbed out, I crossed the room and scrambled back out onto the lawn. We quickly headed down the sidewalk, away from the house. Josh tucked the box half into his jacket, and I kept watch behind us. I half-expected the front door to slam open, and goblins to pour out after us, but everything remained quiet as we left the area.

Once we'd walked a few blocks, I sighed, trying to release the tightly-coiled tension in my chest. I'd fully expected to run into a dead end, despite the Airgeads' insistence that their info was good.

But the goblins had known Shaughnessy—known enough that they'd tried to kill us for asking about him.

No. Not kill us. I stopped dead in the middle of the sidewalk, replaying the fight in my mind. The goblins and the cat-sidhé had had knives, yeah, but the cat-sidhé hadn't even slashed at Josh, despite threatening him with the blade. And every slash aimed at me had been aimed for a non-vital area. No arteries, no gut strikes—the outsides of my legs, the backs of my arms. Injuries to weaken, to wound, but not to kill. Not even to cause severe blood loss.

A chill rolled down my spine. They'd been trying to capture us.

"You okay?" Josh called back to me.

"Yeah." I started walking again. Thank the Almighty they hadn't succeeded.

Chapter 9

JOSH

Eliaster as weirdly quiet as we got back to the hotel room. He went straight into the bathroom and closed the door.

I carefully placed the cardboard box on my bed as if it contained a live snake. Then I dug the case I'd taken from the goblin out of my pocket and opened it, tipping it slightly to one side so I could see the hash marks on the stone. It was tiny, the size of my thumbnail, made of a dark, smooth granite. I pulled the gloves back on and picked up the stone, flicking on the bedside lamp. Under the bright light, I realized the carvings weren't really hash marks. One horizontal line ran across the surface of the stone, with vertical lines cutting through it, some straight, some diagonal. They looked similar to the marks on the bracelet we'd found earlier.

I started to reach for my tablet, then decided against it. Online research regarding the sidhé was sketchy at best. Roe was a source I could trust. Not to mention the fae might have used the runes in a slightly different way than the Celts, and I wanted to make sure I was getting the correct translation.

But before I told her, I wanted to examine the contents of the bigger box again. I took a deep breath and opened the lid, then pulled the bracelet and necklace out of their nests of bubble wrap. The ogham on the bracelet's underside were tucked beneath its decorative wire wrapping. I pried the necklace's round locket open, revealing ogham hash marks carved inside, along with a tiny clump of something that looked suspiciously like hair.

Aw, yuck. Who knew what the locket had been used for? I shut it and rolled the locket in my palm. Something about it was weird—it didn't look *that* old. The golden-colored metal was still shiny, even under the dirt, and it wasn't like I was an expert on jewelry, but there was no tarnish or patina on it. Every other relic I'd seen had definitely been older.

I set the three relics to the side, then pulled out the three books stacked in the box. All of them bore cracking leather covers and crumbling pages. I opened one carefully to a random page. The writing was Gaelic—surprising—but I picked out a few words: *Mag Mell. An cosán i bhfolach*—the hidden paths. I eased the book shut, feeling a grin tug at my lips. Could that be the pathstones? Someone more proficient in Gaelic would know, but if it was, then I'd been right. The Airgeads had led us to a pathstone. I wanted to dance a jig. Bless Cori and Aileen.

I had to tell Roe.

I used my tablet to take pictures of the books and relics, pulled my phone from my pocket, and stepped outside. The air outside was almost chilly now. I checked the time on my phone and winced. Nearly two AM. Hopefully I wouldn't wake her up.

She picked up on the first ring. "Roe Gillam."

"Hey, Roe? It's Josh."

"Josh, good to hear from you! How's the search going?"

"Good." I cleared my throat, looked down at the tablet. "I think we found some things, but I want you to take a look. Mind if I send some pictures to you?"

"Go ahead."

I tucked the phone between my ear and shoulder and emailed her the pictures. Roe's computer dinged on the other end.

She was quiet for a moment, then said softly, "Well, you certainly found an interesting assortment of things here. Let's start with the stone. It's what is known as a *dea-thoil* stone—which means 'peace.'"

"Peace?" I repeated.

"Yes. You wouldn't expect that from a relic, but they were commonly exchanged as signs of good faith as late as a century ago. Sent strictly for peacemaking purposes, often as a gesture of peace or friendship. It's a powerful symbol. Even the most bitter of enemies would honor the dea-thoil. They have glamour, but only to mark the sender of the stone—it's not malicious. The necklace … hmm. It looks to be a standard love charm to weaken the wearer's mental resistance to someone. Not incredibly dangerous, as relics go, but quite nasty. I hate those mind-altering glamours."

"What about the other one? The bracelet?"

I heard clicking, and the line got quiet. Then Roe said, "This one is a bit more concerning." Her tone was a bit sharp.

"How so?"

"Well, my advice would be, don't go touching it unless you'd like to get painful boils in unpleasant areas."

I snorted a laugh. "Could we get more petty?"

"Petty as it may sounds, relics are a serious business, Josh. This means someone is still transporting them. The curators thought they mostly had the black market trade shut down."

"So Cori and Aileen were telling the truth."

"It seems so." She paused, then said, "Please be careful. If this Shaughnessy is dealing in relics, he likely has powerful Unseelie friends."

"I'll be careful. And I promise I'll keep Eliaster from doing anything stupid." We'd already gotten into a fight with three goblins, so I hoped that filled the trip's stupid ideas quota.

"Good luck, and may the Almighty go with you."

"Thanks, Roe." I started to push the phone into my pocket, then thought better of it and opened the contact list. It was a pretty small list nowadays, with only my family, Roe, Cormac, Eliaster, and Lukas entered. And one more ... the only number without an accompanying photo. I stared at the number for a second, then pressed *new message*.

Hey. Looks like you were right about Shaughnessy. Any more tips?

I waited, staring at the screen. After a few minutes, a reply popped up.

I'm going to regret giving you my number, aren't I?
Maybe. ;)
sigh Get Shaughnessy off the streets, and we'll talk.
Aww c'mon. I already said you were right. We know Shaughnessy is dangerous. Anything else? Who's he working with? Why are they taking a risk on relics?

There was a long pause, then ...

People have died because of those questions. Be patient. Please.

I waited. Was Aileen being sincere? Or was she just blowing me off? My stomach jittered. I rubbed the back of my neck and sighed, then rolled my eyes at myself. I just needed to tell her already, it wasn't as if I was asking her to the high school prom. *Eliaster thinks you and Cori have a hidden agenda.*

Because of what Gren said to him, right?
Yeah.

I swear that as soon as you guys are back in Springfield, we'll set up a meeting somewhere safe to talk. That's a promise. But until then, please be careful. Gren meant what he said when he threatened you. As reluctant as I am to say it, he is not on our side.

Nothing more came through, even though I sent a couple more messages asking her for more information.

I sighed and slipped the phone back into my pocket. Was Eliaster right—was Aileen just playing me? But why would she and Cori do that? I scrubbed my hand through my hair. This was ridiculous. I was so tired of not knowing whom I could trust.

The motel door creaked open and Eliaster poked his head out. "Whatcha doing out here?"

"I called Roe."

He smirked. "To report my behavior?"

I rolled my eyes. "Yeah, I'm a total snitch. Tattled to our adopted grandmother that you were being mean to a couple of goblins."

He elbowed me.

I laughed. It surprised me, but it felt good. I'd spent too long feeling wound up like a watch spring. "No, I wanted her to see the ogham on the relics." I told him what she'd said.

"So the stone isn't dangerous, but the necklace and the bracelet ..." He winced.

"Yeah."

Eliaster leaned against the side of the motel, kicking one foot up to bounce against the wood siding. I rocked back and forth from heel to toe, watching Eliaster, wondering if he would bring up anything that had happened tonight. He seemed intent on looking everywhere but at me.

"So ... are we gonna talk about what happened in the fight against the goblins, or ..." I started.

He shrugged. "You can if you want."

Was that an invitation to ask questions, or was he trying to shut me down? I squinted. "You ... killed that cat sidhé."

"Yeah." His voice was hard, brittle.

Would it kill you to be a little more forthcoming? "You could have walked away from it."

"And let it stab me in the back? Or stab you? No thanks. Besides, you shot the other one."

Bitterness touched the back of my mouth. Gee, thanks for reminding me. As I opened my mouth to retort, an SUV pulled into the parking lot, the orange streetlights glinting off its dark sides. Another SUV followed the first.

"Uh oh," Eliaster said. He gripped my shoulder, pulling me back toward the room. "Get inside."

"Why?"

"Trust me, you don't—"

Car doors swung open, and several fae—carrying swords—jumped from the vehicles. fanning out around us. For the second time in less than three hours, we were surrounded. My throat tightened, and I stepped back until my shoulders hit the side of the building. My hands began trembling.

One of the fae, a guy with bright blue hair, glanced up and down the street, then pointed at the door to our room. "Get inside. Now."

Eliaster crossed his arms. "Why?"

I pinched the bridge of my nose.

Blue-Hair stepped up to Eliaster, teeth bared.

Eliaster straightened from his usual slouch and glared back, sneering. "Think you can make me, tough shot?"

The fae's eyes twitched toward me.

Okay, yeah, I was done. The very last thing I wanted was to be turned into a bargaining chip again. I held my hands up, spun on my heel, and walked into our room. If this was the hill Eliaster wanted to die on, I was more than willing to let him fight it out.

A moment later, Blue-Hair shoved Eliaster into the room. Two others followed him in, and they closed the door behind them, leaving the other three fae outside.

Blue-Hair jerked his thumb at the chairs. "You two, sit."

Eliaster crossed his arms and leaned one hip against the chair back.

Blue-Hair rolled his eyes. "Brayan, stay by the door and make sure these two idiots don't try to run. Adam, check the room."

As I sat down, Adam—the one with shoulder-length brown hair—sheathed his sword and started rummaging through the room. The other continued to stand beside the door, eyeing us even as he returned his sword to his side.

"Hey, hey, easy," Eliaster protested as Adam dumped his duffel bag of weapons out onto his bed.

Blue-Hair sat on my bed, facing Eliaster and me. He leaned forward and jabbed his finger at us. Pinpoints of ice blue swirled in his gaze. "What are you thinking, coming here and executing judgement in another fae's territory without permission? What kind of stupid do you have to be—"

"Whoa, hold up a second, Spike." Eliaster held up his hands. "Who are you exactly?"

"My name is Tadhg," the fae spat. He held up his hand. The back of his palm had a tattooed symbol, a small wolf's head in knotwork. "I work for Highlord Keelin."

Eliaster swore. "I didn't realize he lived around here."

"And you thought that'd make a difference?"

Eliaster shrugged.

"Highlord?" I asked.

"Kind of like my dad, but instead of being in charge of a specific community, they're in charge of a certain large area."

"Oh." *Crap.* I glanced across the room, watching Adam as he dug through Eliaster's backpack. The box with the books and relics was on my bed, right behind Tadhg. If they caught us with relics, what would they think? Probably nothing good.

I stood up.

The guy by the door—Brayan—immediately turned to me, shoulders tense.

"Whoa, whoa, sorry." I held up my hands, palms toward him. "Sorry. Just … let me explain." I glanced down at Tadhg.

His eyes narrowed. "So, explain."

"In good faith, I'm going to turn something over to you." I started to step around Eliaster.

"Are you kidding me?" Eliaster hissed, grabbing my arm. His eyes darted around the room, tracking each fae's movements. "We can't just—"

"In good faith," I said sharply. "These guys are Seelie, right?"

"Yeah, but—"

"So they're on the same side as us. And it's in Highlord Keelin's territory, right?" I waited, my eyebrows raised.

Come on, man. Let me try to defuse this since you won't.

Eliaster's lips pinched together. "Right."

"So let's try not to get into trouble with the local authorities any more than we already have, okay?" I eased my arm free of his grip and skirted around the foot of the bed. I grabbed the cardboard box and opened it, then pulled out the bag I'd put the bracelet and necklace into, holding it out to Tadhg.

Tadhg's eyes widened, and he snatched the baggie from me. He glared at Eliaster. "What have you two been doing?"

"I know it looks bad, but if we can explain—"

Eliaster snorted and made a show of studying his nails. "Oh, just doing your boss's job for him, I guess."

Tadhg's hands clenched. "You don't know what you're messing with, Tyrone."

"Actually, I think I do. Either Highlord Keelin is incompetent, or he's in on the racket. I think you can guess which theory I'm going with." Eliaster grinned.

"How dare you—" Tadhg rolled his eyes. "Oh, right. I forget you prefer humans to your own kind."

A muscle in Eliaster's jaw twitched.

No, no, no. This was not how this was supposed to go. "Whoa, okay, can we just settle down here a minute?" I asked.

"It's a little late for that." Tadhg stood. "Get up. We're going to go talk to Lord Keelin."

"You're serious," Eliaster said in a disbelieving tone. "You're gonna stand by and let your highlord sink his—"

Tadhg raised one fist. "You can shut up now and come under your own power, or I can haul you over there like a piece of cargo. Your choice, but you're going."

I tensed.

Eliaster stared at Tadhg for a moment, then nodded once. "Fine. Let's just get this over with."

I'd expected to ride together, but as we stepped outside, Tadhg gripped Eliaster's arm and steered him toward the SUV closer to the street. I started to follow, but the fae named Adam stuck his arm out in front of me.

"This way," he said, nudging me toward the front SUV.

I paused, my throat tightening.

Adam glanced down at me and smiled. Not like he was gloating, but a kind smile, one that understood my instant of panic. His eyes were a steady, consistent dark brown—not flat, like he was trying to hide his emotions, but not the usual gyrating colors I'd gotten used to seeing. He was calm—even in the face of all of this, he was calm.

I could deal with this.

"Hey." Eliaster noticed I wasn't following him. He glared at Tadhg.

Tadhg rolled his eyes. "You can live without your pet human for half an hour."

"No, that's not—"

"Eliaster," I snapped. His name came out a lot sharper than I'd meant it to, but it got his attention. "Just … chill." *I can handle this* and *lay off the mother-henning* were phrases that came to mind, but I bit them back.

I turned and walked to the SUV, pulling the door open and climbing inside. Half of me expected Eliaster to start yelling, so I was a bit surprised when Adam climbed inside after me and pulled the door shut with no incident. I scooted over to the far side, buckled myself in, and leaned forward, elbows on my knees, hands clasped together in front of me.

Adam set my backpack on the floor close to my feet.

As the SUV moved forward, I glanced behind us. The second SUV was following, pulling a wide semi-circle in the motel parking lot and out onto the street. I could still feel my nerves jangling, but it wasn't as bad as it could've been.

See, Eliaster? Totally got this.

After a few minutes, the driver turned on music— smooth jazz. The irony made me snicker under my breath. I sat up and watched the fields go past in dark blurs, clenching and unclenching my numb right hand as if I were trying to work the feeling back into it. Even after a couple of days without the bracelet, it felt weird not to have it on.

Thankfully they hadn't searched my jacket, or they would've found the bracelet tucked in the inner pocket. That *really* wouldn't have gone over well, given Tadhg's adverse reaction to the relics I did show him.

We drove about thirty minutes, heading back out into the Kansas countryside. I watched out the window, thankful this didn't mirror my first car ride with a bunch of fae.

I tensed. That thought made all sorts of memories burst into my mind. The flat cornfield outside became the dark forest, speeding by as I struggled to pull my mind out of a fog. The stickiness of duct tape pulled at my wrists and mouth. My breathing quickened. I curled up, rubbing the back of my neck with one hand. It didn't dispel the feeling of phantom fingers digging into my skin.

"We're here."

Adam's voice made the flashback pop like a dying lightbulb. My hand throbbed. I looked down and realized my fingernails had dug divots into the car's leather interior.

Oops. Adam motioned for me to head outside. I climbed out, waited for the other SUV to pull to a stop. Eliaster got out, jaw clenched. Tadhg didn't look any happier. Somehow I got the feeling that theirs had been a bumpier ride than mine.

We stood on the paved circle drive of a huge Victorian home. I glanced over my shoulder. The circle was filled with a sizable garden and stood quite a ways from the hedge-lined main road, all visible in the soft glow of copper garden lanterns.

Tadhg motioned for us to follow him. "This way, please."

I pulled my backpack over my shoulders and followed him, rubbing my hand. The dark line scoring the underside of my wrist burned as I ran my fingers across it. I pinched the web of skin between my thumb and forefinger, but as usual, felt no pain. Just pressure.

I lifted my eyes from my hand as Eliaster nudged my side.

"How's it look?"

"What?"

He nodded to a blinking light in the corner of the porch. A security camera.

Oh. I glanced around, spotting several other cameras mounted along the porch roof, three pointing outward and two pointing toward the door. There were others, scattered along the edge of the roof as it wrapped around the house.

The front door had no glass panels set into it, as I would have expected. I could lay an easy bet it was solid wood too, or maybe even reinforced with a metal core. A keypad sat below the door handle, rather than a lock, and an intercom was mounted on the wall beside the door at shoulder level.

What was he asking specifically? If the security was good, or if we stood a fighting chance if we had to make a break for it? I settled for a shrug. "I'm not a security expert."

He grunted, looking disconcerted.

Tadhg thumbed a button on the intercom. "I've arrived with Eliaster Tyrone and Josh MacAllister."

The door's lock made an audible *clunk* as it disengaged, and Tadhg pushed it open, motioning us inside. We stepped into a wide hallway painted a soft green.

I couldn't see much more of it, thanks to the two fae who stood in our way. One was dressed in a way I imagined typical security would be, in a dark suit tailored to show off the fact that, despite having the usual slight build, he did indeed have enough muscle to make me think twice about fighting him. The other wore a dark T-shirt and jeans, hands casually in his pockets.

"Figures," Eliaster muttered. He stepped into the house. "I suppose you guys think we need to give up our weapons or something typical like that?"

Suit smirked. "You understand, of course, Mr. Tyrone."

He shrugged and pulled the knife off his belt, handing it over to the guy in the T-shirt. Then he raised his arms, clasping his hands behind his neck. The fae started patting him down.

I sighed, shrugging my backpack off my shoulder and

handing it to Suit.

He set it to the side and started feeling down my sides. I sighed and glanced over at Eliaster. He tapped his fingers against his neck, his expression carefully neutral as always.

Suit grunted and stood up. "Shoes off over here," he said, pointing to a dark welcome mat placed against the wall beside the door.

"You guys should be working for the TSA," I said, sitting down as I pulled off my boots. "If you're gonna keep my backpack, can I at least have my tablet?" I kept my tone polite. If at least one of us was polite and cooperative, maybe we'd get out of here quicker. And maybe they wouldn't catch that I was shaking like a leaf in a gale.

Suit pulled the black leather case out of the backpack and handed it to me. Tahdg slipped past us and motioned for us to follow him, leaving the two security guys behind with our weapons, our shoes, and my backpack.

"If we end up having to run for our lives in sock feet, I'm going to kill you," I muttered to Eliaster.

He flashed a grin. "You'll have more problems if we have to run, because I'm faster than you."

I mimed strangling him.

The hallway opened into a luxurious living room banked with dark bay windows along one side. The sage-green color of the walls gave the place vibrancy, and the sleek, soft-looking leather couches took the inhospitable edge off the large space. Canvases of modern art, some framed and some not, hung on the walls, and lamps created pools of light in the room.

A fae with dark, slicked-back hair sat in a chair beside one of the bay windows, glasses perched on his aquiline nose as he perused a print newspaper. At the sound of our entry, he looked up, then stood, neatly folding his newspaper and setting it on the side table. Must be Keelin.

"Eliaster Tyrone and Josh MacAllister, as requested, sir," Tadhg announced.

Keelin nodded. "Thank you, Tadhg. That will be all." He

motioned to us. "Please, come sit."

Eliaster crossed his arms over his chest and jutted his chin forward. "Not until you've explained why you think you have the right to drag us in here like criminals."

Keelin's eyes flashed, but he kept his tone measured and even. "You came into my territory, interfering in my work, and you have the gall to ask why you're being brought to heel?"

"We're tracking down a lead on a dangerous fae," Eliaster said.

"You still should have checked in with me." Keelin clasped his hands behind his back.

"For all we knew, you were a part of this scheme. You've certainly let it go on long enough."

Keelin raised one eyebrow, dipped his head in a slight nod. "Perhaps a few phone calls could persuade you of my stance."

Eliaster snorted. "Do I look like I'm in grade school? Calling my da won't do a thing."

Keelin smirked. "I was thinking more along the lines of Highlord O'Breigh. He might be interested in hearing about more of your … exploits."

Eliaster's knuckles went white, and his eyes darkened, but I couldn't tell from the stony look on his face if that was from fear or anger. Maybe both.

Probably both.

Not good.

"To be blunt, you coming after wrongdoers in my territory won't do either of us any good," Keelin said. Still in that calm, measured tone.

Yeah, I was one-hundred-percent certain that Keelin had no idea of the storm he was about to unleash. Whoever Highlord O'Breigh was, Eliaster was terrified of him.

Eliaster gritted his teeth. "You mean it won't do *you* any good. It makes you look incompetent—or like you're conspiring with someone for a cut of the profits."

"I had the matter well in hand—"

"Did you?"

Keelin's face took on a thunderous look. His voice cracked across the room, anger and indignation plain in his tone. "What would you have me do?"

"The right thing," Eliaster shot back. His right foot moved back a bit, and he angled his body as if preparing for a fight. "Getting rid of sidhé who were preying on the innocent."

I expected him to keep talking, but Eliaster just stared hard at Keelin. Keelin's eyes narrowed, and with that tiny change, his face suddenly looked a lot more fierce and a lot less friendly. I could swear his eyes even looked like they were glowing a tiny bit. The air suddenly crackled with hostile energy. The hair on the back of my arms rose.

I could *feel* the glamour in the room, but I couldn't see it. That didn't make sense. I could see glamour now, couldn't I? I'd been seeing past glamour ghosts for months now. I'd seen Larae's glamour in the tunnels, and Aileen's when she'd sworn by the rule of three, and left her phone number for me on the napkin.

So *why* couldn't I see it now?

I glanced over at Eliaster. His shoulders were squared, his jaw clenched. He held his hands open, but his fingers were curled in the same way that Keelin's were, in the same way that I'd seen Larae curl her fingers when she summoned her smoke-like glamour.

Crap, he was going to get us killed. I grabbed his shoulder, giving him a shake. "Cut it out!"

Both of the fae ignored me. I balled my free hand. This had to stop. If Eliaster didn't look at me or speak to me in about point-five seconds, I was going to punch him.

Keelin suddenly blinked, and his eyes stopped glowing.

Eliaster took a step back, shoulders slumping.

It felt like oxygen suddenly rushed back into the room, and I could breathe freely again. *What just happened?*

Chapter 10

JOSH

"What. The. Heck?" I glared at Eliaster. "Next time you go all Gandalf fights a Balrog, at least warn me first."

Keelin gave a sharp bark of laughter, hunching forward. I jumped and stared at him, unsure of what that reaction meant. He coughed, then picked up a glass of water from the side table. After taking a sip, he cleared his throat and spoke—staring right at me. "Perhaps you and I should be the ones negotiating here." He tilted his head. "You're not a curator, are you?"

I shook my head.

"I thought not—there haven't been any rumors about Tyrones taking up with the curators again." He looked thoughtful. "You should consider it."

"I'll take that under advisement." I glanced at Eliaster. "Are you done with the pissing contest? Can we talk like adults now?"

Eliaster didn't quite roll his eyes, but he came close.

Keelin sighed and pinched the bridge of his nose. "This was not ..." His voice trailed off. He waved at the overstuffed chairs.

I took a few steps into the room, then paused as Eliaster glared at me. Fine, if he didn't want to play nice with others, I'd do it. I crossed the room and sat down in one of the chairs. The cushions gave under my weight, feeling way too comfortable for my mood at the moment. Eliaster reluctantly crossed the room to slouch in the chair beside mine.

Keelin paused, then took a deep breath and sat as well. He adjusted his jacket. Smoothed his hands over his hair, then rested his hands on the arms of his chair. Open. Ready to talk and negotiate.

I leaned forward, resting my elbows on my knees. "Can you please explain what's going on from your end?"

Keelin tapped his fingers on the arms of his chair. "For a short answer—I've been aware for some time that there's been an unusual number of relics traveling in and out of my territory. It's been difficult, and I've lost a couple of good men, but we've tracked most of them back to a fae named Galen Shaughnessy. I don't know where he's getting them from, but we know he's the main runner in this area. We can't find any information from him—who his people are, what his background is. Six months ago he just showed up, bought shares in one of the nightclubs downtown, and suddenly all these relics began popping up every time we raided a goblin safehouse."

Eliaster made a low growling noise. "So there are slavers in the area?"

Keelin stood, walked over to the kitchen, grabbed a file off the counter, and handed it to me. "Yes. The goblins used enslavement relics in order to kidnap their victims and sell them in in the Underworld."

"Enslavement?" I asked, flipping through the pictures. A necklace, a bracelet, a piece of lace, a ring … most of these were jewelry.

"Relics that control your mind," Keelin said in a quiet tone.

My stomach churned. "Some of these items look … new." I held up a photo of a costume-jewelry ring. "This looks like something you could get in any supermarket." It reminded me of the necklace we'd found earlier tonight.

Keelin nodded.

Eliaster's attention snapped to the highlord. "I thought no

one could make new relics."

"That's what has been assumed for years," Keelin said, propping his chin on his hand.

Eliaster swore.

"My thoughts precisely," a new, feminine voice said.

Eliaster jumped as if he'd gotten an electric shock. He swore again and glanced over at the entrance, scrambling to his feet.

A tall, lean fae with long, platinum blond hair stood leaning against the doorjamb, studying her fingernails. She straightened, looking bored. "That was an impressive display, boys. Are we done measuring each other up now?"

Keelin sighed. "Banshee, why don't you get in here and stop lurking in doorways."

"What are you doing here?" Eliaster choked out.

"Wait, you know her?" I said.

"Hello to you too, lover boy." Banshee sauntered into the room, bright blue eyes flickering.

"Lover boy?" I repeated in a low voice. What the heck?

Eliaster closed his eyes in obvious frustration. "Just … please, for once, shut up, Josh."

I slouched in my chair. Fine, be that way. But if he thought that was the end of the matter …

Banshee passed Eliaster, and she reached up, brushing her knuckles along his jaw.

He opened his eyes and glared down at her, irises shimmering with a dark gray-green color I'd never seen before. "Get away from me."

Banshee stood on tiptoe and leaned closer to him, one corner of her lips curving upward in a smile. "I did so miss you."

He took a step back. "It wasn't mutual."

"Ooooh, my poor fragile heart just broke into a thousand pieces." She put her hand on her chest as she headed for the other unoccupied chair in the room. As she passed me, she winked.

"Banshee," Keelin growled again.

"I'm done, I'm done." She sat and crossed her legs, then leaned to the side, playing with the ring in her lip. "Continue, boss."

Eliaster turned to Keelin. "I am not going to work with her."

He shrugged. "If you want to go home and face Highlord O'Breigh and the possibility of another binding, that's your business."

Eliaster leaned forward, hands planted on the arms of his chair. For a second, I thought he was going to take his chances and bolt.

Eliaster looked between Keelin and Banshee, then sat down and crossed his arms over his chest. "So that's how you're to handle it? We work for you or get into trouble?"

Keelin smirked.

My mind reeled. Okay, so the first thing I needed to do find out why Eliaster was so scared of this Highlord O'Breigh person. And what was a binding? I didn't want to ask right then—it was better that Keelin didn't know exactly how little I knew about the Underworld.

"If you were having trouble, you could have reached out to other ..." I paused. "Highlords, maybe? Or the curators?"

Keelin snorted. "I understand you may not have had any training in fae politics, so allow me to set you straight. To do so would have been to show weakness. There are always other fae circling, waiting to wrest the position of highlord from anyone who shows weakness. No. It wouldn't have been possible." He sighed. "We've been close to closing in on Shaughnessy, but then you two rolled into town and almost blew everything to freakin' hell."

"Buuuut maybe now that they're here, they'll be helpful," Banshee said. She leaned back in her chair, draping her arms along the back of the seat.

Eliaster twitched as if her voice physically pained him. "How?"

Keelin's eyes shifted over to me.

"Umm ..." I swallowed hard.

"Absolutely not!" Eliaster shouted.

Banshee burst into laughter.

"He's a human. Shaughnessy won't even be looking for him," Keelin said sharply. "You know the rules as well as I do, Eliaster. In order to take a fellow fae into custody—to do something this drastic and imprison someone—we have to know he's a danger to the public. Rumor has it that Shaughnessy wears relics, and I think that's what he's using to slip past my men." He shifted and shot a quick, appraising look at me.

I swallowed.

"I want you to talk to Shaughnessy," Keelin continued. "See if you can spot any relics he's using. Not only will this help us formulate a plan, but it will prevent anyone from crying foul when we take him into custody. Even the Unseelie Court doesn't stand for its members wearing relics openly." He checked his watch. "He'll be leaving his apartment tomorrow sometime in the afternoon and head to the Blue Fire." He glanced over at Banshee and Eliaster. "And you two can ransack his apartment while he's at the club."

Eliaster grunted "Tell me one reason we should cooperate, Keelin. One."

Keelin's eyes darkened, and a lean smile pulled one corner of his mouth upward. "Because if you don't, I'll call Highlord O'Breigh here to set a binding on you *tonight*. There's precedent for it."

Eliaster looked like he was going to argue, but I cut him off. "Just stop it, okay? We did interfere in his territory." *Besides, idiot, Shaughnessy is who we're supposed to be going after anyway. Stop protesting so much.* Sometimes I really wished I had telepathy.

Eliaster sighed. "Fine. What'll we do until then?"

Keelin smirked. "I'd suggest you rest." He motioned to the side of the living room, where a set of stairs disappeared into the upper story of the house. "You'll likely have a long day tomorrow—I hope to be able to bring Shaughnessy in. If, of course, you have no objections." The last was said with a sneer.

Eliaster nodded. "The sooner I can get out of here, the better. No objections from me."

"Very well then. Tadhg."

It only took a few seconds for the blue-haired fae to reappear in the living room doorway.

Keelin waved his hand. "Please show them to the guest quarters, and have Eliaster's car brought here."

"Yes, sir." Tadhg bowed his head, then gestured for us to follow him.

As I walked up the stairs, I glanced over my shoulder. Keelin gestured, and Banshee stood, crossing the room to stand closer to him. She leaned forward, resting her hands on one arm of his chair, their voices too low for me to hear.

The upstairs hallway was short and sparsely decorated compared to the living room. Tadhg stopped at the first door and opened it, revealing a small living space with a couch, chairs, a small bookcase, coffee table, and TV. Three closed doors sat at the back of the room.

"Two bedrooms and a shared bath," he said, gesturing. "Be up by noon. That should give us plenty of time to plan out tomorrow before we have to leave."

"Sounds good. We'll see you then," Eliaster said.

"And I swear, Tyrone, if you try anything, I'll—"

Eliaster shut the door in Tadhg's face. He stayed still for a moment, his back to me. "Well, happy now?"

Irritation flashed hot through me. *Thanks for reminding me.* "I thought showing them the relics would help. Show them that we'd come on a genuine lead, rather than just trying to stir up trouble."

"I get it, really, but—" Eliaster turned around, groaned, and ran his hands through his hair. "I guess it wouldn't have been so bad. But why did *she* have to show up?"

"Yeah, uh, about that—question?"

Eliaster gave me a skeptical look. "Just one?"

"Funny. Haha. So who is she? She seems pretty

comfortable around you." I thought back to how close she'd been standing to him and amended that. "*Overly* comfortable."

He groaned again. "That's just Banshee. She thrives on making people *un*comfortable. The trick to working with her is just to keep her at arm's length."

"Yeah, you were doing a *fantastic* job of that earlier."

He growled and walked across the room. Our backpacks and gear had already been brought in and set on the couch. Eliaster started rifling through his backpack, no doubt checking to make sure everything was in its place. "We worked together on a few jobs. She does a bit of everything—bounty hunting, relic retrieval, hacking, tracing—jack of all trades and master of none. She's a free agent and works for anyone who will pay her price."

"Which court does she belong to?"

"Neither. One of her parents was Unseelie, the other Seelie—kind of had a Romeo and Juliet thing going on. Turned out about as well as that story. No Court would ever claim her."

"Okay." I squinted at his back. I wasn't sure what set off my intuition, but he was shutting me out again—fat chance I'd get much more information out of him tonight. Emotions I'd thought I was over—the irritation and frustration from our argument before we met the Airgeads—slammed back into me. I opened my mouth.

"Good job holding your poker face when he gave you Shaughnessy's picture, by the way. You're getting better at holding your own."

I clamped my mouth back together so hard my teeth clicked. "Thanks. Figured you wouldn't want to give away everything we know, at least not before we had a chance to talk about it. So what do you think? Should we tell him about the Airgeads?"

Eliaster leaned back on his haunches and rubbed his chin. "No, I think keeping that to ourselves is the best idea right now. We still don't know what their agenda is."

"I'm telling you, she wasn't lying."

He shrugged. "Lying by omission is still lying, Josh."

Whatever. Maybe they hadn't told us everything, but I got where they were coming from. Wanting to be careful. Wanting to make sure they could trust us. I could see Eliaster's side, too, but his constant caginess was beginning to grate on me. "Think Shaughnessy will lead us to a pathstone?"

"Yeah … I'm still not happy about them making you be the one who makes contact with him."

My stomach knotted. "I don't like the idea either, but it makes sense. Even if he does pick up who I am, he's going to dismiss me. They all dismiss me."

Eliaster was quiet for a moment. Then he rolled to his feet and kicked off his boots. "I'm gonna sleep."

I shuffled my weight from foot to foot. But my mind whirled and jumped with so many thoughts that I knew if I tried to go to bed, I'd ended up lying awake for hours.

That was a good way to set myself up for horrific flashbacks and nightmares.

"What's eatin' you?" Eliaster asked.

I jumped at the sound of his voice.

Eliaster frowned. "Okay, this is weird," he said. "You weren't even that jumpy in the Chicago Underworld. What's going on?"

"Nothing," I said.

He raised an eyebrow. "Pardon me if I find that just a bit unbelievable."

I scratched the back of my neck. I really, *really* did not want to discuss my nightmares with Eliaster. "I said nothing."

He raised his eyebrows, eyes turning a slight blue-green. I shrugged and turned away, heading for one of the bedrooms. Turnabout was fair play.

I dreamed again. At first the images were fuzzy, chaotic. I couldn't clearly see them, but terror, rage, and sorrow swirled around me, dragging at my limbs as if they were physical beings. Someone's face showed white and blurry in the darkness surrounding me. Copper hair—Aileen? Then my view switched. The full moon was shining on me as I slept. This time, I tried to run when the green vines burst from the floor. Didn't work. A vine snaked up one leg, bringing me crashing down. I awoke kicking and screaming.

Someone had hold of my arms, trying to shake me. "Josh! Josh, wake up!"

I wrenched one hand free and punched, hard. Pain shot through my knuckles as they impacted something that crunched.

Eliaster swore and stumbled back, clamping his hand to his nose.

I sat up, chest heaving, and froze at the sight of blood gushing between Eliaster's fingers. Normally I wasn't squeamish, but I distinctly remembered something about blood in my dream. Eliaster. Blood on his face, soaking his shirt. My chest hurt. My stomach lurched. I doubled over on the bed, wrapped my arms around my head, and focused hard on the deep, steady rhythm of breathing. One breath, then two, then three. Nice and slow.

"*Ciorru air*," Eliaster muttered, his voice muffled. His hand pressed against my back. "You okay?"

I shook my head.

He sat down beside me and didn't say anything more. His hand stayed on my shoulder, fingers digging in just slightly, grounding me to this reality. *This* was real. This wasn't another dream. There were no vines trying to choke out my life. It felt stupid, *stupid*, to be so terrified of a dream that I had to have a babysitter, but at the moment, I didn't care. I was just glad someone was here.

After a few minutes, I was able to sit up. My body still trembled, but at least I wasn't going to throw up anymore. I glanced at the alarm clock on the bedside table. Six AM. I groaned and rubbed my eyes. "Did I wake you up?"

"Doesn't matter." Eliaster waved the question away. "They're getting worse, aren't they?"

I shook my head. "This wasn't a flashback. I've … I've been having weird dreams. Just a couple in the last few days." I sighed. "I guess they're starting to get to me."

Eliaster pulled his shirt away from his face, then used a clean part of the hem to wipe the blood off his chin. "About what?"

Seriously? He dodged my questions all the time, but he expected me to answer everything right away? I shot him an irritated glare and started to snap, but the look on Eliaster's face stopped me. Genuine worry pinched the bridge of his nose.

As I described the dreams to him, Eliaster's jaw clenched, and dark threads of green flickered through his eyes. Eliaster sat back when I was done and rubbed his mouth. He pulled his hand away as a bit of dried blood flaked off his fingers, then got up and headed over to the bathroom. He grabbed a hand towel, doused it under the faucet, and scrubbed at his face and hand. In the bathroom light, a darker splotch stood out on his washed-out-black tank top from where he'd used it to stop his nosebleed. He'd done that rather than leave me alone. The thought made me feel marginally better.

I squirmed. It was weird for him to be this non-responsive for this long. "What do you think it means?"

Eliaster shook his head. "I don't know. It was the same dream, both times?"

"As far as I can remember." Something flashed in my memory. "No wait! It was different. This time, I wasn't at home. I was here." I got up and walked over to the room's only window, pushing the curtain back. I couldn't even see the moon—the window was facing the wrong direction. A shiver crawled down my spine. And I remembered another detail. I turned back to him. "I wasn't wearing my bracelet today, but it was on my wrist in the dream."

"Okayyy." Eliaster drew the word out. "Maybe it's some kind of residual effect from the dark magic Larae used to heal your wrist."

I rubbed my thumb along the black scar. "After four months?"

Eliaster shrugged. "Just let me know if it happens a third time."

Three. Three was important—it was a holy number. The Trinity, the number of days Christ was in the tomb … history both fae and human, religious and secular, was full of the significance of the number three. The hair on the back of my neck prickled.

"Wh-what does it mean if it happens three times?"

"I've been taught ever since I was little that if you have the exact same dream three times, it's prophetic," Eliaster said. "Of course, I've had the same nightmares over and over, but they're not prophetic, so I don't really know what counts and what doesn't. But it's weird enough that I think you need to know."

"Oh-kay, then." I sighed. The tightness in my chest eased a little. "Thanks."

He nodded and started for the door. "Try to see if you can get some more sleep. Today might be a bit rough."

I nodded and climbed back into bed as he shut the door behind him. My mind spun so much that I was afraid I'd never fall back to sleep, but before I fully realized what had happened, my eyes had closed and I felt myself drifting off.

Chapter 11

JOSH

By the time I woke up, it was well past eleven. I got up, went to the bathroom, splashed some water on my face, scrubbed my wet fingers through my hair, and brushed my teeth. I had a sour taste in my mouth, with the tang of iron, and my tongue ached liked like I'd bitten it last night. I didn't remember biting my tongue, but I didn't remember much about the dream either. Glamour vines. I knew there'd been glamour vines again. And I'd freaked out. And punched Eliaster.

I smirked. Okay, so given my frustrations with him lately, I honestly wasn't that sorry about that one.

I went out into the living area of the guest suite. Eliaster was up already, with his arsenal spread out on the coffee table. His old, pink-cased mp3 player sat on the table beside his stuff, and I could see he had earbuds in.

I cleared my throat.

Eliaster looked up from cleaning a knife and popped out an earbud. "Hey." He tossed the knife back on the table and twisted the cleaning rag in his hands. "Sleep okay?"

"Yeah, no more weird dreams. You?"

He shrugged and stood. "I stayed up." He stood and grabbed his shoulder holster, sliding the knives back into place. "You ready to go save the city?" The smirk on his face told me he was being a smart aleck.

"Sure," I said. "But I have a few more questions first."

"Josh." Eliaster flopped back onto the couch and dramatically flung his arm over his eyes. "Do you ever get tired of asking questions?"

I bristled. "Pardon me for just wanting to know what's going on here."

I could practically hear the eye-roll in Eliaster's voice. "I was kidding."

Oh, sure. Yeah. He could kid, but I was tired of the unpredictable fae crap. I leaned my hands against the back of the couch. "O'Breigh. I know Keelin said he's a highlord, presumably over Missouri."

"And parts of Oklahoma and Arkansas. He's essentially my dad's boss."

It made sense that Eliaster would be wary of pissing off his dad's boss, but his reaction had been more than that. I turned my mental image of his face at that moment over in my head, still trying to decide—anger, or fear? Fear, I thought, masked in anger. "Why does he freak you out so much?"

"I was afraid you'd ask that."

I dug my fingers into the back of the couch. "I need to understand what's going on."

He sighed and dropped his arm from his face. "I get it. I do. And I'm sorry you're getting frustrated. This is—" He blew out a deep breath. "After my brother died, that whole mess, I ... kinda went crazy."

"How crazy?"

"I tried to assassinate Llew." He paused. "I killed several of his goons. It got really bad. I was reckless. Stupid." He looked down at his feet, then pulled up one pant leg. Just above his ankle was a shiny burn scar in the shape of a hollow circle. There had once been something in the circle, some kind of rune or mark, but a jagged slash mark cut through the center of the circle, rendering the rune inside unreadable. "When Blodheyr sent a sluagh after me a few months ago, those were the two strikes he was referring to. My da was afraid that I'd get myself killed, so he did what's called a binding—it seals a fae to a place, and if they try to venture too far from that place, they get extremely ill. Da bound me to the rath. I couldn't even go to the Market without doubling over in pain."

My stomach flipped. So that was why the mention of a binding had scared him. I waited, but that was all he said. "Okay," I said quietly. "I get why you wouldn't like to talk about it. But this is the type of stuff I need to know, Eliaster."

He leaned back, almost pressing himself into the cushions of the couch. "This pulls up a lot of really painful memories for me."

I raised an eyebrow.

"But I suppose I owe you some kind of explanation." Eliaster gestured to the chair beside the couch. "You might want to sit."

I nodded and slid between the chair and the couch, flopping down into the seat.

Eliaster sat forward and bowed his head, closing his eyes. After a moment, he sighed. "Okay, so—when Banshee and I worked together, we ran into this trafficking ring one time. Remember the slaves you saw in the Market, the first time you were in the Underworld? That kind of thing is more common than you'd think. Goblins and Unseelie steal humans and sell them to other sidhé for sport, for sex, for work. That case Banshee and I worked—it was bad. It still makes me sick to think about. This whole thing reminds me too much of then. I've been trying to rein it in, but ..." He paused, then said softly, "Banshee wasn't a good influence for me back then. Let's just say that my more murderous tendencies tend to show up when she's there to encourage them. She hates the courts and she hates other sidhé, and it's just not a good mix. Of course, it was right after my brother and Emily died, but I have no desire to walk that path again."

The way he said her name ... that caught me. "The

curator?"

He nodded. "Emily was my ... we were engaged." His voice caught.

My stomach squeezed again. I blinked, too surprised to react any more. Eliaster had been *engaged*?

"Not many people knew about it, otherwise I never would've been given the assignment of protecting her." He rubbed his hands together. "Back, umm, in the eighteen-hundreds and early nineteen-hundreds, fae and curators worked together a lot. That's when archeology kind of exploded and people were finding a lot of fae relics, so the curators were busy. And fae warriors were often assigned as bodyguards, of a sort, since curators were never really more than scholarly types." His lips quirked up in a brief smile. "That hadn't really been a thing since World War Two, but a few years ago, my da and a few others thought maybe it was time to try to resurrect the partnership. I was chosen because of my da's influence, and Emily was chosen because her family used to be close friends with my family."

I drew in a quick breath, willing my stomach to settle. "What ... what happened?"

Eliaster swallowed and looked down at the floor. "Well, my older brother Iain worked for Highlord O'Breigh, and somehow or another he ran into Llew and Larae and became convinced the Lucht Leanuna were a rising threat. Iain was obsessed with the pathstones and started trying to hunt them down. He thought he'd found one, and he pulled me and Emily into it because he thought the curators needed to know. Somehow Llew found out, and next thing I knew, my brother and my girlfriend were dead." His eyes flickered bright green, and his mouth pressed into a firm line. "Still not sure why I survived and they didn't. I was the fighter. If I'd done my job, they would be the ones continuing the search today, not me."

I rubbed the back of my neck. Even though his face was like stone, the raw grief in his voice—made worse, I knew, by how recent Marc's loss had been—made me feel like I was intruding.

"I—I'm sorry, Eliaster."

He shrugged, nodded.

My arms prickled, and I turned away, rubbing at them. So much more about Eliaster made sense now—his drive to find the pathstones. His insistence on protecting me, even when I didn't think I needed it. I stood and walked back into my bedroom, grabbing my stuff from the bed and bathroom.

When I returned, Eliaster stood, sheathing his weapons and buckling them on. He turned around. His expression was still hard, but I could see the traces of tears glimmering in his eyes.

"Do you understand now?" he asked.

I stepped up in front of him and held out my hand. "Yeah, I get it. Let's go save the city, huh?"

His stony expression cracked just enough for a smirk. He gripped my wrist in a tight warrior's handshake. "If we have to."

Chapter 12

ELIASTER

I ... had not planned for that to happen.

As Josh headed down the stairs, I stopped in the doorway of our guest suite and pulled in a deep, silent breath. The tightness in my chest eased just enough for me to straighten my shoulders. I blinked and wiped at my eyes with the heels of my hands.

Stupid. Crying in front of people.

I couldn't let Tadhg or Keelin or any of these other goons see me like this. They'd think I was weak. More than ever, I needed to be strong. Bad enough that I could barely pull on enough glamour to make my arms flicker with flames yesterday, while Keelin's whole form had erupted with fire. He knew I couldn't use glamour. So I needed to show him that I was still a force to be reckoned with.

When we got downstairs, Tadhg was the only one in the living room, flicking through the pages of a newspaper. He glanced up, nodded, and pointed to the table, where half-full platters of everything from fruit to scrambled eggs to grilled slices of ham awaited.

"Anything interesting happen overnight?" I asked him.

"No."

I paused and searched his face. Tadhg held my gaze for a

few seconds, looking bored, then went back to his newspaper. I found it hard to believe that no one besides me had heard Josh's screams during his nightmare. But if Tadhg had heard anything, he didn't let on.

Not that it mattered. Everyone who had been through battle had nightmares once in a while, all but the most psychopathic. My mind flashed to Banshee. My gut knotted. I blinked the mental image away.

The problem was how Josh would be treated. Even if Tadhg had the same nightmares every single night, he would still say Josh was weak, stupid. Human.

Josh grabbed a plate and started loading it with food. "Where's Keelin?"

"Busy." Tadhg flicked a page of the newspaper.

Josh glanced at me. I shrugged. Wasn't like we could do anything until Tadhg started talking or Keelin showed up.

While Josh finished getting food, I wandered around the living room, looking at various art pieces on the walls. While the prints were nice, they were familiar. Generic. Pieces you could buy at any department or home goods store in the country.

I turned back to the table, got myself a plate of food, and settled on one of the tall chairs at the kitchen bar. Josh sat, picking at his food as he scrolled through news sites on his phone.

I nudged his elbow. "This place is a safe house, not where Keelin lives."

"Oh yeah? How can you tell?"

"There's nothing personal on the walls. No family photos, no heirlooms, nothing. The place looks like it could be straight from a department store."

"So Keelin's probably not going to show up."

"I doubt it."

"Where do you think Banshee is?"

A muscle in my neck twitched. "As long as she stays far away from me, I don't particularly care."

Josh started to say something, but I heard movement

behind us and turned around. One of the security guards from last night stepped into the living room and cleared his throat.

"Ready to go?" Tadhg asked, slapping his newspaper down on the counter.

"Sure, why not." I stood up.

"Can we at least get an idea of the plan for today?" Josh asked.

"In the car," Tadhg answered.

As we headed to the front hallway, Banshee appeared from one of the side rooms, spinning a keyring on one finger. She shot me a grin. "Ready to come ransack an apartment?"

I stopped. "What, now?"

She glanced at Tadhg, who shrugged, then back at me. "No. I'm going to go watch to make sure Shaughnessy leaves, then I'll come get you, and we'll play cat burglar while your human distracts our little relic-running friend."

"I can't believe no one has searched his apartment before."

Banshee shrugged one shoulder. "We're the experts here, apparently. That's why I was called in."

I snorted. "We're in a world of trouble if they think you and I are experts." I turned to Tadhg. "I'm staying with you."

"No, you're not," Tadhg said evenly. "You're going with Banshee. We don't need you on this part of the job, and it makes sense to go through the apartment while we know for sure that Shaughnessy is busy."

Josh cleared his throat. "It'd be nice if the distraction in question got a say."

Banshee and Tadhg looked at him in surprise. I held back a laugh.

Josh glanced at me and punched my arm. "I got this. You don't need to babysit me."

"I don't like it," I grumbled.

"Yes, yes, I know. Mother hen, blah blah blah." He rolled his eyes, then grinned. "Trust me. I got this."

Trusting him wasn't the issue. Trusting Tadhg and Keelin was.

Tadhg stepped inside the security office and came back with a tactical headset. "You'll be wearing this, so it's not like you'll be going in without backup. You don't have to engage him at all, just see if you can spot anything that might be a relic." He paused and frowned. "If I understand right, you can see through glamour?"

I tensed. Now where had he heard that?

Josh nodded.

"Any and all glamour?"

Josh hesitated, just slightly, then nodded again.

I frowned. What was he hiding? I glanced around at the other fae, but it seemed like I was the only one who had noticed Josh hesitate.

"So you might actually see something one of us missed," Tadhg said. His hand tightened briefly on the headset before handing it over to Josh. He turned to me. "Once Josh confirms that Shaughnessy's at the club, you and Banshee will go search his apartment. See if he has anything stashed there."

I gnawed the inside of my lip before responding, "Got it."

"Make sure you look for electronic stuff too," Josh said to me. "Most fae forget about electronics, but maybe Shaughnessy would be one of the atypical ones. Take his laptop, if he has one, his tablet—he may have a separate hard drive stashed somewhere too."

I rolled my eyes and smirked. "Okay, nerd."

"Well. If that's settled," Tadhg said sarcastically, "let's get moving."

Chapter 13

JOSH

Shaughnessy's club, The Blue Fire, was located downtown between a crumbling brick building and a renovated, vintage shop. We pulled into a parking lot catty-corner to the club. As Tadhg retrieved his headset from the console between the front seats, I studied the club's exterior. Bright blue neon lighting ran around the edges of the sleek, smooth building, outlining the club's name and shape of a flame. A worker was moving a set of velvet-covered ropes and metal stands out front.

I glanced at the clock. Nearly two in the afternoon. I looked over my shoulder. Eliaster was sprawled in the seat behind me, arms crossed over his chest, head tilted back on the headrest. On one hand, it made sense that he was asleep—he felt relatively safe around Tadhg, and he'd been up since I'd had my nightmare at six. But his irritation at being forced into this mission made me think he'd be making sarcastic remarks and snarling at anyone who got close.

A Jeep gunned its engine as it pulled into place beside us. I glanced over, startled, and saw the platinum-haired fae girl at the wheel, grinning at us. Rings on her fingers twinkled in the sunlight as she waved.

I heard a half-sigh, half-growl from the backseat and

snorted.

"Your girlfriend's here," Tadhg said.

"She's *not*—" Eliaster started.

Tadhg held up a hand, tilting his head. A faint crackle told me someone was talking over his headset. He looked over his shoulder at Eliaster and nodded. "Better get moving. Shaughnessy's just gone inside."

Eliaster shoved open his door and climbed out.

Tadhg leaned over until he was nose to nose with me. "No tricks. If you're not back within an hour, I'm coming in to look for you. If you run, I will personally track you down."

"Dude, I get it, okay?" I reached down to unbuckle my seatbelt.

Tadhg grabbed my wrist, pinning it against the seat. "And I'm holding you responsible for him."

I glared back at him. "I'm not his babysitter."

"I don't think you get it. My lord's honor is at stake here. If you screw this up—"

I twisted free. "Don't worry about it. We'll do what we have to do." I got out of the car with my backpack.

"What was that about?" Eliaster muttered.

I told him.

He barked a laugh. "Idiot."

Banshee rolled down her window and winked at us. "Hey, boys." Her voice was light, cheerful. "Whatcha say, Eliaster? Ready to toss an apartment like old times?"

Eliaster rounded the Jeep and got in, and they pulled away. I glanced across the street at the club, took a deep breath, and set my shoulders. This would be easy. All I had to do was get in, confirm Shaughnessy was there, and get out. Easy-peasy.

As I crossed the street, I shoved one of the headset earbuds into place. Hopefully anyone watching would just think I was listening to music. I dug out the fake resume I'd knocked together while we'd been waiting to leave, and straightened the collar of my button-down.

The employee setting out the metal stands looked up as I

approached. "Still closed, dude."

I held up the resume. "Just applying for a job, man."

He nodded and gestured for me to go inside.

I pushed open the door. The place looked bare, almost sparse, with bright fluorescent lights shining down on a glossy dance floor in the middle of the room. It smelled like alcohol, chemical cleaners, and the stale, lingering scent of perfume. The outer rim of the room was raised with a black metal railing around it. Steps led down to the dance floor, and tables and chairs were scattered around. On my right sat the bar, brightly lit, and to my left, there was a staircase that disappeared into the black metal loft. Colored lights and other visual-effect equipment hung from the underside of the loft over the dance floor. I could easily imagine how impressive it looked with dim lights and music pumping through the speakers.

"Hey."

I looked over at the bartender. The guy was shorter than me, with dark hair and a scruffy beard—and fully human. "Umm, I'm applying for a job?" I forced my voice to rise at the end of the sentence in a question. "Any idea where I go for that?"

"Just sit at one of the tables," the bartender told me. "Someone will be with you shortly."

I nodded and settled on the edge of the seat, tapping the papers on the table.

My phone buzzed in my pocket. I pulled it out, half expecting a text from Eliaster, but instead, it was from Aileen.

You were wearing a bracelet the day we met. In the café.

Wow. Observant.

Don't get snarky. You asked for help. I'm giving you help. Keep the bracelet on you at all times. And I don't just mean carry it in your pocket. Keep it on your wrist.

Why?

Another long pause. *It will protect you.*

I ground my teeth. *Why can't I ever get a straight up*

answer? How will it protect me?

After a few seconds, my phone rang with Aileen's number. I popped my earbud out and put the phone up to my ear. The bartender shot me a curious glance, but didn't tell me to get off the call.

"I can't believe I'm doing this," she said sharply. "This is dangerous, for both of us."

"Just give me a straight answer, and I'll get off your back," I snapped back quietly. "I don't know why it's so freakin' hard to get answers from you if you're supposedly on my side."

She sighed, a mix of annoyance and frustration leaking through her tone. "There's no straight answer, Josh. I don't know what that thing is. All I know is that when I grabbed your hand—"

My palm tingled at the remembrance.

"—I could feel the glamour on it."

"It's a—" I started.

Footsteps echoed on the metal stairs, and I looked up in time to see a red-haired fae come clattering down to the ground floor. Shaughnessy. Something flashed on his hand, something that for a split second blinded me even in the dim light and gave me a headache. I winced, squinted.

From here, the ring on his index finger looked like a typical school ring, the kind kids got to celebrate graduation from high school or college. But there was something weird about it—I could see a ghost-image flickering around the ring, moving and shifting as Shaughnessy walked across the dance floor and stepped up to the bar. I squinted and caught sight of the ogham cut deep into the gem. I squeezed my eyes shut, trying to recall the alphabet Roe had taught me.

S. T. and I ...

Stiúir.

Stu-wer. It almost sounded like "steward."

I opened my eyes. Keelin had been right, Shaughnessy did wear relics.

"Josh? *Josh?*" Aileen repeated.

"I gotta go," I said, pulling the phone away from my ear.

"The bracelet," she shouted, her voice sounding far away and tinny. "Don't forget—"

I hung up. Shaughnessy had a relic. I'd confirmed it. It was time to go. I started to stand, glanced over my shoulder back at the bar.

Shaughnessy and the bartender both looked over at me.

Crap. I forced a vague smile, like he was just another stranger I'd accidentally happened to make eye contact with, turned away, and pulled my phone out, pretending to text as I walked toward the door. I put my other hand in my pocket, the one on the inside of my jacket, snagged the bracelet with my fingers, and worked it over my wrist. As it had the first time I'd put it on, the metal shrank so that the sword shards fit snugly against my wrist bone.

My neck prickled and I spun, so quickly my bag slid down to my elbow and smacked against the glass door.

"Hey, whoa, man. Sorry to startle you." Shaughnessy pulled his hand back. The hand with the ring.

The skin on my neck crawled. He'd almost touched me. Why had he been trying to touch me? I forced another smile, pulled my backpack onto my shoulder. "No worries." I looked to the side. The only other person in the club was the bartender, and he was moving bottles around the back of the bar, completely unconcerned.

"Rick said you were applying for a job?" Shaughnessy asked.

"I think I got the wrong place," I said. "My mistake."

His eyes narrowed just a touch. "Do I know you?"

"I just have one of those faces, y'know?" I said, pressing my hand on the glass. I stepped through the doorway. My heart pounded. Was he going to follow me? Would he press the issue?

Shaughnessy watched me, his eyes narrowed, as I let myself out of the building. Then the mirrored glass hid him from view.

I twitched my shoulders, trying to get rid of the creepy-crawly feeling I still had. He'd almost touched me, on the bare skin of my neck, with a relic.

I glanced down at the bracelet I now wore, the metal once again fitting close to the bones of my wrist like a second skin. Had it protected me, like Aileen seemed to think it would? I flexed my hand. What had the word on Shaughnessy's ring—STUIR—meant? What would've happened to me if he'd touched me?

Chapter 19

ELIASTER

Despite what Josh might have thought, it killed me to leave him. I hated it, hated feeling like I was abandoning my friend, hated that I felt so guilty over it. Hated that I'd allowed myself to be forced into a situation where I had no choice but to work with Banshee.

I glanced at her out of the corner of my eye. She lounged back in the driver's seat, nails tapping on the steering wheel as buildings slipped past outside the window. She'd added a few more piercings since I'd last seen her—her ears were pierced all the way to the tips, and the diamond in the side of her nose was new as well. Her long, platinum hair shimmered in the sunlight. Crap, she was as attractive as ever.

I stared at her, trying quickly to sort through the cause of the slow burn at the back of my throat. Had to gather my thoughts before she could use the fact that I was off balance. Anger, nostalgia, disgust, relief, betrayal, and—of all things, longing—all pooled into a vicious cocktail that would probably make me puke if I swallowed.

I took a deep breath. "Okay, Banshee. Give it to me straight."

She turned, blue eyes wide and innocent. "Give you what?"

"Don't play this game with me. Not now. Not ever again. Tell me why you're here."

She spun the wheel, ignoring the car honking behind her. "Secrets, secrets, sweetheart."

I shook my head, blew out a deep breath, and tried to contain my anger. Getting mad at Banshee would accomplish nothing and only make her laugh. She wasn't scared of me. *I'm not scared of her, either.*

But if I was honest with myself, that was probably only half true. I chewed on the inside of my lip. No, I wasn't scared of her. Banshee wouldn't hurt me. Tease me, play games, lie to me, yes. Try to stoke up our old relationship, probably. But hurt? No. She wouldn't dare. But I didn't know what she wanted—and that scared me.

"So where'd you pick up the human?" she asked.

I frowned. "Josh?"

"No, the other human who's tagging along with you." She rolled her eyes.

"You can't tell me that you don't already know."

Banshee tapped her fingers on her knee. "He's kinda cute, in a little-lost-puppy sort of way."

I glared at her. "Don't even think about it."

"Jealous?"

"No." *Yes.* I shoved the thought away. I couldn't go down this road again. She was gorgeous, she was good at what she—we—did, but we were like ammonia and bleach. Toxic. She pulled me down roads I'd rather not travel again.

Her laugh rang out in the car, just as boisterous as ever. "I wondered how long I'd have to dig to bring out the 'cranky guardian' act."

Damnaigh, she'd managed to distract me after all. We pulled into a parking lot, and Banshee parked as far away from the building as she could.

I turned her. "Tell me why you're really here."

She held up her hands, palms toward me. "Keelin called me in because I have a reputation for this kind of work, and he didn't want any curators involved."

"And we're involved why?"

"You pissed him off by interfering."

I narrowed my eyes.

Her lips quirked to the side. "Okay, yes, you have me to thank for that. He was going to have you two hauled back to Missouri, but I convinced him to bring you in, try to get you on board." She studied her black-painted nails. "I didn't tell him to threaten you, no matter what you might think."

Did I believe her? I stared into her eyes. As usual, I couldn't quite manage to read her. Everything about her face, her open posture, told me she was being honest. But was she being *fully* honest? She'd played me before. I didn't want to get burned again.

Guess I'd just have to chance it and see.

I looked up. Across the street was an old-looking brick building, but the steel around the windows and doors glinted, new and shiny, in the sunlight. One of those old factories turned into trendy, hip studios full of exposed brick walls and beamed ceilings with modern furniture. I didn't see the appeal.

"Part ownership of a nightclub can't pay for this place," I said. "How does he afford it?"

Banshee shrugged. "Oh, maybe the fact that he's involved in moving illegal relics?"

I rolled my eyes. "You know I was just thinking out loud. Enough with the sarcasm."

"Pot, meet kettle." She got out of the car.

I shoved open my door and reached for the back door to retrieve the swords I'd propped in the back seat.

Banshee shook her head. "Leave them."

I glared. "You're seriously asking me to leave my swords behind."

"I know they're your security blanket, but you'd barely be able to swing *one* in a small loft apartment, much less both of them." She checked the gun at her side. "Maybe it's time to modernize."

I crossed my arms. "I'll stick to my knives, thanks."

"Suit yourself." She spun and started toward the building. "He's on the second story. Come on."

I jogged up the exterior metal stairs. They reminded me more of an old-fashioned fire escape. The way the metal platforms swayed under my feet was more than a bit disconcerting.

Banshee crouched at the top, pulling a set of lockpicks from an interior pocket of her coat. I scanned the parking lot below, listening to the metal *tchk, tchk* as Banshee rotated the picks in the lock. After less than a minute, she pushed the door open and stepped inside.

I hung back, running my hands along the doorframe. "That didn't seem a bit easy to you?" I asked. "The guy has had Keelin's goons on his tail for the past two weeks, and supposedly he has access to relics, but his door isn't trapped or alarmed?"

"You don't trust me to check that?" Banshee's chuckle drifted out of the apartment.

All right, so maybe I was taking my paranoia a little too far. Banshee knew what she was doing, even if I distrusted her methods. I stepped into the large, wooden-beamed room and closed the door behind me.

The opposite wall was exposed brick, lined with picture windows that revealed Kansas City's downtown below. To one side of the open room was a little kitchenette, with a half-sized refrigerator, a tiny stove and sink, and a couple of cabinets topped with a small counter space, half of which had been taken up by a basket of fruit and a toaster oven.

Banshee stood at the far corner of the room, digging through a standing dresser wedged between the wall and the bed.

I took a few steps into the apartment toward the living room area, intending to search the trunk that doubled as a coffee table.

I heard a scratching sound over my head. I started to turn, but wasn't quick enough. A solid mass slammed into my shoulders, throwing me sideways to the ground. Heat flared through my skin, and I brought one arm up to protect my throat and grabbed a knife with the other.

Thin links of metal gouged into my hand, feeling like needles digging into my skin. I gritted my teeth and slashed backward. Felt the knife catch. My attacker hissed in pain and let the chain go slack. Claws skittered away as Banshee ran toward me. I scrambled to my feet and spun around.

A cat-sidhé lunged for one of the windows. Banshee dove after it, slapping its hand away from the window latch. She palmed its face, slamming the back of its head into the window. The cat-sidhé slumped to the ground, mewling and clutching the back of its head.

I looked down at my hand. Blood dripped from a gash on the back. A thin jewelry chain was embedded in my palm, the ends dangling nearly to the floor. Strangled by jewelry. Now that was new to me. I glared at the cat-sidhé as I peeled the golden chain out, sucking in a sharp breath between my teeth. Damn, that hurt.

I held the chain up and checked it over for ogham. No runes marred the smooth surface of the links. Well, at least I wouldn't be poisoned by some kind of malicious glamour.

Banshee poked at the cat-sidhé with the toe of her boot. "What're you doing here?"

The goblin glared at her, then glanced over at me. "You!"

I recognized him at that moment. The one who had attacked Josh and me in the alley the other night. I smirked. "Nice to see you again too."

The cat-sidhé hissed.

I balled up the bloodied chain and stuffed it into my pocket, then pressed the hem of my T-shirt against the cut. I walked over the kitchen cabinets and started pulling out drawers.

"What are you doing?" Banshee demanded.

"Looking for a towel," I muttered. "I'm not about to leave my blood lying around for anyone to get hold of."

She quirked an eyebrow. "You've learned a few things."

I shrugged off the praise and grabbed a couple of towels. Clutching one in my injured hand to stop the bleeding, I used the other to wipe up the splatters of blood my struggle had left on the floor.

"One more time, goblin ... why are you here?" Banshee demanded.

After a few seconds of silence, there was a *crack*. The goblin shrieked. My stomach lurched. I looked up to see Banshee's foot on the goblin's knee. Its leg was bent at a weird angle. I clenched my hands, swallowing down the bitterness in my throat. This was far too much like old times for me.

"Ready to answer me this time?" Banshee snapped, grinding more weight down on the leg.

Tears streaming from its eyes, the goblin locked his teeth together.

Banshee moved her foot.

"Shaughnessy was working with you, wasn't he?" I said, straightening. Maybe if I led him with some easier questions, I could get him to talk. Maybe Banshee wouldn't have to torture him anymore.

The goblin glanced over at me and nodded. "Ran relics more than anything. That's why I'm here—he called me, told me to clean out the apartment."

Banshee glanced at me. "He's running."

"Keelin's guys spooked him. No surprise there—I don't think subtle is in their vocabulary." I looked back at the goblin. "Where's he keep the relics?"

The goblin pressed its lips together.

"Suit yourself," Banshee muttered.

"Banshee, wait—"

She stomped on the goblin's unbroken leg.

The goblin howled and writhed. I turned away, grinding my teeth together. This was all too familiar. It was all I could do to not press my hands over my ears. I scanned the living room, reached up, and rubbed the cross pendant under my shirt. Tried to focus my mind elsewhere. Where would

Shaughnessy keep relic-related stuff, if he had any in the apartment? Josh had said something once about Marc hiding papers in a video game console, but Shaughnessy didn't even have a TV.

I walked over to the bookcase and began pulling books out at random and shaking them out.

"It's there, in the trunk!" the goblin sobbed.

I turned. The goblin was pointing at the flat-topped trunk in the middle of the living room. I met Banshee's eyes. "Rigged?"

She shrugged.

It looked like an ordinary metal trunk. I knelt next to it and examined the exterior, searching for fine wires, hidden switches, anything that could indicate a trap. Nothing. I moved the dirty dishes, books, and papers stacked on top of it and tried to raise the lid. Locked.

"Where's the key?" I asked.

The goblin's trembling fingers pointed to the bookshelf. I retrieved the key hidden under a few books, then unlocked the trunk and flipped open the lid. Nestled in a cushion of extra blankets and pillows were three items—a red book about the size of my hand, a wooden box, and an external computer hard drive. I shuffled, leaning over so that my body blocked Banshee's line of sight, and slipped the book into my jacket pocket. At the same time, I placed the hard drive in my other pocket, hoping Banshee would notice that instead. Then I grabbed the box and opened it. A couple of pieces of jewelry—a necklace and a ring—winked out at me. I folded the end of one sleeve over my fingers and poked at the jewelry, trying to find ogham engraved on the pieces.

"Where is he getting these?" I muttered.

After a second, Banshee snapped, "Hey, you heard him. Answer the question."

"I don't know," the cat-sidhé sobbed. "Galen knows all sorts of people."

"Relics are expensive! He's not going to get a collection of them just by *knowing* people! How could he afford them?

How did he afford this place?" Banshee poked at him with her boot. You're not gonna tell me it was just because he could manipulate the mind of a few humans."

The goblin shrieked again. "No, no, no! This is recent—he just made a deal. Tipped off someone important about something. He wouldn't tell me what. But about three months ago, he had some woman here—not one of his lovers, either. She was important. She was *powerful*."

"Powerful?" I pocketed the jewelry box. "What do you mean by that?"

The goblin whined. "She reeked of glamour. Of *sorcery*."

"Describe her."

"Beautiful." The cat-sidhé licked his lips. "Pale skin, long black hair with turquoise stripes in it. Her eyes were purple—they looked *delicious*. Like grapes."

"You're *sick*," Banshee growled.

My heart lurched. *Larae*. I walked over to the goblin's side, crouched down, looked into its eyes. "Was she with the Lucht Leanuna? What did Shaughnessy tell her?"

The goblin cringed back. "I don't know. They were talking about some relic—it sounded important—but they stopped when I walked into the room. She never introduced herself to me."

My phone buzzed against my leg. I stood, pulled it from my pocket, and glanced at the screen. *Just talked to Shaughnessy. You should get here.*

"Banshee!" I said, turning away. "Time to go."

Banshee nodded, pulled her gun from her pocket, and pressed the muzzle against the goblin's temple. The creature cringed and shut its eyes. I barely had time to look away before the gunshot echoed in the small apartment. I forced himself to not look at the goblin, to keep my eyes on the floor as I walked out of the apartment, my stomach churning. Good news was, I no longer felt anything other than sickened by Banshee. Out of all the problems that came with working with her, this was my least favorite. I waited on the stairs as she came out the door and locked it.

"That wasn't necessary," I muttered.

"You'd rather he called Shaughnessy and told him to run?"

"I'm just sayin', Banshee—"

She started down the steps. "I don't remember you being such a *lagrachán. Fás píere*, already."

I ground my teeth and followed her, mind spinning. Larae had been in contact with Galen Shaughnessy. And they'd been talking about a relic. An important one, too important to talk about in front of a mere flunky.

It had to be another pathstone.

Chapter 15

JOSH

The Blue Fire would open its doors at 8 PM, so by 7:45, the parking lot had started to fill up. Tadhg and I moved the SUV several blocks away, then walked back. We found a good place to watch from, in an alley across the street. It was dark, flanked by a couple of rundown stores that were closed, and smelled like wet cardboard. Ten minutes later, Adam joined us, and we watched a long line form on the sidewalk.

Soon enough, the lights turned on, and two tall bouncers in suits came out front and began checking IDs and letting people in.

"Do you have someone covering the back entrance?" I asked Tadhg.

"Obviously," Tadhg said.

"You think you worried Shaughnessy?" Adam asked me.

I had absolutely no idea, but I wasn't about to let them know that. "Don't know. He didn't seem rattled." I leaned against the brick and squeezed the handle of the knife at my side. If Shaughnessy ran, would Keelin try to make us chase Shaughnessy down? Could we afford to spend time on that? Right now all I wanted was him in custody so we could get back to Springfield and talk to Aileen.

"Tadhg, what's *stu-wer* mean?" I asked.

Tadhg tilted his head a bit. "Why?"

I shrugged and tried to look like the idiot he thought I was. "I recently saw it somewhere and was curious."

From the narrowing in Tadhg's eyes, he didn't quite buy it, but he answered my question. "Guiding. Like you'd guide a ship."

Well, that didn't bode well.

I went back to watching the front of the club. Before long, Banshee and Eliaster pulled into the parking lot. Tadhg walked over to them as Eliaster got out of the car. As they spoke in low voices, I scanned Eliaster's face. He looked fine, his eyes their normal bright green, his reactions showing attentiveness to Tadhg's voice. Maybe his and Banshee's mission had gone all right.

After a moment, Tadhg nodded and motioned for me to join them. As I did, Banshee stepped out of the car.

I paused and took her in. Instead of her all-black, jeans-and-leather ensemble, she now wore a short, curve-hugging black dress and high heels. I glanced over at Eliaster and noticed that he'd changed at some point too, into dark slim-fitting pants, a green button-down, and a black sports coat instead of his usual ratty, baggy jeans and T-shirt.

I sighed. "Crap. We're going in there after him, aren't we?"

Banshee laughed and tossed me a plastic shopping bag. "Go change."

I glanced around the parking lot and raised an eyebrow. "Where?"

"Behind a dumpster in the alley." Banshee winked. "I won't peek."

Despite myself, I could feel my face reddening. I glanced over at Tadhg and Eliaster. "Seriously, I don't think this is a good idea. He might recognize me. He'll run."

Tadhg scoffed.

"Why do you think that?" Eliaster asked.

"He knows I saw his relic," I said.

"There's another section of the club," Banshee said.

I nodded. "Right, the loft."

"That's a VIP section. As an owner, he'll be up there. So he won't be able to see you right away. By the time he does, it won't matter."

"Okay, but how—"

She grinned. "Trust me, I have ways."

I groaned.

Tadhg shrugged. "It's the best option."

I glanced over my shoulder. "He's going to be long gone by the time we get in there."

Eliaster rolled his eyes. "Just go change already."

I sighed again and trekked into the alley, ducking behind one of the big dumpsters so I was out of their sight. Was I mad about the plan? No. But irritation itched at the back of my neck. No one had even wanted to hear my opinion. Once again, the fae had swept me aside, acting as if I was a dumb human rather than an intelligent person.

"Stupid fae," I muttered under my breath, yanking open the shopping bag. It held slim-fit gray chinos and a dark blue button-up shirt, almost the exact color as one of my favorite T-shirts at home. It all fit me as if it had been tailor-made. Banshee had a good eye. As uncomfortable as it made me, I realized it was likely because she'd done this before. I recalled what Eliaster had said—that he and Banshee used to work together a lot—and wondered how many times they'd sneaked into VIP areas of clubs and dinner parties in order to track down something. Or someone.

I quickly put my phone, wallet, and keys into the pockets of my new pants—at least they'd left me my sneakers— stuffed my jeans and T-shirt into the bag, and went back to the parking lot.

I tossed the bag into Tadhg's car and faced everyone, my arms crossed. "If we're gonna do go after Shaughnessy this way, we have to watch out for everyone else in the club. He might try to take a hostage if he feels threatened."

Banshee smirked. "Don't worry, I'll keep him distracted while you guys move in."

Of course she would. Greeeeeat. I sighed. "Okay. Let's get moving, then."

We stepped down into the street. Halfway across, I could already hear the faint bass line of the music inside the club. Instead of joining the line at the back, Eliaster marched right up to the bouncer, hands in pockets, stride quick and purposeful. The sidhé glared at him, showing off yellowy-brown eyes. Very unusual. I blinked hard, wondering if the guy was able to put up a really good glamour—ever since I'd started seeing through glamour, I'd yet to meet a fae who could trick me with it. I blinked again. Nope, still no ghosting or fuzzing around the edges of his face. So what kind of sidhé was he?

"Line starts at the back, friend," he growled.

Funny how the sidhé all made the word "friend" sound so menacing. I backed up a step.

"Sure, I know where the line starts. Just wanted to introduce myself. Eliaster Tyrone."

The sidhé immediately dropped his gaze and bowed his head. "Your father is well-known in our circles. Welcome."

Well, that part was easy at least.

He moved aside and pulled the door open for us. The music that had so far been mostly bass now blasted out of the door. I felt like I'd been slapped in the face by a soundwave. A headache bloomed above my eyes as I stepped in after Eliaster.

Bright colored lights swirled over the dance floor, painting bodies neon blue and pink and purple. A quick glance revealed that the ratio of fae to humans looked pretty even.

"What was that about?" I yelled to Eliaster.

He grinned. "You just met your first *faoladh*."

First werewolf. At a nightclub. Yeah, that didn't scramble my brain circuits at all.

I pulled off my glasses and rubbed my eyes, half-expecting Eliaster to be gone by the time I opened them again. But he still stood at my side, casually looking around the dim, blue-lit room. I glanced at the bar, wondering if that area would be a little more quiet and secluded, but no. The back of the bar was lit by a wall of electric blue, turning the liquor in the bottles a bunch of weird colors.

Banshee stepped up behind us, brushed her fingers against Eliaster's shoulder. "Keep an eye out."

"Got it."

She passed us and strode around the dance floor, heading toward the staircase, which was now cordoned off by an LED rope light. My gaze followed the glowing stairs upward until they disappeared into a dimly lit space above the back booths.

"Why do you think Shaughnessy is still here?"

"He never went back to the apartment—either he's here, or he ran, and I don't think he had enough warning to run." Eliaster nudged me toward the bar. "Keep moving. The upstairs area is a loft—it overlooks the dance floor and I don't want to chance him spotting us."

"What's Banshee doing?" I asked.

"Just give it a minute." Eliaster scanned the crowd, hands still tucked into his pockets.

We ordered from the bar. So far, no one seemed to recognize us. I started to relax a little and fiddled with my bracelet as I waited for my drink. "So what's the game plan? She's gonna try to get him outside? How does she expect to even get up to the VIP section in the first place?"

"She's *Banshee*. She's really good at suggesting ideas and making them sound like *your* ideas. She'll be fine. We just need to be ready to move when she does."

I turned, leaning my elbow on the bar, and studied him. "You seem a lot more comfortable with this than you did earlier today."

His jaw tensed. "I've … accepted this. Besides, at least Banshee's not an unknown quantity."

"You sure she didn't just make her idea sound like your idea?"

Eliaster rolled his eyes.

Banshee meandered around the VIP area, always keeping in the bouncer's blind spot. A few people—one or two small groups, and a few singles—passed by her, and Banshee's eyes tracked their every move. Oh great. I had a good idea of what she was planning. Sure enough, as soon as a group of eight—with several single guys—approached the VIP area, she slid seamlessly into their group, taking the arm of a guy and smiling at him. He didn't seem to mind.

The bartender—a different guy than the one I'd seen earlier, thank goodness—nudged my elbow and set our drinks on the counter. As I picked mine up, a flick of color caught the corner of my vision. I glanced up. Glamour flickered above me, a lightshow more mesmerizing than the dance floor. I squinted, watching the rainbow of colors swirl overhead. It was weirdly pretty. As far as I could tell, it wasn't attached to anything or anyone, just free-floating glamour that the fae in the club had released to be a mini Northern Lights. I felt myself relax a little as I watched it, the tension loosening from my limbs.

Eliaster nudged me in the side, hard. "Snap out of it."

I swore and straightened. "What?"

Eliaster nodded upward. "That's mesmer. Look at the humans in the crowd."

I looked, seeking out faces that didn't have glamour ghosts flickering over them, that didn't have pointed ears and pinwheeling colors in their eyes. Every single human had a sloppy smile and slack features, and every single one of them was staring at the ceiling as they danced or drank, enthralled by the colors.

Eliaster's eyes flicked over the crowd. "There are some feeders here."

"Feeders? Like vampires?"

"Maybe, but I doubt it. Marraighs, more likely. This feels like them. They feed off human emotion." His lips tightened into a thin line. "I hate feeders."

"So, like sluaghs."

"Yeah, except instead of sucking out your soul, they'll

drain you of their particular type of poison—love, joy, whatever kind of human emotion you can think of, there's probably a marraigh out there who feeds on it."

Lovely. I kept my eyes down.

After a moment, Eliaster started shuffling. "Where is she?" he muttered, glancing at his watch. "C'mon, Banshee, it shouldn't be taking—"

Shaughnessy pounded down the stairs at a full run. I glanced at the stairs, but didn't see Banshee. *Crap, he's gonna get away!* I practically threw my glass back on the bar and took off across the room towards Shaughnessy, Eliaster right behind me.

Banshee dashed down the stairs, somehow staying upright despite the high heels.

Shaughnessy bolted for the emergency exit. I tried to squeeze through a crowd of chatting people.

Banshee caught up and grabbed Shaughnessy's wrist, twisted his arm to the side. Shaughnessy stumbled and lashed out at her with his foot, hitting her ankle. Banshee shrieked and toppled.

I ran after Shaughnessy. He slammed through the emergency exit, and a blaring alarm sounded out over the music. I hesitated, looking over my shoulder for Banshee and Eliaster.

She waved me forward. Eliaster was already right behind me. We burst out into the street behind the club.

I paused, glancing up and down the street. My heart hammered in the base of my throat. Where was he? We couldn't lose him.

"This way." Eliaster tugged on my jacket sleeve, and we dashed down the street.

Shaughnessy was fifty feet ahead of us, running as fast as he could down the sidewalk, his unbuttoned blazer flapping behind him.

"Hey!" Eliaster shouted.

Shaughnessy glanced over his shoulder, and his eyes widened. He ducked his head forward, pushing himself to run even harder.

Eliaster growled and sped his pace. A few months ago, I wouldn't have been able to keep up. Tonight, I stayed right on Eliaster's heels. We were gaining on Shaughnessy when he skidded and scrambled into an alley.

We took the corner, and I promptly tripped over an overturned garbage can. My chin cracked into the pavement. My tongue and teeth started throbbing. Stars burst in my vision, and I rolled off the can, groaning and holding my chin. Blood filled my mouth.

"Crap! Crap, crap, crap!" Eliaster grabbed my arm and hauled me to my feet. "Are you okay?"

I spit out a mouthful of blood and nodded.

"Then c'mon." He skipped a few feet away from me, then sped into a full-out run.

I wobbled after him, doing my best to ignore the ache in my jaw. Shaughnessy wove through the alleys of what I'd guessed had been the old downtown industrial area, now filled with abandoned warehouses and rundown factories. I didn't see Shaughnessy. With the pain in my face, it was all I could do to keep Eliaster in sight. I followed after my friend, trying to focus my mind back on task.

Something metallic jingled ahead of us, like Shaughnessy had climbed a chain-link fence. Eliaster suddenly slowed as we got out from between the narrow buildings, stepping down onto a cracked street with faded markings. Flickering street lights barely illuminated the area. I stopped and leaned over, putting my hands on my knees.

"Did you lose him?" I panted.

"No." Eliaster nodded to the building in front of us. "He ran in there."

I straightened and eyed the huge place. It looked like an old factory, complete with a crumbling smokestack poking from the roof. A chain link fence with warning signs posted all over it surrounded the building. When Eliaster rattled the fence, an entire section crashed to the ground.

"Convenient," I muttered. "Doesn't look very inviting."

"I don't think his intention was to invite us to tea." Eliaster's shoulders hitched in a deep breath.

Something crackled in my ear, and I realized that even with crashing to the ground, I hadn't lost the headset. I pressed the earbud back in place in time to hear Tadhg yelling, "Eliaster! Josh! Answer me already! What's going on?"

Eliaster yanked the earbud out of place, rolling his eyes. "He's been screeching at me the entire time, I just haven't had time to answer."

I nodded. "Tadhg? Can you hear me?"

"*Buíochas le Dia*," Adam said. "Yeah, we can hear you."

"What happened?" Tadhg demanded. "Is Eliaster offline as well?"

Eliaster placed his finger to his lips.

I rolled my eyes. "We've been chasing Shaughnessy."

"Where are you guys?" Adam asked.

I looked for street signs. "Looks like … Fifth and North. Don't know the address, but you can't miss it. It's an old factory made of red brick, partially painted white. Part of the chain link fence around it has been cut. Eliaster said Shaughnessy went inside."

"Okay. Is Banshee with you guys?"

I looked around and realized that no, Banshee wasn't with us. I tried to think back to the last time I'd seen her. "She's not with you?"

"No."

"Maybe we lost her."

"If we could be so lucky," Eliaster muttered.

"Maybe. Well, you guys just stay outside. Wait for us."

"Got it."

Eliaster motioned for me to pull out my earbud.

I removed the device and clenched it in my hand. "He said to—"

"I heard him." Eliaster tucked his hands in his jacket pockets.

"You're not actually going to *do* that, are you?"

Eliaster's jaw clenched. "Shaughnessy is *dansearach*. We know for sure that he has at least one relic, maybe more. So yeah, I'm absolutely going to wait for backup."

My breathing quickened, and I glanced at the abandoned building. "But ... but what if he slips out another way? What if we lose him?"

"Then we'll pick up his trail somewhere else."

"Eliaster—"

He shot me a disbelieving look. "Are you kidding me? *No.* This is how Iain and Emily got killed. We're waiting, Josh."

I clenched my hands, feeling a burning panic in my chest ... and more. Anger. Where did he get off, ordering me around? I knew just as much about this situation as he did. Maybe more, since I'd been the one pushing for it. He hadn't wanted to fully commit until Keelin and Banshee had forced him into it.

We couldn't waste this opportunity.

Fear gnawed at my stomach as I took a few steps forward, then glanced over my shoulder.

Eliaster straightened, eyes narrowing.

"You coming or not?" I demanded.

He sighed, then pulled a small flashlight from his pocket and clicked it on. I flicked on my phone's flashlight, then cautiously stepped on the downed fence. It jingled under my feet.

Eliaster huffed a breath behind me. "Yeah, let's go after the crazy relic-user Unseelie without anyone else. Sounds like a fantastic idea ... and will you at least let me go first?" He shoved in front of me. "Damnaigh, you're going to get yourself killed."

"I don't want to lose this lead," I snapped.

"I get it," he said, not looking back at me.

I sighed, following him into what had once been a parking lot. The old concrete had cracked and tufts of grass grew all over it.

A gaping dark hole stood in the crumbling brick where a

dock door had once been. The dock was still there, chunks missing from the edges of the concrete structure. We hoisted ourselves up on it.

Eliaster drew his knife, and we stepped into the building. Despite the evening sun, the interior of the building was dark enough to make me squint.

I flicked my flashlight along the walls. The huge, open space stretched in front of us, interspersed with concrete support pillars in regular intervals. Some splintering wooden tables had been stacked in a corner, mold growing over them. But for the most part, the place was empty. Our flashlights threw faint circles of light on the opposite wall, about a hundred yards away.

Eliaster growled. "He could be anywhere in—hey. You hear that?"

I stopped walking and tipped my head to the side, holding my breath. For a moment, I didn't hear anything. Then, faintly, the shuffle of a footstep echoed around the large, empty space, making it impossible to figure out where the sound originated.

Eliaster shone his flashlight to the side, revealing a staircase with a metal railing around the top. He crept forward and poked his head over the railing.

I stepped close to him. Reddish light streamed through the open bay door, casting a fading rectangle on the floor. Dust motes danced, sparkling in the sunbeam. And down the stairs, I caught sight of a faint line of light—a door, just barely cracked open. The low murmur of voices came from the room beyond. I drew my gun from underneath my jacket.

Eliaster moved around the railing and started down the chipped steps.

I followed, tightening all but my trigger finger around the gun grip.

Something scuffled behind us. I jerked to the side just in time to avoid a huge metal flashlight whipping at my head. The flashlight struck Eliaster on the shoulder, and he pitched forward into the stairwell with a yelp.

I extended my arms, pointing my gun at Shaughnessy's abdomen. "Step back! Eliaster, you okay?"

Eliaster groaned.

Shaughnessy just stood there, still clutching the metal flashlight with one hand. He grinned. I tightened my grip on the pistol but kept my finger steady on the trigger. My hands shook, and I could feel the sweat on my palms, making the pistol grip slick. My vision tunneled.

No, no, no, not now! I couldn't get a flashback now.

"Eliaster?" I said, my voice pitching higher. I tried to steady my breathing. I had to slow my pulse rate. Blood thundered in my fingertips and temples.

Shaughnessy took a step forward.

"Back up!" I snapped, shuffling my feet into a slightly wider stance. I was gonna have to shoot him. Just like I'd shot the goblin. I could do this. I *had* to.

"Drop the gun," he said, raising his left hand. Even with the low light, the ring on his finger glimmered.

"Or what? You'll zap me with that? Good luck—you have to touch people to get that to work. I'm not completely stupid."

"No, just stupid enough."

Before I could answer, an arm snapped around my throat. I jerked, more out of shock than an attempt to get away, but stilled when the point of a knife dug into my ribcage. Where was Eliaster? Why wasn't he—

"Drop the gun."

My blood ran cold. "Eliaster?" I whispered.

Chapter 16

JOSH

The knife dug through my jacket and nicked a bit of skin.

"Drop it," Eliaster snarled in my ear.

"Okay, okay," I muttered. I took my finger off the trigger and extended my arm. Shaughnessy stepped forward, and, for a split second, I considered jerking it back and aiming it at Eliaster.

No. This made no sense. I glanced over at Shaughnessy. Even in the dim light, I could see the ring glinting on his finger. I went cold.

The ring must be one of the enslavement relics that Tadhg had talked about.

Shaughnessy wrenched the gun away from me and motioned behind. "Down the stairs."

Eliaster stepped backward, and I stumbled along with him as best as I could. He shouldered open the door and dragged me into the brightly lit room. I blinked against the sudden glare as voices exploded around us.

"Galen?"

"Who are these people? What's going on?"

"Relax," Shaughnessy ordered, stepping into the room and shutting the door behind him. He spoke to Eliaster, too rapidly for me to understand, and Eliaster dragged me to the side. I caught a quick glimpse of a mid-size room made up of white cement blocks, the paint thick and peeling, and a few other fae clustered at the other side of the room, near rusting metal shelves. Then Eliaster shoved me.

I staggered, hit the corner with my shoulder, and sank to my knees. I kept my eyes on the floor, not willing to antagonize Shaughnessy by seeming too curious. The ache from hitting my chin earlier spread up my face, probably made worse by my clenched jaw.

"Later," Shaughnessy was saying. "I can't explain and maintain my grip on that one's mind. Just start packing."

Murmurs of compliance, and the rustling of packing materials, accompanied his orders. I glanced under my arm. The other fae were pulling things from the shelves, rolling them in layers of bubble wrap, and placing them in boxes.

I took a deep breath in. "Relics," I whispered.

At that, Eliaster stepped back, the grip on his knife slackening.

"Ah, ah, ah." Shaughnessy held up his hand, and the gem in his ring flared with light.

Eliaster snarled. *Crap.* Before I could duck, he grabbed the collar of my shirt and yanked me upright. Shaughnessy nodded and went back to talking to one of the others in a low tone.

That stupid ring. How was he even controlling Eliaster with it? Shaughnessy'd had no time to touch him. And why was it only working on him? It made absolutely no sense.

"Eliaster," I whispered. "Dude, you gotta let me go."

I could feel him trembling, and, for a second, I thought my words had gotten through to him. Then suddenly he spun, slammed me against the wall, fingers fitting around my neck, and shoved the point of his knife under my chin, lifting my head back. I gagged and kicked at him, but he leaned away. His eyes were a maelstrom of green, and his arms shook.

Doggone it, why couldn't I have waited five minutes for the others?

"That's enough!" Shaughnessy yelled at him.

Eliaster eased the knife away, but didn't loosen his grip. I grabbed his wrist and tried to pry his hand free. He leaned all his weight against my throat, and I couldn't get enough leverage to push him away. I could barely even breathe.

Both times Shaughnessy had moved his attention away from Eliaster, my friend's grip had slacked a little. If I could get his attention long enough and time it right, maybe I could free myself of Eliaster's hold. And maybe I could buy enough time for the others to get here.

"How are you doing this?" I asked.

Shaughnessy laughed. "What, are you hoping I'll monologue long enough to give you a chance to get free?"

Well, yeah, that had kind of been the plan.

"We're ready to load up the van," someone told Shaughnessy.

"Sounds good. Get moving. I need to deal with these two."

I tried to push Eliaster away again. I looked past him at Shaughnessy, held up my hands. "Call it professional curiosity. I assumed that the ring only worked with touch, but unless you call hitting someone on the shoulder with a flashlight a touch, then I guess I was wrong."

Shaughnessy chuckled and shook his head. "I have to admit, I'm a little curious as well. I sent out a strong thread of glamour—if it affected your fae buddy, it should've affected your human mind as well. You should be tearing each other's throats out right now." He stood and swung the backpack to his shoulders, then squinted at me. "Not even curators have this kind of power."

I shrugged, keeping my arms loose and at my sides. My bracelet shifted on my wrist, and I fought the urge to hide it. If, like Aileen thought, it protected me from glamour, then it was the only chance I had.

"Well, as curious as I am, I think Kansas City's finally gotten too hot for me." Shaughnessy waited as the last of his buddies left, then closed the door behind him. He stepped over to us and put his hand on Eliaster's shoulder. "*Maraigh é.*"

Oh no. Bile rose to the back of my throat. I knew that phrase: *Kill him.*

Eliaster's hand around my neck twitched. A spasm made his face tremble. His arms started shaking again.

Galen clenched his fist. "I am your *rialóir*! *Maraigh é*!"

Rialóir, ruler. Yeah, definitely an enslavement glamour. I made eye contact with Eliaster, tried to search for my friend's real self, hidden behind the blazing anger and terror.

His hand tightened.

He was in there. He had to be.

I reached out and put my hands on his shoulders. Pushed. I had to get through to him before he strangled me. "Eliaster? Eliaster, listen to me. You can fight this. He's in your head, messing with your mind, but you're stronger than this, you can—"

Shaughnessy snarled.

Eliaster's thumb pressed into my windpipe, cutting off my voice. And my air.

Panic arced through me like electricity. I tried to twist away from Eliaster's grip. Grabbed his arm, digging my fingers into his elbow joint. "Eliaster! Eliaster, stop it!"

Another spasm crossed Eliaster's face. Then he swung the knife up, the blade arcing for my face.

I yelped and dropped to my knees. Whether it was because of my sudden weight shift, or because his hand had loosened, the move broke his grip, and Eliaster staggered. The knife hit the cinderblock wall with a grating sound.

I scrambled away from him. He swung around, following me, knife held out to the side. I crouched, held my hands out.

"Eliaster, please listen to me!"

He swung.

I scrambled backward, trying to remember our sparring sessions. I'd have to be quick—Eliaster liked to attack relentlessly, not giving his opponent time to recover.

Sure enough, he followed the knife swing up with a

punch. I dodged it, and the next time he raised the knife, I grabbed at his wrist, trying to twist the knife out of his hand. He followed the motion, spinning around and slamming his shoulder into my torso. I folded, breath huffing out of my lungs. He hooked a foot around my leg, and my back slammed into the concrete floor. I groaned, trying to roll to my side, but he planted a knee in my chest and grabbed my hair, jerking my head back.

"Eliaster, *stad*!" I yelled. "*Éreigh as*!"

His hand hitched, and it was just enough. I shoved myself forward, slamming my forehead into his face. Stars burst again in my vision, but the blow threw Eliaster off me. The knife clinked to the floor. He rolled on the ground, clutching his nose. I scrambled to my feet and grabbed the knife.

Shaughnessy backed away from me, bringing the gun up to bear at my chest. "Stay where you are!"

Eliaster tried to grab my leg, and I kicked him in the ribs, harder than intended. I tried to hold back, but at this point, I couldn't let him pin me again. He rolled, tried to get up, and fell back to his stomach, one hand still trying to hold back the blood gushing from his nose. I cringed at his groan as I turned back to Shaughnessy.

The redheaded fae's eyes swirled with every shade of blue, the gun in his outstretched hands steady and trained right at my heart.

"Why?" I asked. "Why are you doing this?"

"Because I can," Shaughnessy snapped. "This power, using glamour in this way? It's the way of our ancestors. Eliaster, Keelin, they're *weak*. They'd never use glamour in this way, the way it was meant to be used. The Tuatha De Danan ruled *this* world as well as Tir Ni-all, and you pathetic curators would have us stand down from that power?" He shook his head. "No. Not a chance. It's unbelievable that you'd even ask—like asking a wolf to ignore a trespasser on his territory. Humans have weak minds—the sidhé deserve to rule over them!"

"Except for me, apparently."

"You're different. You're a curator. They have weird powers, weird immunities ..."

I took a deep breath. And there was my opening. I shook my head and, at the same time, readjusted my grip on the knife. "No, I'm not. I never even knew the Underworld existed until a few months ago."

Shaughnessy's hand faltered, and surprise flicked across his face.

I lunged forward, using my free arm to knock his gun hand to the side. The gun went off, and the shock wave slamming into my ear nearly took me down, but I plowed forward into him. We tumbled to the ground, and I grabbed his left wrist. I had to get the ring off his finger.

He booted me in the stomach, throwing me several feet. I crashed on my side and rolled, thudding into Eliaster. Eliaster rolled, trying to get his hands underneath his body.

"*Fóill ort!*" Shaughnessy snarled.

Eliaster groaned and curled into a ball, wrapping his arms around his head.

I gasped, trying to suck air back into my lungs. Everything hurt, and my limbs felt heavy, weighted down from the kick. I rolled to my hands and knees, tried to get up. Saw the pistol coming at me too late. The barrel crunched into the side of my face, knocking me down onto my back. I curled up, cradling my head. It hurt. It hurt so badly I could barely think.

"I'm sorry," Eliaster croaked beside me. "Josh, I'm so sorry."

"Touching," Shaughnessy snarled, getting to his feet and scooping up the gun. He cocked it and pointed it at Eliaster's head.

The metal door burst open, and Banshee sprinted into the room. She lunged at Shaughnessy. I flinched and shielded my face. A shot echoed in the room, then the thud of a body hitting the ground. I looked up.

Banshee had Shaughnessy pinned to the floor. The red-haired fae thrashed and squirmed, and suddenly the light in his ring flared. Banshee jerked back, flopping off Shaughnessy like a useless rag doll.

Shaughnessy scrambled up the stairs. I dashed after him, past Banshee. Adam stood in the doorway of the factory. He spun at the sound of footsteps. I was suddenly aware of other voices, other sounds of battle in the warehouse. Then Shaughnessy reached out for Adam and my focus narrowed again.

I lunged, hit Shaughnessy in the lower back with my shoulder. We tumbled forward, rolling off the loading dock and hitting the asphalt below. I scrambled up on my hands and knees and pulled my hand back for a punch.

His fingers snaked around my wrist.

Glamour burst around us, and something cold curled up my arm. I looked down. Blue, glowing vines snaked from his fingers, wrapping my arm, but almost as soon as I looked, they flashed green, turned brown and shattered into wisps of dull smoke.

My fist connected into his stomach.

Shaughnessy doubled over, gagging, and let go of my wrist.

I scuttled away from him, panting. Those vines. Those vines had been in my dreams. I rubbed my wrist, felt the cold metal of my bracelet.

Adam jumped down beside me and grabbed Shaughnessy's arm, hauling him to his feet. Adam looked down at me. "You okay?"

I nodded. My legs shook. I leaned against the loading dock, rubbed my hands over my face. My hands wouldn't stop trembling, and after-images of those glowing vines flashed in the corners of my eyes.

Someone groaned from inside the factory, and my stomach dropped. "Eliaster!"

I pulled myself up onto the loading dock and raced inside. Banshee helped Eliaster up the steps. He collapsed to the ground at the top of them.

"I'll get the medical kit," Banshee said, walking past me.

I crouched at his side. Blood still trickled from his nose, and he held his ribs. I waited until she was out of earshot, then crouched beside Eliaster and lowered my voice. "Do you remember what happened?"

"Bits and pieces. Crap, Josh, I'm sorry."

I swallowed back the lump in my throat. "No, I'm a crow-eaten idiot. We should've waited for backup like you said."

He glanced up at me. "You okay? You look kinda pale."

I shook my head. "I'm good. You?"

"I think you broke a rib."

"At least it wasn't your face," I pointed out.

Eliaster let out a sharp bark of laughter, then hunched forward, scrunching up his face.

"Sorry."

"Forget it. You did what you had to do."

A flashlight flared, and Tadhg walked over to us and crouched down, eyes critical and examining. "Where'd he get hit?"

I tried to remember. "Ribs. Umm—I got his nose pretty good too."

"I can see that. And you call yourself a warrior, Tyrone." Tadhg helped Eliaster sit up and pressed his side.

"Ow!" Eliaster glared at him, and I noticed his eyes were slightly bloodshot.

"Yeah, probably broken. Can you stand?"

Eliaster shoved him away and got to his feet, smearing the blood on his face as he wiped his hand across his mouth. "Where's Shaughnessy?"

"Adam's got him."

Tadhg grunted and gave me a grudging look. "Wouldn't have if you hadn't tackled him off the loading dock."

Eliaster glanced up at me. "Nice."

I grinned.

Banshee came back into the factory, carrying a white, plastic-sided medical kit. "Adam's got Shaughnessy." She crouched in front of Eliaster. "How's your side?" Her voice actually sounded a little soft, concerned. She tried to touch his side. "Lift your shirt."

Eliaster made eye contact with her, and something flickered deep in both of their eyes. He batted her hands away. "My shirt's staying where it is."

"Fine." Banshee flicked open the kit and tossed a pack of gauze to me. "Your head's bleeding."

I raised my hand to my temple. Sure enough, my hair was sticky with blood. Must've been where Shaughnessy had clocked me with the gun. I pressed the gauze to the cut and winced.

"Let's check to make sure you don't have a concussion," Tadhg said, turning on his flashlight. He shone the light in my eyes, frowning.

"Sorry again," Eliaster offered.

I shrugged it off, trying not to think about it. One more thing to worry over. One more flashback I'd probably have tonight. Vines glimmered again in the edges of my vision, and I squeezed my eyes shut. That had been glamour. I'd actually seen it this time.

And I'd shattered it.

What was going on?

Chapter 17

ELIASTER

"You need to let me wrap those ribs."

I looked up at Banshee and scowled. "I'm fine."

She sat back and matched my scowl. "Fine. Be that way." She got up and walked away, leaving the medical kit open on the ground.

I hunched over, pressing my arm against my side and trying not to focus on the throbbing pain. Out of the corner of my eye, I could see Josh giving me worried glances as Tadhg examined the wound on his head, then flicked a flashlight beam over Josh's eyes. Why was he so worried? It was just a couple of cracked ribs. I was the one who was supposed to worry about people, and Josh? Josh didn't look great. Blood matted his hair, and a bruise was already starting to spread down his temple. The part that really worried me, though, was how pale Josh looked, and how he'd become quiet, withdrawn. He'd taken down Shaughnessy. Cíorru air, he should be crowing about it. But he wasn't. Something had sent him into a tailspin.

"You okay?" I asked him again.

He shot me an annoyed look. "There's nothing that I want to discuss *right now*."

I raised an eyebrow. So there was something, but he

didn't want Tadhg to overhear it. "Sure. Sorry for asking," I grumbled back.

I glanced around the factory. Adam and Banshee stood near the bay doors, in an intense discussion. I spotted a few other flashlights throughout the factory, searching for any of Shaughnessy's gang who might have escaped capture.

Shaughnessy and three of his men were lined up against the wall near the bay doors, kneeling, their hands bound behind them. Only one guard with a gun watched them. I recognized him from when Tadhg had stormed our hotel room. Brayan, I thought.

Across the factory, I locked eyes with Shaughnessy. A slow smirk curled the corner of his mouth.

Rage burst like a fireball inside my chest. I curled my hands into fists. I couldn't remember anything that had happened in the last half hour, and it was his fault. It was Shaughnessy's fault that I'd hurt one of the only people I truly trusted.

My mind drifted back to the moment. The glamour snaking down the stairway after me, the sudden sharp pain as it filtered into my brain.

I hated that chunk of missing time.

I'd been monumentally stupid.

Enslavement relics. Shaughnessy had given them to goblins to use on slaves. Other fae. *Humans.* And now me. And he'd been talking to Larae about a pathstone.

My eyes fell on the weapons someone had brought up from downstairs. My knife, blood on the blade, sat on top. I grabbed it, tucked it flat against my arm where it wasn't readily visible, and stood. Crossed the room to where Shaughnessy and his cronies sat. The fae guarding them eyed me curiously, but didn't say anything.

I crouched down in front of Shaughnessy and stared at him, gritting my teeth. *Just give me a reason to shove this into your gut. Please, give me a reason.*

After a second, he chuckled. "Think you're gonna stare me to death?"

"Nah," I replied. "I wanted to see what kind of idiot thought it would be a good idea to deal in the black market these days. Especially with the curators cracking down on that kind of stuff."

Shaughnessy straightened, leaned forward. "I'm not scared of a bunch of damn humans who think they can order the fae around." He glanced over my shoulder, in Josh's direction. "Crow-eaten pieces of—"

I whistled, calling his attention back to me. Then I punched him in the face.

Shaughnessy's head bounced off the wall behind him, and he crumpled to the ground. The room exploded into shouts. I ignored them. I stood, grabbed Shaughnessy's ankle, and dragged him away from the others. He kicked, tried to struggle away from me, but his foot slipped on the concrete floor.

The rage still burned in my chest, but I tamped it down, condensed it until it seared like ice. I stepped forward, put my foot on Shaughnessy's throat, and pressed down. He froze, staring up at me, his eyes pinwheeling with the dark colors of fear, hatred, anger. I glared back, using his rage to stoke my own. I leaned forward, resting my elbows on my knee, and twirled the knife in my hand. He watched the blade. I kept most of my weight on my back foot—I didn't want to kill him. Yet.

"So tell me about these relics," I said quietly.

"What about them?" Shaughnessy croaked.

"Who you sold them to. Who you talked to about some of the more valuable ones. Who your boss was. Just simple things, really."

Shaughnessy spat. The bloody spray hit the side of my leg. I rolled my eyes and straightened, leaning more weight on his throat. He choked and started kicking. I could feel the others staring at me, but I avoided their looks and glanced over my shoulder at the rest of the prisoners.

One, dark-haired with a scar that slashed across his right ear, stared at the floor and wouldn't meet my eyes. The other

two stared at me—the younger with a sort of horrified panic.
The third prisoner suddenly lurched to his feet. The guard
yelled at him to sit back down, right before the fae slammed
his shoulder into the guard's stomach and rushed straight at
me.

I shifted my foot off Shaughnessy and stepped to the
side, trying to get out of the guy's way, but the distance was
too short and he slammed into me. We both went down. I
howled in pain and flailed, shoved him away, then his weight
suddenly disappeared.

I rolled to my feet in time to see Banshee slam my
attacker into the ground. Without hesitating, she pulled her
gun and shot him in the temple.

The shot echoed loudly in the space, and I flinched,
instantly feeling sick. *Too far, too far*. I leaned over, pressing
my palms to my knees. Trying to catch my breath.

"Crazy *raicleach*." Shaughnessy half-sat up, staring at
Banshee, eyes darkening. "What was the point of that?"

She ignored him and stepped in front of the youngest
fae. She grabbed his chin and forced him to look her in the
eyes. "How old are you, kid?"

He seemed to shrink. "Nineteen."

"That your big brother?" she asked, jerking her head at
the other one. "Real stupid of him to bring his little kid
brother on a job like this, huh? Even if you are Unseelie."

That got a reaction from both of the fae. The older fae
started cursing her out, and the kid's eyes flashed. "We're not
a part of any stupid court! Why do you think we have a job
like this?"

I winced. Vagrants. Fae who refused to join a court—or
had both courts reject them. Not an easy life.

"Danos, shut up!" Shaughnessy roared at him.

"Oh, you're talking again. Fantastic," I growled. "Shut up
or I'll smash your teeth in." I turned to the kid. "Start talking.
Now."

Banshee put her fingers under Danos's chin and turned
his head back toward her. "Listen, you heard Eliaster," she

said smoothly. "And while I'd much rather prefer to give everyone another facial orifice, I'm willing to let you have another chance before taking such a drastic move again. You're not going to disappoint me, are you?"

Danos cleared his throat and said in a hoarse whisper, "There's a guy in St Louis. I've only met him once, I only started working with my brother a few weeks ago." He paused, glancing over at his brother again.

"You gave your word!" his brother snarled. "Keep your mouth shut, you little bastard!"

"Funny thing about that," I commented. "People usually don't understand how much pain they can experience *before* death."

Danos shot me a glance, eyes wide. Banshee raised her eyebrows and tapped her gun barrel against Danos's arm.

Danos cleared his throat again. "Henry Blair. He's a curator."

Behind me, I heard Tadhg grunt in surprise. I stiffened. "A *curator*? Are you sure?"

Danos kept his eyes on Banshee's gun, cringing away from it. "He never said for sure, but it makes sense—getting his hands on all this old stuff. And he talked about the museum up in Michigan. "

She nodded. "He's Shaughnessy's boss? Your boss?"

"The curator has a boss, but we're not a part of that. He just sends extra stuff here, stuff he thinks won't be missed. Shaughnessy hired us to sort through it all."

"Who is the curator's boss?"

"I don't know."

Banshee Cheshire-cat grinned, leaning a little closer to the fae's face.

Danos drew his shoulders up, cringing away from her. "I swear on all the *aingeals* in heaven, I don't know who is in charge! We're not important enough to know. My brother and I are surface vagrants. We just do this job to get paid and keep out of people's way."

I felt a little sorry for the kid. I stuffed my hands into my pockets and glanced down at the floor.

"You're dead, kid. You know that? We're all dead," Shaughnessy snapped.

"Don't count me in on this!" Danos's brother protested. He looked at Banshee. "I don't care if you kill him or not, but leave me out of it!"

Danos stared at his brother, eyes wide in shock.

"Welcome to reality, where everyone wants to kill you sooner or later," Banshee told him. She stood and faced Tadhg. "I think we're done here."

Without a word, Tadhg motioned to Adam and Brayan to grab the two fae.

Banshee paused beside me. "I was right," she said in a low tone.

"What?" I snapped.

"You have gone soft."

The ride back to Keelin's house was quiet. Since Tadhg and Adam's SUVs held the prisoners, we got to ride with Banshee. I just curled up in the backseat, nursing my ribs and trying to ignore the ache. I could practically feel the tension between Josh and Banshee, though.

If Josh didn't yell at me about this later, I'd know something was wrong for sure.

Banshee pulled into the driveway of the safe house, parking away from the front door to give Tadhg's SUV room. The black vehicle pulled between ours and the house.

I shoved my door open.

"You sure you're okay for this?" Josh asked. "You could wait here. I can take care of it."

"Mother hen," I grumbled, sliding from the car. It hurt to stand upright, but I did anyway, pressing my elbow in against my ribs. I went around to the back of the car, where Josh and I had thrown our more casual clothes, and popped open the hatch. As I grabbed my bundle of clothes, the external hard drive from Shaughnessy's house slipped from my jacket pocket and fell to the gravel driveway.

Before I could lean down, Banshee crouched and grabbed it.

I froze, locking eyes with her. She turned the hard drive over in her hand. For a split second, I was afraid that she was going to call Tadhg over. Instead, she slipped it back into the bundle of clothes and winked at me before sauntering away.

"Okay, you should probably stop staring at her now," Josh said in a low voice beside me.

"Blaming the pain meds," I muttered.

He smirked. "Have you had any pain meds?"

I shoved the plastic bag of his clothes into his chest. "Shut up, nerd."

Keelin stepped from the house. In the dim evening light, it was hard to see his exact expression. The doors to the SUV popped open. Tadhg went around to the back and hauled Shaughnessy out of the vehicle, one hand clenched tight on Shaughnessy's arm, the other yanking his head back to what looked like an uncomfortable angle.

Shaughnessy caught sight of Josh and lunged at him.

I darted in front of Josh. Shaughnessy's fist connected with my gut and I grunted as a shock of pain lanced through my side. I dug my feet into the gravel and shoved the fae back, grabbing his collar. Then I twisted until it cut into his neck. "Back off."

Shaughnessy didn't even try to fight, but he glared past me at Josh, eyes burning with a dark fever. His teeth bared in a feral grin. "Mortals who dabble in fae affairs die, human. You're playing with power you cannot hope to understand. Just remember that when the Wild Hunt comes for you and shreds the flesh from your bones."

"I've faced a sluagh and lived," Josh said steadily. "I think I can handle the Wild Hunt."

I couldn't help but grin. Yeah, he probably could, against all odds.

Shaughnessy laughed.

Keelin stepped closer to Shaughnessy. Adam reached out, putting a hand in front of his employer, but Keelin brushed it aside. He looked Shaughnessy up and down, and his lips curled in disgust. "How did a *gan ainm* like you get hold of a powerful relic?"

Shaughnessy looked at him, eyes flashing. He started to say something, but his jaw stayed locked in place, the muscles of his face trembling. His eyes went wide. "I—I—" The muscles of his jaws tensed, forcing his mouth closed.

Tadhg stepped back, eyes going wide. "He's under an oath of silence."

"Genius deduction," I muttered. *How did I miss this back in the factory?*

Keelin stared at Shaughnessy for a moment longer, his eyes flickering. "It must be a powerful oath to affect him like this." He jerked his head to the side. "Banshee, take this scum away."

"Wait!" Shaughnessy tried to squirm free of my grip. "What are you doing with me? You saw what happened. I can't tell you anything!"

"You'll pardon me for wanting to ensure it's the real deal," Keelin said drily.

Shaughnessy's eyes bulged. He swung his arm wildly. His elbow nearly caught Tadhg in the face. Tadhg grabbed Shaughnessy's arm, digging his fingers in just above Shaughnessy's elbow. Banshee stepped in to help, and I let go of Shaughnessy's collar. Together, Tadhg and Banshee dragged Shaughnessy around the corner of the house.

Keelin waited until they'd disappeared before speaking. "You two look like you got dragged through a meat grinder. Care to explain how that happened?"

I glanced over at Josh, but before we could answer, Adam spoke up.

"One of his relics was a *stuíur* ring, sir." The fae held the ring out to Keelin.

Keelin flexed his fingers, and a thin layer of glamour appeared over his skin, fitting like a glove. He accepted the ring and held it up to the light, rolling his thumb and forefinger around the ring as he studied the *ogham* carved into the gem. His lips compressed into a thin line. "Where did he find something like this? *Cuimhní*, I could understand. Perhaps even some glamoured pendants for human lovers. But this ..."

"Things like that exist?" Josh muttered under his breath.

Keelin shot him a sharp look. "Do you understand why everyone is so worried about a human becoming so involved? Those are not items with strong glamour, and yet humans fall for them all the time."

Josh glanced away.

"Did you find any other relics?" Keelin asked.

I chewed the inside of my lip, considering telling Keelin that I planned to turn over the ones I'd found to the curators. But I doubted Keelin would allow that. I didn't want to push it tonight, not after everything we'd just gone through. Besides ... Banshee already knew about them, so it wasn't like I could bluff my way out of it.

I pulled the box from my jacket pocket and held it out. "This is what Banshee and I recovered from his apartment. I'd send someone to clean it up, if I were you—there was a rather messy altercation with a goblin."

Keelin took the box and grunted. "Well, I suppose it's what I get for hiring loose cannons."

Was he referring to me, or Banshee, or both? I swallowed back the sarcastic words pushing at my tongue.

"We'll send these to the curators as soon as possible," Keelin informed Adam, handing him the box and the ring.

"Do you mind if we take a couple of the relics back to Missouri?" Josh asked. "We have someone who is interested in studying them."

"Roe Gillam, you mean?"

Josh blinked. "You know her?"

"I know of her, and her theories about the greater relics, including the pathstones." Keelin snorted. "Mind you, a few weeks ago, I would've said finding something like this ring was impossible. Regardless, I'm not about to let these out of my sight."

I crossed my arms. "Especially to someone I associate with, is that it?"

Keelin glared. "Get the chip off your shoulder. This is about sidhé surviving in the real world, Eliaster, not running around pretending this is still our history. Humans don't want us to save them—they want to live comfortably in their small existence, happy to pretend we don't exist."

I stepped closer to him.

Keelin raised his chin. Out of the corner of my eye, I saw Adam tense.

"I hope this means we're even." I poked him hard in the chest.

"As far as I'm concerned, we need never speak again."

I smirked and stepped back, raising my hand in a mocking half-salute. "Just take care you can weather the oncoming storm, Keelin. I'd hate to see you break." I turned and walked toward the car. "C'mon, Josh."

"Don't take this as a future license to act in my territory, Eliaster Tyrone," Keelin said. "If I ever see you here without my permission, I'll have O'Breigh—"

"Yeah, yeah, you'll go running to my da and have O'Breigh slap me with a binding or whatever," I snapped as I climbed into the car. "I get it. Far be it from a screw-up like me to try to save the world." I slammed the car door.

A minute later, Josh climbed into the driver's seat. "Home?" he asked quietly.

I nodded, gritting my teeth. I waited until we'd pulled out of the driveway before slamming my fist into the car window. "Stupid idiot."

To his credit, Josh didn't even flinch. "It's easier to bury your head in the sand than accept that there might be trouble. I tried, remember?"

"Yeah, but the difference is that you accepted the evidence and came to a conclusion," I muttered. "Everything is right in front of Keelin's nose, and he won't even accept that there's a problem until it's too late. Look at what happened with Shaughnessy and the goblins. That man is going to lose his territory to some scheming Unseelie because he refuses to acknowledge danger until it's eating him alive."

Josh shrugged, though his expression was pensive.

I side-eyed my friend. Josh gripped the steering wheel with one hand, while the other rested on the windowsill, his fingers tapping out various rhythms. I could practically see the gears in Josh's brain turning, but it was obviously about something else. That was weird. Had Josh seen something?

I dug painkillers from the center console, swallowed several of the pills, and leaned back in my seat with a sigh. I hated this feeling—the gnawing urge to do something, yet being completely helpless. I couldn't force Keelin to believe that the Lucht were real, any more than I'd been able to force my father to believe it.

What does it matter? It's not like I need him as an ally.

"You okay?" I asked Josh.

Josh shook his head. "You?"

"Don't worry about me." I tried to straighten up and winced. "So when we get back to Springfield, let's—"

"Don't lie to me."

I stared at him in shock. "What?"

"You're obviously not okay. Besides the broken ribs, you're the one who got his brain twisted around by that psychopath's glamour." Josh's hands tightened around the steering wheel. "Do you remember any of it?"

Another flash of Josh's face, bloodied and fearful. I flinched. It reminded me too much of the last time I'd seen my brother. "I know I beat you up, and I'm sorry. Josh, you can't—"

Josh abruptly pulled the car over on the wide shoulder of the road. He clenched his hands together at the top of the steering wheel and dropped his head onto them. "You tried to kill me."

The words felt like a punch in my gut, slamming me

back to the choppy memories. I'd held a knife to Josh's throat. I swallowed hard as bile rose to the back of my throat.

"Eliaster, stad! Éreigh as!" Stop. Give up.

My own feeling of out-of-control panic and fear.

My hands trembled, and I balled them into tight fists. Fear? I'd feared *Josh*? The idea would almost be laughable if I didn't have a busted nose and cracked ribs to show for it. Josh had come a long way in five months, but he was far less formidable than Larae, or Llew, or even Ghurdan. I didn't fear Josh. That had to have been the glamour talking.

But the glamour would've needed something to latch onto. I tried to shove the thought away.

I am your railóir.

"Crap."

"What?" Josh snapped.

"The ogham, on the ring. *Stiúir* basically means rule, but its more precise definition is *controlling influence*."

Josh swore. "Tadhg told me it was *guiding*. Makes sense. He didn't take you over completely, because there were a couple of times I managed to get through to you. Even before I hit you. That's what snapped you out of it, right?"

"Maybe? I don't know. It's kind of a blur … I remember the glamour getting into my head, feeling the pain of that, and the next thing I remember clearly is being on the floor. You were beside me, and Shaughnessy had that gun pointed at your head." I thumped my head back against the seat.

How did he get into my mind?

Josh pushed his glasses up on his forehead and pinched the bridge of his nose. His breath sounded shaky. "I should never have insisted on going after him."

I shrugged. "You had a valid point. If we'd waited, we easily could've lost him, and those other fae, and the relics. And then what would've happened? Keelin probably would've tried to blame us, and trust me, if he'd called in Highlord O'Breigh, you and I would be having a very different conversation right now."

"I know, I just—"

"You should've run," I told him. "Kicked me in the knees and run."

"Shaughnessy had a gun on me. Besides, that would've left you to face him alone. While he was mind-controlling you. What kind of friend would I be if I'd done that?" Josh sighed. "I was mad because I felt like I was being railroaded, between you, Banshee, and Tadhg insisting we had to go in the club after him. And after spooking him like that … I just didn't want to lose our only lead. So I pushed to go after Shaughnessy. Turns out I probably shouldn't do that."

Josh thought we'd forced him into that mission? I flinched. "I didn't think—"

"I know, Eliaster." Josh shook his head and accelerated, too sharply, out onto the road.

Why can't I ever just shut the hell up? I curled up in the seat and ran my fingers through my hair. As I thought back to earlier that night, I could see how Josh was right. He'd had objections and I hadn't listened. I winced again and tried to ease into a different position. I didn't want to think about this right now.

How did Shaughnessy get into my head? Glamour like that had to latch onto something. It couldn't just create an intense fear like that where nothing existed beforehand. But I wasn't scared of Josh. Protective, yes. But—

I felt sick. Protective. Just like I'd been protective of Iain. My older brother had been more book-smart than street-smart, the one who had always preferred to sweet-talk his way out of situations when I charged in swinging. Larae's little minion, David, had been right earlier this year. *I'm treating Josh like a replacement for Iain.* And that scared me.

Chapter 18

JOSH

Eliaster had finally kicked me out of the driver's seat—thirty minutes away from Springfield—because he'd claimed I'd nearly fallen asleep. But even once I'd slumped into the passenger seat of his car, I still couldn't fall asleep, despite the fact that it was almost one in the morning. Every time I closed my eyes, I saw those glowing glamour vines wrapping up my arm. Shaughnessy's fingers tight on my wrist. Or Eliaster holding his knife to my throat.

He'd been scared of me. At some point, I'd realized that, while Eliaster had been under the ring's influence. But I still didn't understand why.

As we unloaded our stuff from the car and headed into the rath, Eliaster paused, holding out his hand in front of me. I stopped walking and clenched one hand. Eliaster winced and stepped back, showing me his palms. I breathed, relaxed a little.

Eliaster rubbed at his chest before dropping his hands to his sides. "Sorry. I'll have to be careful from now on, won't I?" When I didn't answer, he shuffled his feet in the gravel. "I'm—look, Josh, I'm sorry. I'm so, so sorry."

I nodded, the knot in my stomach tightening. "I believe you."

Not that it was all his fault. If I hadn't insisted on going after Shaughnessy ...

After a few seconds, he turned and walked into the rath. I followed. We found Cormac and Roe in the library, cups of coffee in hand.

Roe looked up, spotted us in the doorway. Her eyes widened. "What happened?"

"Any leads on your break-in?" Eliaster dropped his bag in the corner and headed straight for the coffee maker.

"No, not yet," Roe said.

I flopped onto the couch and ground the heels of my hands into my eyes.

Roe leaned forward and clasped my arm. "Are you all right?"

"I ... I stopped Shaughnessy from using his glamour."

The reactions I easily predicted were instantaneous: Cormac choked on his sip of coffee, nearly spilling the remainder of the mug down the front of his shirt. Eliaster's eyes locked on me, spikes of panicky mud-green flaring through his irises. Roe frowned, forming a little worry-wrinkle on the bridge of her nose.

"What?" Eliaster said. "What're you talking about? You didn't tell me that yet!"

"You didn't think it was weird," I said, "that the glamour he used went toward you, and not me? You didn't hear him talking about how he couldn't get a grasp on my mind?"

"Not really. It was kind of hard to think with the feeling of hot needles jabbing into my head and all," Eliaster snapped.

I sighed and rubbed my eyes again. I ached from a dozen different scrapes and bruises and felt bone-tired on top of it.

"Josh?" Cormac's voice nudged me out of my own head.

Right, they were waiting on my response. "Shaughnessy used glamour on Eliaster," I said, looking back up at Roe. "He had a ring that allowed him to dig into Eliaster's mind and control him with suggestions and commands."

Out of the corner of my gaze, I saw that Cormac's hand

went to his son's shoulder, worry flicking through his eyes. Eliaster dropped his gaze to the floor, leaning slightly toward Cormac.

"When he tried to do the same to me, I could see the glamour. It looked like a vine, and it tried to wrap up my arm, but almost as soon as it touched me, it turned green and then shattered."

"When did that happen?" Eliaster asked.

"When I tackled him outside of the factory."

Roe rubbed her knuckles against her lips as she thought. I could see the dark color of worry in her eyes. She glanced over at Eliaster. "You weren't able to use your glamour to pull away from Shaughnessy's control?"

He shook his head. "You know how it is. I don't have that much control in the first place, and ..." His voice dropped to barely a whisper. "I panicked. Couldn't think straight as soon as I felt the glamour invade my mind. And—he was strong, Roe. Really strong." Eliaster toyed with the chain of his necklace, his shoulders hunched.

I felt bad for him. Just the brush I'd had with the enslavement glamour had been enough to creep me out. I couldn't imagine how violated Eliaster must be feeling.

"Shaughnessy thought I was a curator," I said. "But curators aren't immune to glamour, are they?"

Roe shook her head. "The best they can do is resist it, using the focus and thought control techniques they're taught as children, but even someone like Simon would be broken eventually. That's why they primarily focus on research nowadays—they're too afraid of being wiped out, or overtaken."

I brushed my hand through my hair. "And I'm not a curator, anyway."

A rap on the door made us all start. Lukas leaned into the room. "Sir, you're needed on the phone."

Cormac nodded and left the room.

I rubbed my thumb along my bracelet. I was starting to worry at it the same way Eliaster always played with his cross necklace. Aileen. I needed to talk to Aileen. She'd been the one to tell me to put the bracelet back on. Because she'd known it would protect me from glamour? Just how much did she know?

Roe watched me for a moment, then raised an eyebrow. "Any theories?"

I smiled. How could she always tell? "When we faced Shaughnessy, I was wearing the bracelet. Could it have anything to do with being able to resist the glamour?"

"What would make you think that?"

I told her about how I'd seen Aileen use glamour in the coffee shop, but how, when Eliaster and Lord Keelin had faced off, I'd only been able to sense the glamour, not feel it.

Roe frowned, but she seemed deep in thought. "I … I don't know. It came from Blake's side of the family. And he was adopted. Authorities found him abandoned in a store parking lot when he was a baby, just barely walking, and the bracelet was tucked into his pocket. We've always just assumed it was a strange heirloom. I've examined it countless times, and there are no ogham, nothing that would indicate it was some kind of relic. But if that's the only difference, there must be some kind of link."

"I thought ogham were always present on relics," Eliaster said.

"As far as I'm aware," Roe said. "But I suppose there could be relics out there that do not have them. They'd have to be quite old, though. Some of the first ever made. The ogham are a human invention, not sidhé, so I'm assuming that relics first made in Tir Ni-all wouldn't have had the markings."

I rubbed my thumb along the slick curve of the bracelet. Great. I could be wearing a literal piece of fae history.

Roe's eyes sparkled with curiosity. "Now, what's this about a dream?"

I swallowed nervously. "It's been the same nightmare twice now. I wake up with a full moon shining on me, and the bracelet starts to constrict, cutting into my arm, and then glamoured vines burst from the floor and start to choke me."

Eliaster turned and went to the coffee cabinet. Even across the room, I could see the tension in his neck and shoulders.

"And you had this dream even the night you didn't wear the bracelet?" Roe asked.

I nodded.

Roe pressed the edges of her fingers to her lips and sighed. "Well, it sounds like I have several more things to put on my research list."

"Sorry."

"Don't be. An unmarked relic is something entirely new to me. And I don't believe I've ever heard of even a fae who had complete, extreme resistance to glamour."

"It's only happened once," I said. "Maybe it was a fluke."

"Flukes in glamour usually end up with someone being dead," Eliaster commented, walking back and holding out a cup of coffee to me.

"Thanks, sunshine." I glared at him as I accepted the mug.

Eliaster tried to smirk, but the expression lacked its usual lightness. He reached into his pocket and pulled out a red book and handed it over to Roe. "Maybe this'll help. I found it at Shaughnessy's apartment."

I raised my eyebrows, trying to push down my irritation. "If Keelin finds out you kept that …"

"Banshee didn't see me take it. There's no way he could know," Eliaster said as he walked back to the cabinet.

Roe took it and flipped it open, slowly paging through it.

"And while we're on that …" Eliaster cleared his throat. "Banshee and I ran into a cat-sidhé at Shaughnessy's apartment. He was one of the goblin slavers—he said Shaughnessy had told him to clear the apartment out."

"So we did scare him off, then," I said quietly.

Eliaster nodded. "Banshee interrogated him." His voice hitched just a little. "The goblin said that a couple of months ago, Shaughnessy had been talking to a woman about some kind of important relic, and based on his description, I think that woman was Larae."

I groaned. Because of course it would be.

Roe looked up. "You're certain?"

"He described her perfectly."

"Great," I muttered. "Well, I'd been wondering if there was a connection—I guess we know now."

"An important relic," Roe said. "You think Shaughnessy knew something about a pathstone, and sold Larae that information?"

Eliaster shrugged, pulling a mug from the cabinet. "Maybe I'm wrong."

"No, I don't think you would be," I said. "It makes sense." I scratched my hands through my hair. "Did the goblin tell you where Shaughnessy was getting his relics?"

"No."

"Okay, so our first step would be finding out that. Where does he get his relics? And we need to figure out if he was involved in selling them, or if he just happened to know the right people." I reached out, grabbed a notepad, and started scribbling down notes as I talked.

"I'd say that based on the fact that you found relics at the house where the goblins were keeping the kidnapped humans, Shaughnessy was at least minorly involved in moving and selling relics," Roe said.

I noted that. "Okay, so how are he and Larae connected? How did she hear about him? Pathstones are big, so something like that isn't going to be trusted to a small-timer like Shaughnessy. It'd go to someone big, someone at the top of the food chain. So we need to find people who are big into black market relics, figure out who's connected to Shaughnessy, who he was moving relics for." I tapped my pen on my leg, mind spinning. "Might have to try to talk to the curators, or maybe Banshee. Maybe Keelin would be willing to share anything they learn from Shaughnessy. Or maybe we can bribe it out of him. And I bet—"

"Okay, okay, whoa, slow down." Eliaster held his hands up. "I get it, this is a new puzzle for you to solve. But I at least need some sleep."

I glanced up at the clock on the mantel. Two AM. The long days and broken sleep of the last couple of nights settled like a weight on my shoulders. I tilted my glasses up on my forehead and rubbed my eyes. "Maybe in a few minutes," I said, glancing over my scribbled notes.

I barely heard Eliaster's sigh as he got up and walked from the room, taking his coffee with him. I tipped my head back against the back of the couch and stared at the wood-paneled ceiling, mind spinning with so many thoughts I had a difficult time grasping all of them.

One stood out in my head—the bracelet. Aileen had known about the bracelet. I pulled my phone from my pocket and opened my texts.

Hey. When can we meet? I have lots of questions.

My eyes felt full of sand, and I blinked slowly a couple of times, then closed them, trying to relieve the feeling.

I vaguely felt the phone slip from my hand as I fell asleep.

Over the next couple of days, I managed to get computers set up at the rath. Then I started working on wifi, which Cormac had insisted he wanted. Yeah, that was basically a joke with a bunch of fae running around. I let it stew in the back of my head for a while as I began helping Roe organize and catalogue all her research on the relics.

Aileen never texted me back about meeting up, even though I checked my phone multiple times a day. Probably more times than was healthy, if I was totally honest.

I didn't really know what Eliaster was up to—he was in and out. I was pretty sure he was giving me space deliberately, which I appreciated. In the little time that I didn't keep myself occupied, I'd find myself turning those moments—Eliaster with his knife at my throat, Shaughnessy telling him to kill me—over in my head until a hot, sickening knot burned in my chest.

If I hadn't pushed for going after Shaughnessy …

"No, Kylie, I'm telling you—"

Roe's frustrated tone snapped me out of my gloomy thoughts. I glanced over at her. She paced in front of the fire, one hand on her hip as she spoke on the phone. I caught her eye and raised my eyebrows.

She rolled her eyes, pressed the phone against her shoulders, and mouthed, "Curators."

Oh, so she was still trying to get hold of someone who would listen. Roe waved at a basket of books sitting on the side table, then pointed up at a blank space at the top of one of the bookshelves flanking the fireplace.

I sighed and got up from my computer desk, grabbing the basket.

"Yes, I work for the Tyrones. That doesn't—" Roe sighed. "That should be water under the bridge. It was proven it wasn't—No, listen. It wasn't his fault, and you know that."

I paused at the foot of the ladder leaning against the bookshelves, frowning. This sounded like how most of the other conversations had gone, even if it was lasting longer.

"All I need to know is where Simon is, and how I can get ahold of him," Roe said. "That's all." She waited a beat. "For multiple reasons, but yes, the pathstones are one of them." Her lips pinched together, and she pulled the phone away from her ear. She glanced at me. "She hung up."

I winced sympathetically. That had been happening a lot. "Because they don't want to work with Eliaster?"

She nodded. "The curators blamed him for Emily's death. Said he had no business taking her with him to help with Iain's wild ideas."

I started up the ladder, balancing the basket of books against my hip and clinging to the rungs with one hand. "So I take it most curators don't think the pathstones exist."

She snorted. "The last couple of generations don't,

anyway. Back when I was a girl, before World War Two, everyone believed in their existence. It was just that no one knew where they were hidden. I'd heard rumors, once, of a stone in Chicago, but had dismissed it. My mistake, as it turns out. I don't want to make the same one again."

I stopped and dug a book from the basket, replacing it in an empty space. "Have you ever found one yourself, Roe?"

"One," she said. "Plenty of rumors, but I've only ever had my hands on one."

I stopped. "Oh yeah? Where's that one?"

"Destroyed," she said grimly. "Back in the nineteen-twenties. A friend of mine, Owan Craig, was hired to track it down. He was cornered, much like you and Eliaster and Mar …" Her voice hitched.

I glanced down at her.

She suddenly looked her age, old and tired and defeated. Roe had lost a good portion of her family to this fight—not just Marc and his father, her son-in-law Blake, but others through the years. She'd dropped enough hints that I knew she'd been involved from the beginning, back nearly a hundred years ago when the search for the pathstones first began. Her daughter and granddaughters were the only ones of her family left.

She cleared her throat. "Anyway. He was forced to destroy the pathstone. He barely escaped with his life, as did his curator partner."

"Craig wasn't human?" I asked.

"Half-fae." She smiled softly. "It made him a very good private eye."

Dang, one of these days, I was gonna have to ask her more about that. A half-fae private investigator, working in the 1920s? That sounded awesome. I reached up, moved a mesh basket, and placed another book on the shelf. As I started to replace the basket, I paused. The mesh was made of metal.

"Faraday cage," I said aloud.

"What?" Roe asked.

I turned quickly, then grabbed at the ladder as my sense of balance struggled to keep up with the movement. "A Faraday cage! I can make one to encase all the electronics, so we don't have to try to keep Eliaster away from them!"

"And here I went to all this trouble to try and contain my glamour," Eliaster grumbled from the doorway as he shrugged out of his jacket. Underneath, he was wearing a black tank top, and his left arm was wrapped in a bandage.

Roe turned, one eyebrow raised. "Focusing tattoos?"

He nodded. "Angel knew a guy—turns out he's one of Opti's buddies. The ink they use is reactive to glamour somehow—I didn't get all of it." He started picking at the edge of the wrap. "Figured it couldn't hurt, anyway."

Roe nodded. "I've heard of them, of course, but most fae nowadays don't bother with them. I'm curious to see if they help you."

I climbed down the ladder as Eliaster unwrapped his arm. Blue ink started at his shoulder with a snarling griffin, a triquetra on the back of his arm above the elbow, an interwoven cross on his forearm, and a shield on his inner wrist. Another, smaller tattoo on his left ring finger caught my eyes, and I squinted. Hands, rendered in precise detail for such a tiny tattoo, wrapped around his finger, holding a heart pointing outward toward his fingertips, with a crown set above it. I recognized the symbol as a claddagh, symbolizing friendship, love, and loyalty.

"How do you feel?" Roe asked.

"Sore, but not bad." He stretched his arm a bit. "I'll get it all filled in with some knotwork in about a month."

"Have you tried using your glamour yet?"

He shook his head, rubbing at his arm. "Figured I'd give this a chance to heal first."

Roe smiled. "Take your time."

I grinned. "Hey, maybe if you can control glamour now, you can help me with a couple of experiments. I have a couple of ideas for keeping all the electronics safe. It might be a bit redundant now, but it wouldn't hurt. And I'd like to set up some security cameras around the rath, but again, I need to know how glamour would affect them specifically."

Eliaster rolled his eyes. "Nerd."

"*Gatlho'*," I said.

"What the heck is that supposed to be? A cat puking up a hairball?"

"No. It's Klingon for *thanks*."

Eliaster blinked at me. "Klingon," he said, in a flat tone.

"Yeah. I recently started learning it."

"Because?"

"Because I needed something fun to do that was a break from all this crazy. Seriously, I used to learn fantasy languages in high school as a hobby, figured I might as well go all out and learn Klingon too." A thought struck me, and I grinned. Time to mess with him for a bit. "And it wouldn't hurt to have a few words for a code, you know."

Eliaster crossed his arms. "Fae are good with languages."

"But are they good with fantasy languages? Like, for instance, Sindarin Elvish?"

"Isn't that supposed to be based on Welsh? And the other one …"

"Quenyan."

He rolled his eyes. "Is based off Germanic and Latin. Off the top of my head I can count at least five fae who know all of those."

We were interrupted by a chiming tone coming from the side table. Roe rushed back to answer it, motioning for us to take our bantering out of the room.

I laughed softly as I followed Eliaster out of the library.

He jerked his thumb at the gym door. "Haven't done any sparring for a bit. Up to it?"

"Sure. So, Klingon for a code language. Sounds great."

"I'm not learning Klingon."

I started for the gym. "I'll get you a printout tomorrow."

"Josh! I'm not joining your nerd club and learning Klingon! I won't do it!" Eliaster shouted after me.

After the last few days, bantering with him felt good.

I rolled out a couple of gym mats as Eliaster sat at the edge of the room, pulling off his shoes and socks. "Swords?" I asked.

"Knives today, I think." He gave a deliberate glance at my side. He started wrapping up his arm again. "Still not carrying your sword."

I shook my head. "Hasn't really been a reason. It's kind of clunky for sneaking around." And I liked the distance that my gun provided me with. Not that I would tell him that. I opened the box of equipment and found the sparring knives, then tossed a sheathed one to Eliaster and chose another for myself.

When I turned around, he was already standing on the mat in a ready stance, the knife nowhere in sight. I stepped within arm's reach, keeping an eye on his right hand, which was partially hidden by his body, and settled into a crouch, my left hand up near my chin ready to protect my face, and my right hand extended, blade ready.

Eliaster lunged forward, raising his right arm in a quick sweeping motion. I spotted the knife, held in a reverse grip.

The blade at my throat...anger and fear freezing Eliaster's face into a snarl... A jolt of fear shot through me.

I stumbled off the mat and landed on my butt, barely aware that I'd dropped the knife. My hands trembled.

Eliaster stopped his charge and waited, bouncing his weapon in one hand. "You okay?"

I shook my head, held up a hand. "Sorry. Sorry, I just ..."

His jaw clenched. "Flashback?"

I nodded.

He looked down at the knife in his hand and shook his head. "I'm the one who should be apologizing, Josh. I didn't think." He tossed the two knives into the equipment box and flopped down beside me, elbows on his knees.

I rubbed my face in my hands, trying to push away the memories. "Does it ever get better?" My voice was hoarse.

"The flashbacks, the new fears … does it get better or do you just learn to deal with it?"

Eliaster was quiet. I looked over at him. He was staring straight ahead at the other end of the gym, a faint blue color swirling through the outer edges of his irises.

He swallowed, lowering his gaze, and started picking at his thumbnail. "Eventually. It took me a while to get over my fear of blades too. In a way, it was a good thing my da had that binding put on me. I was angry, but one glimpse of a blade and I froze up. I would've gotten myself killed if I'd try to go after the Lucht then. It took me six months to even be able to pick up a knife."

Cormac had been the one to bind him to the rath. I felt sick. No wonder they were still working on repairing the rifts the Lucht had caused in their relationship. But I didn't blame Cormac. After losing one son and having another traumatized like that, it was no wonder he'd had Eliaster bound.

A loud, tinny rendition of some classic rock song blared out from the side of the room. Eliaster started, and his head whipped around to stare at his jacket. He swore under his breath and dove across the room, yanking a new phone from his pocket and fumbling to answer.

"Liam. Yeah, what's up?" He pressed one hand to his opposite ear, as if struggling to hear. Then he went very still. "You're sure? I mean, I don't know … what do you think?" A longer pause. "Okay. We'll be there in a bit." He picked up his jacket and shrugged into it, glancing over at me. "Get ready to go."

"Who was that?"

"Liam Conor. He's the owner of the Black Dog, a pub outside of town that caters almost exclusively to faoladh."

"Why're we …"

Eliaster smirked. "Quick rundown. Liam's pack is one of the few that exist in peace with the fae. He and my da have made agreements. One of those is that Da lets them be pretty much self-governing as long as they follow the old laws of the faoladh—vows to protect widows, orphans, the old, the young, those who come to them seeking sanctuary. He just had a girl show up asking for sanctuary and to speak with you and me."

My heart jerked in my chest. "Aileen?"

"What are the odds it would be anyone else?" He gave me a quick look. "I know it sounds weird, but if anyone tried to trap us while Liam was around, they wouldn't last five seconds. We're not close, but I know for a certainty that the vows Liam and his pack have taken will protect us."

I blew out a deep breath. The nice thing about Eliaster's paranoia was that when he placed this much trust in someone, I knew it wasn't on a whim. "Okay. Let's go meet some werewolves."

Chapter 19

JOSH

We pulled into the graveled parking lot of the pub shortly after midday. As expected, the place didn't seem to be very busy at this time. Three cars and a motorcycle were the only vehicles in the parking lot, besides our own. I pulled off my helmet and studied the building's exterior.

The Black Dog looked like one of those log-cabin-wannabes you see in the Ozarks. A front porch held a few rocking chairs and a swing—all in surprisingly good shape. An unlit neon sign depicting a pointy-eared dog with his nose in the air was perched on the porch's roof.

At the sound of our bikes, the front door of the building swung open and a tall, bushy-bearded guy stepped out onto the porch. He looked in his late twenties, maybe early thirties, with a bit of a belly, held in check by the plaid shirt he'd tucked into his jeans.

"Garrett, hey." Eliaster swung off his bike. "Liam here?"

Garrett jerked his thumb at the side of the building. "Around back. Who's this?" He nodded to me. The movement ducked his face into the porch's shadow, and for a split second I saw a flash of yellow in his eyes.

Despite myself, I took a step back.

Garrett grinned. "You must be the newbie."

"Be nice," Eliaster said. "And hey, is the bar open yet?"

"That obvious?" I muttered.

Garrett scratched his bushy brown beard. "Not technically, but I don't think Liam would mind if I brought you something. Still like the Irish honey whiskey?"

"That's like asking if the sun still rises in the east."

"Let me guess, beer for you?" Garrett asked me.

Normally, I wouldn't. But I had a feeling that I was going to need something to get me through the upcoming conversation. "Cider, if you have it."

He nodded and went back inside as Eliaster and I started around the side of the building. An open patio sat behind the building, ringed with grayed wooden fencing and paved with dark red bricks. The colored lights strung overhead looked a bit sad in the bright sunlight. Only one table sat in the middle of the patio—the others had been packed off to the side against the fencing—and the five people sitting around it turned as we came into view.

One of the guys—early thirties, surfer wannabe with shaggy, highlighted blond hair, a sleeveless shirt, and baggy jeans—stood up and waved us over. "Eliaster. Long time no see, man."

Eliaster shook hands and gestured to me. "Josh, meet Liam Conor, alpha of the pack."

I gripped his extended hand. His handshake didn't seem overly strong, which kind of surprised me.

Liam motioned around the table, starting with the dark-skinned, curvy girl he'd been sitting beside. "Patricia, my girlfriend."

She winked.

"And these two are the twins, Charles and James. They're my betas."

Charles was a little stockier than his brother, but they both had the same jawline, the same dark brown hair. James was the more formal of the two, wearing a nice pair of slacks and a button-down shirt with a vest and tie, and I saw a blazer folded over the back of his chair. Charles wore a

Guinness T-shirt and jeans with holes in the knees.

"And finally, our guest of honor. Aileen Airgead."

She stared up at us almost defiantly, head slightly tilted to the side. I blinked a couple of times as purple glamour ghosted away from her hair, revealing again the coarse white locks on one side of her head. Today she was wearing black tights under frayed jean shorts, sneakers, and a vest over a black band T-shirt.

"You gonna sit, or you plan on acting like a couple of stumps this whole time?" she asked.

"Glad to finally meet you too," Eliaster replied. He hooked his foot around a chair leg, pulled it out, and flopped into it.

As I followed suit, I could feel Aileen's eyes on me.

"Rough time in Kansas City?" she asked, pointing to the bruises on my face.

I unconsciously raised my hand to my head, and saw her eyes dart, back and forth, from my face to the bracelet and back. She smiled. A chill brushed my spine. I crossed my arms over my chest, hiding the bracelet, and leaned back in my chair. "A bit. Shaughnessy didn't go down easily."

"But you got him."

"Of course we did."

A smile flashed across her face so quickly that I wondered if I'd imagined it. "Well done."

"Okay, okay, get a room you two," Charles drawled in some kind of British accent.

Heat rose to my cheeks and ears. Aileen shot him a deadly glare, and her grip around her beer bottle tightened.

Liam reached out and lightly swatted the back of Charles's head. "Behave. These are our guests, not members of the pack." His voice carried a low growl.

Charles hunched away from him, looking sullen at the reprimand.

Eliaster picked up his drink. "Seriously, though, thank you for your information. It was invaluable."

I raised an eyebrow. Had he noticed her interest in my

bracelet and guessed why I'd put it back on?

"Laying the flattery on a bit thick, don't you think?" Her warm brown eyes twinkled as she took a drink of her beer.

He shrugged. "Think what you want. But if you have more where that came from, I'm interested. I'd also like to know why you came here, of all places."

At that moment, the door popped open, and Gerald emerged, carrying our drinks. He set the bottle of cider in front of me and the whiskey glass in front of Eliaster. Aileen waited until he'd gone back inside before she finally spoke.

"Josh asked me where a safe place to meet would be." She gestured at the werewolves seated across the table from her. "This is as safe as I could think of."

"You need sanctuary," Eliaster stated.

She hunched her shoulders. "Yeah."

"Why?" I asked.

Eliaster glanced over at me and nodded in approval.

Aileen tapped on the table for a minute, her eyes darting between Eliaster and me. Then she leaned forward, hands clasped in front of her. "I want out. My father …" Her voice trailed off, and her throat bobbed. "Cori and I both want out. Our dad has never treated us well, but lately …" She shook her head. "We're done. We want out."

"And you can't just leave?" Eliaster asked, raising an eyebrow.

"You've figured out who my dad is at this point, and what he's doing, right?"

"We already knew Drake Airgead was an Unseelie living in New York," I said. "But he's been working with a curator and selling relics, hasn't he?"

She nodded.

"And if you want out, why come to us?" Eliaster leaned forward, mirroring her. "Why couldn't you go to the highlord in your area?"

Aileen's amber eyes never moved from his. She clenched her jaw, then pulled the neckline of her shirt to the side, exposing her collarbone. The dark tattoo of a raven stained her freckled skin. "Because of my father, I'm considered Unseelie. You think any Seelie highlord would listen to anything I had to say? He only sees this." She smoothed the shirt back into place. "Is that all you see, Eliaster Tyrone? A lying, cheating, backstabbing Unseelie?"

Eliaster raised his chin. "I prefer to judge by character rather than court."

Aileen glanced over at me.

Her intense gaze pierced into me, and my breath caught in my throat. Eliaster had asked me if her sincerity last time we'd spoken face-to-face had been an act. If her glamour had charmed me. This time, I knew. This wasn't glamour. Maybe her acting was just that good. But … she seemed sincere. She maintained eye contact with each of us and kept her posture open.

I glanced at the wolves. They sat or stood in silence, but every one of them was watching Aileen, muscles tense. Patricia gripped the edge of the table, eyes steady on Aileen, while Liam half-turned, scanning the woods outside the patio fence. Charles and James looked back and forth between the group and the surrounding area. It was like Eliaster had said earlier—no one would be stupid enough to try anything with the wolves around.

"My dad's always been harsh, but it's gotten worse lately. He's becoming … cruel. And his treatment of my brothers has become worse." She started picking at the chipped black nail polish on one finger. "He relentlessly mocks Cori for refusing to show how much power he has, and Gren …well, Gren he pushes to the breaking point. It's not just that, though. He's crossed a line. He has information leading to a pathstone, and he's willing to sell it to the highest bidder. I won't be a part of bringing Fear Doiricht here and setting him on this world. Cori and I'd rather see the pathstone in your hands than in anyone else's."

The air almost crackled with the tension in her voice. I rolled my shoulders, resisting the urge to shrink back a little.

Eliaster sat back, ran his hand through his hair, and blew

out a deep breath. Then he glanced up at Liam. "Okay. So, here's what we'll do. Josh and I will see what we can find about Henry Blair and your dad. If it pans out, great. We can talk further, maybe see what we can do to help your situation. But I'm not promising anything."

"I wouldn't expect you to. Trust me, the only reason I'm here is because Cori and I have exhausted all our other options." Aileen scooted her chair back from the table and stood up. She stuck her hand out to Eliaster.

He shook it, warily.

She turned to me. As soon as our hands met, I felt a faint electrical buzz shoot up my arm. Like last time. I looked up, met Aileen's eyes, trying to hide my surprise.

Nothing on her face indicated that she'd felt anything.

She turned to the faoladh. "Thank you." The calm, sure way she said it told me she meant it.

Liam frowned. "Don't thank me yet. I'll need to talk to the pack. We have decisions to make."

"Still, there's hope. That's enough." Aileen nodded to the rest of the pack gathered around the table, grabbed her bag from her chair, and let herself out of the gate.

We all stayed quiet until we heard a motor start up in the parking lot. A few seconds later, a battered car rumbled past on the highway, Aileen at the wheel.

Eliaster raised his eyebrows and looked over at Liam. "Well?"

He held up his hands. "Like I told her, I have to talk to the pack. This isn't a decision I can make on my own."

"C'mon, dude, give me something."

Liam licked his lips and gazed in the direction the Jeep had gone.

"I think she was sincere," Patricia said.

"I'd agree with that assessment," James said, his voice clipped and precise. "And she seemed genuinely frightened for herself and her brother."

"What's their dad's name?" Charles asked. "I feel like I should know."

"If you weren't drunk, amadán, you'd remember it," James told him. "Drake Airgead. That antiquities expert in New York." He looked up at us and explained, "When we first moved here from England, we stayed in New York for a couple of years."

Charles shook his shoulders, almost like he was a dog shaking water off his fur. "Not a good place for faoladh."

"No, I wouldn't imagine," I muttered, giving Eliaster a sideways glance. Antiquities expert? Sounded like a great cover for a relics dealer.

Eliaster rubbed at his necklace, then abruptly stood up. "Thank you, for even considering this," he told Liam. "If we can get another pathstone …"

Liam nodded and glanced at his pack members. "We have things to consider, for sure. I know what the old laws teach, but in this day and age, I have to take care of my pack. No promises."

We said our goodbyes and headed around the building to the parking lot.

I picked up my bike helmet and spun it in my hands, thinking over the conversation. "What do you think?" I asked Eliaster.

He gnawed the corner of his lip for a second before answering. "We've either been given a huge blessing, or this is a really complex trap someone set up for us."

"Occam's razor."

He gave me a blank look.

"The best solution is the one that is the simplest and makes the fewest assumptions. Which would be that she was telling the truth." Even as I said it, doubt tugged at me. I'd made a mistake last time I'd pushed for a decision—a mistake that had nearly gotten us both killed. Was I making another mistake with Aileen?

He snorted and pulled his helmet over his head. "You really think that works with fae?"

"Probably not, but it's a nice dream."

Chapter 20

ELIASTER

I stood outside the rickety house in the slums, staring up at the second-story balcony and mentally trying to prepare myself. I knew that Da had already sent men to take care of Blaise's body. Clean up the mess. So why was this so hard? All I had to do was go in and search through the room to see if Blaise had hidden any information. Confirmation of Aileen Airgead's claims would be nice, though unlikely, but at this point I'd settle for anything that gave me clues on a reason for Blaise's murder.

I sighed, caught myself absently running my hand through my hair, and forced myself to shove both hands in my jacket pockets. Dang it, I was picking up habits from Josh. I really needed to stop.

If I was honest with myself, going to the trouble of digging through all of Blaise's stuff wasn't the issue. The issue was that I didn't like to be reminded of my failures.

Blaise had never asked for my protection, but I felt like I should've given it anyway.

My left arm itched, and I had to stop myself from scratching. It had only been a couple of days since I'd gotten the tattoos—didn't need to be scarring them up already.

Movement flashed in the window. I jerked back,

withdrawing into the shadow of the building I stood next to, and watched. The window was filthy, but I could make out the vague, blurry shape of a person. Then the shape disappeared. I listened for the sound of squealing hinges, or the shaking of the rickety stairs. Nothing except the far-off rush of sewer water.

I darted across the street and paused at the foot of the stairs, listening. I caught a very soft whisper. And now that I could see the door, I realized it wasn't closed all the way.

Moving slowly and carefully, so as not to shake the entire platform, I eased up the stairs and peered through the open door.

A fae, his long black hair pulled into a ponytail, stood in front of Blaise's bookcase, rifling through a book. As he finished, he tossed it to the side on the floor, swearing under his breath in Gaelic, and grabbed another one.

I should leave. I should absolutely leave. But …

Another book thudded to the floor.

No. I had to find out who this was. How much they knew about Blaise.

I drew my knife. Took a deep breath. Slammed the door open. The fae inside jumped, spun around, backing up against the bookcase. He went for the knife at his belt.

I was faster, angling my knife at the fae's chest. "Hands where I can see them."

The fae complied. I studied him. He was perhaps a few years younger than me, hovering somewhere around his early twenties. There was something familiar about him in his eyes and chin, a look that reminded me of someone.

I stepped all the way into the room and pushed the door closed with my foot. "Who—"

The floor creaked behind me. I half-spun in time to duck under a knife strike. Two of them! I swore under my breath as I backed up toward the kitchenette area. Should've checked by the foot of the bed—I'd known that area was covered by the door, but I'd been stupid.

The two strange fae stood shoulder to shoulder, both

now with knives drawn. The newcomer's hair was buzzed into a crewcut, but other than that, he looked identical to the first one. *Great. Twins. Awesome.* This wasn't going to be as easy as I'd thought.

"Who are you?" I asked.

Crewcut looked over at Ponytail and grinned. "You know who we have here, brother?"

Ponytail flipped his knife in his fingers, catching it by the blade. "Eliaster Tyrone," he said in a mocking, sing-song voice. "Looks like uncle Llew was right. Blaise was a traitor working for the Seelie."

Uncle Llew? My lips curled even as my shoulders tensed at the name. "Related to Larae and Llew? Figures."

Crewcut pointed a knife at me. "Have you not learned respect for our family after what we did to yours?"

Rage spiked in my chest. "Crows eat you all."

Ponytail swore and lunged forward. I caught the knife strike on my own blade and shoved his knife to the side, kicked his legs out from under him. Crewcut was right behind him, knife aiming for my gut, too close for me to counter. I used my left hand to catch the Unseelie's forearm and stopped, staring in surprise.

The tattoos on my arm were glowing bright blue.

What the...

Too late. A fist flew toward my face. I threw my arm in front of my eyes. The blow knocked me against the wall. I twisted. My blade caught, slicing along Crewcut's rib. *Got lucky. Can't expect it to last.*

I lunged forward. Ducked under another of his wild swings. As I raised my hand, I could see blue flames wreathing my fist. I punched Crewcut in the stomach. He gasped and doubled over. I managed to grab his wrist and held tight as I swung him around. Crewcut slammed into the wall. I eyed Ponytail, who was just pushing himself up off the floor.

My ribs throbbed. I pressed my elbow against my side, trying to keep the pained reaction off my face. I couldn't let these two know I was hurt—they'd come after me like raving Wild Hunt. "Just stay there. And get your uncle to actually teach you how to fight before you come after me again."

I backed to the door, tightening my grip on my knife.

Crewcut smirked as he straightened from leaning against the wall. "Oh, don't worry, Tyrone. We'll be sure to tell Uncle Llew you dropped by."

"I think he's got a new knife he'd like to test out on your skin," Ponytail agreed. "All nice and shiny and sharp."

My skin prickled. I swung the door open.

"You're right, Dubh. Better leave him whole."

I dashed down the stairs and away from the building. I kept running until I reached the outskirts of the Market, where the population of the streets slowly increased. I ducked down an abandoned side street and leaned against one of the wooden buildings, trying to calm my hammering pulse.

Llew's nephews were nearly as psychopathic as he was.

What had they wanted at Blaise's house? What had they been looking for? I pressed my hands over my face. A flicker of blue flame caught the corner of my vision. I dropped my hands, then pushed up the left sleeve of my jacket.

The tattoos had stopped glowing, but faint blue tongues of flaming glamour still curled around my fingers. I turned my hand over, watching the glamour dance like sparks. It felt like an iron band squeezed my chest. How was I doing that? Was I doing that? It didn't exactly feel any different than normal. I stretched my hand out and concentrated, trying to imagine a flame dancing above my palm. For a few seconds, the glamour coalesced, and the flickering shape of fire began to spiral into existence. My heart, stuttered, and I gasped. I was controlling glamour. For the first time in my life—

It disappeared.

I growled and lowered my hand. *Maybe I just need time.*

"New ink, huh?"

I started and looked up. Banshee stood at the alleyway entrance, leaning against the side of the buildings, arms and ankles crossed.

"What do you want?" I asked.

She took a few steps forward. "Let me see." Before I could pull away, she grabbed my wrist. The feather-light touch of her fingers trailed along my forearm, tracing the bright blue ink of the shield symbol, raising the hair on the back of my neck.

She paused, then tapped the Claddagh symbol on my ring finger. "Really? Engaged? Don't you think it's time to let her go?"

I yanked my arm free, the warmth in my chest dying instantly. "We're not having this discussion again."

"Touchy."

"Last time we talked about this, you tried to glamour me into sleeping with you," I snapped. "So yeah, maybe I am a bit touchy."

Her eyes flashed. "All I was trying to do was help, Eli."

I put my hands up between us. "Not that nickname. Not from you."

She half-closed her eyes, studying me for a moment. "Very well. How's Josh holding up?"

I frowned. I should leave, but …

I couldn't stop myself. She had information that I needed. "Why do you care?"

"I'm trying to figure out why you do. The Eliaster I knew four years ago wouldn't have picked up a stray human."

"See, that, right there? You think you know me, but you don't. You never did."

Banshee shrugged one shoulder.

She's just trying to get me off balance and use me. As usual. I turned and started walking. Unsurprisingly, she followed like a cat pretending it wanted to be touched. But all she wanted was to dig her claws in.

I slowed my pace a little, let her catch up to me. "So tell me something. Who're you really working for?"

She raised an eyebrow. "How did you know?"

I smirked. "That'd be telling, wouldn't it? Now c'mon, spill."

She smirked back. "That'd be telling, wouldn't it? You'll have to use a better persuasion method." She gently bit on her lower lip and blinked slowly up at me.

I stared at her lips for a second longer than I should've. One corner of her mouth curved into a triumphant smile.

I swore and turned away. "Why are you here, Banshee?"

She bumped her shoulder against me, and at the same time, I felt a small weight drop into the pocket of my jacket. "You need evidence to prove to the curators and to Highlord O'Breigh that you acted for a reason, right?"

"We have the book. The hard drive."

"Hmm, yes. But I think you'll find this helpful." She winked and spun on her heel, walking away.

I waited until she was out of sight before pulling my sleeve over my fingers and using it to drag out whatever she'd dropped into my pocket.

The blue gem of Shaughnessy's ring glimmered up at me.

I swore again and looked around, but Banshee had disappeared.

Chapter 21

JOSH

The screwdriver gouged into my thumb. I yelped and shook out my hand.

From the other side of the room, Roe chuckled. "Need help?"

I shook my head and laid the screwdriver aside. "I'm fine. Just slipped, that's all. I think it's getting too late for me to be handling sharp objects."

Roe laughed.

I laid the screwdriver aside and picked up the metal mesh cage, flipping it over. It wasn't the prettiest-looking thing in the world, but it would—I hoped—provide at least some protection from glamour.

"Hey, Lukas!" I shouted.

The security guard poked his head through the open door and sighed when he saw what I was holding. "Again?"

"Sorry," I offered.

He muttered under his breath as he walked into the room. Lukas had better control over his glamour than Eliaster did, but he could still get technology to go haywire if he touched it and concentrated. I picked up the wireless internet modem on my desk and settled it into the homemade Faraday cage, locking the hinged door into place, then put it down on the desk and scooted my chair back.

Lukas put his hand on the top of the cage and closed his eyes, concentrating. As he did so, a swirl of purple mist began to materialize between his fingers, drifting off his skin in lazy spirals. I studied the way the glamour moved, the way it almost seemed to sparkle in the room's dim light.

In the last couple of days, as I'd walked back and forth through the underworld to aboveground, I'd tested a few theories. Even without the bracelet anywhere near me, I could still see past glamour ghosts. I'd already known that was possible from my time hanging out with my half-fae friend, Marc, but I'd wanted to have a baseline. Carrying the bracelet with me or leaving it behind didn't allow me to see a fae actively using glamour. But as long as the bracelet was on my wrist, I could see the colored, glowing mists that signaled glamour.

I glanced at the lights on the modem. Last time I'd tried this, with a copper-alloy mesh, the lights had gone crazy, then suddenly died. It hadn't harmed the modem permanently, which was why I'd asked Lukas for help. If Eliaster had done this, the modem would probably be a smoldering mass of plastic.

But this time, I'd tried a silver-plated mesh. And the modem lights seemed to be steady. I picked up my phone and checked for available signals, finally finding one that was weak, but usable.

"Yes!" I pumped my fist in the air. "Thanks, Lukas."

He grunted. "Glad I could help."

As he left, I put the Faraday cage aside. I'd have to buy more silver-plated mesh, but it was nice to finally have a workable option for the rath's technology systems. I picked up a book I'd set facedown on the side of the desk and started reading the research chapters Roe had assigned me. It was all in Gaelic, which made the going a bit slow.

Pathstones must at least be used in sets of three to open a path between earth and the Otherworld of Tir Ni-all, but they can be used in greater numbers—six, or even nine—to open greater pathways. Of course, larger pathways lead to greater danger. A single pathway is dangerous enough, but when you force two or three pathways to converge...

"Hey, Roe?" I said.

She looked up from the red leather-bound book Eliaster had given her a few days ago. "Yes?"

"I'm at the section talking about using multiple sets of pathstones to open bigger pathways. But, I'm confused—I thought a pathway was just basically a portal. Just, like *zap*, step through, and you're in one world or another."

She smiled. "Have you ever known sidhé to do anything that simply?"

"No, I guess not," I grumbled, and set the book back down. "So do you think that the Lucht Leanuna are trying to gather more than one set?"

She shivered. "I hope not. Besides, I'm quite certain that there was only ever one set in existence after the pathways were sealed shut."

I ran my hand through my hair. "So Larae's chasing after a hopeless dream?"

Roe shook her head. "No. As long as even one stone is in existence, there are ways to open paths. Dark, dangerous ways, but if she's desperate enough, she might attempt them."

I rubbed the scar on my wrist. *I think she's already pretty desperate.* "How's that book going? Finding any new information on pathstones?"

Roe's eyes brightened. "It's a copy of original texts that were written by monks who lived near a permanent path to Tir Ni-all, back when the paths were still open. Legend has it they were entrusted with these secrets by some of the very fae who began the practice of glamouring objects."

"So, really rare?"

"Extremely. I don't know of anyone who had a copy, even back when I first began my research on the subject."

I tucked the Faraday cage to the back of the desk, grabbed my book, and moved to the couch. It was getting late, but I figured I could get a bit more reading in before I left for home.

I stood up from my bed in my parents' house and opened the curtain, staring out at the moon that was in the wrong phase, the full, bright light shining down onto my upturned face. I stepped back from the window and felt the glamoured vines squeezing my ankles, wrapping around my wrists, dragging me down to the floor.

"Enough!" I yelled around the vines as they began to wind around my face, and somehow, the word made it past their suffocating leaves, ringing in the air like a church bell. I slammed my hands to the ground and forced the vines away, to relax their hold. They crumpled to the floor, brown and withering.

I stared at the back of my fists. More vines rippled over my skin, bending to brush along my hands and my arms, glowing bright green. Then with a sudden rush, they sped into my bracelet and disappeared.

The bracelet tightened. I gasped, doubling forward as it bit into my skin. Pounded my fist against the floor. It felt like the skin was being peeled from my palm. I choked back a scream, looked up. The bracelet had expanded, growing over my hand like a metal gauntlet, melting to my knuckles like a super-heated piece of plastic, the metal glowing in the pane of moonlight shining on my bedroom floor.

The dream shattered around me.

I opened my eyes.

The firelight flickered on the library ceiling, casting dancing shadows into the corners of the room. Not my room at my parents' house. I was still at the rath.

Other than the crackle and pop of flames, it was quiet. I sat up, looked around. The computers were powered down in the corner. Roe's chair was empty, the books closed and neatly stacked, pieces of ribbon and folded paper sticking out of the pages at various intervals.

I raised my hand. The bracelet glimmered on my wrist. It

was its normal size and shape. I flopped back down and sighed, scrubbing my hands over my face. At least this time I hadn't choked to death on the glamour-vines. But why had the bracelet transformed?

I froze. Was it because I'd commanded the glamour? Shown a small measure of control over it?

Before I could continue with that train of thought, the door creaked open. I sat up and looked over the back of the couch.

Eliaster waved to me, blinking heavily. "What time is it?" he croaked.

I fished my phone from my pocket. "One in the afternoon. How'd you sleep?"

He grunted.

Good enough of an answer. I swung my feet to the floor and folded the blanket I'd been using, then stretched. If I kept spending the night at the rath, I'd have to find better accommodations. Constant sleeping on the couch was giving me a crick in my neck.

I walked over to the coffee bar. As I pulled a mug from the cupboard, a flicker of green glamour wound around the corner of the bar. I blinked and shook my head. When I glanced at the spot where it had been, the glamour was gone.

Could I control glamour now? I stretched my hand out in the air in front of me and tried to imagine a spot of green, glowing in the center of my palm. Something flickered, and I clenched my fist closed, my heart pounding.

"You okay?" Eliaster asked.

"Yeah, just … more weird dreams. Same as usual. It's just taking me a bit to shake them."

"Okay. Well … let me know if I can help."

"I will. Thanks."

After getting coffee, Eliaster and I went in search of Roe. We found her in the dining room, her phone to her ear, quickly scribbling some notes into a blue notebook. I listened, sipping at my coffee cup, as she finished up the conversation—something about the relics, from what I could gather—and looked up at us.

"Success?" Eliaster asked.

She nodded. "I finally talked to Simon, and he agreed to meet." Her smile faded a bit. "Though, he only wanted to speak with Josh."

My stomach dropped to my feet. "*What*?"

Roe and Eliaster both glanced at me. I rubbed my hand through my hair. Of course the curators wouldn't want to deal with Eliaster. But why me? Why not Roe or Cormac?

Eliaster crossed his arms. "Where do they want to meet?"

"The Black Dog Pub."

The tension in my chest eased a little. Liam and the rest of the werewolves hadn't been too bad. It wasn't like I was walking into a totally unknown factor there. "But why just me?"

Eliaster smirked. "Think you can handle it?"

Oh no, we were not going to go through that whole conversation again. I ignored him and looked over at Roe, repeating my question. "Why me?"

"He's interested in meeting the human who has been working with Eliaster."

"Oh great, so now I'm an Underworld celebrity. Perfect." Suspicion twinged at the back of my mind. "You didn't tell him that I somehow resisted glamour, did you?"

She shot me a glare over the rims of her glasses. "Joshua McAllister, I would never do such a thing, and you know it."

Cue me wanting to shrivel up. "I know. Sorry."

"However, he would be a good place to start if you're interested in asking."

I looked over at Eliaster. "What do you think?"

He held up his hands. "I trust you to accurately represent the situation. And honestly, the curators will listen better to you."

Roe nodded.

I took in a deep breath, let it out slowly. Yeah. I could totally do this. "Okay, Roe—what do I need?"

I spent the rest of the day preparing for my meeting with the curators. With Roe's help, I went through and gathered together a folder of things we'd discovered—the photos Banshee had given us, a report that Eliaster and I wrote up about dealing with Shaughnessy, photocopies of book pages and other things Roe had on hand about the pathstones and the relics. We picked out a couple of relics for me to take to the curators as a good faith gesture.

I also texted Aileen that we'd gotten separate confirmation that Henry Blair was someone we'd be interested in.

Finally, at around six-thirty, I packed everything into my backpack and turned to Roe. "Any advice on how to deal with the curators?"

She looked up from her book and blinked a moment, refocusing. "I suppose the best thing I can advise is patience. I've been friends with Simon a long time. Given the evidence you're bringing to him, I think he'll make a fair decision. But that might not include you or Eliaster, and I wouldn't push too hard."

I nodded. Like Eliaster had said earlier, even if the curators wanted to handle Henry Blair alone, there were plenty of things we could do. The Lucht may have gone to ground, but that didn't mean Eliaster didn't have resources he could tap or strings he could pull. Cormac wasn't a highlord, but he did sit on the regional council, and that counted for something.

Even though it was underground, now that it was nearing sunset, the Underworld roads were much busier. It took me half again as long to get to the surface as I wove around clumps of goblins, fae, and other sidhé. As I rode, I tried to imagine how I'd convince Simon into going after Anraí. If the curators where anywhere as loyal and pigheaded as the fae, it would take quite a bit of fancy talking on my part to convince Simon that Anraí really was dangerous.

I parked my bike beside my car and rubbed my nose. As usual, the garage smelled like gasoline, always a weird change from the mold and dust of the Underworld. As I neared my car, I caught a whiff of something sharp and metallic. Blood. Fresh blood. I paused beside the car, my hand on the keys in my pocket, and glanced around the parking garage, nerves jangling. Something felt ... off.

The lower level of the garage was dim, lit with flickering yellow lights, and nearly empty. Now that I was used to it, I could tell this place reeked with fae glamour—not the intentional kind. It was almost like a predator marking his territory, a sense about the place that made normal humans avoid it—a sense of danger that triggered the fight-or-flight mechanism. I'd gotten past it for the most part, but it still made the hairs on the back of my neck rise.

Something scuffled behind a car a few feet away. My heart leapt to my throat.

I yanked the keys out of my pocket, jabbed them at the car door. Claws scraped on concrete. I didn't even look, just flung open my car door, dove in, and slammed the door behind me.

The impact against the car made my heart lurch and I twisted to look over my shoulder. A skinny sidhé with patchy fur rimming its face stood at the door. Long dark-colored claws scraped against the glass. This looked more rodent-like than a cat-sidhé, with a snarl full of large, flat teeth, and large ears laid back against its head. A red beanie hugged its head, and trails of something sticky and glistening matted along its lank hair.

My heart sank to my stomach. A redcap—*fear dearg*. The same thing Eliaster had theorized had broken into Roe's home.

Beady eyes stared at me, weirdly animal in a semi-human face.

I put my hand to my jacket pocket, feeling for my keys, my phone. My hands shook.

Quick as lightning, it slammed its other hand into the window. The glass shattered, leaving my only barrier a cracked mess. I yelped and pulled myself to the other side of the car. Its claws poked through the glass, inching toward me in a screeching sound that sped my pulse. It almost sounded like … metal.

Iron claws. Crap. Redcaps were one of the only fae that iron didn't affect. Of course I'd be that lucky. I glanced from the creature to the ignition of the car. I scooted forward, car key clutched in my hand.

The creature got its claws free and slammed its shoulder into the car. The blow knocked me back against the passenger door, the handle digging into the small of my back. For its size, the thing was incredibly strong. The fear dearg punched through the window again. I ducked my head as glass shattered across the seats. When I looked up, the redcap was reaching through the window, a grin baring its teeth. I hit the door handle with my elbow and half-fell, half-rolled out of the passenger side. My phone flew out of my hand and skidded under the car next to mine.

Crap!

I scrambled to my feet and dashed for the ramp to the ground level. As I did, the smell hit me full force. Fresh blood and rotting meat. I stumbled, gagged, slapped my hand over my nose and mouth. Heard the redcap's swift, light footfalls as it raced after me. I fumbled for the gun in my shoulder holster. Everything was happening too fast.

I spun just as the redcap plowed into my side. The blow knocked me off my feet and sent me rolling. My gun clattered to the floor.

I slammed my hand into the pavement and used the momentum to get to my feet—toward my weapon. But the redcap beat me to it and kicked my gun off to the side, grinning. Crap, this thing was fast. Too fast for me to dodge. I grabbed the knife at my belt.

It paused, shifting from foot to foot, beady eyes glancing from my face to my knife and back.

"What do you want?" I growled.

The redcap's eyes met mine. "*Dainséarach.*"

Dangerous. "What? Why? Who told you that?"

It snorted and shuffled closer. I fought down the urge to gag at the rotten-meat smell. The creature suddenly leapt to the side, out of reach, and lunged toward my back. I spun and slashed.

The creature hissed and pulled back, blood seeping along a wound on its arm.

"First blood's mine," I said. Maybe that was something it could respect.

The creature snarled and for a minute it hesitated, head twisting from side to side. Then it sprang at me again. I ducked, feeling claws whistle over my head. It slashed at my side. I blocked the claws with my knife, and the clang echoed through the parking garage.

It had caught my knife blade in its claws. It twisted. My arm wrenched to the side, and my knife skidded across the concrete. The redcap's fist slapped across my jaw. I hit the ground hard on my shoulders and turned it into an awkward roll, coming up into a crouch. I could see my gun out of the corner of my eye. My throat tightened. No way would I reach it in time. I got my second knife out and held it up, the flat of the blade braced against my forearm in a reverse grip.

The redcap halted, the blade inches from its throat. Claws pressed against my stomach, and I gulped, fought down the urge to vomit now that it was so close to me.

"MacAllister has soft skin. Easy to kill." It grinned.

"Why kill me?"

Something in the way it tensed warned me, and I jerked out of the way just as the claws on my belly twitched, tearing my shirt. I scrambled backward, feeling for my pistol. The redcap jumped and slammed into me, driving my shoulders into the ground. I felt something dig into the small of my back and a flare of hope ignited.

Teeth flashed. I threw my arm across my throat just in time. The redcap bit down, teeth sinking through my jacket and into the flesh of my forearm. I screamed as it bit harder and shook, then slammed me down against the ground again, my head rapping against the floor. Still gripping my knife, I drove it upward, between the creature's ribs. The fear dearg shrieked and scrambled off me. It clamped one hand around its side, blood oozing between its fingers.

I sat up and yanked my gun free. Its eyes widened, and with a shriek, it ran for the exit. My first shot went wide, shattering the back window of a car parked at the top of the exit ramp. Surprisingly, no alarm sounded, just the echoing blast of my pistol. I winced, steadied my injured arm, and aimed again.

The redcap squeezed under the fencing on the ground floor. Within seconds, it was out of sight.

I rolled to my knees and stared at the blood spattered across the garage floor, feeling sick as pain throbbed across my arm. *Gotta call Eliaster. Gotta ...* I pushed myself up and staggered across the garage. My knees hit the concrete harder than I wanted when I crouched down to grab my phone.

My hands shook as I brought the phone up to my ear. As soon as I heard the call connect, I stammered, "Eliaster. There was a redcap."

Something dropped on the other end. "A *what*?"

"A redcap."

"Are you okay?"

I looked down at my arm, at the shredded material stained red. "I think so? It bit me. My arm's torn up. But I think that's it." I remembered the claws gashing open my shirt and looked down at my torso. No blood. It had just caught the material. I shivered. I'd been lucky.

"I'm coming, okay? Try to put pressure on your arm. Don't take off your jacket until I'm there. Is there any immediate threat?"

I scanned the garage, sniffed. It didn't matter. I wouldn't have been able to smell a redcap past the blood I was losing anyway. "I—I don't think so."

"Okay. I'll be there in a few minutes. Just hang in there, Josh."

I dragged my backpack out of the car and sat on the curb, then dug out my extra shirt and wrapped it around my arm. As I sat, I concentrated on breathing, deep and even. My body started trembling. My mind slid into a fog.

The hidden door to the Underworld slid open just enough for Eliaster to wheel his bike through. When he saw me, he sighed, then said, "Why do you always get to have the fun?"

I held up my arm. "Yeah, this is fun all right." My hands shook.

Eliaster grimaced. He pulled an emergency kit from his bag, then helped me peel my jacket off. There was less blood than I'd expected, but it still oozed down my arm from the wounds.

Eliaster uncapped a bottle of water and washed off my arm, then flushed the wounds. There were three that were about an inch deep, along with other small gashes, and I could already see the skin around them mottling purple.

Eliaster winced. "Yeah, that's gonna hurt." He sponged at the wounds with gauze. "I don't think there's any muscle or tendon damage, though."

"Thank the Almighty." The last thing I needed was my sword arm completely out of commission.

"You're sure it was a redcap? Those aren't common."

I gestured to my arm. "Trust me, I got a close look."

"Dude." Eliaster shook his head.

As he finished cleaning and bandaging my arm, I cradled my head in my other arm, breathing deeply and willing myself to stop shaking. At least the fog was lifting. Though I wasn't sure whether that was a blessing or not. I could still hear the fear dearg's nasal voice in my head: *Dainséreach.*

Who would think I was dangerous enough to send a monster like that after me? Why? To get a message across to the Tyrones? To get me out of commission for a while?

"Want me to take you back to the rath?" Eliaster asked.

"Tempting." I shook my head and stood up. The shakes had mostly subsided, but now my arm throbbed, and I could feel a headache forming in the back of my skull where the fear dearg had bashed me against the concrete. I opened my car door, swept out the glass that littered the front seat, and dug into the glove box for ibuprofen. I swallowed several.

"Just say the word. I'll call Simon and let him know—"

I shook my head. "I need to get to this meeting. It's too important. Just give me a few minutes."

Chapter 22

ELIASTER

As Josh leaned against his car, inspecting the shattered window, I packed my emergency kit back into my backpack. I picked up Josh's discarded motocross jacket and stuck my fingers through the holes in the sleeve. Josh was lucky—the thick, padded fabric had kept the rodent teeth from seriously damaging his sword arm.

Damnaigh. Why had a redcap been sent after him anyway? I stared at the fence, where smears of blood showed the redcap's flight path. "Did it say anything?"

Josh straightened with a groan. "Yeah. Something about me being dainséreach."

Josh? I almost laughed. "Only if they're worried about a human being part of the Underworld—in which case, they've got others to worry about."

Josh rolled his eyes, then winced.

My stomach clenched, and I placed my hand on Josh's shoulder. "Are you sure you're okay to continue with the meeting?"

Josh's jaw set. "We can't wait. If we do, Henry Blair might hear that Shaughnessy's disappeared, and he's our only lead to a pathstone." Josh looked over at the fence where the redcap had fled.

Human's eyes couldn't change colors like a fae's. They didn't have the d'anam fuienneog. But over the last few months, I'd learned to read Josh's face, and the clouded expression he wore now told me that he'd remembered something disturbing. I kept quiet, let him bring it up on his own terms.

Josh rubbed his hand over his face. "Who have we pissed off that would send a redcap after me? I'm beginning to lose track."

I stifled another laugh. "Fair point. I suppose Blodheyr could've sent it." I ran my hand through my hair. "No offense, but it's weird that it came after you and not me."

Josh's face pinched in a look of worry. "I was thinking about that. Do you think someone else … one of Keelin's people, or maybe one of Shaughnessy's guys escaped? Could someone have guessed that I'm immune to glamour and sent the fear dearg to take me out?"

"Did it say it was sent to kill you?"

Josh shook his head. "I just assumed that because of the stories."

Something twitched in the recesses of my mind, and my hands involuntarily clenched into fists. *Time to go hunting.* I shoved the thought away and rubbed my cross necklace through my shirt.

Josh brushed his thumb along the scar on his right wrist as he stared off into the distance.

"Look, you already survived once," I said. "That'll give whoever's behind this something to think about."

"Thanks. I'd appreciate it." Josh checked his phone and his eyes widened. "I gotta get going."

"You're sure you're good to drive?"

He nodded, glanced over at the shattered windshield on his car. "I'll have to take my motorcycle, but yeah, I'll be fine. Besides, the trail's still fresh. Gotta hunt while you can." As he squeezed past me, Josh slapped my shoulder and smiled. "Thanks."

I nodded absently. *Gotta hunt while you still can.* Had I said "time to go hunting" out loud? At the thought, another shiver spidered its way down my back.

I watched Josh ride off on his motorcycle, then shrugged

off my vague unease. Josh could handle himself, and besides, he was going to meet Simon in the middle of a faoladh pack. It was likely the safest place in Springfield for him at the moment.

I retrieved my second sword from where I'd strapped it across one of my motorcycle packs, changed from the short-sleeved shirt to a long-sleeved henley I kept in my backpack, and pulled my leather jacket on. It was just a little too warm for the long sleeves and jacket to be comfortable, but based on what the fear dearg had done to Josh's arm through his jacket, I had to have as much protection as possible. If both Josh and I were noticeably injured, that left us vulnerable. We couldn't afford that right now, especially since my cracked ribs still prevented me from doing as much as I liked.

I vaulted the railing where the fear dearg had squeezed through and crouched, studying the blood smeared along the sidewalk. A few steps further on, the blood dripped again, and then again. At least Josh had nicked it good.

I jogged along the sidewalk for several blocks, careful to watch for drops of bright red. Clouds still swirled overhead, turning the bright sunset into broken rays and threatening to coalesce into rain at any moment. The threatening darkness wouldn't be a problem for tracking, but rain would wash the trail away. I'd have to move quickly.

The redcap had veered in and out of alleys and across streets with wild abandon, as if hoping that doing so would throw off any followers. Spatters of blood marked where it had stumbled.

In my mind's eye, I imagined redcap teeth sinking into Josh's arm, tearing at the flesh. And just like that, the images of Iain and Emily as I'd last seen them—faces beaten bloody, eyes wide in terror—rose like terrible specters. I gritted my teeth and narrowed my focus, staring at the tiny drops of blood.

Then, in the middle of an alley, the bloody trail ended.

Heart hammering in my throat, I jerked my head upward, scanning the walls and fire escape of the old retail building.

No redcap.

No. This couldn't be happening. I could almost hear Emily's pleas. Iain's cry for help. I leaned into the brick wall and ground the heels of my hands into my eyes. Then I clutched my necklace, hands shaking, and tipped my head back, taking a deep breath.

With Marc's death—with everything that had happened in the last couple of weeks—with finally trusting Josh with my story and then having him so brutally attacked, it was clear I wasn't out of this yet. I could feel the familiar terror rising in me again. The helplessness. The rage of being useless. The mindless itch to lash out and destroy.

I thought I'd beaten that curse.

I balled my fist tighter, and the cross dug into my fingers. The small prick of pain yanked me back to the present.

I let out a breath, opened my eyes. Above me stretched the rain-stained wall, streaks of rust from the fire escape discoloring the brick. And a bright, glistening smear on the fire escape's ladder.

I leaped, and caught the ladder, dragging it down with a rattle that, thankfully, was mostly drowned out by the racket of street traffic. I climbed until I reached the roof, and hauled myself up. Spots of discoloration dotted the black tar paper covering the roof, leading me to a partial, bloody handprint on the far wall.

There, hunkered at the base of the wall in the little side-alley between this building and the next, crouched the redcap. Smears of gore matted its hair and hat, and it was muttering in Gaelic as it attempted to wrap its wounded arm.

Could I drop on top of it from here? And what was I going to do once I caught the thing? Judging by how quickly and unhesitatingly it had run, it had to be familiar with the area. How long had it been in Springfield? And how had something like a fear dearg escaped my notice? I clenched my jaw. How many people had this thing killed?

Now I was sounding like Josh. Always a million questions and never any answers.

I crouched and leaned against the ledge. Clenched my hands. I'd have to kill this thing. Letting it wander away would be condemning countless others to death. Fear deargs did one thing well, and that was kill.

I judged the distance once more, and jumped.

The redcap whipped around to see me, but didn't move fast enough. I landed on its shoulders, knocking it off its feet, and tumbled backward into a roll. As soon as I found my feet again, I lunged, grabbed the redcap around its neck, and slammed it against the wall. Drawing my knife, I pressed the flat of the blade hard against its chin, levering its head back up into the brick wall.

The creature stared at me, huffing sour, rotting-meat breath through its nostrils.

"Do you know who I am?" I demanded in Gaelic.

"You are the one told to avoid," the redcap snarled.

"For good reason. Why did you attack Josh?"

The creature's eyes narrowed. "Dainséreach. All they told me."

"Who told you?"

"Don't know. Just told me there'd be blood." The fear dcarg's tongue darted out, running over its lips, and its eyes glittered. It drew back its lips to reveal its large, flat front teeth and the dagger-like back teeth. "Good at drawing blood."

The familiar burn of rage rose in my chest, and I pressed the blade harder until a thin line of blood appeared on the creature's neck. Then I grinned. "Funny. So am I. Now you'd better tell me who told you to go after Josh MacAllister, because he's under my protection. And so far, you're not giving me much reason to let you live." My hand trembled. I really, really didn't want to give in, to drag my knife across this creature's throat. Yet how could I let it live? It had killed once, and it would kill again. If I ended it, I could save lives. Including people I cared about.

The fear dearg's eyes had been shifting back and forth, but now they suddenly locked in place, staring at a spot over my shoulder. My heart thumped. I almost turned to look, but then hesitated. What if the fear dearg was trying to trick me? Any shift in my attention, and the thing could easily …

Too late. I heard the rush of displaced air and tried to duck out of the way. Something hard smacked into the side of my head. Colored lights burst in front of my eyes, and I staggered, releasing the fear dearg's throat. Claws raked the side of my face, knocking me to the ground. Breath burst from my lungs, and my head bounced on the pavement, making my vision shatter into white.

Through the haze, I picked out fuzzy sounds. Footsteps. Voices. A gurgling, and then something collapsed on the ground near me.

A body! I blinked hard. Tried to get my arms underneath me to push myself up. My entire body felt numb. I could barely move. It had probably only been seconds, but it felt agonizingly long.

Despite the pain blinding my vision, I forced myself up on my hands and knees. *Need to get out. Time to run.*

"Don't."

The cold muzzle of a gun pressed into the base of my skull. I froze. *Dammit.* I started to twist my head to look up.

"Eyes on the ground." The gun pushed harder against my spine.

I obeyed, staying on my hands and knees. Cold shivers crawled up my spine. Was this how I died? Blood dripped down the side of my face and splattered on the ground.

"Who is it?" someone else asked, the voice sharp and low-pitched. "Let me get a look at him."

The gunman grabbed my collar and jerked me up to my knees. I raised my hands, but kept my eyes on the ground. Dark boots walked into my view. Beyond them, the body of the fear dearg lay on the ground, blood pooling underneath its cut throat. I tensed. That would be me in about point-five seconds if I didn't figure out—

After a minute, the man grunted. "Don't recognize him. He's just some fae. Let him go."

"You sure?"

No way. Seriously? How did they not recognize me? *Please stick to what you said, please, just think I'm some typical, normal fae bounty hunter taking out a monster.* It was almost too much to hope for.

"The last thing we need right now is a trail of bodies. For now, we let him go."

"Okay." The gunman shoved me forward, and I stayed there, on my hands and knees, waiting. Sweating. Listening. Willing my pulse to calm.

The gun dug into the back of my skull, making me wince.

The man leaned close to my ear. "You stay like this until we're gone, you hear? If I so much as see you twitch, or catch you following us, I'll shove this gun into your mouth and pull the trigger, understand?" The dry rasp in his throat grated over my nerves.

I nodded, mind racing. Who were these people? How did they know Josh, but not know me?

Footsteps echoed down the alley. I kept my eyes on the pavement, heart in my throat, until the footsteps faded. Then I looked up. The alley was deserted, except for the dead redcap…with iron coins shoved into its eye sockets.

One thing was for sure—those men hadn't been fae. Fae would've known who I was. Fae wouldn't have put iron coins in the redcap's eyes.

I got to my feet, and the world whirled around me. I leaned against the wall and winced. My head throbbed. I touched the side of my face and winced. The redcap's iron claws had raked from temple to jaw—not deeply, but blood crusted my hair and came away on my hand.

Why would humans have hired a fear dearg? And go after Josh, of all people?

Chapter 23

JOSH

By the time I pulled into the parking lot of the Black Dog pub, my arm ached so much I could barely concentrate on keeping my balance on the gravel parking lot. I parked my motorcycle near the road and leaned back, cradling my arm as I studied the pub. The neon dog head mounted on the porch roof was glowing, barely visible in the evening light.

I pulled off my helmet and ran my hand through my hair, feeling nervous. It wasn't the faoladh that gave me the heebie-jeebies—Liam and his pack knew I was a friend, and I knew they'd honor their debt to the Tyrones. But meeting the curators without Eliaster? Not my thing.

I sighed. This was what I'd wanted, though, right? For Eliaster to trust me without having to hover over my shoulder?

Gravel crunched as I walked over to the door and pulled it open. Voices echoed out of the room. Booths lined the left-hand and back walls, with one door interrupting the lines of hardwood tables and benches, and a bar ran down most of the length of the right wall. The overwhelming scent of pine and wood polish filled the room. The bar's polished, shiny wood gleamed in the low yellow light, and shelves of bottles and glasses lined the back wall and hung from a rail on the ceiling above it. Posters of rock bands, old and new, hung pasted like wallpaper on the walls above the booths.

The entire room paused at the jingle of the bell above the door, and everyone's head swiveled toward me. My stomach gave a lurch, and I swallowed hard, unnerved by the dozens of eyes staring at me. Everyone looked human, but there was something weird about them, some kind of feral awareness that manifested in hunched shoulders, slightly-parted lips, and piercing stares. I forced myself inside, letting the door swing shut behind me, careful not to make full eye contact or smile with my teeth showing.

"Hey, Josh." Liam stood behind the bar, pouring some kind of liquor into a tiny measuring cup. He waved me over, set the bottle down, and upended the cup into a larger glass. "Welcome back."

It took me a second to realize he'd spoken entirely in Gaelic. My brain took a second to make the switch. "*Haigh. Buíochas.*"

He grinned. "Sorry." It was in English this time. "Simon and Zeke aren't here yet. You're welcome to wait here, or you can go sit at the reserved booth." He nodded to the back corner, where a large booth was waiting, dimly lit, slightly removed from the rest of the room, and empty.

"I'll stay here." I leaned against the bar. "Aileen been back around?"

Liam cocked his head slightly to the side, eyes narrowing. "*Ní hea.* I'm sorry, I mean, no. She hasn't. Why do you ask?"

"Just had a few more questions for her."

"Sorry. As far as I know, you're the only one who has her phone number. When she called me asking to meet you guys here, she called from a pay phone. Can I get you anything to drink?"

As I leaned against the bar, I bumped against the bandages on my forearm, and a flash of pain made me set my teeth. Painkillers and alcohol wouldn't mix well. I forced a smile and shook my head. "No, thanks."

Liam's eyes flicked toward my arm. "Hurt yourself?"

Dang it. "Had a run-in with a redcap earlier."

One of Liam's eyebrows rose slightly. "A fear dearg? Those things are rare."

"Aw, c'mon," a new voice behind me said. "You don't actually think he had a run-in with a fear dearg, do you? You're getting taken for a ride, Liam."

I turned around. The newcomer was shorter than me, with dark hair and a stocky build. He carried a backpack in one hand, which he shifted to his shoulder as he held out his hand for me to shake.

"Zeke Black. I'm Simon's son and assistant. You must be Josh MacAllister."

I nodded.

"Okay, well ... look, I'm gonna be straight with you. What's the game?"

I blinked, momentarily caught off guard. "What?"

"I know you work with Eliaster. But you're not even a curator. You're some random kid he thought needed to be protected. He's brought nothing but trouble for the curators in the past."

I stiffened. "You think we're lying?"

"I think he's lying to everyone, and I think you're too inexperienced to know what's up or down."

I crossed my arms and glared at him. "I have evidence to back up our claims, but I'd rather not waste my time if your minds are already closed."

"Okay, enough," Liam cut in, and his voice had a feral snarl under the words. "You're in neutral territory. I let you guys meet here as a favor to Cormac, but this ain't a faodladh issue, so you two had better not make it an issue. Clear?"

"Crystal," I muttered.

Zeke nodded.

"Okay then." Liam jerked his thumb toward the reserved booth. "Why don't you two go cool your heels until Simon gets here?"

Zeke trudged toward the booth, and I followed. We

wove our way around the tables filling the main floor. Most of the faoladh seemed content to ignore us, though I caught one or two curious glances as I walked past. Out of habit, I began scanning the tables for phones, receipts, anything that could distract me, but there was nothing. I did notice that none of the wolves seemed to be armed.

I slid into the booth on the opposite side of Zeke. The curator dumped his backpack on the seat, sighed, and turned to me.

"Look," he said. "I don't want to turn this into a fight with you. But honestly, how long have you been a part of this whole mess?"

"I don't think that matters as much as what I've seen in that time," I said shortly.

"Do you even know why my dad told Eliaster he wasn't allowed to be here tonight?"

"I'm assuming because he was involved in a curator's death a few years ago."

Surprise flickered across Zeke's face. He hadn't been expecting that. Had that been his trump card, something he would've held over my head as proof that I couldn't trust Eliaster? Probably.

The bell rang out over the low mutters of conversation again, and I looked over my shoulder. A shorter, chubbier version of Zeke let the door swing shut behind him and adjusted his glasses. Liam gestured toward us, and the man hefted a satchel to about shoulder height and wove his way around the faoladh to us.

"Simon Black," he said as he drew level with me.

We shook hands. As Simon settled into the seat beside his son, my stomach churned. Hopefully Simon would be more open-minded and less hostile than Zeke.

Simon took his round glasses off and folded them into the breast pocket of his sweater vest, then dragged his fingers through his salt-and-pepper, curly hair. "So." He opened his satchel and withdrew a small green pouch and a pipe. He looked past me, presumably at Liam, and raised his pipe questioningly. He must've gotten the go-ahead, because he started slowly packing the pipe.

"So," he repeated. "Roe tells me you've found some interesting things in regards to relics over the last few days."

I nodded. "Did she explain to you what happened with Highlord Keelin?"

"She and Eliaster both." He paused for a moment, then said, "I also spoke to Highlord Keelin after Eliaster called me the first time. That's why I was so readily available when Roe called me."

My palms started sweating. If he'd already talked to Lord Keelin ... I wiped my hands on my jeans. "So you already know about Galen Shaughnessy. Did Roe tell you that we connected him to a curator?"

Simon's hands paused in his work. "No."

Zeke scoffed. "Yeah, right."

"We confirmed it from two different sources, independent from each other. In addition, one of those sources has indicated that Henry may also be connected to Drake Airgead."

"No curator would be stupid enough to align themselves with people like Drake or Shaughnessy," Zeke said. "Especially Shaughnessy. He's too reckless."

I reached into my backpack, pulled out the dea-thoil stone, and set it on the table. "Keelin has more."

Simon shot me a skeptical look. "Keelin has relics?"

A knot formed in my stomach. "He didn't tell you?"

"No. Conveniently. I guess we'll have to have a follow-up chat with him and Highlord O'Breigh."

"If you do, I'd rather my name not come into it."

"Of course not."

Zeke shuffled through some of the photos, lips pursed in a frown. "These could be manipulated photos."

"They could be, but they're not," I said quietly.

He looked up, met my eyes. "Everything we've heard about you says you're good with computers."

"Good with computers and good with photomanipulation

are two different things that don't necessarily combine."

"Tell me about this connection." Simon lit his pipe, then tapped the stem against the folder in Zeke's hands. "Between Shaughnessy and this curator."

I blew out a deep breath. All or nothing, I reminded myself: without putting all my cards on the table, we wouldn't get a shot at the pathstone. Taking Henry Blair out of commission wasn't a necessary step to that goal, but it would be nice. At this point, though, it was out of my hands. All I could do was give Simon the information I had and let him decide what to do with it.

I kept Aileen's name out of it, but explained how we'd been tipped off, gone after Shaughnessy, and how Keelin had pulled us into his own investigation. I wrapped it up by adding, "And I don't know what you think of the rumors that there are pathstones still around, but I can tell you I saw one in Chicago. We have a chance to potentially track down another one."

As I'd been talking, Simon and Zeke had both been quiet, listening intently. At the mention of pathstone, Simon straightened and took his pipe from his mouth.

"I knew there was at least one pathstone, and assumed there were more …" His voice trailed off for a moment, then he sighed. "You make a compelling case, McAllister. As much as I hate to admit it, this doesn't look good for Henry."

Zeke's eyes widened. "Are you serious?"

Simon held up a hand. "We still need to talk to a few others. Get their input. This is a serious accusation. And I wouldn't mind getting the name of your inside source."

"At the moment, I'm afraid that would put them in greater danger than they already are." I thought of the frightened look on Aileen's face when she mentioned her father.

"Very well. Perhaps someday. You don't mind if I keep this, do you?" He held up the folder.

"Go ahead."

Simon gathered up his things and nodded to me. "We'll

be in touch."

Zeke slid from the booth and followed his dad after giving me a long, hard look.

When I heard the doorbell jingle, I leaned back in the booth with a sigh of relief. Simon, at least, had listened to me. Calmly and rationally. Without making crazy, off-the-wall accusations. It was a far cry from the dealings I'd been used to over the last few months—fae tended to make their minds up, sometimes seemingly without any facts at all. I smiled. I could get used to working with humans again.

I got up and grabbed my backpack. The pub had cleared out a bit as we'd talked, and only about half the customers were left. Liam was still behind the bar, tidying up the discarded glasses left in puddles of condensation, but when he saw me, he stepped out from behind the wooden slab.

"Go well?" he asked.

"As well as could be hoped, I think," I said. "Thanks again for letting us host this here."

"No problem. I'll walk out with you. I'd like to talk for a moment in private."

I raised an eyebrow and glanced around the half-empty bar. When he'd promised to discuss the idea of sheltering Aileen and her brother, he'd mentioned talking to the entire pack about it, so I'd gotten the impression that there wasn't much Liam kept from the rest of the faoladh. Still, I shrugged. "Sure."

Chapter 24

JOSH

Liam followed me out, letting the door swing shut behind him with barely a sound. He stepped up beside me on the porch, and for a split second, I was keenly aware of how much of a presence the pack leader had. He wasn't much bigger than me, but the moonlight glinting off his eyes turned them just slightly yellow, and the shadows didn't fall on his face in quite the right way—as if this wasn't his true face. It was a different effect than a glamour ghost—in fact, there was no glamour involved with it at all—and the hair on the back of my neck rose.

He seemed to realize my discomfort and took a step away from me, moving so that the moonlight hit full on his face so that he looked fully human. "I talked to the pack about Aileen. It's a … sensitive subject, which is why I wanted to talk in private." He paused, folded his arms across his chest, looked away.

"How'd it go?" I prompted.

"They're wary. Fae and faoladh in the same pack … it doesn't quite mix. But I've done some asking around about the Airgead kids. There's three of them—Coriander's the oldest, followed by Gren, and then Aileen. Cori's the only full-fae. Gren and Aileen are three-quarters. All from different mothers, all women who have significant glamour capabilities, even the half-fae." Liam scowled in disgust. "Like he's breeding, trying to see which stock is strongest."

"Coincidence?" I asked. "He moved in the same circles as their families or something, and they just happened to have a couple of flings?"

"Doubtful. Aileen's mom is a nobody. I'm not even sure where she is right now." Liam's scowl deepened. "All his kids have college degrees from Harvard. Antiquities, history, that sort of thing. They're brilliant, and Aileen and Gren are rumored to be extremely gifted in the use of glamour."

I'd seen firsthand how easily Aileen used glamour, and from Eliaster's description, it sounded like Gren was just as casual about it—if not more so. "Cori?"

"No one's sure if he's just really good at sleight-of-hand tricks, or if he's hiding a significant talent. Nothing on the explosive level of his siblings though." Liam gave me a sideways glance. "This could potentially be a really dangerous situation."

I sighed. "Typical. But if it means getting our hands on a pathstone before the Lucht Leanuna do, it'll be worth it."

"Well—the majority of the pack agreed to uphold the old laws. I think there's a case for it. Drake Airgead isn't known to be a loving father, and if it's bad enough that Aileen and Cori are asking for sanctuary, then there's a clear precedent for it. There were a few who were nervous about it, but if everything works out, we'll shelter them."

"Thank you," I said quietly. I understood just enough to know the risk Liam was taking. In accepting Aileen and Cori's request for sanctuary, he was putting a target on his pack. I admired his integrity.

Liam nodded and headed back into the pub. I stayed on the front porch for a few minutes, breathing in the humid air. Someone had a bonfire somewhere nearby—I could smell the woodsmoke. There was a bit of a chill that spoke of the coming fall.

I rubbed my arm and winced. It already felt bruised and

stiff. A shiver crawled up my neck, and I looked around.
Nothing rustled. Nothing moved on the edges of the parking
lot. I had a feeling I was going to be jumping at shadows for
a long time to come.

I stepped off the porch and headed for my bike. I was
certain Eliaster would prefer to hear the results of the
meeting in person. But first, I needed to stop by my parents'
house and check in with them.

As I put on my helmet, my phone buzzed in my pocket.
Meet me at the coffee shop.

I sighed. Okay, change of plans. First I had to deal with
this.

I parked in the lot behind the coffee shop and squinted
into the brightly-lit interior, wondering if I could see Aileen
inside. My phone buzzed again and I glanced at the screen.
I'm parked by the alley.

I turned and spotted her Jeep, parked alone in the darkest
corner of the lot, back by the alley that ran past an old grain
elevator. As I walked over, Aileen leaned into the passenger
side and shoved the door open.

Something flickered at the edge of the alley, in the
corner of my vision. I swung around, heart hammering into
my throat. Nothing moved.

"Josh?" Aileen hissed. "Hey, it's okay. No one's here."

The hair on the back of my neck prickled, but I shook
the feeling off. That alley had been where I'd first discovered
that humans weren't the only ones who inhabited this world.
To be totally honest, I was lucky I wasn't in the middle of a
flashback right now.

"What happened to your arm?" Aileen leaned against the
driver's door, eyes alert and on me.

I climbed in and pulled the door shut behind me. "Just an
accident."

She raised one eyebrow. "Riiiight." She shifted forward

a little. "Any word from the faoladh?"

I nodded. "They've agreed to offer sanctuary to you and Cori."

Her eyes closed, and she smiled just a little bit. When she opened her eyes again, it almost looked like she might start crying. "Thank you. You have no idea what that means to Cori and me."

"I, uh … I think I do a little bit." I smiled.

Aileen breathed deeply, as if tucking away her emotions. "I wanted to let you know that I'll be leaving soon. My dad wants me back in New York—I think I've successfully convinced him you guys are chasing a different lead. Do you have any questions for me before I leave?"

"Yeah, umm …" I rubbed my hand over my face. The painkillers I'd taken earlier were already starting to wear off. A deep, dull ache spread over my arm, and my back and neck were stiffening up from the beating I'd taken. "I've been curious—how'd we get on your dad's radar?"

"Since you found the pathstone." She straightened a little. "And no, not because Cori told him they'd seen you and Eliaster in the Chicago Market. I'm the only person he's ever told about that. Drake figured that if there were two groups of people fighting over a pathstone, he should keep an eye on them. Hence my presence in Springfield."

I nodded. "So what's the next plan?"

She reached into her jacket pocket and retrieved a flat, polished stone that looked like jasper. Bits of glamour, like specks of glitter, drifted off its surface as she moved it. "This is a stone that's glamoured to allow you entry into Drake's estate in New York. In a week, he'll be holding a gala, and during that gala, he'll be auctioning off the pathstone he owns. That will be your best bet to get hold of it."

Well, that made it easier. I hesitantly reached out and accepted the stone. As our fingers brushed, I felt that weird tingling again. Some of the glamour clung to my fingers as I studied the stone. "Okay. I'll have to discuss this with Cormac. See if we can raise some funds—" I stopped as

Aileen began to shake her head. "What?"

"Drake's got hundreds of years of wealth behind him. At this point, he doesn't trade in money. And trust me, you don't want to give what he'll be asking."

"So you think we should steal the stone?"

She nodded.

I blew out a deep breath. "That … that goes a bit beyond our usual type of job."

She shrugged, looked out the front window. "We should probably wrap this up. It's not a good idea to sit still too long."

I pushed the door shut and headed back to my bike. Behind me, Aileen started up the Jeep and drove out of the parking lot.

I tucked the jasper stone into an inner pocket of my jacket and smiled. Even if we didn't get this pathstone, seeing Aileen's face tonight had made me realize how much all this meant to her.

I pulled up to my parents' house in Republic and killed the engine. All the windows were dark, so I pulled my phone from my pocket and checked the time. Almost ten. My entire family couldn't already be asleep, could they?

I texted my mom, and a second later her answer popped up on the screen. *Ollie had a basketball game tonight. Working late, aren't you?*

A bit, but I'm done now.

I sighed and tilted my head back, willing my heart to stop pounding so hard. I needed to find my own place, partially so my family wouldn't worry about me, and partially so that I didn't jump every time they were gone.

The bushes near the front doors rustled, and with that faint noise, my blood froze. I placed my hand on my knife and watched the branches sway back and forth.

The neighbor's cat squirmed out from underneath them,

shook itself, and walked off.

I sighed. In that brief second, the image of the redcap going after my family had flashed into my mind. I staggered off my bike, feeling sick, and walked to the front door. My hand shook just enough to make my keys jingle as I started to unlock the front door.

The whisper of sound behind me made me flinch and turn. Before I knew it, I was pressed back against the door, the flat of a knife under my chin. I turned my head up to look the Unseelie in the face.

The fae grinned, clicking his tongue ring against his teeth. In the faint glow of the streetlight, I could see the dark stains of the raven tattoos on his neck and collarbone.

My heartbeat rushed in my ears.

Ghurdan.

The first time I'd met this Unseelie, it had been my first day in the Underworld. He and Llew had decided to try to torment me, because they knew I was under Eliaster's protection. Eliaster's "new pet", as they'd called me. Eliaster had put a stop to it by putting a sword in Ghurdan's shoulder.

This was the first time I'd seen him since.

I gritted my teeth. "What do you want?"

"Been enjoying yourself lately, now that Eliaster's let you off your leash? He must trust you a lot, letting you meet fae girls in alleys and sending you into a werewolf den."

He'd seen me with Aileen. My pulse sped up. I clenched my hands at my sides. "Aww, I'm touched you were so worried. Now what do you want?"

He chuckled and stepped back, easing the knife away from my throat. "Just wanted to check in, deliver well wishes from Blodheyr and Llew and Larae."

Now that he wasn't right in my face, I could see that the right side of his body hunched slightly forward, making his gait off.

I stalked after him, and his eyes flashed in surprise.

If he thought he could threaten my family, he was in for a surprise.

"I don't ever want to see another Unseelie around here again," I said, my voice quiet and slow. Making sure I enunciated each word. "If you do, so help me, Eliaster's vendetta against the Lucht Leanuna will seem like a child's game of tag compared to mine."

Ghurdan sneered. "You think if we cared, your family would still be living? Blodheyr could've sent a sluagh here at any time in the last couple of months to suck out their souls."

That wasn't the way the Lucht operated, I knew that. They wouldn't mass-murder a human family—it left too much to chance, too many questions unanswered.

Still the thought of a sluagh gliding in through my front door made my blood run cold.

Ghurdan's eyes glittered in his pale, thin face. He dipped his head in a nod, then turned and walked away. I watched, making sure he vanished down the street, before sinking down on the front steps, caving forward over my knees like someone had cut my spinal cord. If Ghurdan's only purpose had been to intimidate me, it had worked.

It had been really, really stupid of me to stay here. I got up and unlocked the door, then charged up the stairs to my room. Working quickly, I threw several changes of clothes into my backpack, stuffing it to bursting with everything I thought I'd need. I opened the closet and dug past some boxes my mom had stuck there when I'd moved for college. At the very back of the closet, I'd hidden the sword I'd gotten back in May. I hadn't touched it since I'd gotten home from Chicago.

I grabbed it and slung it over my shoulder, tightening down the belt until it hung at an awkward angle over my back. And I left.

I didn't think too much on the way to the rath. I actively tried not to think.

As I opened the mansion door, Roe and Eliaster were just exiting from the library.

Eliaster looked up at me, and concern crossed his face. "What's wrong?"

I shook my head. "I'm gonna need to stay here for a while. Maybe until I can get an apartment … maybe permanently. Not sure yet."

"Sure, anytime, but what—"

"Ghurdan," I snapped. "Ghurdan showed up at my family's house, Eliaster! That's what happened. I should've known better than to stay there."

Roe crossed the hall and put her hand on my arm. "Coming here was a good decision. With you gone, they won't attack your family."

"Maybe." I sighed and held my face in my hands for a moment. "Hopefully."

Eliaster picked at the edge of his fingernail for a minute, staring off into space. Then he said quietly, "I can ask people to look in on them once in a while. Discreetly."

"Thanks."

"It's probably for the best, anyway."

I gave him a closer look. There was a shadowed look in Eliaster's eyes, a hint of gray swirling around the edges of his irises. "You went after the redcap by yourself, didn't you? What happened?"

"Don't bother with the lecture." He fiddled with his necklace.

"No, that's kinda pointless right now. What happened?"

"I saw a couple of humans kill the redcap. The way they talked made me think that they were the ones who'd hired it."

I felt like I'd been punched in the stomach. I stepped back, clasping the back of my neck with both hands. "What? But … but that thing was sent after me! Why would humans be trying to hurt me?"

Roe grasped my arms. "Josh. We're working on it. Eliaster and Cormac are both trying to figure out what's going on. Why don't you get some sleep? I think you need it?"

"I'm not gonna be able to sleep!"

Despite my protestations, Roe led me into the kitchen, where she pressed tablets of a sleep aid into my hand and talked me into swallowing them. I still didn't think I would be able to sleep, but I was wrong. As soon as I was upstairs and in a bedroom, I could feel my eyelids growing heavy. I crashed on the bed and instantly fell asleep.

Chapter 25

JOSH

I couldn't remember my dreams the next morning, but I woke up with the sheets tangled around my legs, my pulse thundering in my ears.

Whatever it had been, I wasn't sure I wanted to know.

I eased myself out of bed and winced as my arm cramped. Blood had soaked through the bandages, leaving tiny droplets splattered across a portion of the bedsheet. I dragged myself to the bathroom, showered, and wrapped the bites as well as I could after slathering them with an antibacterial ointment that smelled like lavender and rosemary. All I could be thankful for was that there was no sign of infection.

I checked my phone as I walked out into my room. I'd texted my mom last night before I'd fallen asleep, but hadn't been able to stay awake long enough for a reply. There was one now, and the timestamp showed it had been sent a little bit ago. The buzz of the phone was what had probably awakened me in the first place.

We'll miss you, the text read. *Have a good trip!*

That's right. I'd texted her that I'd had to take off on another sudden business trip. I felt a quick pang in my chest. I'd never been super close to my family, but I loved them and lying felt wrong. But it was better. Maybe disappearing altogether would be better too.

As I left my room, my phone rang. I glanced down and recognized Simon Black's number. "Yeah?"

"If you're interested, we're going up to Saint Louis today to speak with Henry," Simon said, his voice crackling through the speaker.

I paused. "That quick?"

I could practically hear his shrug over the speakers. "You presented compelling evidence, and I've spoken to Lord Keelin as well. At this point, call me a skeptical believer of your story."

"You didn't tell Keelin that we met, did you?"

"No. Told him I got my tip from a confidential source. Whether he believes me or not is up to him."

"Well, at least it will take more work for him to pin it on me. Thanks."

"Sure thing."

I pocketed my phone and jogged down the stairs to the foyer. No one was around, but I could smell eggs and bacon and followed the scent. It led me through the dining room to the kitchen, where Lukas stood at the gas range stove in the decent-sized kitchen, stirring a sizzling pan of scrambled eggs. Another of Cormac's security, a scrawny fae with a rifle propped next to his chair, sat at the table with a book in front of his face, squinting through round glasses at the words on the page. What was his name? Jim … no, but it had started with a *J* … Jay. Yeah, Jay.

Lukas glanced up at my footsteps. He focused on the bandages on my arm, then nodded. "Heard what happened."

"Is this going to be another lecture about how humans don't belong in the Underworld and I should get out while I can?" I asked.

He dumped the eggs on a plate, added a couple of strips of bacon from another pan on the back of the stove, and slid it across the counter to me. "Nah. At this point you've made your choice and stuck by it. What we need to focus on now is keeping you alive." He pointed at my arm. "How's that feeling?"

"I can hardly move it."

He nodded. "Not surprising. Get food in your stomach so you can take some painkillers."

I blinked, surprised. While abrupt, his tone no longer had the biting snark I'd become accustomed to from him. I started eating, wincing. Any movement sent throbs of pain up my forearm and bicep. As I finished, Eliaster wandered into the kitchen, looking less than half-awake. He went straight to the coffeepot, found the biggest mug that had been set out on the counter and filled it to the brim.

"Eliaster," I said.

He glanced over at me, rubbing his eyes. "What time is it?"

"Seven AM," Lukas answered. "You want food?"

Eliaster blinked slowly, staring into his coffee cup. "Uh … sure. Wow, I actually slept for eight hours last night. That's weird."

A scene from my dreams flashed into my mind. Dusk. Pouring rain. Lightning flashed, revealing Eliaster's bloodied face.

My elbow cracked into the counter. My hand twitched, and my fork clattered to the ground.

"You okay?" Jay dropped his feet off the table.

"Yeah, yeah, I'm fine." I leaned down and grabbed my fork. What else had I seen in my dream? I tried to search back. Tried to pull the memory from my mind. But it was gone now.

Eliaster gestured for me to hand it to him. "You sure you're okay? What happened?"

I shrugged, held up my injured arm. "This hurts."

He nodded. "Let me take a look at it, make sure there are no signs of infection."

I unwrapped the bandages and let Eliaster examine the wounds. Lukas offered me another fork, but I shook my head. Really didn't feel like eating as Eliaster poked and prodded at my arm.

"Simon said they're going to talk to Henry Blair today," I said quietly.

Eliaster looked over at me, eyes wide. "Seriously?"

"Yeah."

"*Ciorru air*. We've gotta go, Josh. If they confront Henry on their own and he tries to get away…"

I nodded. He didn't need to finish. The Blacks and Henry were all curators, but it was a sure bet that if Henry could use relics, he'd have some stashed away.

"You're sticking your nose in where it doesn't belong," Lukas muttered. "And this time, I'm talking to you, Eliaster."

Eliaster looked over at me, worry flashing in his eyes. "Do you think they'll take it that way?"

Was he deferring to me? I scratched the back of my neck. "I don't know. Zeke wasn't very flattering of you yesterday, but Simon said nothing about you this morning."

I could see Eliaster struggling to remain quiet, to let me make the decision on my own. The fact that he even wanted my opinion showed how he was trying to change after what had happened with Shaughnessy. Trusting me more. Knowing I could handle myself.

Except that this time, I actually couldn't. I held up my injured arm and wiggled my fingers. "I guess I might need some dumb muscle around this time."

Eliaster smirked. "When you can actually defend yourself, you're gonna pay for that comment."

"Sure, tough guy." I got up and headed for the door. "Sure."

Four hours later, we still didn't have a plan.

We met Simon and Zeke in the parking lot of a nice apartment complex near the downtown area of St. Louis. As we got out of the car, Simon came over to us, frowning at Eliaster.

"You're not coming in with us," he said.

Eliaster held his hands up, starting to protest.

"Ah-ah, ah. Don't bother. You're not going in." Simon held up two fingers. "One, because if Henry sees you and recognizes you, we'll have essentially announced that something weird is going on and he's going to immediately be on his guard. Two, you're still not trustworthy."

Eliaster took a step back, hands still up. "Do you hear me arguing? Look, I'll stay out here and keep an eye out, make sure he doesn't get too far if he gets past you guys."

"He shouldn't even be here at all," Zeke muttered under his breath. He gave me a glare. "Why'd you let him tag along?"

Eliaster snapped his fingers. "Hey, I am standing here. You can address your questions to me, you know. I promise I won't take your head off. And to answer, I wouldn't let him come by himself."

Simon sighed, then said, "I'll admit, having someone guard the outside isn't a bad idea. Just try not to get involved."

"I swear I'll stay out of it if I can."

"Good enough. C'mon." Simon jerked his head at me, then turned on his heel and started toward the building. I fell in step behind him, Zeke walking after me.

I glanced over my shoulder.

Eliaster leaned against the trunk of his car, arms crossed, watching us walk away. He caught my worried glance and smirked, then gave me a thumbs-up. "You'll be fine," he mouthed.

Geez, I sure hoped so.

The door of the apartment building didn't have a doorman, but instead it had one of those old-fashioned buzzer systems. Not something I expected to find at a place this fancy. Simon pressed one of the many doorbell buttons, and a few seconds later I heard the front door click open. I followed him and Zeke across a small, posh lobby to an elevator. The elevator doors dinged shut behind us.

Zeke turned to me. "The fae still have you on a leash?"

I glared at him. "I think I already answered that question last night."

He glared back. "Then why's he here?"

"Because he's my friend, and I trust him to watch our backs." I straightened, trying to find another inch or so. "You don't seem to get it yet, but a confrontation with this guy could be life-threatening. I'm injured." I pulled my sleeve back to show him the bandages on my arm. "I want someone here who has pulled me out of the fire before."

Simon planted his hand on Zeke's chest, pushing him away from me. "That's enough. We need to present a united front to Henry."

Zeke settled back against the back wall of the elevator, arms crossed, glaring at the doors.

I took a deep breath. My hands trembled and I shoved them into my jacket pockets. The movement made my arm ache, and I bit back a wince, wishing that they'd let Eliaster come in with us. I was going to be slower than usual if I needed to go for my weapons with this injury.

The elevator dinged, and the doors slid open into a thickly carpeted hallway, which was painted a generic white. Mirrors or framed prints hung in the empty spaces on the walls. Simon led us a few doors to the right from the elevator and knocked.

Almost instantly, I heard the scrape of a bolt sounding from inside, and the door cracked open. A short, slim man with curly blond-gray hair appeared in the doorway, wearing square reading glasses on the end of his nose. "Ah, Simon. I didn't expect you so soon after your phone call."

Glamour slipped away from his face, revealing a fae with bright gray eyes. At least his hair and facial shape were close to the man he'd been masquerading as, but the pointed ears were unmistakable.

Simon smiled. "Well, we were already in the neighborhood—figured it wouldn't hurt to stop and check in."

I shot a glance at Simon and Zeke. Both of them smiled warmly at Henry. Utterly oblivious. I cursed under my breath.

Henry shot a curious glance at me. "You're new." His voice trailed off, and he squinted suspiciously.

As Simon and Zeke walked into the apartment, I stepped up and held out my hand. "Yeah, I'm … Rogers. Steve Rogers." *Please, please let him be as clueless about pop culture as Eliaster is.*

No flicker of recognition lit his eyes, no micro-expression of worry crossed his face. He merely smiled and shook my hand, then waved me in. It made my skin crawl to let him walk behind me, but I did, trying to keep my shoulders loose and relaxed.

The narrow hallway opened up into a living and dining area combined. The kitchen was separated only by a long kitchen island, the gray stone slab on top polished, but covered in stacks of folders and a basket containing odds and ends—various electronic charging cables, a few receipts, a couple of carved rocks. There was a square of black leather couches in the living room, one end closed off by a fireplace with large picture windows showing the St. Louis skyline on either side. A thick, gray area rug covered most of the living area. White tile floored the rest of the apartment.

Henry gestured to the couches. "Please, sit. Does anyone want a drink? Simon, let me run and get some of my other folders. A few things have recently come to my attention that I think will interest you."

"Sure, sure," Simon said.

Zeke walked over and set his bag on the stone-topped coffee table.

I stayed on my feet, looking around the room again carefully.

Henry shot me a concerned look.

I shrugged. "Long hours in the car. I'd rather stretch my legs for a bit, if you don't mind." I pointed to the stone figurines on either side of the fireplace mantel. "Celtic house gods?"

Henry nodded, a relaxed smile appearing on his face. "Non-relics, as you can imagine. Just little trinkets I picked up on a trip to Ireland once. They're not worth much, and not hard to find in our line of work."

"Mind if I look at them? Just professional curiosity."

"Oh, please feel free. Just try not to handle them very much. They're not relics, but they are old."

I nodded and walked over to the fireplace, pretending to study the figurine on the right. In reality, it had been a lucky guess that they were Celtic house gods. I didn't want to just go on Henry's word that they were harmless. I leaned close, pretending to study the little figurine from an angle, and watched Henry from the corner of my eye. So far, so good …Whoever this guy was, he didn't seem to realize that I'd seen past his glamour.

Ice clinked into glasses, and he poured a measure of something from a bottle into each drink. Henry set two on the coffee table's smooth stone surface and slid them over to me and Zeke, then handed one to Simon.

Simon nodded to him and walked around the square of furniture to stand by my side, squinting at the stone figurine on the mantel for a moment. I watched as his dark eyes flicked quickly over the piece, searching for—I guessed— ogham, just as I had.

His eyes met mine in a brief acknowledgment, and then he turned back to Henry. "You said you had some new things to show me?"

"Oh, right." Henry set his glass down. It chinked gently as it met the coffee table. He went to the hallway across the living room and disappeared into one of the open doorways.

I removed my backpack from my shoulder and set it on the end of the couch farthest from the chair Henry seemed to have claimed, but decided to stay on my feet. Zeke reached forward and picked up his drink, took a sip. I raised my eyebrows, watching as Simon unconsciously mirrored his son by taking a sip from his own glass.

Maybe I was picking up Eliaster's paranoia, but drinking from glasses that had been out of sight seemed like a really bad idea.

"Did you watch him make that?" I whispered under my breath to Simon.

He rolled his eyes. "Dear lord, not you too. How long have you known Eliaster?"

"Five months. But listen—"

Simon's eyebrows shot up. "And he's already got you this paranoid?" He shook his head. "Kid, you've gotta—"

"He's not human," I hissed. "He's sidhè. My guess is fae, but—"

Zeke started at me like I was certifiable. "Are you nuts? There's no way you can tell."

A hard knot formed in my stomach. "What?" No, no, no. That wasn't right. Humans could see through glamour if they spent enough time around fae, right? Like I had. Surely curators …

Henry stepped out of the room, closing the door behind him, and Simon straightened. The blond curator carried a small wooden box to the coffee table and set it down. Simon sat down beside Zeke and reached forward, bringing the box in front of him. The two pulled on thin leather gloves and Simon carefully opened the box. Thankfully he didn't look at me—I was pretty sure he would've been able to tell something was up.

I walked around to the back of the sofa as Simon eased a thick golden pendant on a chain from the box. The entire surface of the pedant was covered in ogham, faintly carved and barely visible in the dull surface.

"Fascinating," Simon muttered, angling the pendant back and forth. "Blessings, good fortune, multiple well-wishes … this almost seems like it's a lucky charm of some kind."

"Irish and it's a luck charm. Ain't that ironic," Zeke muttered.

The wounds on my arm itched, and I resisted the urge to scratch at them. When was Simon going to confront Henry like he'd promised? As the curators chatted about the pendant, I found my eyes wandering over the apartment again, searching as hard as I could for something that would give me a clue to Henry's boss. Something to prove to the curators that Henry was a traitor.

Anything.

I looked at Henry's face as he leaned over the coffee table. One gloved hand stayed clenched in a fist, his other hand tracing a line of ogham as he and Simon muttered about the meaning of a particular word. My dad did the same thing—when he put weight on his wrists like that, he balled his hands. If the guy was guilty, he was playing it cool. He didn't look the slightest bit nervous. As Henry straightened, he didn't uncurl his fist—rather, he slipped his hand into the pocket of his cardigan.

Simon put the pendant away, closed the box, and looked up at Henry. "Anything else?"

Henry shook his head. "You're looking at seven months of work, just tracking down that one thing. It was well-hidden. Relics are getting hard to find."

"Interesting. Because I've been told that you've been working for someone else."

Henry froze in the act of reaching for his drink. He looked up, hesitantly, eyebrows raised and stared at Simon in surprise. "You what? Simon, are you ..." His gaze drifted up from Simon to me, and his expression darkened. "You're trusting someone else over me?" He stood up. His hand was still in his pocket.

I gripped the back of Simon's chair. They still thought he was human. Crap, crap, crap.

Simon stood up as well. "They have witnesses and evidence, Henry. More than I can dismiss."

"From who? Other curators? Fae? Him?" He gestured at me.

Out of the corner of my eye, I saw Zeke's hand ease toward his side.

Henry saw it too, and in his eyes I saw a quick flash of

decision. He lunged.

I grabbed Zeke's shirt and shoved him forward, nearly throwing him out of the chair. Henry's hand slapped into the side of my neck, and I felt a pulse of cold and pain radiate up into the side of my head. I jerked back, gritting my teeth, and pressed my hand to my neck. When I pulled it away, a trail of glimmering gray dust followed it. As my neck stiffened, I watched the dust sink into the skin of my palm, turning it an ashen gray. Henry turned, a small disk that glowed with a fiery light in his hand. He reached for Simon.

The side of my neck cracked, and I could move my head again. The gray coating on my fingers cracked, and I could close my hand into a fist again.

I swung hard, driving my fist into Henry's head and knocking him off balance. His hand barely missed Simon's face. He tumbled and fell on his side, slamming into his stone fireplace.

He stared up at me, cradling one side of his head. His glamour was completely gone now. "How?"

"Forgot to mention, I'm immune to glamour. By the way—" I reached down and picked up the stone disk that had fallen from his hand and held it up. "Pretty sure this seals your guilt."

I grabbed his arm, hauling him upright, and glanced over to Zeke and Simon. Both of them looked like they were in shock.

"How?" Simon started.

"Let's focus on getting somewhere safe, and then I promise, I'll explain as much as I understand."

Simon nodded and focused on Henry. His eyes narrowed. "We have a safe house not far from here. Let's go."

I followed him out the door, dragging Henry by one arm. As soon as we got to the hallway, the fae tried to wrench free.

I pulled my gun from my shoulder holster and pressed it into the small of his back, where it would be mostly hidden from view by any innocent passersby. "I don't know about

you," I said, "but a kidney shot sounds like a pretty bad way
to die."

"Who are you?" Henry hissed back. "You're *human*.
How did you resist the glamour?"

Great question, buddy. The elevator dinged, and I
shoved him into it, mind whirling. At this point, all I wanted
to do was get to Eliaster before Henry realized how badly I
was shaking.

Chapter 26

JOSH

Eliaster got out of the car as we approached across the parking lot. His eyes flicked to Henry, then to me.

"Did not expect that," he said in a low voice. "What happened?"

"I'll explain in a bit." *I* still needed time to figure out what had happened. I looked over at the Blacks' SUV. "I'm gonna ride with them and make sure this guy doesn't cause any trouble. You good with following us?"

Eliaster nodded.

Zeke opened the back door for us. As I walked Henry over, the fae started to lean back against me. I jabbed the gun into his lower back, hard enough that he grunted and didn't fight anymore as I pushed him into the back of the SUV.

Eliaster tapped my side and handed up a packet of zip-ties. I sighed, but used the ties to bind Henry's wrists together. Then I pulled the door shut and sat in the middle row of seats, half-turned so I could keep an eye on Henry. I didn't put my gun away, but I did lower it, trying to keep my hand from shaking.

We pulled out of the parking lot, and I spotted Eliaster's car following us.

After a few uncomfortable minutes of silence, Zeke

spoke up. "So how did you know he was fae?"

"I saw through the glamour on his face."

"But—"

Simon interrupted his son. "Maybe we should leave the questions for a more private time."

Henry didn't say anything, but his eyes glimmered with dark anger.

He wasn't going to cooperate. My stomach sank. How were they planning to get anything out of him? My mind flashed back to the factory. Eliaster had looked ready to beat the answers out of Shaughnessy then, but he hadn't because Banshee had stepped in. The thought made me feel sick. What if torture was the only way we could find answers? Was it worth one person's agony to potentially save thousands, if not millions, of others? Because that was the stake here. Relics in the hands of sidhé meant they could cause as much havoc as they wanted.

By the time Simon parked, my stomach was a pit of gnawing acid.

I looked out the window. Simon had parked in the street of a fairly rundown-looking neighborhood. Half of the houses on the block had boarded-up windows with dying, overgrown yards and straggly bushes. The house he'd parked in front of had a piece of plywood over the inside of one window, with pieces of glass still clinging to the busted frame. The other window was grimy and covered with some kind of curtain, and bushes were growing halfway up it anyway. The chain link fence blocking the back yard off from the houses around it sagged in a couple of spots.

"It doesn't look like much, but the nice thing in this kind of neighborhood is that no one asks too many questions," Simon said. "Come on, let's get this over with."

I pulled on Henry's arm. "C'mon."

He barely acknowledged me with a grunt, but slid out of the car after me. I kept a firm grip on his arm as we walked up to the front door. Simon unlocked it and led us inside.

The house smelled musty, and a thin layer of dust coated

the empty shelves that separated the entryway from the rest of the living room. But other than that, it looked decent. A couple of old couches were pushed to the walls of the living room, and a circular dining table occupied another corner, with shelves of books filling the rest of the gaps. An old tube TV and VCR player sat against one wall. Simon led me into the kitchen and opened a door, which led down a steep, dark set of stairs. He flicked on the light.

"There's a couple of holding rooms downstairs. They haven't really been updated beyond a coat of paint since the forties or fifties, but it will do for now."

I pushed Henry's shoulders, nudging him forward and down the stairs. The basement was divided into a couple of sections. To my right, there was a small storage area with a few sagging cardboard boxes and old wooden crates. The room to the left was divided into two parts. One, beyond a half wall topped with thick-framed glass, held a table and a couple of chairs. The other held a few chairs, a table, an old fridge, and a half-closed door to a small bathroom. It looked fairly similar to the police interrogation rooms that populated movies.

A flimsy padlock hung open on the outside of the interrogation room door, a key stuck in it. I steered Henry inside. "I'll bring you some water or something in a bit. In the meantime …" I gestured to the chairs and table.

He snorted but didn't say anything.

I shrugged and slammed the door, then fiddled with the padlock. It was slightly sticky, but I was able to get it latched and turn the key after a minute of struggling. How long had it been since they'd used this place?

I put the key in my pocket and studied the lock. Under concentrated attack, it wouldn't contain anyone, but it would make a lot of noise if Henry tried to break it down. Besides, where was he gonna go?

I studied the glass for a minute and was unsurprised to see strips of black metal placed along the frame of it and the door. Iron. Someone had been thinking. Again, it wouldn't hold against a concentrated fae attack, but there was enough there to make a fae think twice about crossing it.

I headed back upstairs to find Simon and Zeke rummaging in the kitchen, pulling bottled water from the fridge and a few cans of food from one of the cupboards.

"Nice," I said. "When was this built?"

"Originally, back in the twenties. There was a lot of fae activity back then—some Unseelie went hand-in-hand with some of the gangs in various parts of the country, though I doubt any of the humans realized what they were dealing with." Simon shrugged one shoulder. "So, is Henry comfortable?"

"As much as he can be, I think. I don't know how you're planning to get anything out of him, though, Simon. Shaughnessy was under an oath of silence—it would make sense that Henry is as well."

"Well, that's what I was hoping Eliaster could help us with."

I blinked, stared at him. "What're you hoping Eliaster will do, torture him?"

Simon looked away. "Fae have … methods."

"If you're talking about glamour, no, they really don't. Even if they did, Eliaster can't use his glamour in that way. And if you're talking about relics, he won't touch them."

"Why don't we wait until your friend gets here and ask him, huh?" Zeke snapped. "Let the fae speak for himself."

I glared back, feeling my confidence falter. What if I was wrong, and Eliaster could use his glamour in some way to get Henry to talk to us? What if he would use a relic for something like this?

Where *was* he? I checked my phone, but he hadn't sent me a text or anything.

Simon handed me a water bottle. "So, while we have a minute, let's get to the part everyone's waiting for. How did you resist that glamour?"

I tested the bottle's cap. Still sealed. I tossed it from hand to hand. "Long story short, I had a half-fae roommate in college. Marc. The theory is that I spent so much time around him that I became immune to the types of glamour fae use to disguise themselves."

Simon nodded.

Zeke crossed his arms. "Dude, I saw it when Henry touched you with that relic. Your neck started turning to stone."

Crap. Figured he'd seen that. I dug into my pocket and pulled out the flat piece of rock. It was marble, gray shot through with black veins. The disk's glow pulsed in my palm. With each pulse, a small circle of gray spread outward on my skin, cracked, and faded into glittering dust. Awesome. Someone had found a way to channel the White Witch. I briefly wondered what kind of fae liked having stone statues in their garden, then decided that maybe I didn't want to know.

"How … how is this happening?" Simon stepped closer, adjusting his glasses. The glamour reflected off them, hiding his eyes. "Roe said you were fully human."

Zeke snorted. "As if an associate of Eliaster's can be trusted. He's got to be fae, dad. They're lying to us."

"I'm. Human," I muttered.

"Eliaster might, but Roe never would," Simon snapped at his son.

The doorbell rang, and I nearly jumped out of my skin. Simon went into the living room and opened the door, and Eliaster stepped into the house.

I shoved the disk back into my pocket. "Where were you?"

"Letting Roe know that we got him." He looked at me, a grim expression on his face. "How's Henry?"

"Keeping quiet," I said. "He barely said a word on the way here."

Eliaster frowned and looked over at Simon and Zeke, who stood some distance from him, eyeing him carefully. "Any plans?"

Simon shrugged. "We thought we'd wait until you

showed up."

Understanding flashed in Eliaster's eyes, and he took a step back. I raised my eyebrows. It had to be the first time I'd seen him back up from anything that wasn't a direct, physical threat.

He rubbed the collar of his T-shirt. "I don't do stuff like that anymore, Simon."

"Really?" Zeke muttered. "Then why did Highlord Keelin say you were ready to beat the truth out of Shaughnessy, oath of silence or not?"

Eliaster ground his teeth. "It was a momentary loss of control."

"So this time, you voluntarily lose control."

"I said *no*."

Simon crossed his arms. "Someone needs to do something, Eliaster. You said this guy is connected to Drake Airgead. We need to confirm your information from Henry Blair so we can move forward. Don't you have some fae tricks you can use?"

Eliaster growled. "Roe said the two of you have been friends for years, right?"

"Ye-es," Simon said slowly.

"Then why in hell do you think I can use 'fae tricks'? If you've known Roe as long as you say, you should know better. I can't control my glamour enough to be that precise. Besides that, Sidhé who have lived on this side of Mag Mell this long can't access glamour like that without relics. And I'm not touching any of those damned things." Eliaster's voice rose. "And if you think I'm willing to do something like that, we're done here."

Fear flickered in the two curators' eyes. I put my arm across Eliaster's chest, pushed him back a pace. "Hey, chill." I reached behind him and pulled open the door. "We'll be back in a minute, Simon."

I pushed Eliaster out onto the porch and let the door swing shut behind me. "Look," I said in a low voice. "We don't even have to interrogate him. We have it confirmed by two other sources that Drake Airgead hired this guy. We could just go."

Eliaster shook his head. "If we go off on this half-cocked, and Drake Airgead decides to make things difficult for us, that means Highlord O'Breigh will get involved. And if we don't have enough confirmation, he'll bind us both to the rath."

Since when was he worried about asking permission? I studied him. Eliaster stood leaning against the porch railing, arms crossed over his chest, legs crossed at the ankle. Totally closed off. Blue threads of color flickered through his eyes.

"Are you worried you'll lose control again, like you did with Shaughnessy? Or is this because of Highlord O'Breigh's inevitable visit to the rath?"

Eliaster looked down at his boots, and his mouth quirked to the side. I waited, letting the buzz of insects in the yard fill the silence. Was he going to answer me, or was this something else I'd have to wonder about?

Eliaster sighed and dropped his arms to his sides, his hands clutching at the porch railing.

"Both, I guess. But mostly about losing control. I don't want to be that person." Eliaster shifted slightly. "But at the same time I'm scared that if someone doesn't do it, a lot of people are going to get hurt. I'm scared that people like Shaughnessy are gonna hurt people like you, and that they'll use people like me to do it."

Okay. I could work with that. "I get it, I do. We're both scared. But that's why I'm here, right? To help."

His eyes clouded.

"Look, I know it's probably not going to help much, but I know what I'm getting into. Don't make yourself vulnerable because you're worrying about me." I shrugged. "I realize that's probably hopeless, but I figured I might as well try."

He chuckled. "Okay, okay. I still want to talk to Henry. If we can get something concrete from him, then Highlord O'Breigh won't be able to protest no matter what happens. Or—well, he will, but I think that would be enough evidence for the council to get him off our backs."

I nodded, playing with the flat stone disk in my pocket. I could feel the glamour tightening across my skin, turning it partially to stone, and then crumpling away. I focused for a second, trying to see what would happen if I consciously held off the glamour, imagining it hovering just above my skin but not touching it.

Nothing. My hand stayed flesh. I pulled the stone out and examined it. Something glimmered over my skin for a second, then vanished, and the slowly pulsing gray circle began to appear on my palm again.

Eliaster watched it for a moment, frowning. He leaned forward, examining the disk, the shivered. "Okay, enough. That's creeping me out. Did Henry have that?"

I nodded.

"That's really weird." He was quiet for a minute, then said, "But it does give me an idea." He pulled his car keys from his pocket and held them out to me. "Trunk of the car. There's something that might help."

I hesitated.

"I trust you with this." Eliaster's gaze never left my face. "I trust that you can handle it. Do you trust me?"

I nodded and grabbed the keys. I waited until I heard the door's lock click into place before I headed over to the car. I popped open the trunk and dug into Eliaster's duffel bag. My fingers brushed the ring box, and I immediately felt the jolt of glamour hit my skin. A familiar glamour.

I pulled the box out and closed my fist around it, breathing deep. I think I could guess what Eliaster had in mind. This was probably stupid. So many things could go wrong, and we'd lose this chance—a chance Eliaster already lost his brother and his girlfriend for. A chance I'd already lost my best friend for.

That was probably worth doing something a little stupid.

Chapter 27

ELIASTER

I hope I'm doing the right thing.

I let the front door close behind me, resisting the urge to look back. Pushing down my panic, my fear. Josh could make the right decision—he knew his strengths. I'd had to make a choice, and I knew I'd made the right choice, to trust him.

But it was hard to step away.

I could hear Zeke and Simon's voices floating up from the basement as I opened the door in the kitchen.

"He's *fae*, Dad. How did none of us pick this up before?" Zeke sounded angry, his voice almost hoarse in his intensity.

"We'll figure it out. At any rate—" Simon's voice stopped as soon as I stepped onto the stairs.

I clomped the rest of the way down. "By all means, don't stop talking on my account."

The two curators stood near the stairwell, about as far away from the holding cell as they could get while still being in the same room. I glanced over at the cell. Henry Blair sat at the table, staring at his clasped hands.

"What can you tell me about him, Simon?" I asked, pushing between the two curators and crossing the room. Henry did not look up at my approach. "You taught him at the Musuem, right?"

"Back then, I would've said he was loyal to a fault. Driven. He made small connections, extrapolated theories. He was a good curator. Some thought he was better than …" His voice trailed off.

I could fill in the blanks pretty easily. "Emily's heart was what made her better. She actually cared about people. This idiot apparently didn't, since he's been selling relics."

Simon cleared his throat awkwardly, then said, "Well, clearly Henry isn't the same man I trained years ago."

"Fae, Dad," Zeke repeated. "He probably never cared."

Simon rubbed his forehead, but didn't say anything.

Footsteps on the stairs announced Josh's arrival. He crossed the room, face scrunched in thought. I studied him. He kept both hands clenched in the pockets of his jacket, shoulders stiff. He looked up at me and nodded.

Okay, so we were on the same page.

"So what—what's the plan here?" Simon asked Josh.

Josh sucked in a breath and leaned back on his heels. "Henry's the only fae I've seen besides Eliaster who wears gloves while handling relics. That tells me that he's scared, or at least nervous, around them."

"So?" Zeke interrupted.

Josh didn't bat an eye. "So, we scare him."

I smirked, disguising the surprise that fluttered through me. Trust Josh to figure out an angle I hadn't anticipated.

"How do you propose to do that?" Zeke said.

Josh pulled the ring from his pocket.

Simon's eyes widened. "What do you have there?"

"Our ticket to get Henry to talk," Josh said.

"Wait a second." Zeke spluttered. "You can't just walk in there and use a relic on him!"

"He won't have to," I said. "If Josh's idea is correct, then we might be able to scare him into telling us what we want."

"And if not?"

"Using this would be preferable to other methods," Josh said.

Zeke rolled his eyes. "Right. You think you're just gonna walk in there and freak out a fae."

"Trust me, if I wasn't on Josh's side, a human who could resist glamour like this would freak me out too," I said.

Simon adjusted his glasses. "Yes, I've been meaning to ask you about that…who are your parents? Grandparents? Is there a possibility that you're from a curator family? Did you see through glamour as a child? There are theories out there that young children can see through glamour, but that most grow out of it."

Josh blinked, and I could see that he'd just hit information overload.

"Later," I said, putting my hand on Simon's shoulder. "You two can get all nerdy with your theories … but later."

Surprisingly, he didn't flinch away from my grip.

"Of course, of course." Simon gestured to Josh. "Please. Let's see if your plan works."

Josh rolled the ring in his hand and blew out a deep breath. The blue gem glittered in the yellow light of the overhead fluorescents. I looked away, tucking my clenched hands into my pockets. What if this didn't work?

A chill crept over my neck. What if it did?

Josh took another breath, closed his eyes, and slipped the ring over the third finger on his right hand. After a second he rocked back, staggering a little. His eyes flew open.

I caught his arm. "You okay?"

"Yeah, I—I'm fine." Josh straightened and shook his head, blinked a few times. "Okay. Let's talk to Henry."

Simon unlocked the door and opened it for us.

As we stepped inside the room, Henry raised his head. His eyes flicked warily from Josh to me, and then he smirked. "Oh, so the curators do still have a few pet fae at their beck and call. Interesting."

I growled.

"Yeah, now you get why being called a pet is annoying," Josh muttered to me. He faced Henry and held up a water bottle. "Thirsty?"

"I suppose I won't get that unless I answer a few questions."

"Nah, it's a freebie." Josh tossed it to him.

The ring flickered in the corner of my eye. I ignored it, kept my eyes on Henry.

He caught the water bottle clumsily and cracked open the lid, his eyes following Josh's hand as Josh sat down across the table from him. "Well, are we going to discuss this or not?"

"There's no discussing anything," I said. "You're going to tell us who you sold relics to. We already found Shaughnessy and his little gang in Kansas City. So who else paid you to get relics for them?"

"Oh, you found them too? Well done." Henry mockingly applauded. "Well done."

I slammed my hands on the table, making the curator jump a little. "Do you not understand what you're doing? There's a reason using the relics was outlawed! Shaughnessy was using his ring to control people and run a slaving ring. How do you think that's going to affect the visibility of the sidhé? For all we know, there could be some human law agent out there slowly coming to grips with the fact that the fae exist because he's run across a crime committed with a relic!"

"Funny that you're worried about that, what with your history and all," Henry snapped. "Real funny, Eliaster the curator-killer."

It took me a split second to register what he said, and then I went cold. My hands curled into fists. I looked from Henry's hands to his neck and imagined wrapping my hands around it, squeezing my thumbs into his windpipe.

Josh planted his hand on my chest and pushed me back. I startled and looked down. Not the hand with the ring.

"Let me deal with this," he said, face serious.

I nodded, not trusting myself to speak, and stepped back away from the table. As Josh pulled his phone from his pocket and set it to the side of the table, I focused on breathing. Tamping down the cold rage that had flooded me the instant Henry had said the words 'curator-killer'. Is that how the other curators referred to me behind my back?

"Look, I get it, okay?" Josh said to Henry. "It's not easy being part of the Underworld. Look at me—I'm human. I get treated like dirt. But sometimes even fae have a rough time of it." He leaned his elbows on the table. "So, we can make a deal, right? Just a little give and take. Maybe we can make it worth your while too."

"What is this, good cop/bad cop?"

"Ehh, more like bad cop/snarky cop, but I'll let you decide which one is worse."

I snorted.

Josh pulled the stone disk from his pocket and starting playing with it like it was a fidget toy—spinning it, turning it over and over. The ring on his finger glittered, and bits of white-gold flame flickered off the stone disk. It was almost mesmerizing.

I looked away.

Henry's eyes widened, and he leaned back in his chair. He replaced his glasses. "So much for taking the moral high ground there, curator."

"You saw what happened to me in your apartment," Josh said quietly. "I've seen this ring in action before, and while it didn't affect me, I'm pretty certain it would put you through the wringer. So let me explain how this is going to work—you're going to tell us what you know about your employer. Or I'll compel you to tell us."

"Skipping the torture and straight to the compulsion," Henry muttered. He stared at his water bottle for a long moment, then sighed, removed his glasses, and rubbed them with the tail of his shirt. "Look, let's just get down to the point. I don't want you using that thing on me. I don't have many options, but I do have one big bargaining chip." He pulled at a chain around his neck and revealed a silver pendant from underneath his shirt. The pendant itself shimmered like an oil slick as he removed the chain from around his neck and passed it across the table.

Josh studied it for a moment, then picked it up by the chain and held it out to me.

I pulled my sleeve over my hand and accepted the necklace. As I held it, I could feel a faint vibration in the jewelry. I rubbed the smooth, round pendant between my fingers and looked up at Henry. "And this does what?"

"That's a way into my employer's house."

I grunted. "If your employer is who I think he is, then we already have an in."

Henry stared at me as he slipped his glasses back into place. "If you already know who my employer is, why are you talking to me?"

"People ask for second opinions all the time."

Henry nodded and folded his hands on the table. "My employer is an Unseelie by the name of Drake Airgead. As far as I know, he is not affiliated with any specific Unseelie lords, although he seems to think he is one. That pendant gives you access to his house—"

I snorted again. "Yeah, like I said, we already have access. You're gonna have to do better than that."

Henry leaned forward. The lenses of his glasses flared as he tilted his head up to glare at me. "Let me finish. It gives you access to *all* of his house. He's paranoid—he has wards over wards within wards. You won't be able to sneak in, not unless you have some pretty powerful glamour, and I'm guessing you probably don't, even if you"—he gestured to Josh—"have a bunch of tricks up your sleeve. And if you do indeed have an 'in,' it's probably what essentially counts as a visitor's pass. It will get you in the door on the day of his choosing, but no more. That pendant will allow you access to anywhere you want to go."

Josh tapped his fingers on the arm of his chair. "So how much of your soul did you have to sell to get something like this?"

Henry grinned. "The nice thing about fae is that if you make yourself invaluable enough, they'll reward you handsomely. Remember that—it's the only way guys like you and me survive in this world. The rest of the curators will figure that out soon enough."

I paced back and forth behind Josh, half-listening as he tried to get more information from Henry. I felt … useless. Usually people were looking at me like I was the greatest threat in the room, but Henry's eyes never left Josh.

It was weird.

Part of it was that I was used to being the one questioning people. And even though he seemed to be pretty good at it, I had to wonder just how much of it was actually Josh, and how much of it was the ring.

I shook the thought. Josh wasn't actually using the stupid thing. There hadn't been a flicker of glamour from it.

Something buzzed in the room, and Josh and Henry stopped talking and glanced at me. I rolled my eyes as I fished the phone from my pocket. *Angel.* What was Angel doing calling me now? I put it up to my ear. "Yeah?"

"You're not gonna like this."

"I rarely like anything urgent enough for you to call me about. Spill it."

Angel grunted. "There's been another death. And I heard … things … scratching around my place last night."

A chill brushed the back of my neck. I turned, rapped on the doorframe and waited until Simon pulled it open and I could step outside to answer Angel. "Things? What kind of things?"

"Something with claws."

Now that I was listening for it, I could tell that Angel was trying really, really hard not to let his voice wobble. I swore under my breath. More redcaps. "Shoulda realized that there wouldn't be just one. Who died?"

"Maira."

The fortune-teller.

I clenched my fingers tight around my phone. I walked to the corner of the basement and leaned against the wall, fighting the urge to slam my phone against the wall.

"Eliaster?" Angel sounded very far away.

"I'll head home as soon as I can," I said. I put the phone in my pocket and opened the door to the interrogation room. "Josh. A word?"

Josh came out of the room and closed the door behind him. "What?"

"Maira is dead, and Angel says it looks like a redcap," I said in a low voice.

Josh paled and slumped against the door. He pushed his glasses onto his forehead and pinched the bridge of his nose. A glint of color snapped in one of his eyes.

My gut knotted. I took a step back from Josh. Had I just imagined that ... had that been a glamour spark?

Josh didn't notice. "Do you think everything he said in there was enough? If we go after Drake, with this evidence and the evidence that Aileen and Danos gave us, will it be enough to keep Highlord O'Breigh off our backs?"

At the moment, Highlord O'Breigh was the least of my concerns. I studied Josh. He was still slumped against the door, looking pale and worn. Part of that, I guessed, could be the fluorescent lights overhead.

I took a deep breath. *Maybe I just imagined it.* "I think we'd be stupid not to. We'll walk in with our eyes wide, but yeah ... I think we have enough to be able to defend ourselves if O'Breigh throws a fit."

Josh nodded and stood upright. Then he wobbled. Before I could grab his arm, Josh half-fell against the wall and slid down to crouch on his haunches. I knelt beside him. Josh's gaze swung upward. I gasped.

Josh's brown eyes had an amber glow to them, weirdly bright under the fluorescent lights. "Eliaster—" He grasped my arm. "I don't—I don't feel so good ..."

My pulse sped up. "Take the ring off." I tried to keep my voice steady even as panic gripped my heart in iron fingers. Heat flared along my arm, along my focus tattoos.

"Oh, yeah, I'd forgotten I even had it on." Josh reached down and tugged on the silver circling his finger. For a split second, it looked like the ring caught on his knuckle, but then it slid smoothly off. The pale glow died from his eyes, and Josh looked around, blinking. He swayed and planted his hand on the ground, barely keeping himself upright. He swore under his breath.

I tightened my grip on his arms. "You're all right," I whispered. "It's okay."

"What was that?" Simon hissed.

Cac. I'd had forgotten the curator was in the room. I turned and looked up at him. "We've had a rough few days, Simon, it's just—"

The shorter man stepped toward us, jaw clenched. He jabbed a finger at my face. "You're playing with fire. Again. This kind of thing is what got Emily killed."

I flinched.

"More fae arrogance," Zeke muttered from behind him.

Heat flared in my chest, and I flipped the younger curator off.

Zeke's face reddened.

"I'm fine, seriously." Josh got up, rubbing his arm. Red stained the edge of the bandage peeking from beneath his jacket sleeve. "Eliaster's right, we've had a rough few days, I'm probably just overtired."

"Josh." Simon's voice was even. "Humans *cannot* control glamour. I don't know what you did, or what he"—he glared at me—"has convinced you of. But you're just endangering yourself."

Josh crossed his arms and stuck his chin out. "I'm *fine.*"

I glanced between the two of them, unwilling to get into the middle of their stare down. I'd just make it worse, at this point.

Simon looked away first. He sighed and massaged his forehead. "You know … Fine. Fine. At least we got answers without any violence."

Okay, that was unnecessary. I rolled my eyes.

"So we're good then." Josh pushed his way past the two curators and jogged up the steps. I started to follow him.

"Wait, wait, wait," Simon said. "So what do you suggest we do with Henry for now?"

I shrugged. "He's a curator. He's your problem."

Josh was waiting on the porch, swinging my car keys around one finger.

"Think they'll be okay, dealing with him?" he asked.

I snatched the keys away. "They'll figure it out. It's time the curators stop sitting around on their butts and actually do something useful." I paused, scanning Josh's face. He still looked a little haggard, but at least his eyes were no longer glowing.

Just one more thing we've gotta figure out.

When we got back to Springfield, I woke up Josh—who had uncharacteristically fallen asleep almost as soon as we'd pulled onto the highway—and then we made our way to the market of the Springfield Underworld. Just inside the gate, I heard a familiar voice.

"Eliaster!" Angel trotted toward me. "We've been waiting for you. Your da's even here."

My stomach sank. Crap. It had to be really bad if my da had even come to look at the crime scene. I followed Angel through the twisting streets of the Market, my muscles winding tighter with each step I took. Maira's tent had been at the far northern edge, past the street to Opti's smithy.

Maira's tent was draped in opulent silks of purple and orange and green, gold embroidery twinkling in the light of the thousands of tiny fairy lights she'd strung through the translucent fabric. A curtain of beads hung in the doorway. My nose wrinkled at the scent that wafted from the doorway—hippy incense mixed with iron and viscera.

Josh made a weird, half-gagging noise behind me. I turned. Josh stood frozen a few paces away in the middle of the road, eyes flicking back and forth over the tent in front of them.

"Josh?"

No answer. But I could see his breathing quicken. He curled his arms in as if protecting his torso from a blow, shoulders hunching forward.

A spike of fear shot through my chest, and I reached out, grabbing Josh by the arm. As soon as I touched him, he jumped and his eyes focused on me, startled.

"Wh-what?" He gasped, sounding oddly short of breath. "What happened?"

"You just froze, dude."

Josh blinked and shook his head. He was still slightly hunched forward, breathing hard as if he'd just finished sprinting from the parking garage aboveground. "I don't …" His eyes widened, and he clamped a hand over his mouth. "Holy crow, that smell."

Angel grunted and I winced.

"Sorry," Josh muttered through his fingers.

"You sure you'll be okay?" I asked.

"Mother hen," Josh grumbled.

With good reason, I wanted to say. Instead I smiled briefly, then turned and followed Angel into the tent. The glass beads of the curtain chinked together, grazing against my arm as I brushed past.

The inside of the tent looked much like the outside—draped in colorful swathes of translucent silks backed by fairy lights. The burnt-out stubs of several candles dripped tall piles of wax on a scarred wooden table in the middle of the tent, and wooden shelves at the back held little bags of carved bones, dice, and other fortune-telling paraphernalia.

Da stood on the other side of the table in a loose half-circle with three other fae. Two of them I recognized as other council members. Lukas was surprisingly absent. The other fae, a councilwoman—Lily—looked pale and drawn, the dark makeup around her eyes standing out starkly.

Da looked up sharply as we entered and gave us a nod. "Glad you're here." His tone added the word *finally*.

A tiny stab of irritation rose in my chest. Da had been

more lenient in the last few months, but there was still that old resentment that threatened to rear its head at any time. I tried to shrug it off, to realize that Da was probably feeling much as I did at the moment—angry with himself, helpless.

Maira lay huddled on the ground behind her table, a pool of crimson soaked into the knockoff Persian rug under her. Someone had thankfully closed her eyes.

Josh made another gagging sound.

He stared at the table, his eyes wide with shock. He looked over at me, face pale, and shook his head. "I—I can't … I'll wait outside."

Angel snorted. "What's the matter, Overworlder? Can't hack it?"

Josh just glared at him as he left.

"Hey, lay off. He can hack plenty of things, including your security, and at the moment I'm inclined to let him," I growled.

Angel glared at me.

"Are you done?" Cormac demanded.

The sharp tone made me straighten my shoulders. "Yes, sir." *Under pressure. He's under pressure. I'm under pressure. Don't say something you'll regret.*

Cormac nodded to the woman. "Please repeat your story to my son."

"Your friend," the young woman said, looking up at me. "The human. He's the one who got her killed."

I felt my hackles rise. At these times, I really missed Josh's tempering effect on me. "Really? He's the one who got her killed? He only talked to Maira once!"

Da shot me an annoyed look, then reached out, put his hand on the girl's shoulder. "Sarenna, right? Maira was your grandmother?"

I winced. Damnaigh. Why couldn't I just have kept my mouth shut?

The girl nodded.

"Sarenna, why don't you repeat for my son what you just told me."

Sarenna glanced over at me, then at Da, then dropped her gaze to the ground and crossed her arms. "Last night, I was out back packing up a few things. We were just getting ready to leave for the day and make deliveries—Gran has a few customers who buy potions and things from her." Her eyes flicked up to me. "Harmless, you understand. Mostly just herbs and essential oils. The humans go nuts for that stuff."

I nodded, hoping I'd schooled my face into something resembling encouragement.

"So I was packing up, and I saw these two humans come in through the front door. Men. Kinda unusual—the few humans we do get down here typically tend to be female. And I recognized them because they'd visited once before. The first time they talked to Gran, they just acted like they were interested in the shop, in having their fortunes told. But this time they started asking about who runs the city, who keeps it safe, that sort of stuff. Then one of them mentioned Eliaster by name."

I did not like where this was going. I shifted my weight from foot to foot.

"Gran says yes, she's seen Eliaster Tyrone pass by, he generally wanders the market on most days. They say, have you ever read his fortune, Gran says no. They ask, you ever read fortunes of anyone associated with the Tyrones, and Gran admits yes, a couple of their employees. The smaller guy asks, a scrawny human kid with glasses, and Gran says yes again. And then the bigger guy, he says, we hear you pass along more than just the fortunes. Gran got all bristly and said she doesn't know anything about that, she's just a respectable upstanding citizen trying to make an honest wage, and that she was about to close up shop if they didn't mind.

"They kept pushing at her, trying to get her to admit she'd passed along sensitive information, and Gran got all mad, saying she was going to put a curse on them if they didn't get out.

"Now, the thing is, Gran didn't have that much glamour to her name, not anymore, but she had enough to push a nasty curse or two, and everyone knows it. So they left, swearing her up and down the street, and I thought that was the end of it. She was so upset she sent me home early, saying she'd take care of the deliveries, but she never came home last night, and when I checked here ..." The girl broke down, sobs choking her voice.

Crap. I looked at Maira's body again, rubbing the back of my neck.

Lily reached out and put her arm around the girl's shoulders, gently leading her out the back door of the tent.

Cormac glanced over at me. "When did Josh last talk with Maira?"

"Like I told her, just the one time about a week, week-and-a-half ago." I sighed and scraped my fingers through my hair. "I can't believe this."

I crouched down, studying Maira's body from a distance before shuffling closer. The blood was tacky, the rug stiff to my touch. Blood soaked the front and back of Maira's layered dresses and shawls, but several puncture wounds marred her chest and back. The punctures looked deep enough to have stabbed her through. I held my hand up in the shape of a claw and compared the pattern to her wounds.

"So, the redcaps yet again," Da said.

I nodded, stood up. "Yeah, and Angel says he heard something scratching around his place last night too."

Da looked over at Angel, who nodded.

"You really think it was a redcap?" Angel asked. "I mean, other than this, what do you have?"

"One came after Josh the other day, but he's dead, so this has to be the work of a second," I said.

"Josh killed a redcap?" There was so much disbelief in Angel's voice that it was almost comical.

I snorted, trying to keep from laughing. "No. I tracked it down and watched two men murder it."

Da's eyes narrowed. "The same two men who talked to

Maira?"

"Based on Sarenna's description, it sounds likely. Besides, I don't think there could be that many humans who associate with redcaps."

"Humans," Angel muttered. "Fascinating. Ex-curators, I wonder?"

"Possibly, but I don't think there are that many ex-curators in existence," Da said. "Even if they stop working in the field, so to speak, they tend to stick to the community. Like tends to stick with like."

And where does Josh come into that? I wondered. *Like tends to stick with like, but Josh isn't fae, and he's becoming ... what, less human?*

As soon as I thought it, a chill rolled down my spine. No. That wasn't what was happening.

I stood up, dusted off my knees, and stepped out the back door. Sarenna sat slumped against the rickety boards of the next building, with Lily standing beside her looking extremely uncomfortable.

I crouched down in front of Sarenna. "Two questions, and then I'll get out of your hair. Did the two men say where they were from?"

Sarenna shook her head, wiping her eyes.

"Okay. Second, do you know who could've told them that your gran had given my friend Josh information?"

Sarenna bit her lower lip as she thought. "I ... maybe Cordella? She's a goblin fortune teller a few blocks away. She and Gran didn't get along very well."

Of course not, I thought. I stood. "Look, I'm really sorry about your gran." I tried to make it as heartfelt as I could, but I'd never met the woman, and my words rang hollow. I think Sarenna knew that.

I walked around the outside of the tent.

Josh sat on the curb, hunched over with his knees drawn up to his chest. He looked up as I approached. "Well?"

"I think it's the same guys who I saw kill that redcap, and it looks like there are more redcaps out there than we thought."

Josh winced.

We sat in silence for a minute.

"Look," Josh said finally. "I'm sorry I couldn't go in there."

"It's okay. It was brutal. You didn't need to see it."

"I … I think I did see it, though."

I ducked a little so I could look my friend in the eyes. His irises were still a little too bright, making his eyes stand out more sharply and giving his face an almost drawn, hungry look.

"What do you think is happening to me?" he asked, his voice small and quiet and scared.

"I don't know, but we'll find out." I reached over and gripped Josh's shoulder. "But like you told me earlier, I'm here. I won't let you walk this road alone. I swear."

Chapter 28

JOSH

The ring felt heavy in my pocket as Eliaster and I made our way back to the rath. The weight scared me. It felt more and more like I was carrying the ring to Mount Doom, and I knew how that had turned out for Frodo.

I'd seen Maira, dead, before I'd even stepped into the tent. Based on what Eliaster had described to me, I'd seen the scene perfectly. I could've told him where to find every deck of cards, every potion, every crystal in the mess scattered across the floor. I could've told him that there was a crumpled ball of paper spilled from the trash can under her desk. I could've told him exactly how the body lay, and the exact shape of the stain in the rug.

I did, as we walked. And the more I talked, the more Eliaster's face turned grim, until it was like his features had been carved from stone.

We stopped outside the gate to the Tyrone rath, and I reached over and grabbed his arm. "What's happening to me, Eliaster?"

"Do you still feel weird?"

I shook my head. Once I'd taken the ring off, the little spots of light and shadow had vanished. The strange double-vision, like everything around me had a glamour ghost that wasn't quite disappearing as I looked at it, had also gone away. And I hadn't seen any glowing vines since I'd first put the ring on. But even now, hours later, I still felt *weird*. There was an itch in my skin that I couldn't get rid of. It wasn't the ring, because I had absolutely no desire to put it on again. But something … something had been awakened in me. That was the only way I could describe it.

"We'll talk to Roe. I'll hunt down those redcaps and the men manipulating them, and we'll figure this out."

I noticed his use of *I*. "You can't do that by yourself."

"At the moment, I'd rather you pursue what's going on in your head."

I cringed. Great, it was going to go back to that. He'd started trusting me, but he was probably right—who knew what was going on. Maybe I wasn't trustworthy now.

"Hey." Eliaster jerked me around to face him. "Not because I think you're lying to me, or dangerous, or anything else is going on in that big brain of yours." He poked my forehead. "But I'm worried. This is not normal for a human— at least, not in my experience."

I smirked. "I feel like that's a sort of backhanded compliment."

"Sure, we can call it that. Either way, I'd rather we try to figure out what's going on now than have something weird happen that isn't so good for us later, at a vital moment."

"What about later, at Drake Airgead's gala?" I glanced down at the gravel under my feet, resisting the urge to kick the rocks like a little kid. "I should probably stay home from that, shouldn't I?"

"Not a chance."

I looked up, surprised.

"I told you. I'm trusting you, Josh. One hundred percent. We're a team, and I know we'll need your help at the gala. Besides—" Eliaster smirked. "Aileen trusts you more than she trusts me. And that's important right now."

I nodded. I still felt a little sick, but it was nice to know that he was going through with his promise. Trusting I could contribute to the problem, that I could take care of myself. *He thinks Aileen trusts me more than him*? The idea lit a bit of a warm glow in the center of my chest.

We headed into the house, and Eliaster disappeared almost immediately, leaving me to walk to the library by myself.

Roe sat in her customary chair by the fire, which crackled and spread the scent of clean campfire throughout the room. She looked up as I flopped into the chair beside her.

"Long day?" she asked.

I nodded and leaned forward, cradling my head in my hands. "Yeah. Did you hear about Maira?"

"Yes. Very tragic, and unsettling, considering your own attack." She paused.

I glanced up between my fingers. Roe was regarding me with a quiet watchfulness, perched on the edge of her chair.

"I saw it all, Roe," I said quietly. "Without even stepping into her tent, I saw it. The body, the blood, the wounds, even the things on the shelves, all down to the last detail. And that's not all." I desperately tried to keep my voice steady, but it trembled anyway. "Those dreams, about the glamoured vines? I had another one. But this time I was able to control the vines. And look at this." I pulled the stone disk from my pocket and held it out in my hand.

It was still mesmerizing, watching the glamour spread a layer of granite over my skin, only for it to crack and crumble into dust. Over and over. Hypnotic. I pulled myself out of the rhythm and imagined a thin glove of glamour between my skin and the stone, pushing my will forward. This time, I could watch it happen. A layer of green glamour instantaneously wrapped my hand, and the disk just sat there, flickering but unable to affect me any longer.

Roe frowned. "Where did you learn that trick?"

"I watched Keelin do it once. *Once*, Roe. And ..." I hesitated, then forced myself to keep speaking. I wasn't going to start keeping secrets. I told her how I'd worn the ring, messed with the stone disk while I was talking to Henry. How I'd felt dizzy afterward, and even after Eliaster had made me take the ring off, I'd been tired and fallen asleep in the car.

I looked up at the older fae woman, feeling a little like a penitent at confession. Roe was staring, not at me, but at the fire, her brows furrowed and her lips pursed. After a moment, she glanced over at me, then reached forward and grasped my hand with hers.

"I don't know what to tell you, Josh," she said softly. "But one thing I am certain of—you are here for a purpose."

I smiled weakly. "Yeah? It feels like a cosmic joke."

"There are no accidents. At times of need, heroes will arise …" her voice trailed away, and she abruptly got up and walked over to the bookshelves. She ran her fingers along the spines of the books, the old leather and cloth crackling and wrinkling at her touch. She picked one out and came back, showing me the title.

Mort d' Artur.

I looked up at her. "The Legends of King Arthur?"

"Merlin, specifically. There's a legend in the British Isles that if they are ever in need, Merlin will come back to rescue them. Some people believe some of their most famous leaders—William Wallace, Churchhill—were reincarnations of Merlin."

I took the book, weighed it in my hands. "Please don't tell me you think I'm a reincarnation of Merlin."

She chuckled. "No, but I do ascribe to the theory of heroes rising when there is a need. And I believe that you and Eliaster are two such heroes. Nothing is coincidence, Josh."

I nodded, looking down at the book in my hands. Knowing Roe cared was the only reason those words didn't make me feel worse. It felt too vague. I need something concrete.

I remembered the way Aileen had looked at my bracelet. The way that she'd told me to put it back on. She *knew* something about it. Maybe she knew why I was suddenly able to use glamour.

I pulled my phone from my pocket and texted her. *We got Henry. We should probably meet to discuss plans for your dad's gala this weekend.*

I didn't even have to wait thirty seconds this time before the little typing icon popped up. *This is becoming something of a habit of ours. :)*

I blinked. She was using emoticons now? Wasn't quite sure what to make of that. *Yeah, sorry.*

Pfftt. Don't be. The Black Dog again, tomorrow morning? Eliaster can come too. I have to leave tomorrow afternoon to get back to New York.

If she possibly had the answers I thought she did, Eliaster wouldn't just *want* to come along. The Wild Hunt wouldn't be able to keep him away.

Chapter 29

ELIASTER

I sighed heavily and leaned back in my chair, twisting the pen in my hands. Another piece of crumpled paper rolled away from me.

"Sounds like it's going well," Liam commented from the bar.

I shot him a glare. The faoladh had already turned his attention back to the TV mounted in the corner. Except for me and Liam, the place was empty. Even though the pack had agreed to shelter Aileen and Cori, they weren't needed for planning what was essentially a heist at Drake Airgead's.

I rubbed my forehead. A heist. Who would've ever thought that I'd be planning a heist? Josh was giddy over the idea. Not me. I looked up at the TV, trying to see what Liam was watching. "Didn't know you were a soccer fan."

"I'm not, but it's less painful than watching you."

I rolled my eyes and dragged out the map that was crumpled under my notes. "Okay, *béalastán*." I spread the map out on the bar. "Tell me, if there was a group of redcaps hanging out in Springfield, where would they be?"

Liam raised one eyebrow. "Redcaps. Didn't Josh say he was attacked by a redcap?"

"Yeah. So?"

"And so now you're planning a one-man vendetta against them."

"No, I'm trying to figure out who's hiring them."

Liam's ear twitched, and he scratched it. "Why would you think—"

The doorbell jingled. I spun around on the barstool.

Aileen let the door swing shut behind her, then noticed my gaze. She held her hands out. "Didn't know there was a welcoming party. Figured it'd be just me and the wolves today."

"Faoladh," Liam corrected. "The first thing you need to know about getting along with us—call us faoladh. We're not wolves, and we're not werewolves."

"Okay, sorry." She glanced around. "Where's Josh?"

"I dunno, he was running some sort of experiment involving glamour and a video camera last I saw, so …" I shrugged. "Hopefully soon?"

Aileen laughed as she sat beside him. "What's all this?" She gestured to the stuff spread over the counter.

I exchanged a glance with Liam, then said, "Have you heard about the redcap killings?"

She wrinkled her nose. "No. There are redcaps in Springfield?"

"Seems like."

"Awesome. And here I thought maybe I'd be getting away from stuff like that." She sighed.

An awkward silence consumed the room. I started gathering up my notes and the map, stuffing it all into my backpack.

After a few minutes, Liam plunked a beer down on the counter in front of Aileen and leaned on the bar. He started to say something, but the bell jingled again, and Josh stepped into the bar, grinning.

"Experiment go well?" I asked.

"Inconclusive. The video camera blew up." Josh shot a grin at Aileen. "Hey."

She smiled. "So, shall we get started?" She pulled a thin laptop from her bag and opened it. "I could've drawn a map, I guess, but it was just as easy to snag a digital copy of the blueprints to Drake's house. The only one we'll need to worry about is the first floor, anyway."

"Do you have pictures of the pathstone?" I asked.

Aileen shot me a look. I couldn't quite tell if it was annoyance, or surprise. "Of course." She picked up her phone and scrolled through the apps, then set it down on the counter between us.

The screen showed a white granite stone about the size of my palm, sitting on a black cloth surface.

Josh put his backpack on an empty table and stepped between us, reaching for the phone. "Do you mind?"

"Go ahead," Aileen said.

Josh picked up the phone and zoomed in, scrolling through different parts of the picture. "Do you have proof that this is in your dad's possession?"

"Swipe right."

He did so. The next picture that popped up was a selfie of Aileen, tongue stuck out, holding the stone up next to her face. Josh raised an eyebrow and shot an amused glance at Aileen. She shrugged, a shy smile on her face. Again, Josh zoomed in, studying the photo, especially around Aileen's hand.

I sat and watched them—the way they both unconsciously leaned toward each other, the way they occasionally glanced up at each others' faces and then quickly looked away as if they were afraid of being caught. If there were any more sparks they'd catch the building on fire.

This would make things … interesting.

Josh handed the phone back to her. "Looks legit to me."

She nodded. "Now that we're done with that—"

"Just a second. I have a couple of questions I want to ask first." Josh crossed his arms.

I leaned an elbow on the back, swiveling my chair so I could see both Aileen and Josh's faces. *What is he up to?*

Aileen raised her eyebrows. "Okayyy."

Josh held up his right arm and motioned to the bracelet. "You're the one who told me to put this back on, and you seem interested in it. I'd like to know why."

"Is this information important?"

"Besides the fact that we're now allies, and allies share information? Look, I know you fae love your secrets, but I've been able to do stuff I'm not supposed to." He pulled the stone disk from his pocket and flattened his hand so Aileen could see the circle of stone growing and fading on his palm—which still made my skin crawl. "It protects me from glamour, and I've even been able to use it a little. I need to know what this bracelet does."

Aileen slid off the barstool and extended her hand. "You trust me?"

Josh nodded. He took the metal band off and handed it to her.

Aileen turned it over in her hands. Her fingers ran along the ground-down edges of the blade-like pieces, lifted the edges of the leather bands that bound the pieces together. After a few minutes, she sighed and press her lips together. "There are no markings on this, so I don't know its origin." She handed it back. "The first time we met, I could tell that this was a powerful relic. So when you said you didn't have it on, that worried me. I knew it would protect you."

"How? For all you knew it could've been an enslavement glamour, binding him to me," I cut in.

She shook her head. Her eyes flashed a light gray. "I didn't think your mind was *that* twisted, Eliaster."

Josh snickered. "But you still think it's a little twisted?"

Liam snorted and hid the laugh behind his hand.

Aileen grinned. "All fae minds are slightly twisted. Might as well get used to it."

"Oh, trust me, I've noticed."

"Hey." I shoved on Josh's shoulder.

Liam leaned forward on the bar, waiting for our laughter to die down before saying, "How did you know it was protective?"

Aileen climbed back up on her barstool and faced him. "What color are the stripes in my hair?"

"White," Josh said, at the same time that Liam and I said, "Purple."

Aileen pointed at Josh. "That's why. My glamour is strong enough to hide the color of my hair even from other fae. But Josh saw through it, when he should be the least likely person to do so. And, he told me on the phone that he was no longer seeing glamour. The only difference was that he wasn't wearing the bracelet."

Her glamour must be really strong, then. I recalled what Josh had told me about Liam's findings on the Airgeads. Aileen and her brothers had basically been bred for strong glamour. But even that didn't explain how strong her glamour supposedly was. I squinted at the colored stripes in her copper curls, but they stayed purple, no matter how much I tried to convince myself that they were actually white.

I glanced over at Liam. The faoladh hadn't moved from his casual lean against the bar, but his hand had tightened on the white towel he held. Something was making him nervous. Liam raised his eyes and caught me looking. He gave me a slight nod. What had he picked up?

Well, time for that later.

I swung my seat back around and motioned to Aileen's laptop. "Okay, time to get serious."

Aileen nodded and called the blueprints back up on the screen. "Drake usually holds galas in this room." She used her finger to circle around a huge foyer-type room. Then she eyed Josh. "You're going to stick out a bit."

"Not many humans?"

"Not many who are free-minded, anyway. The people my father hangs around tend to treat them as more playthings. There will probably be a few escorts who are humans—some fae think humans are exotic and exciting to have as lovers, but trust me, the humans there will be mesmerized or glamoured in some way."

Josh sighed. "Fantastic."

"How do we deal with that?" I asked.

"There's different ways, depending on what we decide to do." She swiped across the screen, calling up a blueprint of the second floor. "Drake pulls people out of the gala for private auctions, so at some point during the night, one of you will have to indicate that you're interested in that." She glanced over at me. "Josh and I've already discussed this. Did he explain?"

I nodded. "Favors, memories, basically curiosities other than gold. Yeah, I don't think we can afford his price." I made a face. "As much as that would simplify matters."

Josh grinned. "So it's a heist."

"Oh no." I pressed my hands to my temples and leaned my elbows on the counter. "Josh, this is not *Ocean's Eleven* or James Bond or whatever you've got going through your head—"

"Actually, you'll have to wear tuxes, so it'll be a little bit like James Bond," Aileen said.

I shook my head. "Stop encouraging him."

Josh held his thumb and forefinger a fraction of an inch apart. "Just a little, tiny, teensy-beensy bit like James Bond."

Aileen's face scrunched in disgust. "That means I'm the femme fatale."

"Ehh, wouldn't be a heist without one." Josh's ears immediately turned red, and his eyes rounded. "Umm—I shouldn't have—"

Aileen threw her head back, laughing.

I shot a glare at both of them. "You two are going to be the death of me."

"Where's his office?" Josh asked.

Aileen pointed. "Down this hallway, on the right. It's right off the foyer, but the problem will be that it's glamoured to appear as part of the wall. To get past it, you need this special pendant. I suppose I can pass off mine to whoever is going to try to break into the office, but—"

Josh plunked Henry Blair's necklace on the counter.

"Next step. Any glamoured traps or anything in the office?"

Aileen raised an eyebrow. "Well done. And no. But he has a safe hidden in the floor."

"Sounds like your thing then, Josh," I said.

Josh reached for his backpack. "Yeah, I can start looking up different ways to—"

"Actually, and hear me out on this, guys—I think Josh should be out here the whole time." Aileen tapped the big room again. "And here's why. You're human—you'll attract a lot of attention just by being there. But if you're with Cori or me, you'll be safe."

I could feel the tension knotting up my muscles with every word she spoke. Put Josh in the spotlight? That was a stupid idea.

"No offense," she said. "But you're not trained in fighting as well as Eliaster or I are. I'm worried what would happen if you ran into someone."

Josh nodded quickly—a little too quickly, as if he was trying to talk himself into it as well. "Yeah, it makes sense."

It did. And Aileen had shown every cooperation. Nothing I'd seen about her set off my alarms—like Larae had. Everything Josh and I and even Liam had found indicated that she had every reason to want to get away from her father. And Coriander … well, it said a lot about him that he hadn't pulled Josh into this because of the owed favor.

I still didn't like the idea of leaving Josh with Cori and Aileen, but I liked the idea of sending him to steal the pathstone even less.

I half-listened as Josh and Aileen finalized the plan, turning my own fears over in my mind. But as Josh stood to leave, I snapped my attention back to them. Josh left first, and I nodded goodbye to Liam and Aileen and started gathering my stuff.

"Aileen." Liam finally straightened up from leaning on the bar.

She stopped in the middle of grabbing her jacket from the back of her bar stool and glanced up at him, eyes clouding faintly with a darker gray.

"What was it you weren't saying? About you having strong glamour?"

Aileen looked at me, then dropped her gaze to the floor. She fiddled with the piercings on her right ear. "I already told you that my brother and I were br—"

"There's more to the story," I said. I nodded to Liam. "He sensed that you weren't telling the whole truth. Better get it out now—if you break a faoladh's trust—"

"I don't mean to break trust!" she snapped, eyes flashing. "If you have to know, we're cursed."

I blinked. Cursed? Was that even a real thing any more? I looked over at Liam. He looked just as perplexed as I felt.

"Airgeads die young." Aileen's voice was rough, as if she was angry that we'd dragged this confession from her. "Family legend says that back when the paths to Tir Ni-all closed, our ancestor bargained with someone to keep his glamour strong, but it came with a cost. Airgeads never live past one hundred, and all of us die gruesome deaths. Da never let us forget it. So I hate talking about it."

I felt a bitter taste in the back of my throat. What kind of person was sick enough to make that kind of bargain? To continually remind your kids about it?

"So…" Liam said slowly. "How does this affect you wanting to leave?"

She shook her head. "It doesn't. I just want out. I'm sick of all of it and this is just another thing that I'd rather forget."

Liam looked at me and nodded. This was the truth. All of it. He turned back to Aileen. "I don't think you have to worry. Josh and Eliaster are good at what they do."

Well, now I just hoped we could live up to that hype.

As I turned to go, Aileen reached out and gripped my arm. "I didn't want to say it around Josh, but you know I'll take care of him, right?"

I spun around. "Why do you think you need to tell me that?"

She made eye contact with me. "Because I can tell that

he means a lot to you. You're practically brothers."

I smirked. "And it's not because of anything you feel towards him?"

Aileen didn't break eye contact. "You have a problem with it?"

I shook my head. "It's the best place for him. Josh is smart, got a good head on his shoulders. As long as you and Cori can keep an eye on him, he'll probably be wheeling and dealing with the best of them." I put my hand over hers. "Thank you."

She nodded.

Chapter 30

JOSH

At least Eliaster got a kick out of me being fitted for a tux. I got poked by three needles and the smart-mouthy seamstress who, as my luck would have it, was an old friend of Roe's, pulled my ear when I complained.

But finally the torture was done, our stuff was jammed into the tiny trunk of Eliaster's super car, and we were off.

When I plugged the address Aileen had given us into Google, it pinged a place in upper New York state, about three hours away from New York City. Nothing except a dark blur showed up on street view, but it was a substantial-sized blur, which just added to my nervousness. This was so far above my pay grade.

I sighed. It was also almost too close to the Indiana Jones stereotype of evil, rich art collector. Except that Airgead was trying to rid himself of the relic instead of tricking us into finding it for him.

And after that, it was just a matter of not losing our minds on a nearly twenty-four-hour car trip. There were a few moments of snarling at each other, and I was mightily tempted to bean Eliaster on the head with one of the huge research books I'd brought along. More than once. The long trip did have one perk, though—it was long enough that

Eliaster was forced to let me drive his fancy supercar.

Finally, though, the long trip was mostly behind us. Our last stop, when we'd changed into our tuxes at the local mom & pop gas station, had been over an hour ago. Eliaster was back in the driver's and I was adjusting and readjusting the bowtie around my neck.

"I think it would've looked *maith* arriving on motorcycles, personally," Eliaster muttered, gripping the steering wheel.

I tucked my chin to my chest, lowering my voice. "My name is Bond. James Bo—"

"Oh shut up!" Eliaster rolled his eyes.

I laughed, then reached over and adjusted my phone. I'd propped it up on the dashboard to function as a GPS, even though Eliaster grumbled about not using proper paper maps.

My stomach churned with nerves, but I kept repeating our plan in my head. Once we got in, I'd stay with Aileen or Cori. Be the distraction so Eliaster could sneak off and get the pathstone. I glanced out the window, watching the dark forest whip past us. I couldn't believe how dark it had gotten once it had hit late afternoon.

We came down a hill and around a curve, and the headlights flashed over an unobtrusive set of metal gate posts framing a blacktop driveway that wound away through the woods. The metal posts shimmered faintly, wrapped in some kind of glamour. Eliaster stomped the brake and turned sharply, screeching onto the pavement. I caught a quick glimpse of the symbol of a hand etched into the arch of the gate. Palm open, facing outward as if warding off something.

I swallowed. This would be fine. We'd be fine.

I fished the stone out of my pocket. It was slightly warm to the touch—warmer than it should have been from just sitting in my pocket. As Eliaster continued down the driveway, it gradually grew warmer and warmer.

"Umm, Eliaster—"

He looked over just as the stone flashed. Both of us flinched, and I yelped, throwing my free hand in front of my face. A hot spark snapped against my hand.

The car slammed to a halt.

The light died out as quickly as it had appeared, leaving faint sparkle of glamour floating around us. I blinked, trying to clear the spots from my eyes, and looked down at my hand. In my palm were a few flakes of ash, and my skin looked a little red and irritated.

"Holy crap," Eliaster muttered.

I followed his line of sight and gasped. We'd stopped on a curving hill. Below us, the trees fell away to the graceful, manicured lawn of a huge Gothic mansion. Light spilled from the windows, and old-style lamp posts lined the driveway, which circled in front of the doors and then curved off behind the house. All of it was framed against the rising backdrop of the just-visible Adirondack Mountains, black against the last streaks of red sunset.

"Holy crap," I echoed, my heart dropping into my stomach. I ran my hand through my hair. Sure, Eliaster and his family were rich, but they'd never flashed it beyond Eliaster's expensive modes of transportation or their ability to pull strings that I thought immovable. But this ... this was so far beyond my depth.

As Eliaster eased the car forward, he glanced at me out of the corner of his eye. "Ready?"

"As I'll ever be. How about you?"

Eliaster grinned, his teeth catching the moonlight that shone in through the sunroof of the car. "I'll be on my best behavior."

"That's what I'm afraid of." I sighed. *It's okay. He knows the plan. It'll be fine.*

He shrugged and started the car forward again.

I stuck my hand back in my pocket, double-checking. Shaughnessy's ring still felt cold to the touch, despite having been in my pocket since we left Missouri. I patted my wrist—my bracelet was there—and felt at my side for my knife and gun. Everything was in place.

We pulled up to the massive wooden front doors. Both

of them were heavily carved with deep-rooted, many-branched trees bordered by Celtic braids. At each corner of the door, a dragon's head joined each braid.

"Heist time, baby," I said, trying to push back my nerves.

Eliaster snorted and rolled his eyes.

A valet jogged down the steps as Eliaster and I got out of the car. Eliaster palmed something—another set of keys?—from the driver's side door and tossed the valet his remote opener and the key he kept on the same ring. We headed up the wide, shallow steps to the front door.

Two other fae in suits stood waiting for us. One's frame and face were a bit square for a fae, and the other was tall, thin, and bald. Baldy stepped forward, nodding politely to us.

"Eliaster Tyrone and Josh MacAllister," Eliaster said.

"My name is Altru." He looked back and forth between us, his ice-blue eyes piercing. Whatever he saw, we must've passed muster, because he glanced at the screen of his phone, then stepped to the side and gestured. "If you would be so kind, please, step inside."

The square fae pulled open one of the doors. I blinked, trying not to stare. That door looked massively heavy, and he'd just swung it open as if it weighed nothing more than a cheap hardware store screen. We followed Altru inside.

The first room we stepped into was richly paneled in wood, with carved cubbies set into the wall on either side of us. Some of the cubbies held neatly folded coats, others contained weapons.

Altru gestured to the cubbies. "Unfortunately, due to the nature of his work, Mr. Airgead asks that his guests enter weaponless. I'm sure you understand."

I swore under my breath and started to reach for the gun tucked under my tux jacket.

Eliaster gripped my arm and glared at Altru. "Come on," he said. "You really think I'm going to leave my stuff here? Anyone could take off with it. Furthermore, I'm not about to walk in with a bunch of unknown fae—"

So much for being polite.

"Each cubby is armed with glamour to prevent anyone other than you retrieving your belongings," Altru interrupted. "Keyed to your touch. I give you my word and the word of your host that no one will take your belongings while you remain under his hospitality."

Even I caught the caveat there. *Under his hospitality.* So if we did anything to piss off Drake Airgead, we would no longer be considered under his hospitality, which would give any front door guards the right to grab our stuff before we could get to our weapons. I glanced at Eliaster and could tell from the pinched, sour look on his face that the same thought had occurred to him. But there really wasn't any alternative. I took off my jacket and shrugged off the harness that held my gun and knife, then placed it in a cubby and slid the jacket back on.

Eliaster hadn't moved.

"Well, am I gonna have to go in alone?" I asked him.

"I don't like this," he growled.

"Yeah, neither do I. You're welcome to go sit in the car."

"I'm not your stupid valet," he snapped at me, reaching down and pulling up his pant leg. He'd exchanged his usual motorcycle boots for sleek, shiny leather boots, still tall enough to allow him to shove a couple of knives down the leg. He removed a knife from each boot and another from his side, and stowed them in the cubby under mine, then he turned toward the door.

"Just so you're aware," Altru said pleasantly, "the door is warded. Anyone who tries to smuggle in weapons will receive an extremely unpleasant shock."

Eliaster muttered in Gaelic and yanked a throwing knife out from under his sleeve, tossing it so that the point stuck into the back of the cubby where he'd shoved his other weapons. Then he straightened his jacket and jerked his head toward the door.

Altru nodded, somehow making it almost look like a formal bow, and stepped to the door. As he opened it, sure enough, I could see a faint shimmer around the doorframe. I had a brief moment of panic as I followed Eliaster over the threshold. Would the ring somehow set the thing off? I tucked my hands into my pockets and braced for the shock, but nothing happened.

Altru stepped to the side and allowed us to enter. I couldn't help it—as we walked into the room, I gasped.

If the outside of the house had been impressive, the inside was doubly so. The outside of the large room was slightly raised, and at the far end ran into a double-branched staircase that curved around to the next level. Pillars supported the lower, ten-foot ceiling on the raised portion of the room. The middle of the ceiling was at least twenty feet high, if not higher—I couldn't tell for sure because it looked like it was draped in gauze. Thousands upon thousands of tiny twinkling lights peeked through the fabric, throwing a gentle glow over the room, enhanced by the flickering lanterns hung at intervals along the walls and from long chains dangling from the ceiling. Some of the lanterns had patterning on them that cast shadows in a pattern of tree branches. The floor was a golden hardwood, flecked with tiny, branching mosaics in earthy colors of dark green, brown, red, navy blue. The walls were painted a deep, rich gray, and sparsely patterned in veins of gold, as if to mimic veins of the precious metal in a mine.

A few people sat or stood at tables and chaise lounges along the raised sides of the room, but the majority milled around on the sunken middle of the floor, where all the mosaics spiraled into one large, circular whorl. It seemed to be functioning as a dance floor. Fae waltzed slowly across it, their hair a rainbow kaleidoscope, each one's clothes fancier than the last. Delicate music played in a strange, slow melody that twined electric guitar together with pipes, gentle drums, and typical string instruments, along with something that had a weirdly tinny, picked sound. The air hung heavy with the smell of wood smoke, wine and other alcohols, perfume, and some other earthy scent—like the smell of the forest after a heavy rain—that I identified as fae.

My head spun, and I wobbled a little bit. It felt like the first time I'd seen an Underworld Market, but *more*. The glamour in the room danced along my exposed skin in a tangible way, raising the hair on my arms and neck like a mild electric shock. Glamour ghosts floated and mingled in the crowd, so that I felt like I was looking through a haze of fog. I hunched my shoulders and drew my elbows close to my body. This was more glamour than I'd ever felt in my life.

Altru brushed past us, tapping both Eliaster and me on the shoulder, and motioning for us to follow him. Eliaster glanced back at me, his eyebrows pinching together.

"You okay?" he asked in a low voice.

I rubbed my eyes and nodded. "Just feel a little fuzzy-headed."

"Your gut doing all right?"

"Oddly, yeah." I didn't even feel the slightest bit of nausea. That was weird. I wondered if the bracelet had something to do with it, just like it protected me from the glamour of the relics.

We'd made it less than a quarter way around the room, heading for the tall double staircase at the far end, when I heard a familiar voice from behind us.

"Don't worry, Altru, I've got it from here."

I spun around. Cori Airgead stood behind us, flashy as usual in a red tux, spiked boots, and fluffed Mohawk. He nodded to Eliaster and me, and then flashed a wide grin at Altru.

Altru frowned and raised an eyebrow.

"Aw, c'mon, wouldn't want Dad's special guests to be bored waiting around for him, would you?"

Altru just nodded, turned, and walked away, still heading for the stairs.

Cori's grin remained fixed in place until Altru disappeared up the stairs. "Okay," he said, motioning us toward a few chairs set close to the wall. "I bet we have less than five minutes before he shows back up saying Drake wanted you immediately." He looked between me and Eliaster. "Let me get you some drinks." He led us to a bar at one side of the room. The bartender was serving a fae couple, but as Cori slid behind the bar, he glanced over at him and nodded, hands never stopping as he mixed liquors together in a tall, clear glass.

I raised an eyebrow. He was human—the only other human I'd seen so far. As I watched him for a minute, the hair on the back of my neck prickled. His movements were swift and smooth, but there was a glazed look to his eyes, and he didn't blink nearly enough.

I glanced over at Cori.

He shrugged. "Just ... watch yourself around here, okay?"

Eliaster leaned with his back against the bar, observing the rest of the room. I let him, focusing instead on the smooth dark wood of the bar and carefully breathing in and out. In high school, I'd been around a couple of people who smoked pot, and just breathing in the secondhand smoke had made me loopy. This was similar, but instead of being lethargic, I felt jittery.

Cori handed us a couple of glasses and said in a low tone, "I went light on the alcohol for you guys."

"Appreciate it," Eliaster said.

Cori gestured around the room, pointing to various doorways set into the wall. I was careful to follow his hand motions and not look at the mesmerizing dancers in the middle of the floor.

"There's probably a few games there, if you're up for some gambling. Those over there you might want to stay away from." He snorted. "My dad provides spaces for all sorts of carnal activities at these feasts."

Eliaster's nose wrinkled. "Duly noted."

I chuckled. "Fae are all just overgrown high schoolers, you know?" As soon as the words were out of my mouth, I regretted speaking them. Holy crow, what was wrong with me? I felt like anything I thought would just fly out of my mouth with no restraints.

Eliaster gave me a worried look. "You sure you're okay?"

I coughed and made an effort to think through what I was going to say. "I think … I'm getting high off all the glamour in here."

"*What*? But …" Eliaster glanced at my wrist, but held his tongue. He looked around the room, and the fingers of his left hand twitched. "I guess there's more in here than usual." He looked over at Cori. "Your dad likes to pretend he's one of the old fae, I guess."

Cori's eyes clouded to a darker shade of blue. "My dad's family *is* old, and yeah, he's obsessed with glamour."

I remembered what Liam had told me, about Drake's experimentation with his three kids and their varying fae blood.

"You're here. Good." Aileen's voice at my side nearly made me jump out of my skin.

I turned and glanced at her. Unlike most of the women, who wore bright, eye-catching colors—if they wore much at all—she wore an all-black, lace-sleeved dress with a corset-like bodice and a sleek skirt slit to her knees. Her lips were purple-red, and her gray eyes flickered under dark eye makeup. The only bright color was her hair, which the firelight turned a deep copper-red.

Man, she looked … I stopped myself, slamming the thought to the back of my head. My inhibitions were already lower than I'd expected—the last thing I needed was the distraction of thinking how good she looked.

But man, does she look hot.

"Cori," she said in a low voice. "Gren's watching."

Cori stiffened. "Where?"

"The stairs landing." She looked at me and Eliaster, then held her hand out to me. "You want to be noticeable, right?"

I swallowed hard, glanced at Eliaster.

"You sure?" he asked quietly. "We can always switch

roles."

I shook my head. "I'm human. I'll be a better distraction." I let Aileen put her hand on my arm and forced a grin. "I'll be fine. Let's just get this done and get out of here."

My heart rate spiked as Aileen pulled me to the edge of the dance floor.

Dear Almighty, I was going to dance with the daughter of Drake Airgead. I could only hope that he didn't decide to twist my head off if he saw me.

Aileen twined her fingers into my right hand—her palm was warm against my cold skin—and carefully placed my left hand on her waist. Then we spun into place among the dancers. A chill rippled down my spine. It was not a good feeling. Every muscle in my body tensed.

We danced for a few minutes in silence. Thankfully it was a slower number. Without really seeming to, Aileen led, pulling me slowly toward the center of the dance floor until we were surrounded by other fae, quite a few of whom were taller than us. She sighed, and I could feel her relaxing.

I wished I could've done the same. Glamour swirled around the edges of my vision, making me dizzy. I actually felt like I might throw up. I blinked hard and focused on Aileen's face, watched as she gently counted under her breath, her lips moving to the time of the music as we settled into the correct rhythm.

She looked so different from most of the other fae women I'd met. I couldn't even really say *what* it was that made her different. She looked hard-edged, but there was something—a softheartedness that I only saw in quick glimpses.

She glanced up, caught me staring. Her cheeks and the tips of her ears turned a bright red.

I coughed and glanced away. "Sorry."

Aileen twisted her hand in mine, wincing. "You can relax a little bit, you know."

I glanced at our hands. Her fingers were white, as were my knuckles, and I realized I was gripping her hand really,

really hard. I forced myself to relax. "Sorry. Again."

"Are you feeling okay?"

"I'm a little off," I admitted.

"Sidhé sometimes have that effect on humans. Can I do anything to help? Some kind of glamour, maybe?"

"It won't stick."

"Oh, the bracelet." She frowned. "I'd like to try something, if I may."

"Uhh … sure."

She reached up and placed her hand over my chest. A cool, mist-like sensation brushed over my face, then dissipated. She studied my face and I cleared my throat. My turn to go red under her intense scrutiny. The warmth of her hand in mine suddenly grew blazing hot.

The song ended on a high note, and then another one started, just as slow and seductive as the first. I shrugged my shoulders, wishing they'd play something fast, something that wasn't a waltz. I gathered memories of the dreams of Larae's betrayal that still haunted me and pulled them to the forefront of my thoughts.

"You're still tense, and Gren is still watching," Aileen murmured. "He's not going to leave until you look like you're enjoying yourself."

I resisted the urge to glance upward at the balcony. Instead, I pulled Aileen a little closer to me and took in several deep breaths, willing my shoulders and arms to relax.

Her eyes twinkled, and one side of her lips curled into a little half-smile. "Most guys don't need an invitation like that."

"Yeah, I … uh … I don't have a good history with fae women. Sorry."

She laughed softly. "Honestly, that's the last thing you should be apologizing about."

I tried to chuckle, but it turned into a cough. Dang it, why was I being a bumbling idiot? Everything about her was the exact opposite of Larae. Aileen didn't ooze seduction and pleasure like Larae had—rather, her open smile and confident way of carrying herself seemed genuine.

But Gren probably wouldn't stop watching us until I looked relaxed, just as she'd said. So I blew out a deep breath and tried to smile as we swept back and forth in time with the couples around us.

My ankle hit something hard, and before I could stop myself I'd tripped backwards, dragging Aileen down with me. I twisted in midair and cracked my shoulder against the hard marble floor, but managed to keep my head from hitting as well.

Around us, the other fae gasped and yelped, pulling away. I winced and looked over at Aileen. She'd only been pulled down to her knees, but her eyes weren't on me—they were fixed on a point past me.

I turned my head.

A fae with pale skin stood over me. His jet-black hair, one single streak of turquoise cutting through his bangs, was swept over one eye. I didn't recognize him.

The fae sneered down at me, then looked at Aileen. "The human bothering you, Aileen?"

She stood, eyes flashing Airgead. "No one asked you to interfere, Dubh."

I started to roll to my feet. Dubh kicked at me, and I dropped flat, feeling the heavy boot whistle over my head. He laughed as I scooted away from him and stood.

Aileen hooked one elbow around my arm, as if she were afraid someone would try to drag me away from her. "Watch our backs. Where there's one Son of Carmen, there's always two others."

Carmen. I recognized that as the screen-name of the leader of the Lucht Leanuna, when I'd found their online message board back in May. My stomach sank. Great, the Lucht were here after all.

Two fae stepped forward from the crowd surrounding us, but didn't advance. They looked nearly identical to the one who had attacked me, except that one wore his hair tightly braided at the back of his neck, while the other had short hair and teased a lip ring with his tongue.

"This human is under Airgead protection," Aileen said, her voice raising so she could be heard over the murmurs around us.

The Son of Carmen with the lip ring scoffed loudly and said something in Gaelic that I didn't quite catch, but judging by the snickers from the other two, it couldn't have been complimentary.

Aileen ignored him and continued. "I'll let this go, but only once. Any other attacks against him, unprovoked or provoked, will be taken as an attack against the house of Airgead and the offender will be dealt with by my own hand."

I watched the two facing me as Aileen talked. Neither reacted, their expressions slack in what appeared to be casual boredom. There was something about them that seemed familiar, and it nagged at the back of my mind.

"Aww, that's sweet," one of them said. "Very cute, Aileen."

That phrase stuck in my mind. The word choice, even the inflection in the words … I felt sick. Llew. It reminded me of Llew.

A loud clap echoed through the room. I flinched. A tall, square-jawed fae stood on the stairs, slowly and deliberately clapping, his ice-blue eyes locked on me. Once he'd caught everyone's attention, he walked the final two steps down onto the ballroom floor. The crowd of dancers parted for him, giving him plenty of room as he strode up to Aileen and me.

"I see my daughter has already caught someone's eye." His voice was deep, almost rumbling, with a hint of Celtic burr to his words.

Heat flushed my face. He stopped in front of us, one side of his mouth curled into a smirk. His ice-gray eyes glittered as he stared at me. Despite the outward air of geniality, something dark and dangerous radiated from the man. My stomach knotted, and it was all I could do to stand my ground and not take a big step away from him. I shifted, straightening my jacket sleeves so he couldn't see the bracelet on my wrist.

"I—I didn't mean any offense," I stammered.

Drake waved one hand in a dismissive gesture. "Aileen, didn't I tell you that I wanted to see VIP guests as soon as possible?"

There was nothing harsh about her name from his tongue, but his gray eyes glittered, turning cold and hard, unlike Aileen's own warm-toned gray eyes. Her hand grew tense in mine, and her body stiffened.

"Sorry, da," she said softly. "I just … I thought … you always tell me to make sure everyone's entertained."

Crap, she was absolutely terrified of this man.

Drake waved his hand in a dismissive gesture. "Josh MacAllister. It's very nice to meet you." He looked me up and down, cold, calculating. His eyes rested on Aileen's and my clasped hands.

"Nice to meet you too, sir."

"If I could drag you away from your charming companion for a few minutes." He smiled.

No, no, no. I was just supposed to be a distraction. I resisted the urge to look through the crowd of fae, to seek out Eliaster for rescue.

I squared my shoulders, forced my voice to remain steady. "Ready when you are." I could do this. It wasn't the plan—I wouldn't be with Aileen—but I could still be a distraction. Could still play my part.

"Good. Come along." He put his arm around my shoulders and steered me away from Aileen. Her fingers gave mine a quick squeeze.

I squeezed back and released her hand, praying quietly under my breath. I just hoped this worked out.

Chapter 31

ELIASTER

I watched Josh and Aileen spin across the dance floor, worrying gnawing at the back of my mind. I took a small sip from my drink. I hated this. Hating using Josh as, essentially, bait. It was probably one of the stupidest ideas we'd ever come up with.

But it was working.

Heads turned as Josh and Aileen danced, and I could see a few fae on the edges of the dance floor elbowing each other. An Unseelie and an obviously free-minded human, dancing together. It was scandalous on the level of Romeo and Juliet.

I allowed myself a small grin, then turned to Cori. "You'll stay out here, right?"

Cori's gaze darting between me and Josh. "I'll keep an eye on him, don't worry."

"If he gets hurt, I'm taking it out of your hide."

Cori nodded.

He really meant it. I turned and wandered off toward the back wall, pausing every now and then to look around as if in awe. As I did, I scanned the room, looking for people who might be watching me. I spotted Gren standing on the stairs landing, arms crossed, eyes on Josh and Aileen.

So far, Josh's idea of distraction seemed to be working. I took a slow breath, then pushed my glamour to the forefront of my mind. I could feel the slight warmth of my tattoos beginning to glow. An answering warmth bloomed on my chest, where Henry's pendant rested just below my cross necklace. As long as Henry hadn't been lying about the pendant allowing him access to all parts of the house, I'd be fine.

Yeah, trust a turncoat curator. Seems smart.

I turned so that my body mostly blocked my arm as I ran my hand along the wall, where Cori had pointed. Cool, smooth marble slid beneath my fingertips, and then I staggered a bit as my hand dipped through an illusion into a hallway. I glanced quickly around the room again, then backed into the wall, feeling the glamour around me, slick and clinging like a fine mist.

When I blinked again, I was standing in a dark hallway. A shimmering mist blocked off the entryway, mimicking the pattern of marble on the walls. If I squinted, I could see beyond it into the ballroom, where the fae still danced and the music still played.

It worked. I sighed.

I scanned the dimly lit hallway. There was only one doorway, set on the right-hand wall about ten feet from the hallway entrance. I pulled leather gloves from my pocket, slipped them on, then stepped up and pressed my hand flat against the door's surface, listening. No sounds came from within.

I gently pushed it open. At the motion, light flared up in the room. I glanced at the row of lantern-like sconces on the walls on either side of the door as I let the door swing shut behind me.

Drake's office was richly paneled in dark wood. Weirdly, the walls were bare, except for the bookshelf to the left of the door that was stacked with neat, orderly books of all kinds, though most of them looked old. I stepped up to the shelf and ran my finger across some of the spines. Most of the titles had to do with curses, the occult, or magic. I snorted. "Power monger."

Did Drake really think that this kind of thing would help him in his quest for stronger glamour? And why did he want more anyway? From what Aileen said, Drake had to be one of the more powerful fae in America, at least.

I quickly riffled through some of the papers stacked on his desk around a central workspace on the hard wood surface. Business receipts, orders, inventory—apparently the guy didn't believe in using electronics for any part of his business. I found an old-style ledger and flipped it open, scanning through the pages. Nothing caught my eye.

I growled in frustration. Josh would be better at this kind of thing than me. I slapped the ledger shut and moved back from the desk, rolling up the edge of the rug on the floor. I could just make out the square cut into the flooring. I pried it up and set the square aside.

The hidden safe was set into the floor. I swore again, reaching down to jiggle the knob. What had Josh said about cracking safes? I closed my eyes and tried to recall the crash course he'd given me, based on his research and the type of safe Aileen thought Airgead had.

Which way did the handle turn? I jiggled it again. It clicked a little going counterclockwise, but barely moved if I tried to turn it clockwise. I made a fist and slammed the heel of my hand into the safe just above the digital display, then quickly wrenched the knob counterclockwise.

Nothing.

"Damnaigh." I hit the safe again and turned the knob.

Once again, the safe remained firmly closed.

I leaned back on my heels for a second and took a deep breath. If this whole plan failed because I couldn't get the safe open, they were screwed. The Lucht would get the pathstone. The whole *world* would be screwed if that happened.

I slammed my fist into the safe again and jerked the knob counterclockwise.

The locked clicked, and the door popped open.

I huffed out a laugh. "Thank you, Almighty," I whispered, flipping open the safe. It only took a moment of digging to unearth the wooden box Aileen had described. I opened it and dumped the stone out into my gloved hand.

My heart skipped a beat, seeing the white palm-sized stone. After years of searching, I was finally holding one of the relics Iain and Emily had died for. I pressed my lips together. Swallowed the lump forming in my throat.

"Eliaster?"

My pulse sped and I spun around, stuffing the stone into my jacket pocket.

Banshee.

Crap.

She stood in the doorway, wearing her usual dark clothes. I couldn't see any weapons on her, but with the party going on, she would have to be discreet. She took one step forward, mouth open, her eyes darting around the room, taking in the disturbed papers on the desk, the open safe.

"So you're working for Airgead now. Can't say I'm surprised." I smirked.

Her eyes locked on me, and her lips pressed into a thin line. "Hand it over." She held out her free hand.

I kept my hands to my sides.

"Don't make me shoot you, Eliaster."

"Will you?" I snapped back, stepping up to her. "Will you shoot me, Banshee? I've gotten in your sights plenty of times before now, and you've made that threat plenty of times before. Somehow I doubt this is the night you'll make good on it."

Her voice trembled. "You don't want to do this. If you make an enemy of Drake Airgead—"

I snorted, started to walk past her.

She grabbed my shoulder.

I spun, aiming my elbow at her midsection.

Banshee twisted to the side. Her boot crunched into the back of my leg. I grunted and stumbled to my right knee. I kicked my left leg out, trying to sweep her feet out from under her. "Banshee, I don't want to hurt—"

Her foot cracked into the side of my head.

I lost my grip on the stone, and a second later I hit the ground, the room spinning around me. I blinked hard, was barely able to focus on Banshee's face. She planted her knee in my gut, pressing her hands against my shoulders, and stared down at me for a moment, breathing heavily.

Then she swore. "How'd you get this?" She pulled Henry's pendant from under my shirt. Yanked hard enough to snap the chain. She shoved it into her pocket, then grabbed the pathstone from where it had fallen on the ground.

I growled and scrambled up. "Give that back."

"I'm sorry. I can't."

"Banshee—"

"Do you know what Drake Airgead would do to me if he found out you'd stolen this?" she snapped. "He knows we're friends, Eliaster. He'll take this out on me!"

"And are you aware of who he'll sell it to?" I flung my hand outward. Warmth skittered along my skin, gathering along my left forearm. Had she even *thought* about this? "Do you *want* Fear Doirich to rise from the shell of Tir Ni-all and begin slaying and enslaving us all again? Do you want this world broken and destroyed like Tir Ni-all?"

Banshee hesitated, just enough. That was all I needed.

I lunged forward, closing my hand around her wrist and twisting it. The stone dropped from her fingers and I scooped it up. I looked up at Banshee's face. Her eyes were wide with surprise.

Then she wrenched her wrist hard and kneed me in the gut.

I staggered to the side, gasping. Banshee's fist grazed the side of my face. I stumbled back, caught her next blow, and shoved her hard against the wall. Then I turned and ran for the entryway.

Banshee hit me low in the back, catapulting me through the glamour. A loud, shrill chime echoed over my head as we hit the ground and rolled, slamming into the legs of several people. I heard screams as I stood. Banshee was already stomping back toward me. Another chime sounded, louder than the first.

Well, at least the noise would alert Josh. I stepped my right foot back, tightened my grip on the stone, and raised my fists.

Despite all our planning, looked like we were going to have to fight our way out after all. Josh was right—it was just like a heist movie.

Chapter 32

JOSH

As we headed up the stairs, Drake smiled and nodded to the fae we passed. I tried to keep relaxed, tried to walk naturally, even though every nerve in my body screamed at me to run. My stomach rolled, and not just from nerves—this guy had my fight or flight instinct doing pinwheels.

"So," he murmured in my ear. "I'd be interested in knowing how a human got hold of one of my invitations."

I let my smile widen a little as I pulled away from him. "Aw, c'mon, Drake, you don't expect me to reveal my sources just like that, do you? Surely you can respect the secrecy that comes with this kind of business."

Drake raised his chin slightly, eyes narrowing. "Go on."

I shrugged. "I was just given the invitation and told that you might have a few ... items I'd be interested in acquiring."

Drake smiled thinly. "You'll have to be more specific than that. I have many items that may be of interest or all sorts of people."

Breathe. Keep breathing. Keep acting. "This would be one of the more rare things you've found, potentially the only one of its kind. One that could potentially open worlds of possibility."

Something flashed in Drake's eyes. "Ah." He stepped

back from me, and his smile widened. "I'm sorry, but I very much doubt you could afford the asking price for such a thing."

Panic thrummed through me. "I—I might not be able to, but my employers certainly would."

"I thought you said you were a free man."

"Free body and soul, but I have certain ... skills ... that are in high demand." My palms were sweating. I pushed my hands into my pockets.

Drake looked me over again, and I could practically see him calculating, reassessing. "Who are your employers?"

"Cormac and Eliaster Tyrone."

I saw a flash of recognition in his eyes when I said Eliaster's name.

A second later, his smile widened. I liked the look on him even less than the small, smirk he'd first worn. "Of course," he said. "Please, come this way."

The sudden shift in attitude actually genuinely scared me. I honestly hadn't expected that to work. How did he know the Tyrones, and especially Eliaster, by name? Why did that make such a big difference?

He motioned, and Altru walked ahead of us by several paces. He reached for a spot on the wall, and a door, so seamless as to be practically invisible, swung open. Drake went inside. I looked over my shoulder, scanned the crowd. No Eliaster. Hopefully he'd managed to slip away unseen.

I stepped into the room. A large stone fireplace occupied a good portion of the back wall, with a bar to one side and multiple leather chairs arranged around a coffee table. Oversized bookshelves dominated the windowless walls. Unlike the library back home, these bookshelves were neat, orderly, each leather bound book precise and straight.

"Please, sit." Drake motioned to one of the chairs. Without asking, he walked over to the bar and began pouring a couple of drinks.

I turned to glance over my shoulder. Altru stood behind me, close enough to make me jump. The door was already closed. I hadn't heard it close. Sweat broke along my forehead and back, and I shrugged, adjusting my jacket. Why did I suddenly feel like I was trapped in here? I really wished Eliaster were here. I swallowed and walked over to the chair that Drake had indicated, sitting down. It made my skin itch to be sitting with my back to the door, but I tried to shrug the feeling off. It wasn't like Drake would kill me. I was a potential customer. He had more to gain by not harming me.

Yeah, I didn't believe my little personal pep talk for a second. I licked my lips as I sat down, flexed my hands. Tried to remind myself that it was okay if I screwed this up. Aileen had said her father would never let a pathstone go to a Seelie buyer. So now, I just had to make him believe that I trusted his integrity enough to seriously negotiate with him.

Drake came over and handed me a glass of something golden brown, then sat in the chair opposite. "Now that we're in private, do you mind speaking plainly? What relic is it exactly that you're hunting down for the Tyrones?"

"A pathstone," I quietly.

Drake leaned back in his chair and half-closed his eyes. "That's fascinating. Not generally the kind of thing I advertise. I wonder how you came upon that piece of information."

"Am I wrong?" I asked.

Drake held his glass up to the light, spun it slowly so that the liquor sparkled. "No. No, you aren't wrong. It's just … well, this should make things interesting." He looked over at his bodyguard. "Altru, would you please go fetch our other guests? Thank you."

Other guests? I tried not to stiffen up as I thought about that. As far as I knew, there weren't that many other people who knew about the pathstones.

Altru was gone barely a minute before the door creaked back open, He stepped to the side, holding it as two fae walked into the room. My stomach dropped to my toes, and I had to fight the urge to scramble out of my chair and get it between me and them.

Blodheyr didn't notice me. His blue eyes settled right on Drake. Larae, however, did see me. Her eyes widened a fraction, then narrowed even as her lips bloomed into a smile that was mocking yet somehow oozing seduction.

Crap. Larae would never believe the Tyrones had let me come here on my own.

"Well, Josh MacAllister. Fancy meeting you here." As Larae said my name, Blodheyr stiffened, and his attention snapped to me.

A slow smile crept across his thin, wide lips. "Joshua. So nice to see you again." He paused, then added, "Shame about Marc."

I set my glass down on the side table by my chair, because if I held onto it, I'd end up throwing it in that self-satisfied Unseelie's face. Gah. I *hated* it when fae smiled. I glared at him.

Drake stepped into the middle of the room, rubbing his hands together. "Would either of you care for a drink?"

Blodheyr nodded. "Yes, please. I have a certain mix in mind—here, let me show you."

They walked over to the bar.

I casually put my hand in my pocket and slid the ring into place on my index finger. It was probably a bad idea, but this whole situation was rapidly turning into a choose-your-own-adventure of bad ideas.

As I spun the ring so that the gem faced my palm, I closed my eyes and took a deep breath, trying to steady myself. Blodheyr's voice pulled at me, and memories flashed in the edge of my vision—memories I'd rather forget. I had to keep hold of myself, had to keep the flashbacks at bay. *Not here, not now.*

Silk rustled, and something brushed my leg. I opened my eyes. Larae had sat on the arm of my chair, legs crossed, one sandal-clad foot brushing against my leg. She smiled down at me, bright violet eyes almost glowing against the backdrop of pale skin and dark, turquoise-streaked hair.

I shoved myself back, my heart nearly bursting from my

chest. Cold shivers raked down my spine, and the scar on my wrist sent a hot throb of pain into my fingers. I slowly clenched and released that hand, trying to work the arthritic feeling from my knuckles.

"It *is* good to see you again, Josh," Larae said quietly. "Despite the fact that we're on opposing sides. I worry about you."

"Don't," I snapped. "I can take care of myself."

She put her hand on my arm. "But can you?"

I stared at her, brain whirling. What kind of game was she playing? Her eyes glimmered, and for a split second, I almost believed. Almost thought, *maybe she does care.* Almost smiled.

Then I saw the glamour weaving light around her face, softening the edges of her smile, of her eyes. I blinked, and the image popped. Her smile almost had a predatory edge to it now. I reached out, fumbling for my drink. My hands wouldn't stop trembling as I took a sip, the liquid burning down my throat. Fine, let her see. She already knew I was afraid. Maybe I could use it against her.

"Where's Eliaster?" she asked.

"None of your business." I kicked her foot away from my leg.

She nearly fell off the chair arm.

"Larae, leave him alone," Blodheyr muttered. "You've had your fun."

Larae's stare shot daggers at me as she got up and moved to the other side of the room.

I smiled and said loudly, "Hey Drake, when are we gonna get to the proceedings? I'm getting bored."

Blodheyr turned from the bar, his glare matching Larae's.

That's right. Underestimate me all you want, old man. I'm not cowering any longer.

Drake chuckled and took his seat. He waved for Blodheyr and Larae to sit. "Well, of course. By all means, let us get to business."

He gave Larae and Blodheyr a moment to get settled before continuing.

"I don't think there's any point in being secretive any longer. You're all looking for pathstones." He grinned, propping his elbows on the arms of his chair, and clasped his hands under his chin. "The epic struggle of the ages, Seelie and Unseelie, each battling for dominance over the long-hidden paths. Who will bring Tir Ni-all back to us?"

"May I remind you which Court you've sworn loyalty to, Airgead," Blodheyr said drily.

"But that doesn't mean I can't enjoy myself!" Drake leaned back. He picked up his drink, then waved it back and forth between the sides of the room. "Who wants to open the bidding?"

I swallowed, recalling Aileen's warning that her father wouldn't be looking for money. For a relic this rare, this powerful, he wouldn't be asking for cold, hard cash. He'd be asking for something else. A trade in relics? A favor? I shuddered at the idea of owing Drake Airgead a favor. Either way, there really wasn't a lot of good I could do here.

Dang it, Eliaster, hurry.

"Perhaps this." Larae leaned forward and held out a small, clear crystal, about the size of a marble and in the shape of a teardrop. Something smoky swirled inside, but from where I sat, I couldn't quite make out what.

Drake raised his eyebrows. "I feel like I should be insulted that you began the bidding so low. A memory? What would I do with that?"

"I'll remind you who and what I am," Larae said. "I remember things you have no knowledge of, Drake. I could make another, with a memory of your choosing. What do you want to know? A secret of glamour? An old way of the sidhé that will grow your power?"

Drake laughed. "I'm pretty sure I have that well under control, so I'll decline." He looked over at me. "Do you have anything to offer, Mr. MacAllister?"

I froze, my brain spinning like a hamster wheel. What

did I have that—

An idea hit like a snowball between the eyes, and I blurted it out before I had second thoughts. "Information."

"Hmm. An interesting choice as well. Please, elaborate."

"You asked me earlier how I'd gotten my hands on an invitation. I could tell you that. How we found you. How we figured out that you knew where a pathstone was." I could so easily spin this. Slide suspicion away from Aileen and Cori. Shaughnessy would probably suffer for it, but I was having a really hard time feeling sorry for him.

He snorted. "Don't insult me. I know you've spoken to Galen Shaughnessy and Henry Blair. One of them had to have told you. It's what I get for trusting idiots."

"Yeah, yeah, and I know, you must think I'm a special kind of stupid," I shot back. "But do you know where Henry Blair is? How about Shaughnessy?"

Drake stilled, and his eyes glittered. "You'd offer me their locations in exchange for the pathstone. You do realize that I'm not likely to welcome them with open arms?"

I shrugged, tried not to feel sick. Would he actually take the offer? I couldn't believe it. That had been a shot in the dark.

Drake sipped his drink. "Interesting move from someone allied with the Seelie. Not at all what I'd expected, so points for that."

I shot a smirk at Larae. She stared at me, hands clenched, eyes dark purple. Good. Let her get pissed. Apparently the cocky act was getting on her nerves. I'd have to remember that.

Before anyone could speak again, a loud chime echoed through the room. I jumped. Drake and Altru both froze. When a louder, more insistent chime sounded, they both darted up from their chairs and ran for the door.

Eliaster. I got up and started to follow them.

Larae grabbed my arm. "Where do you think you're going?"

Crap, I don't have time for this. I spun around. Her eyes

twinkled, and she had a cruel smile on her lips. My heart sank. *She knows we're up to something.*

I didn't even think—I reached up and placed my right hand over her hand on my arm. I felt the gem come in contact with her skin and mentally reached out. *Obey.* The room pulsed, and phantom glowing lights flickered into the space around me. Glowing green vines twined around my arm, trapping her hand underneath mine. They snaked up her arm and shoulder and dug into her neck. Larae's eyes flashed an unnatural, poison-green for a split second, and her hand went limp.

Oh my gosh. It worked. I blinked again, and the vines and flashing lights vanished. Faint traces of mist swirled around our clenched hands. I pulled Larae's hand from my arm and gripped her wrist tightly.

"What have you done to her?" Blodheyr snarled, standing from his chair.

I glanced over at the older fae. His hands were clenched—no sign of a weapon, but I couldn't be too careful. I pushed Larae between me and Blodheyr and wrapped my arm around her neck. She wasn't resisting me, but her movements were stiff and clumsy. I got the feeling that I only had tenuous control and that if my concentration slipped for even a second, her mind would be her own again.

But for now, I was in control of the situation, and it felt … good. I could feel Larae's pulse against my arm, and for a split second, I was tempted to squeeze just a little harder. Guilt and disgust washed over me. After this, I was going to destroy this stupid relic.

I raised my hand toward Blodheyr so he could see the ring on my finger. "Stay back and let me leave in peace."

His thin lips twisted into a sneer. "Do you think you're some hero of old, able to use our relics, boy?"

His choice of words struck me. Humans had never been able to use relics—had they? I pushed the thought away. Not the time to think about it. I backed up, out the door and across the open hallway to the stairs, dragging Larae with me. Drake stood at the top of the stairs, fists clenched by his sides, and panicked shouts and yells echoed from downstairs. I got close enough to the railing to see what was going on.

The entire crowd had pushed to one side of the foyer, staying well out of the way of the fight below. Banshee and Eliaster traded blows back and forth, while Aileen and Cori stood to either side, holding off the three Sons of Carmen with knives and shouted threats.

Out of the corner of my eye, I saw Drake turn, and his eyes widened at the sight of me and Larae. I swore and shoved Larae at him. They tumbled to the side of the balcony, and I dashed down the staircase as fast as I dared.

"Eliaster!" I yelled, skidding onto the marble floor and scrambling toward him.

Eliaster glanced at me. Mistake. Banshee lunged and snapped her arm around his throat, dragging him to his knees. Her free hand went for his jacket pocket.

Eliaster elbowed her, grabbed something from his pocket, and threw it toward me. "Catch!" he yelled.

I snatched the smooth, polished piece of white granite from the air. As soon as my fingers closed around it, as soon as it came into contact with the ring, a massive concussion slammed into my chest. I flew backward and rolled, coming to a stop when I hit the stairs.

I half sat up, blinked, shook my head. My vision swam, and my ears rang like I'd been in the center of an explosion. I slowly opened my hand, feeling like my fingers had been glued together, stiff and unwieldy. The blue gemstone on the ring had cracked, one of the pieces missing. The pathstone lay in my palm, untouched.

Voices filtered through my brain. I rolled to my side, tried to push myself up. The world rolled with me and dumped me onto my back again.

"Josh!" Aileen's voice sounded as if it were underwater.

I turned my head toward her in time to see a black tendril of glamour snake forward, throwing her to the ground. Where was Eliaster? Cori? I couldn't hear them anymore. I rolled up to my hands and knees and tried to push myself to my feet.

Someone kicked me in the back of the legs. I pitched forward. My hands slipped on the slick floor, and my forehead cracked against the stone floor. The world went black.

Chapter 33

ELIASTER

I kicked, feeling Banshee's arm around my neck tighten. Black spots swam in my vision.

"Why'd you have to show up here?" she hissed in my ear. "Of all people, I didn't expect *you* to be stupid enough to try to steal from Drake Airgead."

I reached back. Sure enough, she was leaning close enough that I could get hold of her hair. I dug my fingers into the strands closest to the nape of her neck and yanked as hard as I could. Banshee screamed and staggered, loosening her hold just enough for me to wrench free.

A deep *whumph* concussed the room. I looked up and saw Josh go flying, hit the ground, and roll. My stomach lurched. What had hit him? I dashed forward, and out of the corner of my eye saw Aileen do the same, yelling Josh's name.

"Hold!" Drake Airgead's voice rang out across the room.

I heard a slithering rush across the floor. I looked down in time to see a flame of glamour whip around one of my ankles. I crashed to the ground, kicked and scrambled upright before the glamour could latch onto the rest of my body. It enveloped both legs to the knee and with a crackling sound, crystalized. Instantly, a dry chill seeped through my pant legs. I reached down and pressed a hand against the substance.

Ice.

I looked up, panic nearly making me sick. Aileen was on her knees just a few feet from Josh, clawing at black glamour wrapped around her throat.

Black. That was Larae's. I looked toward the stairs. Sure enough, there she stood, halfway down the stairs. A thick thread of glamour wrapped her hand and streaming down toward Aileen. Where was Cori? I looked around and spotted him off to the side, two of the fae who had attacked them pinning his arms behind his back.

Crap. Both of our allies were down.

I looked back to Josh. He was slowly getting up, shaking his head as if he'd been stunned. What had happened to him?

Altru kicked Josh in the legs, sending him tumbling forward. Josh's head cracked into the stone floor and his body went limp.

"No!" I shouted, trying to lurch forward. The ice held my feet fast.

Drake looked at me, eyes darkening.

"Don't worry, sir," Banshee said from behind me. "I'll deal with him."

I flinched as her gun pressed into the back of my head. Clenched my hands into fists. "Banshee, don't."

"Stay quiet," she hissed, her voice cracking. "Just, *please*, Eliaster, stay quiet before he kills you."

Drake clasped his hands behind his back, looked at the remaining crowd of fae who had all stepped as far away from the conflict as they could. I could tell some of them had fled as soon as the fighting had started, but there were still a good twenty to thirty people in the room.

"Leave," Drake snapped at them.

Without a word, they all obeyed. As the fae hurried out the door, I kept my eyes on Josh. He was still breathing, thank the Almighty. It tore at me that I couldn't break free of the glamoured ice binding me in place and go to my friend.

The glamoured mist swirled around us all, but it never actually touched Josh's body. It skimmed around his legs and torso, giving him an eerie halo.

As the last few fae left, Altru walked up to the front doors and pushed them shut. Then he stepped back, grabbed Josh by the collar, and hauled him up to his knees.

Pieces of the ring Josh had worn clinked to the floor, along with the stone. Altru glanced up at Drake.

Drake nodded, eyes as dark as chips of ice.

Altru slapped Josh.

Josh gasped in shock and jerked upright, hands clawing at Altru's arm. Before he really had time to recover, Altru slapped him again. Josh's head snapped to the side, and he went limp again, but his eyes were still open.

Altru hit him three more times, the sound echoing in the eerily-quiet ballroom. I snarled and wrenched my feet again, nearly toppling over. I wanted nothing more than to close my hands around the bastard's throat.

Josh collapsed on the ground, and Altru stepped forward, raising his hand again.

"That's enough!" Aileen suddenly yelled. She tore free of the black glamour around her and ran forward, pushing between Josh and Altru. She reached back, gripping Josh's arm.

Altru looked up at Drake again. In the respite, Josh turned his head to the side, choking and gagging. He spit out a wad of blood and mucus.

The muscles in Drake's face twitched. "You dare to betray me like this, and now you're asking me to show him—to show a *human*—mercy?" he snarled at his daughter.

"Josh isn't alone in this," I said, digging my fingernails into my palms. "Take on someone your own size, Airgead."

"Shut it!" Josh snapped, his voice thick.

Drake glanced over at him. My blood turned to ice. The Unseelie's eyes had gone a dull, flat gray. Drake Airgead smirked and raised his hand, glamour coalescing around it. "So the human did have a handler. Figures. Let me guess, one of Tyrone's lackeys?"

"Better than that, sir," Larae said from beside Drake.
"That's Eliaster Tyrone himself."

A sneer curled Drake's lips. "So Cormac Tyrone sent his
own whelp to steal from me. Bold move. Too bad he's going
to lose his only living heir tonight."

I squeezed my fists tight, feeling as sick as if he'd
punched me in the gut. Out of the corner of my eye, I could
see a faint glow rising from my left arm.

"Get out of the way, Aileen," Drake said.

Aileen's eyes flared, but she said nothing.

"Gren. Control your sister." Drake shot a glance at his
youngest son. "She's obviously not thinking clearly."

Gren's jaw clenched, and he stepped forward. Aileen
balled her fists and struck at him, but he caught her wrists
and dragged her out of the way. She screamed and kicked,
but he quickly spun her around, trapping her back against his
chest and pinning her arms crossed over her own chest. He
leaned forward, speaking quietly in her ear. Tears tracked
from the corners of her eyes and trickled down her chin.

I glanced up the stairs. Larae and Blodheyr stood at the
top of the steps. Black flames roiled around Larae's hands,
but she stayed still, her flat purple eyes fixed on Josh.

Altru grabbed the back of Josh's jacket and jerked him
onto his knees again. Josh glared at Drake as the fae walked
down the steps and stood in front of him.

"Maybe I'll squeeze your neck until your head pops off,"
Drake said. "Or maybe your heart. That sounds more
satisfying. How's that sound, Eliaster?"

I snarled. My entire left arm felt like it was burning now,
the glow from the tattoos so bright that it was shining
through my sleeve. I lowered my left hand, rested it against
my leg. My fingers just reached a shard of ice that was
digging into my thigh.

Josh shifted slightly, and something glinted at the edge
of his jacket sleeve. A knife? Where'd he get a knife? He shot
a sideways glance at me.

Aileen. She'd passed him the knife somehow.

"Sir, look out!" Altru shouted.

Josh shot to his feet with a yell, the knife in his hand flicking out at Altru.

I closed my eyes and imagined my glamour flaring. Imagined my fingers pressed against the screen of a computer. Stoked the fire in my chest, my rage and fear, and imagined channeling it into a burst of glamour that flowed through my tattoos, down my fingers, and into the ice, blasting it apart.

Something cracked against my leg, and pain raced through my hand. As if I'd slammed my fist against the marble floor. The ice around my legs shattered into glamour mist.

I swiveled to face Banshee, flexing my hands, ready to knock the gun away. Her eyes widened and she took a step back. Then she lowered the gun and looked away.

She'd given me a chance.

I laughed and dashed forward.

Josh and Altru were locked in combat, Josh's knife flickering as he struck over and over at the tall bodyguard. Altru dodged from side to side, arms bleeding from a few minor gashes. I sprinted for them, slammed my shoulder into Altru.

Altru staggered forward.

I looked up, scanning the room for Blodheyr and Larae. Where had they gone ...? Something moved in the corner of my vision. Drake flung his hand forward, glamour flaring out at me. I ducked, felt it brush my side and slice like a razor. Pain knocked me to my knees. I gasped and clamped my hand to my ribs. It came away bloody.

Drake lashed out again, too fast for me to scramble away. Josh ducked in front of me, and the fire broke in a useless spray against him.

"What are you?" Drake snarled.

"What? Not so useless after all, am I?" Josh said, grinning.

The two stared at each other. I could practically hear Drake's teeth grinding together.

To the side, Gren released Aileen and reached into his pocket. Aileen's eyes widened, and she spun to me.

"Close your—"

Suddenly light exploded over the room. An enormous wash of glamour burned over my skin as it picked me up and threw me to the floor like a rag doll. I heard panicked screams, surprised shouts, but the entire world was a blaze of dancing, pure color.

Then it was gone, leaving me in darkness. My ears rang and my head spun. I rubbed at my eyes, but all I could see were spots.

Someone grasped my arm. "Up! Eliaster, c'mon! Aileen, Cori, run!" Josh shouted.

I staggered, let Josh drag me to the edge of the room. My vision returned enough, and I looked over my shoulder, blinking hard.

Swirls of yellow-green glamour spun off Gren Airgead's arms and shoulders as he walked after us, face set into hard, grim lines. Behind him, Altru, Drake, Blodheyr, and Larae all lay on the floor, unmoving.

I stared at Gren in shock. He had done that? Had he killed them?

We pushed through the foyer and into the night air. The chill slapped me to full alertness, and I shook my head. It throbbed. My entire body ached from being tossed around like a toy.

Gren slammed the door behind him and leaned on it.

"Gren? You okay?" Aileen asked tentatively.

I noticed that a half-dozen pocket watches hung out of Gren's pockets on short chains, their lids hanging open.

"Gren?" Cori reached out, touched his brother's shoulder.

Gren shrugged away. "I just used up an entire month's worth of glamour, okay? Give me a minute." He took a few more deep breaths. "And what was that about, taking his side?" He jerked his head at Josh.

Aileen straightened her shoulders. "Cori and I are leaving. We asked Josh for help."

Something like pain flickered over Gren's face. "And you didn't ask me?"

Aileen bit her lip. "You—we didn't know—" She looked over at Cori.

"We thought you were with Drake," Cori whispered. "The few times we even tried to bring it up, you shut us down. We thought you wanted to stay."

"Of course I did!" Gren snapped. "Because your plans were all idiotic. I tried to tell you that!"

"So why'd you do that?" I asked, nodding to the door.

Gren shot me a disgusted look. "Because after what they just did? It was the only solution I could live with."

"Well, now that you did that—" Josh shrugged and glanced at me. "I mean, I don't think another fugitive would make all that much of a difference at this point."

"Yeah, probably not," I said.

Gren nodded and stepped forward, holding his hand out to Josh. Josh grasped it.

Quick as a flash, Gren's other hand slammed into Josh's stomach. Josh gasped and dropped to his knees. Gren spun around him, wrenching Josh's arm behind his back, using it to drag Josh up to his feet. My stomach wrenched as Josh screamed in pain, and I started forward, balling my fists.

"Gren!" Aileen yelled. "What the hell are you doing?"

Gren locked eyes with me and laid the flat of a blade against Josh's throat. "Come closer," he snarled, "and I will slice him open, Eliaster. You know I will."

I met his eyes and believed him. I'd do the same if I felt cornered—had done the same. I stopped, held my hands up, palms open toward Gren. "Don't," I said, and hated the way my voice shook.

"I don't want to." Gren let go of Josh's arm. "Give me the stone."

The knife bobbed against his throat as Josh swallowed and nodded. "It's in my right hand jacket pocket. You want to get it, or me?"

"Gren, why are you doing this?" Cori demanded.

"What's wrong with you? I thought—"

Gren dug into Josh's pocket. He looked over at his siblings, pain creasing the corners of his lips and eyes. "I'm sorry, but we're not. We've never been. I can't live like this."

He kicked Josh in the back. Josh staggered forward, slamming into Cori. The kick was powerful enough to knock them both to the ground. Gren turned and ran.

I snatched Josh's gun from the ground and leveled it at Gren's back.

"No!" Aileen grabbed my wrist.

I gritted my teeth and let her force my arm down. I couldn't have shot Gren anyway. But I glanced over at Josh. "Please tell me that was the fake and not the real thing."

Josh got up, wincing and holding his shoulder. He looked over at Aileen. "You got it, right?"

She smiled and tossed him the stone.

I tried not to laugh. So they had found time to switch it. I handed the pistol back to Josh, the tension in my tense muscles fading. "C'mon. Let's get moving before everyone inside wakes up."

Chapter 34

JOSH

We couldn't all fit into Eliaster's car, so with a nod that said he knew I could handle it, we split up. Cori slid into the passenger seat of the supercar with Eliaster, and I followed Aileen to the garage, where she unlocked the doors of a dark blue, squarish Bentley.

I scrambled in. We were quiet as she accelerated after Eliaster. As we approached the gate, I gripped the armrest—would we have a problem here?

"Relax. This thing is only glamoured to deal with people trying to enter."

Sure enough, both cars passed through without a hitch. I let myself sag back against the seat and breathed out a deep sigh. Then I chuckled. The sound came out a bit distorted.

Aileen bit her lower lip, but a laugh escaped anyway. She rubbed her hand against her face, smudging mascara under her eyes. "I can't believe we pulled that off."

I couldn't either. I rubbed my jaw and uncurled my fingers from the stone. My blood left smears on the white surface. I stiffened, bracing for the flashback. The motion set jabs of pain throughout my body.

Aileen's hand closed around my wrist. "You okay?"

I glanced at her, startled. She didn't look at me. Her eyes

were on the road. I looked down at the stone again. Whether my pain and Aileen had sufficiently distracted me, or if was something else, the flashback didn't hit.

I was okay.

"What comes next?" she asked quietly.

"What d'ya mean?"

"What do you plan to do with the stone, now that you got one away from the Lucht?"

"Not sure. I don't think Eliaster ever thought that far ahead. But Roe will know what to do with it more than us."

Aileen smiled, risking a quick glance at me. Her amber eyes sparkled in the dim light of the car's dashboard. "Well, whatever happens, I'm glad we could help. And … I'm glad you took a chance on us, Josh."

I shifted my arm so that instead of holding my wrist, her fingers rested in my palm. I glanced up at her. She didn't look over at me this time, but a faint touch of a smile teased at the corner of her lips. I squeezed her hand. A frisson of energy, smaller this time, ran through my my hand and arm, as if I was touching a live electrical wire. "Me too."

She pulled her hand away, placing it on the wheel. Had she felt it this time too? I studied her face, but there was nothing to indicate she'd felt anything weird.

I closed my eyes and relaxed back into the seat. We'd done it. We'd taken a pathstone right from under the Lucht Leanuna's noses. If Larae, Blodheyr, and Llew hadn't been angry enough at us before, this would definitely paint targets on our backs. Hopefully we'd find a safe place for the stone. And hopefully we wouldn't get in trouble with anyone else.

But honestly? At the moment, it didn't matter. For once, it just felt really good to win.

Epilogue

JOSH

One Week Later…

I stood on the porch of the small house, shifting the weight of the box of books on my hip as I struggled to knock at the front door.

Eliaster snorted and pushed me to the side. "You're worse than a colt. Let me." He rapped on the doorframe.

A woman's voice called, "Just a second!" Footsteps rushed towards us, and a minute later the door opened and Patricia smiled out at us, her freckled face framed by wild, dark curls. She grinned and called over her shoulder, "Josh is here, Aileen!"

"What am I, chopped liver?" Eliaster muttered.

Down the short, bright hallway, Aileen appeared in a doorway, blinking sleepily as she clutched a coffee cup in one hand. "What…" Her eyes widened. "Patricia!" she hissed. "I'm in my pajamas!" She clunked her coffee cup on the counter and darted out of sight.

"Oh, I'm sure Josh won't mind *at all*, would you, Josh?" Eliaster shot a wicked grin at me over his shoulder as he stepped into the house.

My face felt like it was on fire. "Shut up, idiot." I shoved the box of books at him and wriggled out of my jacket, hanging it on the peg by the front door.

The house was smaller than I'd expected for something owned by the faoladh. Just ahead of us there was a kitchen, with a living room to the right. The hallway took a sharp left down to what I assumed were the bedrooms and bathroom. Cozy, but small.

Patricia caught the question in my eyes and smiled. "The faoladh own this whole subdivision," she explained, motioning for us to go into the kitchen. "This is designed for guests, mostly, or members who prefer to live a bit more isolated lives." She tapped the top of the box in Eliaster's arms. "What's this?"

"Books." Eliaster rolled his eyes. "Last time Josh and Liam talked, they somehow got on the subject of books, and how Cori had been browsing the bookstores around town. So Josh decided he should loan him some fantasy novels, and they got to talking, and...well." He lifted the box, shrugging. "I think they got carried away."

The kitchen actually wasn't as small as it had first looked, with a breakfast nook to one side and a big bay window that looked out to an unfenced backyard scattered with a small flower bed, a vegetable garden, and the thick Ozark woods not far away. Eliaster put the box of books on the table and we took seats in the breakfast nook as Patricia served us coffee and she and Eliaster chatted about the pack.

A few minutes later, Aileen reappeared, now dressed in jeans and simple tee, running her fingers through her rumpled curls. I smiled at the "Bite Me" slogan, complete with vampire fangs, on her t-shirt.

"That's a bit on the nose, isn't it?" I asked.

She glanced down, then grinned. "Yeah, well. Haven't run into vampires yet, so I think I'm safe for now."

"Hey, where are you guys going?" I asked as Eliaster and Patricia started for the back door.

Eliaster jerked his thumb at the door. "Liam called on the way over and wanted to talk to me."

I raised an eyebrow. How true was this, exactly?

He gave me an overly-sweet grin. "Don't do anything I wouldn't do."

"Doggone it, Eliaster," I muttered, feeling my face flame up again.

He snickered and ducked out the back door. Patricia shook her head and followed him.

I stared down at my coffee mug, suddenly unsure of what I was going to say. *Hi, I think you're cute, let's get to know each other better?* That was stupid. She'd just essentially lost her father and her brother—and even if her father was an abusive jerk, it was still a major life change. I needed to be sensitive to that.

Aileen suddenly reached over and gripped my hand, squeezing gently. I jumped.

"How're you feeling?" she asked.

I smiled and looked up at her. "Do I look that bad?"

She studied me for a moment, a small wrinkle of concern appearing between her eyebrows. She moved her hand from my fingers to my wrist, brushing both my bracelet and my scar.

Warmth spread across my hand and arm, and my breath caught.

"Have you and Roe figured out anything about this yet?"

I shook my head.

Aileen made eye contact with me, a warm almost-brown tone flickering through her eyes. "Do you want me to help?"

I blinked, surprised.

After a second, she shook her head. "Sorry. Never mind."

"No…" I put my free hand over hers, tightened my fingers so she couldn't pull her hand away. "No, I'm sorry. I was just surprised, is all. Help me with…figuring out what exactly the bracelet is?"

Aileen bit her lip. "What is it, what it's doing to you…" She hesitated, then said, "You know you blocked the worst of Gren's light blast, right?"

I thought back, trying to remember that moment. I'd

blocked Drake from throwing more glamour at Eliaster, then I'd heard Aileen shout to close our eyes. I'd turned away from Gren, and wrapped my arms around my head. I remembered feeling a blow to my back, like I'd just been sucker-punched, and a bright light I could see even with my eyes squeezed tightly shut.

Then I'd grabbed Eliaster, dragging him outside.

Just remembering it made my stomach twist.

"Gren used all the glamour he'd been storing for three months for that blast," Aileen said quietly. "He didn't target Cori or me, but everyone else in that room should've been on their backs like Blodheyr, Larae, Altru, and Drake."

Drake, now. Not 'Da'.

"But you stayed up. And even though Eliaster got knocked over, he wasn't unconscious. He should've been, but you were between him and Gren. It's not just that you're a human, Josh. You're using glamour strong enough to block *my father*. The Airgeads some of the strongest glamourists out there."

My stomach knotted. "You think that's a bad thing?"

"No," she said, drawing the word out a bit. "But it's an unknown. And with glamour, unknowns make me nervous." She tightened her fingers. "I'll help you figure it out. I owe you, for getting Cori and me out of there even when things went badly. I don't think any of us were expecting that fight."

I snorted. "You don't owe me anything."

She looked up at me, startled.

"I'm not doing this whole trading favors thing with you, Aileen," I said. "I know that's how fae usually operate, but I don't do that with my friends. I would be glad for your help. But we're not trading information or favors any more, all right?"

The corner of her lips turned up into a half smile. "Okay," she said. "I can work with that."

Yeah. So could I.

If you enjoyed this book, please remember to rate and review on Amazon and/or Goodreads! Reviews mean a lot to authors, and are one of the ways you can help support my effort to bring you more fabulous stories. (And if you're interested in other ways, please sign up for my newsletter at my website, hatitus.com!)

ACKNOWLEDGEMENTS

So I guess I should start out the acknowledgements with an apology.

When I published Forged Steel back in 2015, I thought I was ready to go. I had everything planned out. I would have all the books out by 2020 and be on to other series.

Well…yeah, we know how that worked out. Between a nine-month break during my rough third pregnancy, a disrupted schedule once the new baby was born, burn out, and a severe case of Sequelitis, it's just been in the last year or so that I'd been able to face this book again, even though I still adored Josh, Eliaster, Aileen, and the host of other characters that populate this world.

If it wasn't for the fans that kept gently prodding me, I'm not sure I would've ever gotten this second book out in the world. So, you guys—thank you!

To Justin, my husband, who has never stopped encouraging me to chase my dreams, and my boys, who consistently remind of the everyday magic in the real world. I promise I love you guys even if dinner ends up being late six nights out of seven. ;)

To my critique partners, J.J. Johnson and S.D. Grimm (who is also my fabulous editor and a member of my Paladins)—thank you guys for helping me iron out all the (many, many) bumpy parts of this book.

The Paladins, my writing/D&D/framily group…guys, where even to start. Thank you for reading false starts, for shredding things and telling me I could do better, for listening to my rants, for sending me funny memes when I was having a bad day, and for providing fun creative breaks through our D&D games and Minecraft calls.

You're all fantastic and I thank God for each and every one of you.

H. A. Titus can usually be found with her nose stuck in a book or spinning story worlds in her head.
She loves mythology, RPGS, and a good cup of coffee or tea. She lives in Missouri with her weather mage husband and two supervillain sons (don't mind the robotic dinosaurs, they're friendly) who enjoy dragging her into real life adventures.
Some claim she is half fae, but that's just unfounded rumor.
When she's not reading or writing, she enjoys mountain biking and hiking.

She can be found online at hatitus.com, Facebook, and Instagram.

FAYETTE
PRESS

If you enjoy *The Crucible*,
you'll probably love these other clean fantasy series:

THE
SENTINEL TRILOGY

THE
THREE ROYAL CHILDREN
AND THE **BATTY AUNT**

THE
STONES OF TERRENE

Blood-bonds with angels. Surreal mental abilities. Elemental gods. Maze Runner meets The Mortal Instruments in this adrenaline-laced urban fantasy.

When Prince Torrin sees a light in a forgotten palace tower, he meets a mysterious aunt who unlocks a world of adventure he and his siblings will never forget.

Welcome to Terrene— where dragons exist, the past haunts, and magic is no myth. Welcome aboard the Sapphire.

www.ingramcontent.com/pod-product-compliance
Lightning Source LLC
Chambersburg PA
CBHW020246200626
46816CB00001BA/149